A BEAST NO MORE

20-2-

Emerging from the

PHYLLIS MAGOLD

Joan Of Arc Press

A Beast No More
Emerging from the Middle State

v5.0

This is a work of fiction. The events and characters described herein are imaginary and are not intended to refer to specific places or living persons. The opinions expressed in this manuscript are solely the opinions of the author and do not represent the opinions or thoughts of the publisher. The author has represented and warranted full ownership and/or legal right to publish all the materials in this book.

Joan Of Arc Press

Paperback ISBN: 978-0-578-18463-0

Library of Congress Control Number: 2016955022

PRINTED IN THE UNITED STATES OF AMERICA

Virginia Woolf once wrote that, to be a writer,
"A woman must have money and a room of her own."
This book is dedicated to my husband, Ray, who has provided both.

Chapter 1

St. John's Hospital, Cleveland, Ohio
June 1, 1950

Brigid Delia Nagy gave birth to Brigid Delia Nagy.

Rose Margaret Vanetti gave birth to Rose Margaret Vanetti.

Barbara Ann Turyev gave birth to Barbara Ann Turyev.

Fateful irony brought together the three mothers, who passed down ancient family names to their daughters on the same day, at the same time, in the same place. The irony of similarities transcended the circumstances of name and birth: each woman delivered her first child; each woman married a distinguished World War II veteran; each woman was deeply linked to a generational matriarchal tradition; and each woman bubbled with ethnic Catholic blood flowing like holy water through her veins. Fate had planted the seeds of friendship within the daughters long before the mothers ever heard the wails of their babies' exits from the wombs.

The baby business boomed that day, as St. John Hospital's delivery room welcomed six male infants along with baby girls Brigid, Rose, and Barbara. The three girl babies were placed in a row in the maternity ward. Sisters of Charity, who served as administrators and nurses of the hospital, enjoyed the unique namings and circumstances of the girls' births. As a result, they treated the mothers like queens, and the babies like princesses. The mothers of the female babies received extra time, with sponge baths and with extra bowls of Jell-O during evening snacks. Baby girls Brigid, Rose (whom they called Rosie), and Barbara, were the first to be comforted, and the first to be fed.

Mothers of the male infants took offense, but the nuns knew that the sons would eventually get more than their due of attention from the mothers and the worlds in which they would live.

The idolatry of the boy babies could already be heard in the chatter among the visitors.

To the mothers of the boys:

"Oh, thank God you have a son."

"Everyone should begin a family with a boy."

"Boys are so much easier to raise than girls."

To the mothers of the girls:

"Ooooooh, maybe next time you'll get your boy."

"You know, if you drink cranberry juice while you're ovulating, you are more likely to have a male."

"Girls are so expensive."

This chatter had no effect on the great joy the mothers felt at the births of their daughters, and when their husbands came to see the babies, there was no hint of disappointment. The husbands and fathers offered untainted, unconditional love to their women and their girls.

Brigid's husband, Miklos Nagy, her high-school sweetheart, adored his wife, never "knew" another woman, and showed no desire to do so. He was a Hungarian whose fiery passion for life was overshadowed only by his fiery passion for Brigid. Miklos and Brigid graduated in 1941 from West Technical High School located on West 73rd, a few blocks from the hospital. Miklos Nagy was a football hero, a receiver of passes thrown by Gabe Nagy, one of the best quarterbacks ever to play high-school football in Cleveland, who just happened to be Miklos's older brother. The Nagy brothers were strikingly handsome—the darlings of the hallways of West Tech High. But while seventeen-year-old Gabe chased every willing girl on the West Side, sixteen-year-old Miklos set his eyes and heart on Brigid. Miklos and Brigid were a couple opposite in nature (Brigid was unassuming and private; Miklos was gregarious and outgoing), but they both held a mystically deep faith in God, and shared an intense commitment to faith, family, and friends. They married in 1947, shortly after Miklos returned from the Philippines, where he had earned a Purple Heart for an injury incurred during a battle in the Guadalcanal Campaign. The injury, though painful and serious, did not prevent Miklos from pursuing his childhood dream of becoming a firefighter, and he had recently been hired to the Parma, Ohio Fire Department.

Rose's husband, Massimo Antonio Vanetti, called MV by his friends, was also a war hero. He received the Silver Star for valor in the Middle East theater of war, in North Africa, for going back to a battlefield in a hail of gunfire to carry a wounded buddy to safety. He did this not once, not twice, but three times, on three different battlefields.

Far from these battlefields, MV and Rose had grown up a few blocks from each other. She lived on West 61st Street and Detroit Avenue; he lived on West 65th and Detroit. In elementary school MV was a protector to Rose, and in high school he was her first and last crush. They, too, graduated from West Technical High, but before the reign of the Nagy brothers, in 1937. Like Miklos and Brigid, these two lovers had opposite personalities. Rose was brash, blunt, and bold; MV was considerate, reflective, and reserved. Rose and MV married in 1940, and when the war was over, he began his lifetime career as a public servant, elected to Cleveland City Council. Rose never left his side.

Barbara's husband, Richard Turyev, was the eldest of the group. At fifty, Richard Turyev was considered an old husband, and an old father. He was born in Germany, of Jewish parents, and raised in the Jewish Orthodox tradition. By 1930, Richard was a respected physicist in Germany, and as a result, was privy to the many ominous secrets that swirled in the fumes of rockets, weapons, and swastikas. In 1936, he sailed to America with hundreds of artists, scientists, and freethinkers who fled the dark shadows of war and uneasiness that crept over and menaced their homeland. He begged his parents to come with him, but they refused. He never saw them again, learning much later that his mother disappeared into Auschwitz with his father, who committed suicide there. During the war, Richard worked clandestinely on top-secret weapons and aircraft for the United States government. He carried a deep sadness in his soul, which was penetrated only by Barbara, whom he met when she was a student at John Carroll University, where he was a professor. Their brilliant minds provided a metaphysical bond that would transcend the obstacles of religion, gender, and culture. They married in 1949 and settled in Shaker Heights, Ohio, one of the wealthiest communities in the country.

It was Richard's Jewish heritage that brought a priest named Father James Templeton to Barbara's bedside on the day her daughter was born. Father Templeton served at Our Lady of Peace, the Shaker Heights Catholic Church where Barbara attended Mass. Tanned and handsome, with a crew cut and white-hot teeth, he seemed charmingly uncomfortable that day in his hot, white collar. The charm masked a stern dedication to his vocation. His main purpose in visiting the hospital on June 1, 1950, was to ensure that Barbara and Richard were planning to raise their child in a Catholic household. The Vatican frowned upon mixed marriages between Catholic and non-Catholic. Both the Catholic and the non-Catholic in a marriage had to solemnly promise to raise any children from the union in the Catholic faith.

Too much pain and suffering in Richard's life had hardened his ability to embrace religion or a loving God. He was, however, willing to make the Catholic promise for his wife and daughter. After Father Templeton was assured of the Turyevs' commitment, he blessed the baby and gave a nod of greeting to Monsignor Anthony Giuliani, who was just entering the maternity ward. Monsignor Giuliani served as Rose's pastor from her home parish, Our Lady of Mount Carmel, located on Detroit Avenue, about ten blocks from St. John's Hospital. He was a burly, hairy man with a heavy Italian accent, who spoke loudly and forcefully. The brusque exterior disguised a gentle soul, who guided his flock with love and tenderness. He gave Mama Rose and baby

Rose a special blessing, because June 1 is, after all, the feast day of St. Candida.

The final shepherd to care for his sheep that day was Monsignor Murphy, the Nagys' pastor, who came in from St. Charles Borromeo in Parma. He was a kindly man with an identifiable Irish, elfin twinkle in his eye and a thick Irish brogue in his throat.

When first seeing baby Brigid, Monsignor Murphy lifted her up, holding her over his head, and said, "Whoa, now look at the big noggin on this one! You'll have a hard time catching a man with that head!"

Baby Brigid, with wide-open eyes, responded to the kindly priest with projectile vomit that landed in his wide-open mouth.

•

On June 4, 1950, Barbara, Richard, and baby "Babs" Turyev left St. John's Hospital, and went home to their Tudor house in Shaker Heights. Rose Vanetti and MV took baby Rosie home to their three-story house at West 65th and Detroit Avenue. Brigid Nagy and Miklos headed home with baby Brigid to their Parma bungalow. The mothers said goodbye to each other, vowing to stay in touch. Although they all returned to St. John's over the next ten years to give birth—Brigid had five more daughters, Rose had one more daughter and three sons, and Barbara had one son—their paths did not cross again for many years.

*

Chapter 2

Parma, Ohio, 1950–1964

With a population of about twenty-nine thousand, and a burgeoning influx of Cleveland families of Eastern European descent, Parma, Ohio was emerging as a popular place for newlyweds and young families to start their postwar lives. Miklos and Brigid Nagy lived like pioneers in this suburb, which they moved into just nineteen years after it had secured city status. The fire department's Station No. 1, on the corner of Snow Road and Dresden Avenue, became Miklos's second home. It was situated around the corner from their bungalow. He walked the one block to work every other day -- firefighters in Parma averaged a 56-hour workweek, and at the time no one complained.

A strong sense of community and neighborly helpfulness nurtured new churches, new schools, new businesses, and new clubs in postwar Parma. The children of immigrants, having paid the price for global freedom, were now ready to start anew, espousing the middle-class values of hard work, hard play, and soft hearts. If anyone were to think to ask the question, "What is the American Dream?" the answer could be found in 1950s Parma, Ohio. That is, if one was white. The black man's dream is another story, in another city: there were no black families living in Parma, Ohio in 1950.

Miklos relished the newness of it all, and recognized that here was a place where a man could make a difference--a place where a man could stand on the ground floor of innovation even as he stood on the solid ground of tradition. Brigid was joyful that here was a place where she and her family could be safe. Here was a place where she could live happily with the only man she had ever loved. Here was a place where she could be free from the screeching sirens and beer-joint squalls that pierced through the frightful nights in her old Cleveland neighborhood. A bungalow on a corner lot in Parma under the comforting glow of a city streetlamp, a short walk from Standard Drug Store, Fisher Foods grocery, the Parma Theater, Tassi's candy store, Tal's Deli—here was a place to call home.

Although Irish passions burned deep in Brigid's soul, and Hungarian roots grounded Miklos's heart, the pair were first and foremost, Catholic. Monsignor Murphy baptized Baby Brigid two weeks after she came home from the hospital, being careful to stand clear, in case she decided to share her half-digested breakfast with him.

Great-Grandma Brigid, Grandma Brigid, and Mama Brigid attended as Baby Brigid was ritually accepted into the Holy Catholic Church. Later that day, the first of many baptismal bashes was held at the house on the corner of West 79th Street and Essen Avenue in Parma. The godparents, Hungarian cousins Tilly and Andy Kollar, proudly wore the corsage and boutonnière, and all present enjoyed a feast of *stobhacj gaelach* (Irish stew), Hungarian *gulyas* (goulash), and *toltott kaposzta* (stuffed cabbage), chicken paprikash, poppyseed streudel, and a triple-layer nutmeg cake with buttercream frosting.

Grandmas, grandpas, great-grandmas, aunts, uncles, great-aunts, and great-uncles joined the celebration, along with a group of firefighters and their families.

These were the players on Baby Brigid's stage. These were the bearers of her history and would be the cornerstones of her future. The DNA linked in all these genes provided her with a love of learning, laughter, life, and liquor.

•

Soon after settling in with the baby, Miklos was dealing with the slight annoyance of having two Brigids in the house as well as two more close by. (Great-Grandma was in a nursing home on Cleveland's west side, and Grandma Brigid had also moved to Parma.) The slight annoyance had nothing to do with the women themselves. Miklos loved and cared for them all with great affection. Instead, the annoyance came in the wake of a plethora of conversations that sounded like this:

"Hey, Mik, how is Brigid?"

"Which one?"

After the hundredth time Miklos Nagy confronted this banality, he had a talk with his wife.

"Brig, do you remember what I used to call you when I first came home from the war?" he asked her.

Mama Brigid glanced fondly at a bracelet that was ever present on her wrist. On the bracelet was a heart, engraved with the words "To my Dar." Miklos had sent it home from California before he shipped out to Guadalcanal. The heart was gold and it cost him his last dime. After paying for the bracelet itself, he had only seventy cents left for the engraving. Letters cost ten cents apiece. So, the "To my darling" which he had originally planned, was reduced to, "To my Dar." "Dar" became a pet name between them.

After a discussion regarding the annoyance that Miklos had come to call Brigidmania, Mama Brigid agreed that "Dar" would be a lovely everyday moniker, and soon everyone called her that. Miklos was thus relieved of the banality of Brigidmania and freed to be busied with the banality of suburbia.

•

Cerebral specialists have hypothesized that human beings can retain memories from the womb. It was an incident that happened in 1953, when Brigid was barely three, that seared a memory which lasted her a lifetime. At 3 a.m., the shrill ring of the yellow wall phone shook the kitchen and woke the Nagy household. Dar ran to the phone. Brigid, barely awake, listened to her mother speak in soft, worried tones.

"When was the last time you saw her? What was she wearing? How'd she get out? We'll pick you up in ten minutes."

By the time Dar had hung up, Miklos was by her side, holding a frightened Brigid. Dar, who was eight and a half months pregnant with Baby No. 2, explained: "Grandma escaped from the home. She was last seen on a bus on Lorain Avenue, barefoot and in her nightgown. When the bus driver questioned her, she exited the bus and ran away. We need to pick up Ma and go look for her."

Great-grandma Brigid started showing signs of dementia shortly after baby Brigid was born. At first, it appeared to be the forgetfulness that often comes with the aging process, but it soon deteriorated to full-blown insanity, with bouts of violence, detachment from reality, and uncontrollable outbursts of emotion. Great-grandma's condition was diagnosed as severe dementia. At family gatherings, the members of the kindly clan simply said she was "off her rocker."

Everyone in the family took a turn caring for her, but when great-grandma went after Sister Mary Abraham with a paring knife at a school bake sale, the family came to the horrifying decision that the old woman would "have to be put away."

They found a place on the west side, not far from their family home, on Clark Avenue. The facility was administered by the Sisters of the Sacred Heart, a caring and loving group of nuns who ministered to the elderly. The sisters were diligent and watchful, and the grounds were secured. Or so they had thought. Great-grandma Brigid apparently found a way out.

The Nagys dressed hurriedly, and as they were going out onto the side steps, the phone rang again and Miklos rushed to answer it. It was Muncie, his sister, who lived next door.

"Mickey, what's going on? I saw your lights go on and then saw you all moving around. What's all the commotion?"

Miklos explained the situation, and by the time he locked the house and walked to the garage to get the car, Muncie's husband, Joe, was already pulling up in his pickup truck, giving a sign that he would follow and help in the search.

They drove quickly to Grandma Brigid's house, a few blocks away. Dar's cheeks dripped with silent tears as they passed through the deserted streets of the center of Parma, spotting only a few people tumbling out of the bar of the Ridgewood Inn. When they reached the house, Grandma took Brigid and held her on her lap in back as the 1953 Ford Victoria headed out of the suburban solitude into the flashing neon lights and erratic traffic of the west side of Cleveland.

Dar was the first to see the old woman in a long green nightgown strolling down West 25th Street toward Denison Avenue.

"There she is!" she cried as Miklos slowly edged closer to the curb. Rolling down the window, Dar shouted, "Grandma!"

Three-year-old Brigid would never forget her namesake's frightful countenance. The old woman stopped suddenly with a wild, crazed look in her eyes—like a scared animal desperate to escape a kill. Her white hair was tangled and hung far below her shoulders; she screamed a horrifying, cackling shriek. Little Brigid clung to her grandma, who was quietly sobbing, as Miklos and Joe went to the sidewalk and lifted the screaming woman, then pushed her into the front seat of the car, where Dar hugged her and tried to comfort her.

When Miklos slid back into the driver's seat, he held the old woman's shoulders and stared into her cold, zombielike eyes. Suddenly, for a moment, the wild, crazed look was gone. The green eyes were clear, and glinted with recognition.

She looked at Miklos and said, "You damned, daffy Hunky—I almost got away!"

Before Miklos could respond—in an instant—the haze and the craze came back to her eyes, and Great-Grandma Brigid once again slipped into her own reality. She became subdued and was eerily silent as they settled her back in with the good Sisters. Her retreat was permanent, and within two days her reality became a coma, and then became death.

At three years old, little Brigid was instilled with the one great fear of her life: going off her rocker.

•

When Brigid turned five, she started afternoon kindergarten at St. Charles Elementary School, the largest Catholic school in the country. Brigid loved her morning routine of watching Pat Boone on the Arthur Godfrey show, followed by *I Love Lucy,* and playing with her younger sister, Michele, who was born shortly after Great-Grandma's death. After lunch she would get dressed and ready for school.

Dar had been reading to Brigid every night for three years, and the five-year-old could already read primer books. She had also memorized the first few verses of Edgar Allan Poe's "The Raven." However, her main source of confidence came in the form of her best friend, Patti DeSantis, who lived across the street. Patti's and Brigid's mothers had visited almost every day since the girls were babies. The girls shared playpens and buggies and toys and first steps. They developed a bond that sustained them through the fears and foils of the first days of school: losing their lunch, breaking new crayons, and last to be picked in the schoolyard games of Farmer in the Dell and Sally in the Water. Patti was vivacious and uninhibited, while Brigid was quiet and introverted. Together they made the best mud pies, drew the straightest hopscotch squares, and collected the most beautiful marbles in their class. They were both in the group for the best readers and earned the most holy cards for reading without error. They both had crushes on the same boys, but while Patti dreamed of marriage, Brigid dreamed of college and writing and travel. Even as five-year-olds, they had goals that seemed settled. They thought one thing was for certain: they would always be friends.

During the summer of 1957, when Patti and Brigid both turned seven, Patti's father was transferred to another city, and Patti moved away, suddenly, with no time for farewell parties or long goodbyes. The night before Patti left, they were chasing lightning bugs in the yard. While running onto the sidewalk, they both fell, skinning their knees. Blood covered their knees in a meshed, tic-tac-toe pattern. Suddenly, Patti took Brigid's knee and rubbed it on hers.

"We're blood sisters now," she said. "Just like the Indians and white men on *Rin Tin Tin:* we will always be with each other in spirit."

Brigid looked at Patti and they both started crying and hugged each other for several minutes until their mothers pulled them apart.

When Brigid told her mother about the blood-sister act, Dar lifted her up and put her in the tub and scrubbed her with harsh Lava soap. Apparently the idea of mixing blood did not set well with Dar, and she reprimanded Brigid, saying it was a filthy thing to do. Across the street, Mrs. DeSantis was too busy loading the moving van to discuss anything with Patti, but she did take time to bandage her knee and put her to bed, and tell her they would be leaving very early in the morning.

That night, as the glow of the streetlight filtered into the two corner houses at 79th Street and Essen Avenue, the two mothers and the two daughters cried themselves to sleep.

•

Patti and Brigid did not keep in touch. Brigid often wished her friend was close by; schoolyard and neighborhood games and explorations were not the same. Her cousin Josephine, called Jojo, who lived next door, became her closest confidante and daily playmate. They would find secret places behind the garages and the rosebushes, where they would build fairy houses and camps, and create plans to save the world from all evil and hunger. Sometimes they roller-skated on the smooth floor of their garages, and would sweep with the push broom, pretending they were trapped in a fairytale-ish scenario of witches and wicked stepmothers, forced to labor all day. In all of their endeavors, they were helpers, saviors, and nurses. The nuns at St. Charles instilled a sense of universal love for mankind in these young girls. Brigid and

Jojo often felt sorry for the poor souls who were not Catholic—because people who were not Catholic were all going to Hell, of course.

When baby Sally was born, in February of 1958, Brigid retreated into the quiet solaces of school, reading, and watching the stars from her bedroom window. She was content to be the oldest sister, to help around the house and concentrate on schoolwork. She never paid attention to the snickers of "teacher's pet" and "brownnose" that slithered off the tongues of the other second graders.

The event she most dreaded was First Confession, receiving the sacrament of Penance. Learning the prayers—Apostles' Creed, Act of Faith, Act of Love, Act of Hope, Act of Contrition—was the easy part. She loved learning new prayers, because each one taught her something new about being Catholic and what was expected of her as a child of God. The Examination of Conscience and the Confession of Sins, however, made her squirm. At night, she would examine her conscience for sins against the Ten Commandments:

Have I had strange gods before me?

Well, sometimes I would prefer watching "Mickey Mouse Club" to saying the nightly rosary, so I guess TV can be a strange god. So yes, I've committed a sin against the First Commandment.

Have I taken the Lord's name in vain?

No, but Sister said that using foul language is a form of cursing, so yes, I committed a sin against the Second Commandment when I said the word "crap."

Have I kept holy the Lord's Day?

Not completely, in the summer I wore shorts on Sunday when it was hot and didn't wear my Sunday best. So yes, I committed a sin against the Third Commandment. But fortunately it was not a mortal sin, because I never ever missed Mass.

Have I honored my father and mother?

Many times I've made faces behind their backs and sometimes I did not clean my room right when I was told. And I also refused to eat the hot red beets even though Mommy said I must. So yes, I committed a sin against the Fourth Commandment.

Have I killed anyone?

Haha. No, I haven't, but this commandment also means we should be nice to everyone, and in school Martin Gorman pulled my hair and I told him he looked like a hairy gorilla, so yes, I committed a sin against the Fifth Commandment.

Have I committed adultery?

Of course not. But impure thoughts are also a sin under this commandment. Hmmm, after I told Martin Gorman he looked like a gorilla, I wanted to kiss him and that night I thought about kissing him, so yes, I committed a sin against the Sixth Commandment.

Have I stolen anything?

Noooooooooo!! Yaaaaaaaay! But, oh no, oh dear, I did find a penny in the schoolyard and I kept it, not even trying to see whom it belonged to. So yes, I've even committed a sin against the Seventh Commandment.

Have I borne false witness against my neighbor?

Yes, I told my mother that Jojo ate the last cookie, and really I did, and well, yes, I have told a few other lies. So yes, I committed sins against the Eighth Commandment.

Have I coveted my neighbor's wife?

Okay, for sure this is a no—no sins against the Ninth Commandment.

Have I coveted my neighbor's goods?

Yes: I wished I had Marlene's color TV, and I wished I had Yvonne's xylophone, and I wished I had Timmy's baseball glove, and, ooooh, many times I have coveted my neighbor's goods. So yes, I committed sins against the Tenth Commandment.

By the time Brigid had finished examining her conscience, she was sobbing, on her knees, begging God for forgiveness. When she finally made her First Confession, she cried so hard that the priest stopped her by the Fifth Commandment, and told her to say a Hail Mary for her penance. He assured her that she was a good girl, and that God loved her and appreciated her efforts to know, love, and serve Him. When she came out of the confessional, eyes red, blowing her nose in her babushka, her classmates stared, convinced she was a non-churchgoing murderer.

Later that year, however, Brigid's dismay turned to joy. On Saturday, May 3, 1958, Brigid received her First Communion. There were a hundred and twenty students in Brigid's First Communion class. As a result of this large number, only parents were allowed to attend the Mass. Grandmas Brigid and Mary snuck into the last pew. Grandma Brigid had made the dress: a white chiffon, layered pattern, covered with lacy insets and speckled with rhinestones. The veil was the same veil her mother had worn on her First Communion day. These would both be the First Communion attire for future generations of Nagy girls.

The Mass was always a special encounter for Brigid. There was something about the mystical flow of Latin chants and the golden tabernacle and the anticipatory bells that filled her soul with a sense of wonder. It was otherworldly. It made her believe in an existence outside herself, outside her world, outside her universe. The Mass somehow connected her to a great spiritual otherness, in which she found deep comfort. Even though many years later she would reject many of the precepts of her beloved Church, she would always keep this connection with a greater reality, and she would always relish the Eucharist as the bridge between the realities of the flesh and the spirit.

After returning to her pew, she said her Act of Contrition, and looked around at her classmates, wondering whether they felt the peace and connection that she was feeling. She found herself thinking of Patti—they had often spoken of how they wanted to be partners for this ceremony. Putting her face between her hands, she said a prayer for Patti's happiness and her eternal soul.

She was surprised to hear the clicking of cameras and the popping of flashbulbs. Sister John Berchman, a tall, stern woman with rimless eyeglasses, who was in charge of the arrangements, had firmly asked that no photos be taken during the ceremony, since it would prove disrespectful to the solemnity of the event. Also, some of the students were getting sick, and two vomited in the pews and had to leave before the final blessing. Everyone grew apprehensive about how the nuns would handle these unplanned and unwelcome events. Brigid looked at Sister John Berchman, and although the nun looked a tad annoyed, Brigid marveled at her peaceful demeanor and forgiving countenance. The sisters were a source of great comfort to Brigid and she admired and tried to emulate their humility and dedication. She had heard that sometimes the sisters would lose their tempers and hit students, but she had never witnessed such behavior, nor had she ever felt a hint of animosity from the nuns toward the students.

As the children walked in perfect step out of the church, Brigid did not hear Sister John Berchman mutter to herself, "Damn these kids!"

•

By the time Brigid entered fourth grade, she had established herself as an avid reader, a model student, and an accomplished player of the saxophone, playing in the respected St. Charles Advanced Band. The teachers loved her, but her classmates called her a "goody-woody," and while they were not openly vicious, they effectively ignored her—which was, in some ways, worse. A few weeks into the school year, Brigid was afforded an opportunity to escape her classmates' neglect. Sister Marie Canice, Brigid's teacher, contacted Dar and Miklos and requested a conference. This was very unusual. Communication between parents and teachers was minimal in the Catholic schools of the 1950s. The teachers taught, the parents parented, and the students obeyed. Teachers and parents were almost always on the same side, which meant that if the student was in trouble at school, the student was also in trouble at home. There was no need to confer.

The Nagys were concerned about the request. They had paid their eight-dollar book bill, so they were confident that the conference was not about money, and they knew Brigid was succeeding in school. On Miklos's next day off, they went to Room 301 of the new St. Charles school building, and met with Sister Marie Canice and the principal, Sister Mary Judyth.

Sister Canice, soft-spoken but businesslike, started the conference. "Mr. and Mrs. Nagy, as you know, Brigid is doing quite well in school. She is doing so well that we would like to accelerate her."

Dar and Miklos looked embarrassedly at each other, because they had no idea what Sister was talking about.

Miklos said to the nun, "Would you please explain what that means?"

Sister Canice took out Brigid's report cards from the previous years and laid them on the desk. "You see," she said, "there is a red line drawn across the grade section of the report card. This indicates the intelligence quotient, or IQ, of the student. Brigid's is very high, as you can see, near the A plus grading mark. When we enter the grades on the report cards, if a student's grade falls below the red line, that indicates that he is not achieving his academic potential. Conversely, if a student scores above the red line that means he is working hard and rising above his predicted success. So for some students, a C or even a D is a respectable grade, considering their ability to learn."

Dar interjected, "What does this have to do with acceleration?"

Sister Canice continued: "Brigid's IQ is very high, and her achievement is even higher. We would like to recommend that she skip the rest of fourth grade and move, or accelerate, if you will, into fifth. It would academically challenge her, and perhaps put her on a more congenial level with her peers."

Sister Judyth, who had sat authoritatively silent, now joined the conversation. "We also feel that the students in the higher class are more attuned to, shall we say, the spiritual nature of vocations, and to performing the Lord's work. The sisters think that Brigid has shown evidence that she has a calling to the be a nun."

That last comment jolted Dar and Miklos. Having a child called to a vocation was a heavenly dream. The comments regarding Brigid's intellect were completely overshadowed by the notion of a vocation—a child of theirs, serving the Lord in the convent.

"Can we discuss all of this and let you know next week?" asked Miklos.

"Next week at the latest," said Sister Judyth, and shook the Nagys' hands and left the room. The conference was over.

Later that night, Dar, Grandma Brigid, and Muncie were having coffee at the kitchen table of the Nagy house while Dar related the conference to her mother and sister-in-law. Muncie, who embodied the free spirit of the gypsies that was hidden deep in the family tree rooted in the wild forests of Hungary, was not a fan of the rigid rules and personal controls of the Catholic Church.

"She's nine years old, for heaven's sake. Everyone wants to be a nun when they're nine years old. Don't go pushing her in a direction she might not want to go later on. Keep her with kids her own age—she will grow up soon enough. She can be holy without being shoved into a vocation."

Grandma Brigid, who longed for someone in the family to be a priest or a nun, suppressed her own desire and agreed with Muncie. "We are all called to something higher. Brigid has plenty of time to discover that calling. Let her travel her path in her own time—no need to accelerate the journey."

Miklos came in and joined in. "What about that IQ thing? If we keep her in fourth grade, are we holding her back? Will she get bored with school?"

"It's not up to the school to keep her interested and entertained," said Dar. "That nun has sixty kids in the class. I am not going to expect her to make individual lessons for one child. If Brigid learns everything there is to know in fourth grade, then we'll get her books, and she can come up with her own sources of knowledge. We have enough know-how sitting at this table to keep her busy and educated long after the school day ends."

No one ever considered asking Brigid. A nine-year-old's opinion meant nothing to the adults drinking coffee and deciding her fate. She was a child. The proverb "Children should be seen and not heard" was the order of the day.

If they had asked her, she would have told them, in a most scholarly, accelerated manner, that she wanted to stay in fourth grade. She did not want to leave Martin Gorman.

•

The decade of the 1960s began in a frenzy for Brigid. John Fitzgerald Kennedy brought his presidential campaign to St. Charles Borromeo, and Dar made sure that her four daughters—baby Joan had been born late in 1959—were there to witness history. Brigid sat enthralled, watching his sizzling smile and listening to his charming New England intonations. She would never forget the feeling in her stomach as their eyes met and locked for a heartbeat. (Later, she would write about it, capturing all the mystique and wonder of the moment by eloquently proclaiming, "I turned to mush.")

Kennedy's victory in November filled the school with a howling wind of celebration. The nuns were visibly excited with shining, happy smiles so permanent that even the most unruly student could not but be affected. If there were any Republican families at St. Charles School, they did not dare express their politics. This day belonged to Catholics and Irishmen, and no one infringed upon the euphoria—no one, that is, except Brigid's classmate, Thomas Smith.

During a classroom discussion of the effects of the election on government and on the role of the United States in the world, Thomas Smith whispered across the aisle to Brigid, "You know that mick is just a nigger-lovin' papist, don't you?"

The whisper was not quite whispered enough, and before Brigid's mouth had time to drop open, Sister Mary Raphael was on Tom's back like a hawk on a rabbit. She was pounding on his backbone with her open hands, the slaps shaking Tom's desk and the desks around it. Tom was shaking, too, but he refused to give in. Instead, he laughed. The more she struck him, the harder he laughed. He buried his head in his hands on his desk, bearing the relentless slaps with a defiance that Brigid could not imagine. Once it became obvious that the laughs had turned to sobs, Sister Raphael turned to the class, and spoke in a strange, calm, icy voice: "Don't ever say anything bad about our President—ever."

Apparently, calling an Irishman a mick and a Negro a nigger was acceptable, as long as it was not directed at President Kennedy.

After school, Brigid went to band practice, and by the time she arrived home Dar had already gotten calls from several fifth-grade parents, discussing what was now being called "Sister Raphael's attack on Tom." After dinner, Brigid fed baby Joan while Dar readied Michele and Sally for bed. Dar settled them in front of the RCA Victor television for an episode of *Huckleberry Hound* and a bedtime snack of Charlie's potato chips and Coke. Then she put her arm around Brigid and asked her to come into the bedroom for a chat, after Joan finished eating.

Sister Raphael's attack on Tom had unsettled Brigid to the core. She never would have imagined a nun hitting a student, never mind beating on him that way. Tom's reaction also troubled to her. His unrepentant defiance showed her a side to human nature that she could not grasp—an insane refusal to be conquered. Finally, the comment that sparked the firestorm was also zooming through her brain. She heard hate in those words, a hate she'd never heard before. Hatred of the Irish, of Catholics, of Negroes ... and coming from the soul of a classmate whom up until that time Brigid had seen as a fun and wholesome boy. Brigid was a mess. She knew that what Tom had said was very bad, but, to her, the beating was far worse. The words were awful; the beating was evil.

Most of all she dreaded this conversation with her mother, because she knew that her mother never spoke against the nuns. She knew that her mother would say that Tom was disrespectful and, no matter what, the nuns and all teachers must be respected because they are doing the Lord's work. She knew that her mother would talk about the workload and the minimum pay for the nuns and say that there could be no Catholic education without them. She knew that her mother would forbid her to talk about the situation, or about Sister Raphael, and say that the matter was closed. She knew that her mother would think this was an adult situation and that children should not be asked to comment.

As it turned out, she knew nothing.

Dar was sitting on the rocker in her bedroom when Brigid slowly walked in. She opened her arms in a welcoming gesture and called Brigid over to sit on her lap—an invitation that Brigid often longed for but rarely received. With three younger sisters, Brigid was more often the giver of hugs, not the recipient. It wasn't that she felt unloved: she was always secure in the love and care that her mother and father gave her. But because she was rather independent, and seldom showed neediness, demonstrative affection was spread more evenly among her three younger sisters.

So when Dar lifted her ten-year-old and held her to her breast and said, "Tell me about your day, sweetheart," Brigid just cried. They rocked silently for a while, and finally Dar spoke gently and firmly.

"I know I have always told you to respect your teachers, especially the sisters, who have a very special calling. But no one, not even a nun, has the right to hit another person's child, no matter what that child has said or done. And certainly no one has the right to beat another person's child to tears. If anyone—teacher, nun, relative, or anyone else—ever strikes you, you tell me or Daddy immediately. It is never okay."

Overwhelmed with relief, Brigid couldn't speak. With her arms around her mother's neck, she just squeezed with love and gratitude.

Dar went on, "Tomorrow, you will have a new teacher. Sister Raphael is going away for a rest. Thomas will be there and he will most likely be struggling with embarrassment or confusion. I know you will treat him with kindness. The comment he made about the president was most likely something he heard at home and repeated, so we will not judge him too harshly."

Brigid kissed her mother's cheek, said, "I love you, Mommy," and headed for the door, feeling firmly rooted again, in a world that once again made sense.

Dar called to her before she left the room, and said, in the same sweetly firm voice, "Brigid, you know, of course, that if I ever hear you refer to anyone as a mick or a nigger or any other bad name, I will give you a lickin' far worse than Thomas received today."

•

The months after Sister Raphael's attack on Tom brought peace to Brigid, a peace enhanced by music. Although, at ten years old, she had already decided that teaching was her calling, she also felt in tune with a rhythm underlying the world—a rhythm that accented the iambs and trochees of her favorite poems. It was the rhythm of a heart pumping. Or the rhythm of a weeping willow on a windy day. Or the rhythm of a baby's laugh. Or the rhythm of a mother's sigh. All around her, she felt a beat; she felt the music of humanity.

When she played her saxophone, she became one with that beat. The school band became a peaceful refuge from the world of fifth-grade angst. When Brigid knelt and prayed each night before going to bed, she counted among her many blessings the band director at St. Charles. He was a man who demanded excellence from students and taught not only the fundamentals but an appreciation of the power, beauty, and universal truth of music. He gave the students an array of the classics, pop, and jazz, in an environment where other elementary-school bands were playing "Pop Goes the Weasel." In an era when specific gender norms were the rule, he displayed no gender bias and based his decisions on talent. So when Brigid decided to take up the saxophone, the only female in the school to do so, he did not hesitate. If she was good, she would play in the band. Brigid was, indeed, very good.

Music was a treasured gift in the Nagy household. Dar was adept at the piano, and she and Miklos and the girls would often gather around it to sing show tunes, with Brigid occasionally adding the swing of the sax.

However, the music idol of the Nagy girls was not a saxophonist; it was Judy Garland. The one luxury that Dar afforded herself was buying any—all—of Judy's recordings. The daughters were raised on the sounds of "Over the Rainbow," and "For Me and My Gal," and "The Man That Got Away." Judy's voice was Dar's sanctuary; she got lost in the joy and sorrow of Judy's blues.

During the month of April, 1961, a rattling in the dinner-table conversations of the Nagy ensemble shook the rhythm of the family vibes. Miklos had taken a part-time job as an explosion supervisor (any new construction needed a firefighter on site to supervise blasting). He was often working late, and Dar noticed he had become withdrawn and unusually quiet. She also noticed that although the check stub indicated he was making fifty dollars a week, he was giving her only twenty-five. The man who had shared every thought and every penny with his wife for fifteen years was keeping a secret. Dar knew it. Dar felt it. Dar hated it.

Brigid felt the tension but did not dare mention it. Finally, on the last Monday of the month, which also coincided with the last paycheck of Miklos's extra job, the bubble of anxiety burst at dinner. Dar started crying—a rare and formidable occurrence.

She blurted out, in front of the children (another rare and formidable occurrence), "Miklos—what is wrong with you? Why are you hiding money from me? Why are you silent in the bedroom? Who have you been talking to on the phone in whispers? What—"

Miklos interrupted, in a tone much too jovial for the occasion. "Jeeez, Dar, what on earth are you so upset about? Can't a man have some quiet time and personal spending money?" He winked at Brigid. Her mood immediately changed: this was going to have a happy ending.

Dar was too shocked to speak, and before the lump had disappeared from her throat, Miklos got up, took an envelope from his shirt pocket, walked over to Dar, and handed her the envelope, giving her a hug that warmed the chilly atmosphere in the kitchen.

"I have an early present for you. Happy Mother's Day, darling. I am so lucky to have you as the mother of my children. I love you more than you will ever know. I've been quiet because I've never kept a secret from you and I was afraid if we spoke at any great length I would blab what I was doing. And ... well, in a minute, you'll see where the money went."

The trance that seemed to engulf Dar deepened as she opened the envelope. She pulled out two rectangular tickets. Brigid assumed they were Cleveland Indians tickets, since Dar was an avid fan. The look on Dar's face, however, convinced Brigid that the tickets indicated something much finer than a baseball game. Dar turned pale, her eyes became glassy, and her hands glistened with sweat. Miklos was afraid she would faint. In a moment, her color came back; her eyes cleared, and her hands were strong enough to squeeze Miklos's arm until it turned purple.

She turned to her oldest daughter, and said, "Brigid, next month, on Mother's Day, you and I are going to see Judy Garland, in person, at Public Hall."

•

May 14, 1961, cemented in Brigid an unshakable love for the arts. Music, language, emotion, family, expression, understanding, rhythm, love, oneness—all of them swirled in the vortex of Judy Garland's voice.

Public Hall, on East Sixth and St. Clair in Cleveland, was an overwhelmingly beautiful venue for even the most seasoned of concertgoers. For a child of ten, it presented a wonderland of architectural splendor. Brigid clung to her mother's hand as she gaped at the windows, the ceilings, the vastness of it all. When they were seated, twelve rows from the stage on the center aisle, Brigid stopped gaping and sat in amazement. Dar studied the program and softly groaned in satisfaction as she read the songs that Judy would sing.

The mood changed a bit, at 7:45, when the concert had not yet started. The audience—a sellout crowd—began to clap, in a steady, nervous beat. It reminded Brigid of a *Little Rascals* episode where the audience, sitting in a barn awaiting a Spanky production, started clapping and shouting, "We want the show to start! We want the show to start!"

Dar whispered nervously to Brigid, "You know, Judy has developed a reputation for being very late, and sometimes not even showing up for performances."

Before Brigid could fully comprehend these words, Mort Lindsey's orchestra started playing "The Trolley Song," and the audience convulsed. The orchestra's sound was astounding, and Brigid wished she could just sit and listen to the music all night.

Then the lights dimmed, the orchestra stopped, the spotlight shone on stage right, and there she was, a diminutive lady with a full chest, slightly disheveled hair, and weary-worn bags under big, sparkling brown eyes, dressed in a plain black dress and black high-heeled shoes. For the slightest of moments, many in the audience were taken aback—one could feel the surprise—this is not what most of them expected Judy Garland, Dorothy of Oz, to look like.

Then, the voice.

"When you're smiling, when you're smiling, the whole world smiles with you.... When you're laughing, when you're laughing, the sun comes shining through...."

Brigid was weak with awe. The voice, a gentle whirlpool of sound, sucked everyone into glorious depths of emotion. Judy's voice swallowed the audience. The voice, endlessly deep, pleasant, soothing, joyous, yet filtered through melancholy. Brigid would never experience anything like that moment again. She glanced at her mother, and Dar was holding her hands to her heart, tears in her eyes and her mouth slightly agape.

When Dar caught Brigid's glance, she squeezed her daughter's hand and said, "I love your father for this gift."

This would be Brigid's most treasured memory of time with her mother. The emotion and the depth of Judy Garland's concert did not let up. Each song, each word, each note took the audience into a world they had never imagined—even though it was the world in which they lived. Two men who sat in the row in front of Dar and Brigid held hands, and whispered through the entire concert, "Judy. Judy."

A few thousand people sat spellbound for two hours. There were several encores, no one wanted to leave.

After Brigid and her mother finally exited the hall, another fantasy awaited.

When Miklos arrived to take them home, he told them that he'd discovered where Judy was leaving the building. He parked the car, and they walked over to a garage where they saw dozens of people milling around a slightly open overhead door. Brigid, the only child in the crowd, thus quite shorter than the rest, went down on all fours and peeked under the door, and saw a white limousine with the motor running. When people asked her what she saw and she could tell them, they applauded, appreciating both her agility and the fact that they were in the right place to get a glimpse of the star.

The garage door began to open, and the limousine edged slowly into the crowd, which respectfully made a path for the vehicle to pass. The tinted windows shaded any clear glimpse of Judy, but suddenly the back passenger's-side window began rolling down, and there was

Judy Garland, peeking out, smiling and waving to her fans, still wearing the sequined jacket she'd worn during the second half of the show. Then the limousine stopped. Judy Garland caught sight of Brigid and beckoned her over to the car.

Dar walked over with Brigid and stood speechless as Judy Garland reached out and gently touched Brigid's wrist. In a deep, raspy voice, the idol of the Nagy household, the diva of all divas, spoke to Brigid with a sweet, gentle, laugh.

"Thank you, dahling, I do hope you enjoyed the show.... Now go home and go to bed."

•

During the summer following the concert, Brigid felt a stronger commitment to excellence: her music, her schoolwork, her writing—everything she did—was now executed in the light of what she perceived as artistic perfection, the performance of Judy Garland.

It is easy to lose oneself in the sometimes-nebulous world of artistic expression, but everyday living provides a direct route to reality. Brigid discovered this truth in the summer of 1961.

The Hungarian branch of Brigid's family tree was more entwined than the Irish branch. Even though Grandpa Nagy remained married to Grandma Nagy, he was living with his mistress on a farm in rural Medina, a few miles south of Parma. While the rest of the family accepted this arrangement, Miklos was adamant that the *kurva* (whore) was never to step foot in his house. Miklos and Dar brought their daughters to the farm only when the *kurva* was not there. This put a strain on the relationship between Miklos and Grandpa Nagy. Nevertheless, Grandpa Nagy visited the Parma bungalow once a month, bringing fresh corn or chicken from his farm to share with Miklos's growing family.

A tall, grizzled man with his gray hair in a high, wild mound, he had a mean snarl snapped permanently to his lips, which made Brigid somewhat fearful of Grandpa Nagy. The fear was somewhat eased by the warmth of his embrace and the prickly tickle of his beard on her cheek. He always smelled of whisky, and Dar always had a bottle of pálinka and a shot glass ready for him.

In July of 1961, Grandpa Nagy died. Viewing a dead body was a new experience for Brigid. She had never been taken to the funeral of her great-grandma. This made Grandpa Nagy's death more tangible, more sensory, more emotionally eerie. Her first look at his dead body, along with the deathly smell of fresh funeral-parlor flowers, sickened Brigid. The wailing of her Hungarian aunts and the all-permeating tension between the wife and the *kurva* became too much for the narrow worldview of an eleven-year-old child. She gladly took Michele, Sally, and Joan to the basement of the parlor where others gathered to smoke and drink coffee. Never before had she used babysitting to make a comfort zone.

While the sisters played in the basement, Brigid could overhear tales from her grandfather's past. She recalled some of them, which he had told at family gatherings.

Several years before, he had disappeared from Ohio for a year. He later revealed that he had returned to Hungary, to fight in the revolution against the Soviets, who had occupied the country since the end of World War II. Grandpa Nagy lost cousins and uncles in that uprising, and "communism" became a word not to be spoken in his presence. During one of his tellings of this story, the big, strong, wild-eyed freedom-fighter-turned-farmer-adulterer suddenly began to weep. It was the only time Brigid had ever seen her father hug another man.

Now that man was gone, and the smell and sounds and tensions of his death seeped into Brigid's soul with a nauseating awareness of mortality.

•

Sixth and seventh grades went by in a flurry of human achievement and folly that Brigid observed from a distance. With her classmates she watched as Alan Shepard shot up into space and, shortly thereafter, the Ohioan John Glenn circled the earth. Astronauts became the heroes of the day; Russians, the villains. Once a week, Brigid and her cousins would retreat to the basement and pray the Rosary for the conversion of Russia. Mary, the Mother of God, had promised that if children prayed the Rosary, Russian communism would be defeated. Brigid faithfully acted on that promise and held on to it through the Cuban missile crisis and beyond. While the threat of Russia's atomic weapons frightened her, the overall optimism of the space endeavors and the safe, stable rhythm of daily suburban life provided Brigid with an ample comfort zone of hope and security.

Dar and Miklos added twin girls to the Nagy family, Cindy and Suzy, in 1962. They also added two extra bedrooms to the bungalow, where Brigid and her five sisters lived and loved and laughed their way through peaceful days, starry nights, lightning bugs, and saxophone interludes. Brigid had a nucleus of trusted friends with whom she shared the adolescent joys and sorrows of crushes and broken hearts and menstrual cycles and middle-school anxieties. These friends all played instruments in the band, so Brigid always had pals by her side. Martin Gorman, who had grown to become the heartthrob of her class, was always close by. He called Brigid a few times a week, walked her home from school occasionally, and became her closest confidant. There was no physical attraction; they were friends, and Brigid relished the male companionship, Martin serving as the brother she would never have.

She seldom gave in to the petty jealousies that hormonally creep into twelve-year-olds, but she did long for a "better" body. Brigid was very thin, with tiny breasts and skinny legs. One day she overheard a boy in her class smirk to another, "That Nagy girl is totally shapeless." That hurt. She cried that night in bed. But as she gazed at Orion's Belt through the window of her new bedroom, the wonder of the heavens and the warm sounds coming from her parents' bedroom soon lulled her into a cozy sense of belonging to the universe. She didn't need a better body to be happy. She just needed her mind, her faith, her family, her saxophone, and a book.

She would need all of these to survive her eighth-grade year.

•

While other thirteen-year-old girls had bulletin boards with posters of Fabian or the Beatles or the Supremes, Brigid adorned her room with large pictures of Charlie Parker, Charlotte Brontë, and a local celebrity, Ghoulardi. Charlie Parker was the jazz saxophonist whose sound and approach to music filled her with inspiration; he was a standard of excellence in sound to which she aspired. Charlotte Brontë wrote the novel *Jane Eyre,* one of Brigid's favorites because it was written about a woman, by a woman. Even at thirteen, Brigid appreciated the social and literary relevance of female perspectives. Finally, there was Ghoulardi, whom Grandma Brigid simply called "a nut." Brigid thought he was a genius. Ghoulardi was a Cleveland TV personality who hosted the *Shock Theater* program on Friday nights. Using satire, technology, slapstick, and any other entertainment technique he cared to use, he seduced his audience into a night of fun and laughter and surprise. His show conquered Cleveland. Clevelanders loved it. So did Brigid.

Most families in Parma society in 1963 did not regard becoming a teenager as a noteworthy milestone. In Brigid's family, thirteen-year-olds were ignored on a greater scale than small children, who themselves maintained no noteworthiness except their need to be fed and loved and tended. A teenager was in the limbo between childhood and adulthood, and so Brigid passed her first summer as an invisible teenager babysitting for her five sisters, playing her saxophone, reading novels, writing in a journal, and watching Ghoulardi on Friday nights. Occasionally her parents let her spend an overnight at one of her friends, but Dar frowned on that adolescent practice.

"You'll be out from under my roof soon enough. And there's

nothing for young girls to be talking about after 11:00 p.m. that nourishes the soul. I want you home at night."

Brigid did not mind. One night, she was especially grateful to be with family. It was the night Grandma Brigid died.

Friday, July 19, was a hot, humid night, and the sky was shadowy with wispy clouds and dim moonlight. Grandmothers Brigid O'Malley and Mary Nagy were walking home from the annual St. Charles Borromeo carnival, where they had played bingo. They were, as Grandma Mary frequently said, "chums," often playing bingo or going for walks together.

Brigid was sitting on the front porch, watching the two old ladies stroll up the avenue, holding on to each other's arms, chatting gaily, swinging their pocketbooks, and breathing in the summer night. When they reached the curb under the streetlight in front of the house, Grandma O'Malley's knees suddenly buckled, and she fell forward, her face crashing into the sidewalk.

Grandma Nagy reacted with an "Oooooh oooooh!" and tried to lift the other old woman by her elbows. But Grandma O'Malley was not moving.

Brigid screamed in through the screen door to Dar, who was lulling one of the twins in the rocking chair. "Mom, Grandma fell! I think she's really hurt!"

Dar, holding the baby, ran with Brigid to the curb, where they came upon the two matriarchs, one flat on the ground, frighteningly still, her face covered in blood, and the other kneeling beside her, clutching a rosary and murmuring Hail Marys in Hungarian.

A neighbor, Paula Keegan, was witnessing the situation from her porch. She called the Parma Fire Department. An ambulance from the Snow Road station arrived within five minutes. Miklos was one of the firefighters on duty.

Although Brigid was shaken at the sight of Grandma O'Malley's motionless physical condition, and Grandma Nagy's frenzied emotional condition, she could not help feeling admiration and pride as she watched her father take control of the situation. He calmly and professionally moved his mother and wife away from his mother-in-law, and immediately stabilized the neck, put gauze over the wounds that were bleeding, and, with the help of the other firefighter on duty, lifted Grandma O'Malley into the ambulance on a stretcher.

He looked at Dar and said, "Come to Parma Hospital. I'll wait for you."

Paula Keegan took Brigid, the baby, and Grandma Nagy back to Brigid's house. Dar called her father to inform him of what had happened, then drove to the hospital, picking him up on the way.

Grandpa O'Malley was a quiet, studious man who worked as a truck driver for Wonder Bread and as a part-time scorekeeper for the Cleveland Indians. The relationship between Grandma Brigid and him was strained. He provided her with steady financial security and he was home every night. She, in return, cooked his dinner and made their home a comfortable place to live. Yet, at family gatherings he was very quiet, sometimes turning his hearing aid off to avoid the noisy familial interactions. He and Grandma Brigid—he called her by her middle name, Delia—slept in separate bedrooms, and rarely sat by each other or conversed congenially. There was a deep, hurtful secret lurking in their relationship. It was always present but never revealed.

The drive to the hospital was a silent ride. Dar loved her father, but there was little warmth or emotional connection between them. She had never seen his tears, never felt his hug, and never heard his praise. But he was always there. When she was a child, he was there when she woke up, there when she had dinner, there when she went to bed, there when she had appendicitis, and there when she saw Wes Ferrell pitch a no-hitter for the Cleveland Indians. And he was there, with the cash for the wedding, when she married Miklos.

Almost an hour had passed since Grandma O'Malley collapsed. When Dar and her father arrived at the hospital, Miklos was waiting by the Emergency Room door, red-eyed and serious. He shook his father-in-law's hand, put his arm around Dar and walked them into a private waiting room, where a doctor was sitting, expressionless and official. He addressed the old man.

"Mr. O'Malley, your wife has suffered a traumatic injury to her head. Despite valiant and continuous resuscitation efforts by the fire-fighters in the ambulance, I am very sorry to tell you that she did not make it through the ordeal. She passed away at eleven o'clock this evening. Her remains will be sent to the coroner's office to determine an exact cause of death."

Miklos wrapped both arms around Dar as she wept uncontrollably into his shoulder. John O'Malley sat as rigid as if he, himself, were a corpse. He stared unflinchingly at the doctor, and whispered, "I want to see her."

The doctor led them all to the hospital morgue, where the frail body of Brigid Delia O'Malley, covered with a taupe-colored sheet, was lying, face and arms ghostly white, bluish fingers hanging slightly over the side of the gurney.

Holding her father's hand, Dar walked over to the body, gulping in her sobs. John O'Malley, who still could not find his full voice, looked down at his wife of fifty years and whispered, "I'm so sorry, Delia."

Those were his last words. He collapsed onto the floor of the morgue and died of a massive heart attack.

The autopsy later revealed that Grandma O'Malley had died of a ruptured brain aneurysm. The suddenness of the deaths shook Brigid's soul. One summer's night her Irish grandparents were in her life; the next night, they were gone. At thirteen years old, she grasped the reality of the cliché, "Here today, gone tomorrow."

•

The Nagy household seemed to dwell in a silent fog of surreal activity for the remaining days of summer, after Grandma and Grandpa

O'Malley died. Dar had lost the spark of vigor that supplied the energy for family activities. Miklos faced every endeavor with solemnity. Brigid could find no peace; she found no consolation in faith or music or literature or family. Her cousin Jojo had moved from the neighborhood last year, and Martin Gorman was away for the summer. She was alone.

Although she thought frequently of her grandfather, it was the loss of her grandmother that made a hole in her soul from which she could not escape. Every night, Brigid lay in bed thinking of how every important moment of her life carried with it an image of her grandmother. The search for Great-Grandma, awakening from the ether after a tonsillectomy, her First Communion, St. Patrick's Day parades, each and every one of her band concerts, Confirmation (Brigid had chosen Abigail as her Confirmation name—the same as Grandma Brigid's), the births of her sisters, every holiday and holy day Mass . . . Grandma Brigid's face and love pervaded every moment. Now she was gone.

One night, late in August, while Brigid was reading to Michele and Joan, Miklos walked into the room and asked Brigid to come chat with him and Dar in their bedroom. Brigid hadn't "chatted" with her mother since Sister Raphael's attack on Tom. She guessed the topic would be the deaths of her grandparents.

Miklos began the conversation: "Brigid, we hope you know how proud we are of you. A lot of guys at the station talk about how their teenage daughters sass them and sneak around. Some of them have even started smoking. And a lot of them pile on makeup or get Ds in school. They don't help at all around home. And Jeez, I'm just so thankful you're such a good kid."

This isn't what Brigid was expecting and she wondered where the chat was heading. Her father often muddled through important conversations, never clearly articulating his thoughts. Her mother now quickly got to the point.

"We have all been preoccupied with the loss of your grandma and grandpa," she said. "Losing both of my parents so suddenly was a shock and has overshadowed me with a sadness that will linger for quite a while. But it's time to move on, and—more important—it's time to rely on God to provide us with strength to live our own lives and use the blessings He has given us."

So this is a "We have to move on" talk, thought Brigid. *Okay, I get it.*

But then the talk took a turn.

Dar continued, "Grandma and Grandpa left us a nice amount of money. Dad and I have paid off our loan for the room additions and we have enough left over to send you to any high school you choose to attend. We . . . ."

Brigid was so stunned she barely heard what followed. She had dreaded going to the Parma public high school. Not because of the school, or the people, but because she longed to explore life outside Parma. Parma was her home, and she did love it, but she also loved the grit and the rhythm of the streets of Cleveland. Grandma Nagy lived on Carroll Avenue, and on Saturdays when the family would visit her they would all walk to the West Side Market on West 25th Street, and Brigid relished the smells of the various ethnic foods and the sounds of the Hungarian, Puerto Rican, Italian, and Polish customers. In that same neighborhood was an all-girls Catholic school, Lourdes Academy, on 41st Street, which Brigid had always wanted to attend. She had visited it at an open house the year before and had fallen in love with the spirit of the place. Some of her friends were going there and she prayed every night that somehow her parents would find a way to pay the $122 plus transportation fees, to send her there.

"Thank you! Thank you! Thank you!" she said, hugging her parents and jumping up and down with glee.

"We're proud of you, Brigid," Miklos said, his voice cracking with emotion.

"You can move on and keep Grandma and Grandpa in your heart," said Dar, not holding in the tears that welled from her eyes.

Brigid went to her room and took up her sax. She found the sheet music for Charlie Parker's rendition of "Summertime," Grandma O'Malley's favorite. Her saxophone never sounded so mellow as it sounded that day, in the joyful sadness of life and death, the joyful sadness of playing the blues.

•

Autumn arrived with a heat spell, as hot, dry air held on to the leaves of summer. Brigid eagerly awaited the cool chill of fall and the burst of orange that radiated from the maple trees of Patti DeSantis's yard. (She still called it Patti's yard, even though there had been several occupants in and out since Patti left.) There had always been a sense of order to Brigid's world, and the predictable behavior of the seasons was an integral part of that order. Although Parma weather was prone to sudden dips in temperature, the summers were usually hot and sunlit yellow, the autumns were chilly and reddish orange, the winters were cold and snowy white, and the springs were wet and emerald green. There was a rainbowed rhythm to this world, and Brigid slid through its beat.

This year, the quartet from Liverpool, England, the Beatles, had provided the beat for the lives of most thirteen-year-old girls. There was something so fresh and vibrant about these young men that even a scholar like Brigid succumbed to their charm. Seen from the eyes of a thirteen-year-old girl, John was intellectual and cerebral, Brigid's favorite. George was pensive and spiritual, the favorite of isolated and detached adolescent souls. Ringo was quiet and easy-going, the favorite of sensible youngsters who liked the music but did not get caught up in the frenzy. Paul was everyone else's favorite, the cutest, funniest, and most likely to make moms and dads happy. In between high-school entrance exams, band concerts, and literary club meetings, the Beatles provided a unity in Brigid's middle-school social structure. High achievers, low achievers, cheerleaders, and musicians would all swoon to the sounds of "She Loves You."

Yeah, yeah, yeah.

But there was not enough love. At 1:00 p.m. on November 22, 1963, Principal Sister Mary Judyth's voice came shakily over the school's public-address system.

"Teachers, boys and girls, please give me your full attention. President Kennedy has been shot, in Dallas, Texas. We do not know his condition. Please silently form a line and proceed to the church, where we will pray for our president and our country."

Mrs. Howard, Brigid's homeroom teacher, slammed her book on the desk, threw her pencil in the air, and groaned, "I knew it! I knew he should never have gone to Dallas!"

She quickly regained her composure and asked the students to get their coats and books, and anything else they would be taking home.

"We will most likely be dismissed right from the church," she said. "Please be silent and begin your prayers now. There will be troubled times ahead."

Hundreds of stunned and frightened children walked in complete silence into the church to pray for their wounded Irish Catholic President. Within the hour, a worker from the rectory came in and handed Sister Judyth a note. She paused from her recitation of the Rosary, and tearfully announced that the president had died. Teachers bowed their heads in sobs; children looked around for some sort of comfort or for guidance on how to react. Brigid turned automatically to the person beside her in a search for comfort and support. She received a warm embrace.

It came from a weeping Thomas Smith.

•

The days after the assassination were a blur of shock and sadness. The murders of Dallas Officer J. D. Tippit and then of the accused assassin, Lee Harvey Oswald, coupled with the never-ending news coverage of the Kennedy family and the president's funeral, cast a grimness over the entire country and, indeed, the world—including Brigid's world. Brigid loved President Kennedy. There was a charm and confidence about him that inspired her and her friends. He was youthful and funny and had exuded an optimism that she would never again experience from a political leader.

When the Nagys and O'Malleys gathered over the holidays, she would overhear heated discussions of "philanderer" and "adulterer" and "silver spoons." She never overheard enough to understand the underlying contention of several family members that President Kennedy was not the altar-boy cherub that she envisioned. Her vision of President Kennedy—as a savior, an icon, a role model, a motivator—would last well into her adult life. His assassination spun her back into the cloudy silence that had engulfed her after the deaths of her grandparents. It would take a foreign invasion to shake her out of the fog.

•

The Beatles arrived in New York City on February 7, 1964. Brigid and her friends were consumed by the television screen, this time looking for any glimpses of the Fab Four. Ghoulardi showed film clips of the Beatles' early years, in English basement pubs and Hamburg taverns, which whetted the girls' appetites for the upcoming treat on *The Ed Sullivan Show.* Fortunately for Brigid, Dar and Miklos found the music of the Beatles to be acceptable, and Dar often commented on the beautiful harmony of the voices and guitars of the young performers. Many parents disdained the long hair and the rock sound, but the lyrics were not yet tainted with sexual innuendos or drug mantras, so the Nagy girls were free to listen and involve themselves in what the news reporters labeled "Beatlemania."

When Brigid was invited to a Beatles party at Melanie Burke's house, to watch the group's first Ed Sullivan Show appearance, Dar did not hesitate to give permission. She did double-check with the Burkes to make sure that no boys would be present. St. Charles had a strict code forbidding "boy/girl parties"—the only sin worse than a boy/girl party was smoking in the restroom.

The invitation surprised Brigid. Melanie was a main character in the "popular group" (girls with steady boyfriends and weekly pajama parties and stylish clothes and Maybelline eyes), and although Melanie had always been cordial to Brigid, they did not socialize at all outside school. Melanie was the steady girlfriend of Martin Gorman, so Brigid suspected he had nudged Melanie to include her in the grand event. A few other band girls were also invited, so Brigid was excited to spend an evening with classmates screaming out a welcome to the British invasion. And scream she did.

Shy and quiet, Brigid rarely had outbursts of emotion. She liked to be in control, especially of herself. But now, the frivolous chatter of her friends and the resonant energy of the moment, pushed Brigid into the frenzy. When John, Paul, George, and Ringo appeared on Ed Sullivan's stage and Paul began to sing, Brigid began to scream.

She screamed away dementia; she screamed away lost friends; she screamed away kurvas; she screamed away aneurysms; she screamed away heart attacks; and she screamed away assassinations.

•

Springtime budded quickly that year, and soon Brigid's time at St. Charles had come to an end. In the final Mass of her elementary-school journey, Brigid joyfully sang her favorite hymn, "Holy God, We Praise Thy Name," and was ready for the next evolution of her life. Brigid's world was back in order, and her hopes for herself and for mankind rested in the orderly rhythms of her God, her family, her music, and her books.

*

Chapter 3

Gordon Square District
Cleveland, Ohio, 1950–1964

The National Civic League had awarded Cleveland, Ohio, its coveted All-America City Award in 1949, and by 1950 optimism and hope permeated the mood along the shores of Lake Erie. Though many returning veterans surrendered to the lure of new suburban adventures, clean air, and economic opportunity, many more firmly planted themselves back in their family roots, in the city that many people were calling "the best location in the nation."

Such was the case of MV and Rose Vanetti. They brought their new baby, Rosie, home to West 65th Street, to a house they shared with Mama Rose's mother, Grandma Rose Clemente. It was a large three-story house, with five bedrooms, dark cherry woodwork, and colorful stained-glass windows. It was the house where Mama Rose had grown up and where she would raise her own family.

Around the corner, on Detroit Avenue, was a small grocery store, owned and operated by the Vanettis. It was one of many stores run by Italian families in the area. The widow Marie Magaldi owned a religious gift store, with merchandise ranging from First Communion books to handmade handkerchiefs to lacy scarves. Mr. Vinnie Magooch owned the wine store, with wines ranging from expensive imported Italian to Cleveland specials from the local lake wineries. Tony Parete owned the gas station with services from fill-ups to oil changes to windshield washing. The children's favorite, Cookie's Candies, was owned by Concetta and Cornelio Barone and carried treats of wax lips, Bazooka bubble gum, delicacies of Cadbury Fudge and Whitman's Samplers.

The neighborhood's crowning glory was the Gordon Square Arcade, a magnificent structure built in the 1920s, which housed a theater, a hotel, offices, shops, a billiard room, and a market. Though not as grand as the Arcade's market, Vanetti's Groceries was the hub of the neighborhood culture. Everyone needed eggs and bread and flour or other staples and so at some point everyone within a ten block radius stopped in at Vanetti's. They would chat, exchange woes, bemoan rising prices, and in the same breath curse all things made in Japan. MV was a good listener, who possessed the proverbial broad shoulder upon which people could cry, or laugh, or be comforted. He often settled disputes among quarreling neighbors and, because he was fluent in both Italian and English, he regularly acted as translator and mediator if an Italian-speaking neighbor had dealings with public utility companies or with the government. Because of all these traits, the neighborhood had elected Massimo Vanetti to represent them in City Council.

Mama Rose was a caring person, too. Most of all, she cared for her husband. MV's parents had died very young of heart disease, a genetic omen not overlooked by Rose. She affectionately monitored MV's workload and stress levels.

If someone went on talking to MV for more than a few minutes, Mama Rose, working at the cash register, would tenderly shout to the customer, "Hey—you gonna buy somethin' or not?"

•

Rosie was baptized into the Catholic faith in a duplex home on Detroit Avenue, which, at the time, was serving as Our Lady of Mount Carmel Church. A new church and parish hall were under construction, but for now the neighborhood Catholic Italians gathered in this house for fellowship and special ceremonies. Monsignor Giuliani performed the sacramental Baptism ritual, as Grandma Rose, Mama Rose, MV, and the godparents, Aunt Maria and Uncle John Vanetti, lit the candles and held the baby. Immediately afterward, they all went back to the house on 65th Street, where over a hundred friends, relatives, and neighbors joined the celebration to welcome Baby Rosie into their world.

Globe string lights that were hung from the house out to the clothes lines were lit when the party lasted into the darkness of the summer night. Tambourines tapped and jingled the rhythm as Uncle Michael Clemente played the accordion, and the Clemente and Vanetti families, along with their *paesani,* danced and sang and ate and gave thanks for the newest member of their community.

Baby Rosie occasionally suckled at her mother's breast, and the rest of the time gave back the greatest gift a baby has to offer: she slept in silence.

•

As the first years of Rosie's life passed by, her neighborhood and her family grew around her. Riccardo Vanetti was born when Rosie was two years old. Rosie immediately formed a bond with him, enchanted by this tiny, fragile being who now shared her room and her parents' love. MV and Mama Rose instilled in Rosie the notion of what it takes to be a "big sister," and even though she was still essentially a baby herself, she often helped her mother by running to fetch the baby powder or the hooded terry towels for bath time. Sometimes she stood gazing at Riccardo asleep in his crib and wondered at his tiny fingers and his head of thick, dark hair.

By the time Riccardo was one, Rosie had signed on as his caretaker. Now three, she could entertain her brother with peekaboo, patty-cake, ball rolling, and tea parties. She was enthralled with her playmate, and Mama Rose appreciated the tender ways in which Rosie occupied the baby's time.

Grandma Rose was home with the children on most days, but whenever she visited friends' homes or attended Italian Women's Club meetings, Rosie and Riccardo would stay in the back room of the store, where a playpen and crib were set up. Rosie watched *The Howdy Doody Show* on the tiny TV in the back of the store, and barraged her baby brother with Flub-a-Dub songs and "I Love Bosco" jingles. Watching her parents work, listening to the neighborhood chatter, and caring for her baby brother—Rosie would later remember these days with a joyful heart.

The memories from that third year would sustain her through the traumas of the coming year.

*

One afternoon, Mama and MV were working late at the store, stocking the shelves for the onslaught of 4th of July shopping. Italian-Americans celebrated all the holidays with gusto. They favored summer picnic time celebrations because the pasta feasts were now accompanied by steaks and barbecued pork and sausage. The Vanettis made sure that all essential items of food were readily available and fresh for their neighbors and friends, many of whom would be celebrating in the Vanettis' own backyard at their annual cookout.

Rosie and Riccardo (enamored of *I Love Lucy* episodes, she had started calling him Ricky) had stayed home with Grandma Clemente, and they were all watching the landscapers supplement the beauty of Grandma's flower bed with a waterfall. They themselves had been working all morning helping to clear out rocks, making a space near the tulips for a soothing and beautiful refuge. Grandma sat on a lawn chair and kept an eye on the men and on Rosie and Ricky, who were now playing on the backyard swing set.

When Ricky started to climb the ladder on the sliding board, Rosie went up right behind him, as she always did, to make sure he did not fall backward. Ricky was adept at climbing, but Rosie was too cautious to let him climb to the top of the eight-foot sliding board unattended. They both giggled and sang songs as they ascended the ladder.

When they reached the top, Ricky's foot slipped through the side arch of the metal railing and, before Rosie could grab any part of him, he plunged straight to the ground, with an unintentional somersault in midair which sent his head plunging toward one of the garden rocks that had been strewn throughout the yard. Rosie heard him squeal with laughter. It was not a sound of fear, it was a sound of delight, a sound that would forever reverberate in her ears.

Ricky giggled all the way down until his head hit the rock. He died instantly. The sound of his laughter added an uncanny horror to the incident and the memory of it. Rosie's memory was a vision of Ricky having the time of his life—at the time of his death.

•

Riccardo's death emptied the joy from the Vanetti household. The accident occurred while Mama Rose was pregnant with her third child, and that child, Rebecca, was born prematurely, a few months after the death. Mama Rose was happy to have another girl; she did not want to feel that another baby boy could ever replace Riccardo. She was also relieved to have the extended hospital stay. The loss of her little boy had annihilated her spirit and wracked her body. Nothing and no one could calm the volcano of emotions in her. After a fretful and laborious Caesarean section during the birth of Rebecca, when the doctors told her that both she and the baby must remain in the hospital for at least two weeks, Mama collapsed in exhaustion and for once in her life allowed others to care for her. She did not allow herself to worry about her husband, or her daughters, or her mother. If she was going to move on, she knew she had to heal herself first. Tending to the rest of the family would come later.

At home, Rosie, MV, and Grandma Clemente walked and talked in a glum world of grief and shock. Rosie spent her nights reliving the fall in her mind; the birth of a baby sister brought no excitement or happiness to her, and she spent her days sitting on Grandma's lap in an old rocking chair, rocking wistfully and aimlessly, watching the leaves fall outside the window. Grandma no longer had any interest in the garden, and MV lost himself in the business dealings of the store and the council. The backyard lay in a waste of weeds and scattered rocks.

Three days before Mama Rose and Rebecca were to be released from the hospital, MV stayed home from work, leaving the store in the hands of his brother, John. He cooked breakfast for Rosie and Grandma that morning, and announced that for the next few days there would be workmen in the house, painting and redecorating the nursery.

"It's time for life to come back into our home," MV said that morning to Grandma Rose and Rosie. "Ricky's spirit will always be with us, and we have to cling to that spirit. But we also have to cling to physical life. We don't want Rebecca coming into a house of sadness. She's going to enter our world like you and Ricky did, Rosie, with love and joy."

At four years old, Rosie, thanks to her big-sister persona with Ricky, possessed an aura of maturity and responsibility that belied the chronological fact that she was just a little girl. During the months following Ricky's death, however, she reverted to babyish behavior. She sucked her thumb, sometimes wet her bed, and would often wake screaming during the night. It would take more than a new baby and fresh paint to fully extinguish the flames of guilt and loss that were consuming her.

As the year passed, her nightmares of the accident did diminish, and some gaiety returned to Rosie's life. There was an eternal spot of sadness in her heart that she returned to now and then, cementing the memory of Ricky in her spirit, but family and faith again filled her life. Baby Rebecca was a peaceful infant, and by the time the next summer's flowers bloomed, Rosie was again relishing her role as big sister, and Rebecca looked at her with loving, joyful eyes.

For her fifth birthday, Mama and MV surprised Rosie with a puppy. He was a boxer, and when he flopped toward Rosie, she shrieked, "Oooooh, he is so tiny—but he has muscles! I love him."

She named her puppy Muscles, and she and Grandma Rose took

complete charge of his care. They trained him to be housebroken, how to treat Rebecca, and the boundaries of his domain. Rosie cheated a bit on disciplining him when he wept and whimpered in his bed-box. She would often sneak to pick him up and hold him. One time he fell asleep in her bed and when she woke up she was covered in puppy urine. The next night she let him weep and whimper in his bed-box until he slept.

That summer, Rosie's days were filled with helping Grandma in her garden. On the anniversary of Ricky's death, the family gathered in the backyard and prayed for the repose of his soul. Rosie and Grandma had planted a small section of lilacs around a statue of Saint Riccardo, imported from Italy, that Grandma had mail-ordered through a catalogue.

4th of July celebrations went on as scheduled, but this year, instead of the backyard gala, the Vanetti and Clemente clans picnicked at Edgewater Park, to get a better view of Cleveland's prime fireworks display. During the afternoon, Rosie and her cousins enjoyed the cool waves of Lake Erie while listening to the mild cussing of their elders playing the annual softball game at the nearby baseball diamonds. This was a gender-segregated group, with the mothers and daughters minding the food and the children while the fathers and sons engaged in sports and wine.

Muscles ran between the groups like a crazy mutt, not knowing which way to frolic. He calmed down long enough to rest his head on Rosie's lap, when he found her, sitting in silent sadness, by a rock next to an eight-foot sliding board at the Edgewater playground.

•

When Rosie started kindergarten in the fall, Mama Rose treated it like any other day. "You are going to a wonderful school, with wonderful people, and you will learn, and you will succeed," she said as she handed Rosie her Dale Evans lunch box, a treasured birthday gift from her father.

Rosie had felt no anxiety about attending school; she had longed for the adventure of walking to Our Lady of Mount Carmel Elementary School with her cousins and neighborhood friends. The others rushed readily to their classrooms, but Rosie was a dawdler, stopping to examine anthills or pokey caterpillars. Although she was not fond of alphabet lessons and printing exercises, she did enjoy the recess activities and the playground circle games, like *How Many Miles to Bethlehem?* and *Bow Bow Bow Belinda.* She loved being outside, and often sat collecting fallen leaves from under the maple trees that lined the schoolyard.

Kindergarten and first grade passed by swiftly, with no major incidents. Rosie was a quiet, average student who behaved properly and slid under the radar of the nuns' all-seeing eyes. At home, she was a bit more vocal about what she perceived as the nonsense in some of her lessons. During second quarter of her first-grade year, Rosie received a U, for "Unsatisfactory," in the category "Pays attention in class."

When Mama Rose saw it, she asked for no explanations. She told Rosie to bend over and proceeded to swat her backside a few times with a belt, exclaiming, in a clear, measured tone, "We pay four dollars a year for you to go to that school! You damn well better pay attention, all day, every day!"

At dinner that evening, Mama Rose quietly gave Rosie an extra portion of her favorite dessert, chocolate pudding with whipped cream, and gently squeezed Rosie's shoulder while they were washing the dishes. Later, when Mama Rose finally asked Rosie why she was not paying attention in class, Rosie, still stinging from the belt and not soothed by the pudding, unexpectedly blurted out, "Because Sister Hortense is a dumb ass."

Mama Rose did not need a belt for this reply: her open hand slapped Rosie's open mouth, and effectively ended the conversation. Rosie never brought home another U.

•

First Communion Day was cause for great celebration, both in the neighborhood and in the family. Rosie reveled in the special attention from family and friends. Mount Carmel parishioners stood on their tree lawns and waved to the Communicants as they paraded around the block. Rosie's dress was covered in lace, with hand-stitched embroidery and pointed satin sleeves. Her veil, worn thirty years before by Mama Rose, and sixty years before by Grandma Rose, was slightly yellowed with age, and Rosie considered it a holy relic. As the procession made its way into the church, Rosie broke from the line to hug Grandma Rose, who was standing by the doors, rosary in her hand, tears in her eyes.

As the priest was reciting the Communion antiphon, a bluebird made its way into the church, and while other parishioners seemed greatly distracted by its frenzied chirping and flying, Rosie felt a rare, spiritual sensation, not so much with the other people in the church as with the earthly kingdom of all creatures. As she walked to the Communion railing, her seven-year-old mind was thinking not of Transubstantiation or of the Act of Contrition but of Jesus' words "Behold the fowls of the air: for they sow not, neither do they reap, nor gather into barns; yet your heavenly Father feedeth them."

Later that day, a grand party was held at the Vanettis' home, and Rosie gratefully accepted the numerous gifts and offerings, and the giving and getting of hugs and kisses from relatives and friends. When everyone had left, Rosie sat in the garden with Grandma Rose, watching Muscles feast on the dropped scraps of meatballs and spilled remnants of pasta. They spoke of God and nature and Ricky, as Rosie drowsed to the hooting of an owl and the clanging of dishwashing. MV carried her upstairs to bed, and Mama Rose undressed her, all while Rosie slept. The house quieted and settled for the night as Mama Rose and MV counted the hundreds of dollars given to Rosie on her special day.

"We are indeed blessed," said MV.

"That we are," Mama Rose agreed.

They, too, settled in for the night. Nine months later, Renaldo Riccardo Vanetti was born.

•

Our Lady of Mount Carmel Elementary School provided Rosie with the basic tools of reading, writing, and arithmetic. Her approach to learning was to do what was necessary to please the nuns and her mother. After all, Grandma Rose had told her, "Real learning happens outside the classroom."

Every day after school, Rosie would run home, where Grandma would have milk and cookies waiting on the lace-covered dining-room table. The milk was served from an old family teapot of Capodimonte porcelain, made in Italy. Cherubs with mischievously smiling faces adorned the pot and the matching cups. This daily activity became known as "teatime." Rosie loved sitting quietly, sipping from a family heirloom as Grandma told stories from her youthful days, spent in the vineyards of Naples. When Grandma's mind wandered, ancient Italian history crept into the stories, tales of Hannibal mingling with the narrative of the family fables. When Rosie would ask how the battles of Rome connected to the vineyards of her forebears, Grandma would just say, "We are all linked in time—everything and everyone connects."

One story that held Rosie's interest was the story of the Punic Wars, when many of Hannibal's elephants drowned in the Ofante River. Intrigued by the use of such magnificent, peaceful beasts for warfare, Rosie developed an intense interest in and love for elephants, which would eventually direct her life's path. She read and reread Golden and Wonder Books like *The Saggy Baggy Elephant,* and *Happy Animals.* Her favorite was a French book called *Babar.*

When teatime was over, Rosie would take Rebecca and Muscles for a walk to Vanetti's Groceries, where she shared the events of her day with her mother and father. MV and Mama Rose closed the store for an hour every day between four and five o'clock to spend the time talking with Rosie and cuddling Rebecca.

In 1960, Kennedy fever struck the Vanettis and the entire Mount Carmel congregation, as the miracle of Americans electing a Catholic president excited every Catholic community. When the president's motorcade drove down Detroit Avenue, students from Mount Carmel lined the streets, applauding and waving flags. During this time, Rosie developed the habit of cutting out newspaper articles, magazine covers and articles, and saving them, along with political memorabilia having to do with John Fitzgerald Kennedy. She collected hundreds of stories and reports and slogans and photos, and put them in a scrapbook.

While she was accumulating items for this collection, Rosie became fascinated by the space program of the Russians. She read about Laika, the first Russian dog in space. Laika did not survive the trip. Again the use of animals with little regard for their well-being dismayed Rosie. She was pleased, however, to read that Mrs. Kennedy and the new president were great animal lovers, and it delighted her that the premier of Russia, Nikita Khrushchev, presented the Kennedys with Pushinka, a puppy produced by two stray dogs, Belka and Strelka, that the Russian scientists took from the streets and sent into space to orbit the earth.

The pride in having a Catholic president, the awe of putting men into space, and the chill of the Cold War dominated the conversations at the dinner table and in the classrooms. Rosie participated in the Rosaries said for the conversion of Russia, and attended Masses specified for the intention of President Kennedy, but her thoughts mostly strayed to the stray dogs of the Soviet Union.

School became less and less appealing to Rosie as she progressed to junior high. The inevitable hormonal changes in her body and her moods left her wanting either to fit in or to tune out. "Fitting in" meant constantly competing for boys' attention, wearing stylish clothes and makeup, having weekend sleepovers, and sneaking to the doughnut shop instead of attending Mass.

Having a best friend was the ultimate goal of fitting in, because being alone was the ultimate sign of rejection. A girl needed just one friend to rely on, share secrets with, borrow clothes from, go to movies with, talk to on the telephone, to be able to belong. Best friends, however, were as interchangeable as spaghetti and rigatoni—one could be substituted for another, and either would eventually be gone. Rosie tried to have a best friend, inviting girls to her home for sleepovers or tagging along to Saturday matinee movies; but not belonging to a specific group left Rosie depending on beauty and style to gain acceptance. She had neither—at least not by the junior-high standards of teased hairdos and cover-girl skin. Her social life consisted of listening to the Beatles and Fabian with her cousins, and watching *The Donna Reed Show* with her parents and siblings. On Friday nights she retreated with Muscles to the big family room and watched Ghoulardi as she snacked on potato chips and Lawson's French Onion Dip. Sometimes her father would join her, and Rosie enjoyed the companionship and the neighborhood stories he shared with her. His job as a councilman and his responsibilities at the grocery store gave him few moments to spend alone with his oldest child, so these Friday nights were precious to both of them.

Nonetheless, Rosie would have preferred to have a best friend.

•

On November 22, 1963, at 2:00 p.m., Rosie heard shrieking in the hallway of Our Lady of Mount Carmel school. Mr. Lorenzo, the school custodian, came running into the eighth-grade classroom, shouting, "The president has been assassinated! The president has been assassinated!"

The eighth-grade teacher, Sister Mary Peters, turned ghostly pale and asked the students to put their heads on their desks and pray Hail Marys while she went to see what was happening. Rosie looked around as the other students immediately obeyed, but she kept her head up and sat erect at her desk, frozen in shock at the thought of a murdered president, a murdered Catholic president. Sister Peters came back into the classroom, announced that President Kennedy was dead, and said that the students were dismissed to go directly home.

Instead of going home, Rosie went to her parents' store, where she knew neighbors would be gathering. Her mother, now eight months pregnant with her fifth child, was waiting for Rosie in front of the store. When Rosie saw her mother's tear-streaked face and her open arms, she ran to her, on legs heavy with the gravity of grief.

Mama Rose embraced Rosie, and cried, "They've killed our president—they've killed him, Rosie!"

MV had moved the tiny television into the front of the store, which was now filled with neighbors and relatives, all watching in quiet shock as news trickled in from Dallas, Texas. Rosie and Grandma took Rebecca and Renaldo home. Mama and MV followed shortly after, and the Vanettis, like the rest of America and the world, watched the horror and sadness of history unfold.

In the following weeks, Rosie found every magazine and newspaper available and neatly pasted these articles and photos in her scrapbook. Long walks with Muscles down to Hermann Park, a mile from her home, helped to soothe her constant heartache at the violence she could not comprehend. The death of President Kennedy took a personal toll on Mama and MV, because they had met the president and spent time with him at some political events in Cleveland. They felt that President Kennedy offered a vision of strength and youth to the whole country, and they had become attached to his personal charm as well as his political philosophy.

December brought new life to the Vanetti household, when Mama Rose gave birth to another baby boy. Mama Rose and MV decided to honor the late president by naming their child after the man they thought would carry on the hope and the vision of John Kennedy's legacy. They named their new son Robert.

•

At the beginning of the New Year, Grandma Rose and Rosie discontinued their daily teatimes, because Rosie was going to work every day after school in the family store. Mama Rose now worked at the store only on weekends, choosing to stay home during the week with Rebecca, Renaldo, and Robert. This change in arrangements gave Rosie a new feeling both about her home and about herself. The responsibilities at the store opened new worlds of conversation and observation for Rosie. She often thought of Grandma's words that real learning happens outside the classroom. Nature had been her favorite out-of-classroom so far, with her dog, her elephant books, and Grandma's garden. Now, working in the store, she found a new non-classroom, where she learned about human nature. It came as a shock to her when she decided that humans were not so different from elephants. They had the same life expectancy; they had strong family units; and it was the females who kept the family units intact. She saw the same interdependence of humans on one another, observing how a neighbor helped another when necessary. But neighbors also hurt each other, sometimes for no apparent reason. This dual nature was confusing to her, and she wondered whether, at the root of it all, these wonderful Italian people were no better or no worse than the elephants, the beasts.

At home she observed a change of structure. Mama Rose, no longer the business manager, was a mom and a housewife. This softened her demeanor a bit. It seemed to nourish her spirit with a peace that Rosie hadn't seen before. Where Grandma Rose had given her the comforts of family history and of nature, Mama Rose was now giving her a different view of motherhood and of feminine strength. She often surprised Rosie with books about animals and with pictures of animals from the National Geographic magazine. Mama Rose told Rosie how she appreciated her help at the store and with the three little children, and that she knew thirteen was not an easy age. But, she believed if Rosie was true to her faith and her family's values, she would surely eventually succeed at any task that presented itself. They did talk about love and marriage and options for Rosie as she grew older, but Mama Rose told Rosie early on that she would go to college and get a degree. This was not the norm at the time. Many people thought that college for females was a waste of time and money, since they would end up getting married and leave it to their husbands to have careers. But Mama Rose was determined that her daughters would have the opportunities that she herself had been denied—whether they wanted them or not.

One night, during one of these conversations, Rosie asked, "Mama, what do you like better, being a mom or being the store manager?" She had expected her mother to give a tenderhearted answer about the joys of motherhood along with a reassurance that for her nothing could replace the satisfactions of loving and caring for one's children.

Mama Rose gave Rosie a quick hug and responded, "They're both a pain in the ass."

•

When the Beatles made their first appearance on The Ed Sullivan Show in February, Rosie was invited to her cousin Beth's house to witness the event. With her own lack of best friends, Rosie had become close with Beth, who was a junior at Lourdes Academy (Mama Rose had already decided that Rosie would also attend Lourdes Academy). The daughter of Rosie's godmother, Aunt Maria Clemente, Mama Rose's sister, Beth served as Rosie's surrogate big sister. If someone was teasing Rosie at school, she told Beth, and the teasing soon stopped. When Rosie had a question, about where babies came from, or about what to do on a date (if she ever had one), Beth always provided her with an honest answer, an answer that Rosie was certain was not the same as the answer her mother would give her.

So Rosie had looked forward to sharing the Beatles' American television debut with Beth and Beth's friends. That night, some of her other cousins were there, too, and Rosie was excited to be part of a scene with girls her own age, as well as high schoolers. The adults had left Beth and her friends in charge—having decided to have a Beatles party of their own at the Vanettis' house.

The Beatles' appearance was met with "Woo-hoos" from the older girls and sighing giggles from the younger ones, but there was neither screaming nor emotional fits of crying. Beth and her friends made fun of the audience of screaming teens at The Ed Sullivan Show, calling those girls "ugly little things who couldn't get a guy of their own."

Rosie thought that was a little harsh, especially since no one in the room had a guy of her own, but she laughed and enjoyed the music and camaraderie. As the night went on, she knew she would remember the occasion, both as the night that she first watched the Beatles and as the night that she first smoked a cigarette.

•

Rosie's job at the store, her new relationships with her mother and with Beth, her grandmother's ever-whitening hair, and the blooming of spring, forced a melancholy into Rosie's spirit. Her life was changing. The air said spring, her heart said autumn. She began, for the first time in her eight years there, to notice things and people at her school. She noticed that Mary Ann Pendolino walked with a slight limp; she noticed that Michael Russo had a long scar on his neck; she noticed that Susan Benecchi lived with her grandmother and not her parents. Why hadn't she paid attention to these things before? For the last few months of her time in Our Lady of Mount Carmel, Rosie began to reach out to her classmates. She reached out beyond herself and her dog and her garden and her family. She reached out to the world.

She was ready for high school, and as the eighth-grade class of 1964 marched in its final procession around the neighborhood, Rosie Vanetti prayed to God that high school would be ready for her.

*

Chapter 4

Shaker Heights, Ohio
1950–1964

Lush green lawns, wide boulevards, architecturally approved houses, and idyllic lake scenes filled the landscape of Shaker Heights, Ohio in 1950. A meticulously planned community that included a train to connect it with downtown Cleveland, Shaker Heights was designed to be a utopian suburb offering easy access to the big city while simultaneously offering an easy escape from it. Originally, it was a semi-closed community, with strict real-estate codes that allowed the city planners to refuse housing permits to people they felt were undesirable—people like Negroes, Catholics, and Jews. Prompted by government intervention and changing times, the codes were relaxed, and Shaker began to evolve into a multicultural haven of fine schools, fine restaurants, and fine society.

Barbara Schneider Turyev had been raised on the east side of Cleveland, on Superior Avenue, where her parents, Bruce and Barbara, still lived. Both of her parents were of German descent, her mother a homemaker and her father a successful jeweler. Her maternal and paternal grandparents had all died in the great influenza epidemic of 1918, which took the lives of millions of people, five years before Barbara was born.

In Shaker, Richard and Barbara Schneider Turyev lived not far from her parents. The Turyevs were quiet, studious people. Baby Babs cooperated with their regimented, calm lifestyle by settling into a schedule of sleeping for four hours, feeding for one hour, and going back to sleep for four more hours. She rarely cried, and when she did, Barbara immediately held her and comforted her with soft German lullabies that she had learned from her own mother many years before. Motherhood suited Barbara, although she had never imagined herself the motherly "type." She was an accomplished, published scholar, and the only passion she developed was scientific theory, which Richard also shared. Although Richard had, after the war, turned to the serenity of academia to escape the scientific horror of atomic weaponry, he longed for the intellectual and problem-solving environment of hard-core scientific experimentation. Shortly before Babs was born, Richard left his professorship at John Carroll University and accepted a job at the National Advisory Committee for Aeronautics (NACA), in Brookpark, Ohio, in a new facility that was exploring and developing cutting-edge research techniques in jet propulsion and wind tunnels. The looming lure of space exploration was too enticing to resist, so when the chief of the NACA had called him, Richard readily accepted the offer. A magnificent bonus had been the NACA's inclusion of Barbara in the contract. She could go to the Brookpark facility once a week, to collect data from a specific research project, and otherwise work from home, analyzing and reporting on the findings.

Four weeks after Babs was born, Father Templeton administered the sacrament of Baptism at Our Lady of Peace and, after the ceremony, shared a quiet dinner with the Turyevs and Schneiders at the Turyevs' house. They talked of Catholics, Nazis, astronauts, and jewelers.

•

Richard and Barbara were totally immersed in the work of the NACA. Working side by side with the most brilliant astrophysicists of the era, they found that their evenings, too, were filled with theories of Mach speed, three-dimensional effect on airflow, and fuselage placement on aircraft. But the cold scientific jargon melted away when Babs was in the room. Even as an infant, Babs had a sweet demeanor, and Richard and Barbara doted and cooed like any loving parents.

Weekends were reserved for family outings, usually culminating in a train ride to downtown Cleveland and a walk along the lake. Pushing Babs's baby buggy, strolling along the East 9th Pier, the Turyevs would treat themselves to ice lemonade from Captain Frank's restaurant as they enjoyed the view of ships sailing into Cleveland's harbor. As Babs began walking, the jaunts came to include stops at Boukair's ice-cream parlor and walks downtown on Euclid Avenue. By the time she was three, the suburban Shaker Heights toddler already considered herself a Cleveland girl, and the weekend excursions now expanded to Cleveland's renowned planetarium, aquarium, and art museum.

Shaker Heights possessed its own gems of beauty and tranquility, and on some Sundays the Turyevs enjoyed a quiet picnic on the grassy greens of the Shaker Lakes Park. It was an observation made during such a picnic that changed the weekend routine of the Turyevs. In fact, it was an observation that changed everything.

Three-year-old Babs had napped on a blanket after lunch while Richard and Barbara quietly enjoyed the natural sounds and beauties of the park's willows and songbirds. When Babs awoke, she seemed to struggle to stand up. Once she finally made it to her feet, Barbara noticed a limp in the child's gait, and a wince in the child's smile.

"Is something wrong, Babs?" Barbara asked as she lifted Babs into her arms.

"It hurts, Mama." Babs moaned as she pointed to her knee.

Barbara examined the knee and noticed that it was warm to the touch, but she saw no scrapes or bruises. When she felt Babs's forehead, she realized that her entire body felt feverish.

Turning to Richard, Barbara nervously exclaimed, "Richard, she has leg pain and a fever! She—"

Richard said at once, calmly but firmly, "We will get to the clinic immediately."

As they hurried to the car, Richard stopped at a telephone booth to make a call to the NACA. By the time they reached the Cleveland Clinic, which was a ten-minute drive away, a leading specialist in childhood diseases was waiting for them at the front desk, wearing a mask and heavy protective gloves and clothing.

The Turyevs were taken to a ward at the far end of the clinic, and as Babs was examined, poked, and probed, they were quarantined.

By 1952, tens of thousands of children world-wide had contracted a disease called poliomyelitis, commonly known as polio. Thousands had died or suffered paralysis from it, or were kept alive by means of machines called iron lungs. There was widespread dread among parents everywhere that their children would become infected.

Two of the early symptoms of polio were leg pain and fever.

•

Richard and Barbara were scientists; they lived and breathed research and logic and data. As they were responding to the medical survey given to them by the doctors in the quarantine unit, parental fear accompanied their scientific discipline.

Has the child spent much time in public places? YES

Has the child drunk from public water fountains? YES

Has the child had contact with foreign visitors? YES

Has the child complained of pain or weakness in the limbs? YES

Has the child been feverish? YES

As they checked the affirmative beside ever more queries, their dread grew and their spirits quailed. They were now convinced that a long, painful journey lay before them.

Richard took Barbara's hand and told her, "We don't yet know what awaits us, but our child will survive this, and we will all be stronger as a result. We are in the best care facility in the world—hold on to that thought."

Barbara could think of nothing but quarantine, iron lungs, painful shots, and maybe even death for her baby. One of those fears was to become a reality.

Babs was asleep when the nurse rolled her portable crib back to her anxious parents. Barbara picked her up and cuddled her and gently rocked her. The nurse informed them that the doctor would be in shortly with test results. When she left the room, Richard put his arm on Barbara's shoulder and whispered, "The nurse was not wearing protective clothing, not even gloves."

Barbara nodded. "I noticed. I noticed."

When the doctor came in, he sat down behind a desk and invited the parents to sit in the chairs closest to him. The look on his face was neither hopeful nor worried. Richard thought that the doctor was probably a good poker player, but that benign thought vanished as the doctor began to speak.

"Your daughter does not have polio," he said, making direct eye contact with them. He enjoyed seeing the intensity of relief on the faces of a mother and father who were receiving good news. But before Richard and Barbara could express their relief or even catch their breath, he added, "However, there are problems. All signs indicate that she is in the beginning stages of rheumatoid arthritis. This is a very painful condition for a child. Hopefully, in time, the pain will diminish, but early treatment is essential. We need to begin further testing, and possibly begin a regimen of injections and—"

"Doctor!" Barbara interrupted. "Please, slow down. We deeply appreciate the swift and excellent attention you've given us and we are relieved more than we can express that our little girl does not have polio—but, before we discuss this new ailment, can you please tell us what tests were done regarding polio? And, before we discuss treatments for the arthritis, can you tell us how you came to the conclusion that this is what we are dealing with?"

The doctor was not used to being questioned, especially by a woman, but he patiently answered the questions.

When they were satisfied with their understanding of the diagnosis, the disease, and the likely treatment, Richard and Barbara carried Babs to the pediatric rheumatology wing and made an appointment to see the head of that department the next day. When the chief physician at the NACA had called the clinic, he had ensured that Babs would receive the finest and most expeditious care. The work of the NACA was appreciated and respected by powerful institutions in Cleveland and all over the country; the NACA scientists and their families received the best health care in the world.

As they were leaving the clinic, the Turyevs stopped in the chapel. Richard had always honored his commitment to raise Babs in the Catholic faith, and he supported Barbara's devotion. What's more, he held to a steadfast belief of his own, that humanity was called to something higher than the animal kingdom, something spiritual—something perfect. Richard sat stoically in thought as Barbara and Babs knelt in the chapel. When Barbara broke down, with silent tears of fear and worry streaking her face, Babs offered strength. She took her parents' hands and whispered the prayer she said every night before going to bed: "Angel of God, my guardian dear, to whom God's love commits me here. Ever this day be thou at my side. To light, to guard, to rule, to guide."

The three of them said, "Amen" in unison and left the hospital. They were to return there many, many times.

•

Injections, hospital visits, and pain filled the two years that followed the initial diagnosis. The arthritis spread to other joints in Babs's body and she needed support from two orthotic leg braces to be able to walk. As time passed, her spine and arms also weakened, but her spirit and demeanor remained gentle and conciliatory: she often apologized to her mother for the trouble and worry she felt she brought upon their household.

"Mama, I'm sorry that you have to worry so much. I will get better soon—I know I will."

Such comments were more hurtful to Barbara than the physical illness.

"Babs, you never have to say you're sorry for being sick. Mama and Papa are so proud of you for being so brave. God will bless us all through this suffering."

Barbara did see positive results arising from the pain and suffering. As a result of Babs's painful immobility, her attending kindergarten classes was deemed ill-advised. The Shaker Heights school system grudgingly permitted the Turyevs to provide schooling at home, but Babs would have to pass a rigid exam to enter first grade the following year. Although Babs was disappointed not to be able to start school with the other five-year-olds, Barbara and Richard were happy to provide lessons of their own.

Soon, it became obvious to them that Babs possessed a keen mathematical mind and an uncanny knack for understanding abstract concepts like distance, size, and space. On one of their outings to Lake Erie (they took their daughter to the pier in a wheelchair), five-year-old Babs commented on how small the ships looked from far away, and how she was always surprised at how big they were as they came closer.

"Why are we tricked like that, Papa? Why do the boats look smaller than they really are?" she asked.

Richard, pleased at his child's insight into the difference between perception and reality, explained to her the concept of size-distance relationship. Before he could finish, he noticed a eureka flash in Babs's eyes as she spoke.

"Oh my, oh my!" she exclaimed. "The moon and stars must be ginormous!"

Barbara and Richard, the mathematician and the astrophysicist, exchanged a look of unbridled parental pride.

The next day, Richard came home from work with a telescope, a

Newtonian reflector on a German equatorial mount. He also brought home a young engineer and pilot with whom he had been working for the previous two years. Babs sat quietly during dinner, listening to her mother and father and their guest discuss the moon, the stars, and machines that could possibly provide mankind with a trip to these places.

After dinner, Richard set up the telescope, and they all took turns looking at the moon. Babs sat on the young pilot's lap as he told her the name of every visible area on the moon's surface. She was speechless with wonder, but she listened and she learned, and since he returned every month for dinner and stargazing, Babs gained a good knowledge of the solar system, and of the Earth's place within it.

The pilot never came on the weekends. On the weekends, he returned to his home and family in Wapakoneta, Ohio.

•

While Babs learned the secrets of the lunar surface, the local kindergartners learned "B says Buh." The following year, Babs easily passed the "rigid exam" and entered first grade at Our Lady of Peace Elementary School, in the fall of 1956.

The arthritis in her legs and spine continued to require leg braces, forcing Babs to sit quietly on the playground bench while the other children ran around at recess and before school. Some of the ruder classmates made fun of her, calling her "Step-and-a-half" or "Limpy." She never mentioned this to her parents, and she suffered the childhood sneers in silent misery.

One friendship did emerge from the murk of the playground. A frenetic girl by the name of Karen Grovac befriended Babs and became her protector. Karen, labeled a "tomboy" by her peers, played baseball and basketball with the boys, and even managed to win a few playground brawls.

"If someone bothers you and won't stop when you tell them to, you just gotta slug 'im once in the nose and that will make 'im stop," she told Babs. "Since you ain't up to sluggin' them yourself, I'll do it for you."

Barbara was delighted at Babs's new friend, and Karen often visited with Babs after school, for snacks and playtime. Sometimes on Fridays she would stay until past dark and they would look through the telescope together. Although she didn't understand any of Babs's explanations of size and distance, she always gasped at the moon's glow and its craters.

Occasionally, Karen's mother saw Barbara picking up or dropping off Babs at school, and she always made a point of telling her how happy she was that Karen and Babs had become friends.

"Karen's attitude toward school is so much better now," Mrs. Grovac told her. "She is starting to like to read and likes looking up at the stars. Babs has been such a nice influence."

As first grade passed and second grade brought First Communion, with its sacramental grace, the effects of the friendship also showed in Babs's personality. After the Mass, which was torturous because of the sitting, kneeling, and standing that dominated the ritual, Babs hobbled out of the church. Despite her pain, she felt very special in her imported German white lace First Communion gown.

When one of the tyrants from the playground came up to her and said, "Hey, Step-and-a-half, I'm surprised you could make it up to the altar," Babs slugged him in the nose.

•

In 1958, the NACA became NASA, "National Aeronautics and Space Agency." Richard was very pleased with the direction in which President Eisenhower was taking the space program. While the country at large was alarmed and distressed at the progress the Russians had made (they had launched the first satellite, Sputnik, into space in 1957), Richard and his colleagues welcomed the president's non-military approach to space exploration. NASA was a civilian agency, and although national-security and military concerns were certainly addressed, academics and scientists emerged with the authority. Richard felt this was a brave and righteous move and, though nonpolitical by nature, he moved to the Republican side of the spectrum.

Even as Richard's professional work grew more fulfilling, Babs's monthly injections, the refitting of her braces, and the continual new medications began taking a toll on the family. By the time Babs finished fourth grade, she had become weary and weak in spirit. Barbara herself had become discouraged by the ineffectiveness of the treatments. The hope and the expectation had been that Babs would be better by now.

To celebrate Babs's tenth birthday, Richard decided to treat the family to a delectable meal at Gruber's, one of the finest restaurants in the Cleveland area, and the swankiest in Shaker Heights. Interesting and famous people ranging from the artist Salvador Dalí to the baseball player Bob Feller often dined there. Dressed in their Sunday best, Grandma and Grandpa Schneider, Barbara, Richard, and Babs joined the elite diners on June 1 and enjoyed a five-course meal, highlighted by beef and lobster served on flaming swords.

During the peak of their enjoyment, a beautiful, buxom vision of white fur, white dress, white-blonde hair, and white décolletage entered the room. The Hollywood actress Jayne Mansfield and her new husband, the actor Mickey Hargitay, sat down at the next table. Even the calm and cool scientist Richard giggled with excitement.

The evening at Gruber's concluded with a birthday cake glittering with sparklers, which was brought to the table as the entire restaurant, including Mr. and Mrs. Hargitay, sang "Happy Birthday" to the diminutive ten-year-old girl in leg braces.

When the Turyevs returned home that evening, they sat in the backyard, among well-manicured bushes and blooming magnolia trees. They gazed up at the night sky, and each told their favorite mythological story of the constellations.

"I love the Lyra constellation," Barbara began. "It represents the lyre of Orpheus. Some of the ancient Greeks believed that music was a link between the spiritual nature of man and the mathematical precision of creation. Pythagoras used a lyre as the basis for his philosophy that there is a universal truth or principle that governs everything. Math and music is a combination I can't resist."

Richard took her hand as they shared a soft glance. Babs, nestled in her mother's lap, relaxed in the comfort of their love.

"Well," said Richard, "I prefer Sagittarius. Half man, half beast, which to me represents the most profound struggle within mankind. Are we an animal? Are we man? Are we something higher? Sagittarius makes me ponder those questions. This constellation also lies near the densest part of the Milky Way and contains many star clusters and nebulae." Richard sighed, and added, "Someday, man will visit and explore these wondrous neighbors."

Babs yawned and looked up at the stars. "I like Hydra, the water snake," she said. "It moves across so much of the sky, and it doesn't need legs."

•

The election of President Kennedy held little excitement for the Turyevs. Although Kennedy had made numerous comments regarding his commitment to the space program and the research being done by NASA, Richard and Barbara had little confidence in the elegant idealism that the president worked into his speeches and promises. Richard was especially fearful that under Democratic leadership the program might yet come under military control. Barbara and Richard followed the way of the majority of Ohio voters and cast their ballots for Richard Nixon. When the election was over and Kennedy was in, they just hoped for the best. The frenzy to compete with the Russians, who had already put two men into space, weighed heavily on NASA. When President Kennedy announced his goal of "landing a man on the moon before this decade is out," Richard groaned in frustration.

"This is a grandstand promise designed only to promote national pride. There are other things we should be doing," he lamented to Barbara.

With the president's goal, however, came federal money, and with federal money came job security and more research funding for the NASA program in Cleveland. Richard and Barbara played an integral role in the development of everything from rockets to space suits, and they hobnobbed with the likes of Alan Shepard and John Glenn and other Mercury astronauts, the elite American heroes of the era.

Babs never became lost in the Catholic adulation of the Kennedys, nor in the secular adulation of the prestigious visitors who frequented the Turyevs' dinner table in the months that followed. She did share in the excitement of her classmates as they watched Alan Shepard shoot into space and John Glenn circle the earth, but, even in the midst of her close-up experience of scientific history in the making, she preferred to focus on strengthening her legs and ridding herself of the braces and of the pain that still burned throughout her joints. This focus was rewarded in the autumn of 1961.

Joseph Pentello, a newly hired assistant trainer for the Browns, Cleveland's National Football League team, moved into the house next to the Turyevs in early September, along with his wife, Madge, and his son, Louie. Barbara invited the Pentellos over for a backyard barbecue the first Saturday after they arrived. Mr. Pentello, who preferred to be called Joe, was a stocky former lineman for the football team at the University of Notre Dame, where he earned a Bachelor of Science degree with a major in business and a minor in health. His previous job was as a trainer for the Indiana University football team. Mrs. Pentello worked as a seamstress for the Notre Dame athletic department, where she had met Joe. Louie, who was beginning his freshman year at Cleveland's Cathedral Latin High School, aspired to be the starting quarterback for the Latin Lions.

The families meshed immediately. The Pentellos brought a fresh world of football and athletics into the Turyevs' circle of doctors, physicists, and astronauts. The Turyevs brought stimulating intellectual conversation into the Pentellos' circle of playbooks, pigskin, and ankle tape. When nightfall came on that first Saturday, their eyes turned to the stars, but Joe was covertly observing Babs.

"What's the diagnosis on your daughter's physical condition?" he asked Richard as they withdrew from the rest of the group to smoke. Richard enjoyed a pipe, and Joe lit a Cuban cigar.

Richard's face clouded with worry, and he replied, "She's been being treated for rheumatoid arthritis for seven years. We had hoped she would be better by now, but she has remained in pain and now even has some slight deformity in her legs. The main treatment has been drugs and injections of gold salt and vitamins."

Joe looked hesitant, but spoke confidently. "Well, I know I'm the new kid on the block here, but there's a whole new field of physical therapy that shows great results in improving mobility and lessening pain. In the past, kids were told to take it easy and rest the aching joints, but in many cases moving around and using the joints is a much better road to take. That's part of my role with the Browns: to treat injuries by strengthening the muscles that surround the afflicted areas. I have equipment in my basement that Babs could use. We could start a regular schedule of exercise that just might help her."

Later that night, Richard discussed the matter with Barbara and Babs, and they all agreed that Babs's stagnant condition called for a new approach. Without discussing the matter with their doctors, they arranged to have Joe Pentello create and supervise a consistent, gentle exercise regime for Babs.

Although it was painful at first, Babs enjoyed the movement. She felt hope for the first time that she could win the battle against the braces. She exercised three afternoons a week. Louie Pentello often shared the equipment room with her while he lifted weights, keeping in shape for the football season. He and Babs developed a sibling-like bond, and Babs shyly relished the moments when Louie's high-school friends came to work out with him. Adolescence began to offer a delicious foretaste of innocent desire.

At school, Babs would tell Karen about the workouts and the Cathedral Latin boys with whom she spent her afternoons.

Karen salivated and squealed, "Oooh, oooh, oooh! Hot, sweaty Lions, bulging muscles, all of them treating you with attention and care! It doesn't get any better than that, girl! Go get 'em!"

Babs loved Karen's lack of inhibition and the raw perspective on life that colored her every word. When Karen spoke that way, Babs would just blush and giggle. At night she would include a prayer of thanksgiving for all the wonderful people in her life. Her parents, Karen, and the Pentellos were at the top of her list. The Cathedral Latin Lions also made the cut.

•

Joe Pentello gave Cleveland Browns season tickets to the Turyevs, and Babs quickly became a fan of the team's leaders, Milt Plum, Jimmy Brown, and Ray Renfro. Although she was still in braces, her muscles were beginning to benefit from the exercises and she could climb the steps of Cleveland Municipal Stadium with only minor discomfort. This year, school had become a distraction from what she considered her real life: astrophysicists and astronauts for Friday-night dinners, and Cleveland Browns football on Sundays, with a smattering of galaxy-viewing on crisp winter nights. She relished the thought of Christmas vacation, away from the schoolyard and classroom.

The Turyevs' Christmas was always a quiet celebration, with attendance at midnight Mass on Christmas Eve (the only occasion on which Richard joined them), followed by the giving and receiving of gifts with Grandma and Grandpa Schneider. Christmas Day was a peaceful celebration of food and family, and the occasional friend dropping in with a fruitcake or a poinsettia. On Christmas evening of 1961,

Barbara shared with the family that the following year there would be a baby in the house. She was due to bring another Turyev into the world in September. Grandpa Schneider jumped up and slapped the 61-year-old Richard on the back. "Atta boy, you old coot!" he cried. "I didn't think ya still had it in ya!"

•

A few months into 1962, Babs's sixth-grade class went on a field trip to the National Shrine of Our Lady of Lourdes, not far away, in Euclid, Ohio. Realizing that her time alone with Babs would be limited once the baby came along, Barbara signed up to be a chaperone on the trip.

Barbara had passed on to Babs a reverence for the deep mystery of the faith that she carried in her soul, but the scientific environment of Turyev household did not dwell at all on emotional Catholic attachments to relics, votive candles, holy cards, and statues. Except for a crucifix in each bedroom, and a framed picture of the Sacred Heart of Jesus, which had been given to them by Father Templeton and hung in the foyer, there were no outward signs of religion adorning any of the halls or rooms. These things were not disdained; they were just deemed unnecessary.

It was a surprise to both Babs and Barbara to find themselves deeply touched as they walked through the beautiful setting of the shrine. The life-sized sculptures of saints, the spiritual meditations relating to the Stations of the Cross, and the silent walking to the grotto that bore the chiseled engraving "Ave Maria" over its entrance arch took their minds and spirits out of the physical world. The grotto housed an actual piece of stone from Lourdes, in France—a stone that believers said was from the very place where the Virgin Mary, the Mother of Jesus, stood when she appeared to Bernadette over one hundred years before. Bernadette's story was well known among Catholic schoolgirls, and though Babs had never thought it fully credible, as she stood in the garden of the grotto she felt a strange connection to something that was holy—something that was extraordinary. Since she was a bit weary from the long walk, and the braces were beginning to scrape her skin, she received permission from her teacher, Sister Mary Arthur, to remain behind on a bench outside the grotto with her mother. The class moved on through the grounds to explore the rosary made of stones, that surrounded the grotto.

When they were alone, Babs said to Barbara, "Doesn't this place feel nice, and peaceful, and special? I am going to go into the grotto to touch the special stone and pray. Please stay here—I would like to go in alone."

Barbara agreed to wait on the bench outside the grotto; she, too, was enjoying the peace of the setting. As she watched Babs hobble into the grotto, she began to pray to Mary—something she'd done only as a child, when mandated to participate in novenas and holy days. But this place beckoned Barbara from within, and she had a conversation there with the Mother of God.

"Mary, Queen of Heaven and Earth, you know the pangs of motherhood and the ache of empathy when your child is hurt. Please, please, although I am unworthy of any favors, please take the pain from my child. I will not make idle promises, I come before you just as a mother and ask for your intercession with your Son to heal my child. Amen."

Meanwhile, Babs struggled to kneel by the stone of Lourdes. It hurt. She, too, was praying. While touching the stone, she prayed, "Dear Mother of Jesus, thank you for bringing me here today. I don't know why or how, but somehow I do feel your presence and love and I hope this makes me a better, stronger person."

Then, suddenly and inexplicably, Babs unbuckled her braces, removed them from her legs, placed them on the stone, and walked firmly, and pain-free, out of the grotto.

When Barbara saw her, she stood in stunned disbelief, and then a swift realization settled in and she knew that Babs was cured, healed, better—whatever the facts of the situation. Her daughter was walking without wincing or wobbling.

She went running up to her. "Babs! Where are your braces? Are you okay? What happened in there? How—"

Babs interrupted and in a whisper said, "Mama, I was touching the stone, praying for strength, and my mind told my body, 'The pain is gone—it's time to move on.' And I knew, I just knew Mama, that my body was healed."

The remainder of the day was filled with the students gaping at Babs, some crying, some giddy with joy, many convinced that Our Lady of Lourdes had performed a miracle on their classmate, many more convinced that it was all a hoax.

Barbara and the nuns from both the school and the shrine filled out lengthy reports and witness forms. The braces were put in another building on the grounds, the building where crutches, eyeglasses, wheelchairs, and other artifacts of "miracles" and answered prayers were enshrined. Barbara declined to sign a public-relations release that would have allowed the nuns to sell or communicate the story to local news stations.

"We are a private family," she told the nuns. "Whether this is an act of God or an act of therapy, we will keep the discussion between God, our doctors, and ourselves."

The school nuns did make a phone call to Father Templeton, however, and when the bus rolled into the parking lot of Our Lady of Peace parish, there were camera crews from the three television stations, waiting to cover the story of the miracle of Shaker Heights. The students exited the bus. Most were swept off into the cars of their parents, but some remained, enjoying the glare or glow of public attention.

"Oh, I saw the whole thing. She is such a good friend, I just always knew there was something special about her," lied Linda Cherry, who before today had not known Babs's name.

Jack Farkas, a high school chaperone, who was planning to join the seminary, told one reporter, "I was walking in the woods and, at the exact time of the miracle, I saw a vision of Mary holding Babs's braces in her lily-white hands. It was marvelous, just marvelous."

A reporter shoved a microphone in Karen Grovac's face and shouted, "We are told that you are the best friend of the girl who has been healed. Were you with her at the time of the miracle?"

"Nah," Karen said. "I was sneaking a cigarette at the third mystery of the rosary."

•

Barbara and Babs managed to dodge the reporters and Father Templeton, too. They made it home and welcomed the sight of the magnolias and rosebushes in the quiet solitude of their backyard. Barbara stifled her strong urge to call Richard. The activity at NASA was so intense at this time that only the most critical emergencies got past the switchboard. They would have to wait for his return from work to tell him the news.

Barbara made some lemonade and, after making an appointment at the Cleveland Clinic for the next morning, sat down under the weeping willow and beckoned Babs to sit and talk about the events of the day. Babs refused to be sedentary. Despite her mother's beseeching her to rest until she'd been examined, Babs stayed in motion. She chased a butterfly; she trudged through a swale at the very end of their property boundary; she idly kicked a ball around the perimeter of the property. Her thoughts were not focused on the spirituality of the healing, but rather, on the pure physical joy of her ability to move without pain.

As Barbara watched her daughter frolic like a sprite, she fought with her psyche. Was it indeed a miracle? Was it the years of injections and drugs that finally just spontaneously became effective? Was it Joe's exercise regime? Was it Babs's fantastic mind over her weakening matter? Barbara didn't know. What she did know was that her exultation was peppered with a lingering dread: maybe the recovery would not be permanent.

Babs finally decided to take a break from her frolicking and she settled her adolescent body on Barbara's lap.

"Mama," she sighed, "you have no idea how good it feels to move without having to say 'Ouch.' Or how the wonderful freedom of moving without pieces of leather and metal poking into my skin makes me want to jump for joy and scream with laughter. I just feel so very, very good."

She closed her eyes. Soon her breathing became slow and noiseless, and Barbara could feel her grow heavy with sleep. Her head first, then her shoulders, then her torso, and, finally, her legs. Barbara cradled Babs in her arms with a gentle grip, and she wept. She wept for the pain that had been endured, and the pain that had gone away. Her mind wept. Her body wept. Her spirit wept. Finally, exhausted, she, too, yielded to slumber, and, together, mother and daughter slept.

When Richard arrived home, he found them in that sweet repose. Pouring himself a glass of lemonade, he sat down on a lawn chair in the yard, and stared quietly at his two best reasons for living and he thought for a while of the days long ago when his own mother would hold and comfort him. Even now, after so many years, the loss of his parents ached at the core of his being. He stifled a sigh, and that slight sound wakened Babs, whose leaping to her feet startled Barbara awake.

"Papa! Papa! Look!"

Babs danced around her father's chair, twirling her way into his arms. She pulled him to his feet and forced him to dance. She led him over the lawn in a wild two-step, then a three-step, until they fell to the ground in raucous glee. Richard, amazed, raised himself on an elbow and looked from Babs to Barbara and back to Babs in a bewildered state of excitement. When Babs finally stopped laughing, she and her mother told him the entire story of the visit to Our Lady of Lourdes shrine. At the end, Barbara told him that she'd made an early-morning appointment with Babs's specialist the next day, in order to confirm as soon as possible the extent of the healing.

Later that evening, after Father Templeton and Grandma and Grandpa Schneider had paid a brief visit to share in the excitement, Joe and Madge Pentello came over for drinks and a discussion of Babs's condition.

"You know, I'm a believer in God's love and power," Joe began, "and I do believe in miracles. But I also have to say that I have seen several instances where an injured person just says he's had enough, and wills himself to get better. There are other times when the exercises and treatment culminate in one instant, and it appears to be a spontaneous healing. My professional opinion? It could be any one of those."

Madge laughed and said, "I always tell him he should have been a lawyer—he can talk circles around any topic."

"But I understand what he means," Barbara said. "There's no way to really prove definitively what spurred the recovery. I must say though, that the shrine possessed unique and almost supernatural ambience," she added.

Richard, who had been sitting in silence throughout the evening, finally spoke. "My little girl is the happiest I have ever seen her in her eleven years on this earth. Whatever the cause of her cure, it is both a physical and spiritual healing, and if the doctor confirms that the physical healing is real and lasting, we should all just rejoice and not dwell on that moment but on what lies ahead. Babs will believe what she feels is right, and we will respect that belief."

Barbara lifted her glass and said, "A toast to Babs's health."

The others joined in and that marked the end of the discussion and the end of the evening.

Babs would spend the next two days in the Cleveland Clinic for tests and examinations. The following conclusive medical opinion was recorded in her file:

"Patient responded favorably to treatments and therapy. X-rays indicate no signs of the arthritis, and blood levels are normal. Prognosis favorable for full recovery."

•

The remainder of the school year brought Babs fame and scrutiny. Both the school and the shrine were featured on national television-news shows when a brick with Babs's name on it was dedicated outside the grotto. The school hosted a parish-wide Mass of thanksgiving, and afterward numerous organizations invited Babs to speak at meetings and conferences. On May 20, 1962, she made a presentation at the Women's Sodality's May Crowning ceremony. Her closing comments summarized her feelings.

"We will never be sure what healed my legs," Babs said, "but I know in my heart that it was a mother's love that gave me strength to move on. I thank Mary, the Mother of Jesus, for her very special presence in my life and I thank my own mother for her endless sacrifices in getting me through my pain. I hope that the tremendous blessings I have received will inspire me to help others who are in pain.

This will be my last statement on the subject of my healing. There are so many exciting things going on in the world. Last month a man by the name of Scott Carpenter ate dinner at my house. In four days, he will be orbiting the Earth. I am so proud to say that my father helped design the systems that will put Mr. Carpenter into space. You see, there are many miracles happening all around us. The power and love of God is within all of us to change the world, to change ourselves. Mary gives me faith, my mother gives me love, and my father gives me hope. Thank you to everyone for your support. It's time for me and all of us to take our miracles and reach for the stars."

Late that evening, Babs called her father, who was staying at Cape Canaveral, in Florida, with the other NASA scientists who were preparing for the launch. She read him the speech. After a few seconds of silence, Richard spoke in a voice that cracked with uncharacteristic emotion.

"I am filled with pride and joy," he said, "and, in case I have not told you enough, I love you, my daughter. I love you so much."

Five days later, Scott Carpenter returned safely to earth, and Richard Turyev returned safely to Shaker Heights. A week after that, the Turyevs celebrated Babs's twelfth birthday at a family friend's cottage in Cape Cod, Massachusetts, where they would stay for the summer, enjoying private time, away from rockets and relics. Babs ran every day on the beach, and swam every day in the private pool. She continued to maintain the exercise program designed by Joe Pentello.

At night they gazed at the stars and studied the moon through the telescope that belonged to the cottage. For Richard, the vacation was lifesaving. Now sixty-two years old, the stresses of Babs's illness, Barbara's pregnancy, and the space flights had penetrated his bones and muscles. The peace of the Cape and the joys of his family provided him with the contentment he needed to rejuvenate his aging body. For Barbara, the vacation was necessary. Now six months pregnant, her mood varied from moment to moment, and her body leaked and lagged from step to step. The Cape provided her with a worry-free tranquility that refreshed her mind, her body, and her soul.

Occasionally, television crept into their oasis. In July, they watched the launching of the first communications satellite, Telstar. Richard and Barbara explained to Babs the mathematics and physics that enabled television signals, radio transmissions, and telephone messages to be transported through space. The challenges of the physical systems of the universe, Babs thought, far outstripped her own challenges with the physical systems of her body.

When Grandma and Grandpa Schneider visited the Cape during the last weeks of August, they were astonished at the physical transformation of all three of the Turyevs.

Grandma hugged her daughter and granddaughter in relief.

"Barbara," she said, "you look wonderful. So rested. Your ankles aren't swollen anymore, and the puffiness in your eyes is gone."

"Well, I guess I didn't realize what a hag I looked like before," Barbara joked, though slightly irritated. *Only a mother,* she thought, *could insult and compliment a daughter in the same breath.*

As Grandma hugged Babs, her eyes held tears. "I had almost given up hope that I would ever see you running on a beach—or running anywhere. You look so ravishingly fit. The epitome of answered prayers."

Babs responded with a hug around Grandma's waist, and they all walked down to the beach in quiet contentment.

In the cottage that evening, the men smoked their pipes, and Grandpa Schneider told Richard how happy he was to see the family looking so well.

"You're an amazing man, Richard, and a blessing to the family. And it's so nice for me to have a son-in-law I can talk to, about, well, just about anything. We sure have an exciting year ahead of us, don't we?"

"Yes," said Richard. "At work, we are reaching for the moon, and at home we are reaching for a healthy baby."

"Oh, well, um, yes," Grandpa said. "But actually I was talking about the Browns."

•

Babs entered seventh grade reborn. Puberty treated her kindly, and the exercise and basking in the Cape Cod sunshine rewarded her body with a bronzed glow of health and sensuality which she wore with a confidence that made her irresistible. Back at Our Lady of Peace, she became popular. She noticed boys—and boys noticed her—and she liked it. Her weekends were filled with Friday night Ghoulardi pajama parties, where boys in the class would sneak peeks and speaks through open windows. Sundays brought matinee movie shows at the Colony Theater, where she held hands with Mark Malone, an eighth-grader, and later received her first kiss and more from her classmate Joey Dietrick. The miracle at the shrine was almost completely buried in the communal memory of Our Lady of Peace parish. For the first time in her brief life, Babs was free to be what she considered a normal adolescent.

David Richard Turyev was born on September 10, 1962, and Babs took time from her social activities to swaddle and coddle her baby brother, and to help her mother with housework and laundry. But she still managed to have fun and frolics. When Grandma Schneider had come to stay for two weeks to help out, however, Babs's seventh-grade boy-crazy romp was about to cease.

Grandma volunteered to take the baby's 2:00 a.m. feeding shift, so that Barbara could sleep through the night. As she walked past Babs's bedroom that first night, she heard giggling and muffled talking. She listened through the closed door and determined that Babs was not talking in her sleep. Babs was on the telephone. The conversation was too muted to hear clearly, but it didn't matter: a twelve-year-old talking on the telephone at two in the morning was completely unacceptable. Her first inclination was to barge into the room, but she hesitated and then knocked. The sound of the click of a receiver followed immediately, and Babs opened the door. Grandma could see the lighted dial of the blue princess phone on Babs's bed, and asked her, in an agitated, determined tone, "What on earth are you doing awake and on the phone in the middle of a school night? Never mind. Don't even bother to answer, I need to get to the baby. We will discuss this tomorrow. Get to bed."

Babs obeyed without question and lay down, fretting about what tomorrow would bring. Ever since the family returned from Cape Cod, her father was away most of the time, and her mother was first preparing for the baby and then caring for the baby. Babs was not neglected, but she was granted tremendous freedom, with little supervision. In addition to late-night phone conversations and Sunday-movie necking dates, she would also occasionally sneak a cigarette or two, which in her household had almost the same stigma as standing on East 105th and

Euclid beckoning to men in cars. Trickles of guilt would sometimes escape from her conscience, but no Jiminy Cricket was strong enough to combat the temptations of puberty, popularity, and Pall Malls.

The next morning, Grandma waited at the kitchen table, where she had prepared a breakfast of pancakes and sausage, Babs's favorite. Relieved at not seeing her mother, Babs hugged her grandma, and began her prepared lie.

"I'm sorry about last night, Grandma. I know I should not have been on the phone so late, but one of my friends found out her grandfather is very sick and she just needed to talk. Are you going to tell Mama?" The ease of her deceit stunned her.

Grandma's lips quivered a bit; she clearly recognized that her granddaughter was lying to her, and she was hurt.

"Yes, I am going to tell her, young lady. And don't think for one moment that I believe your dreadful fabrication. I also fear that late-night phone conversations are not the worst of your offenses. Your mother will have much to say to you, I am sure, when you return from school. Eat your breakfast and move along."

For Babs, the day went from bad to worse. Karen was absent from school and there was no one to whom she could confide her anxiety. She moped through the lessons of pronouns, protractors, and Protestant blasphemies, and at two-forty-five her anxiety morphed into full-scale fear. It was report-card day.

Her parents were accustomed to, and expected nothing less than, straight As, or A pluses. Babs feared she might have slipped to an A minus in a couple of subjects. When Sister Agatha handed Babs the report card, the nun looked at her contemptuously, smirked, and said, "What has happened to you? I think you may need another trip to Our Lady of Lourdes shrine for a miracle of the brain instead of the body."

There, well below the red line of potential, was a C. Next to the C was a B. She had a C in Religion and a B in English. The five As in the other subjects did not matter. She could not breathe.

More surprises awaited her at home. Her father's car was in the driveway; he was apparently home from Cape Canaveral a day sooner than expected. When she came in, he was talking on the telephone and her mother was taking a bath. Grandma, it seemed, was out for a walk with David. Feeling slightly buoyed by avoiding immediate wrath, she went to her room with the sense of a temporary reprieve. That's when she noticed that her princess phone was no longer on the nightstand. Spread out open on her bed were her diary and ten notes that she had written and received from her friends. In them were descriptions of Sunday matinees, cigarette breaks, and clandestine parties disguised as study dates. Consumed by an overwhelming nausea, she fell on the bed, pounded her fist into the mattress, and burst into tears of rage and shame.

"Babs, come down to the living room," she heard her father call.

She wanted to scream at him that not only was she not coming down to the living room; she would never speak to him or her mother again. Whatever guilt her conscience had burdened her with dissolved into anger at the thought of her parents invading her privacy and property.

"Babs, come down to the living room—NOW!" her father bellowed.

There was no avoiding the showdown. She walked to the living room slowly, defiantly, preparing in her mind her attack on their audacity. Her father stood holding her report card, and her mother sat on the davenport, both looking unexpectedly calm. Babs opened her mouth to speak, but her father interrupted before a word could come out.

"Do not say a thing. We, in fact, do not want to hear anything you have to say. And please remove that bold look from your face, it will serve no purpose other than to worsen the consequences of your acts. We have afforded you freedoms because we trusted you. Please note the past tense. We know that you are aware that lying is wrong, that sneaking is wrong, that smoking is wrong, that engaging in public displays of affection is wrong, that neglecting your studies is wrong. You knew they were wrong and you chose to do them anyhow. That, my dear, according to the tenets of your faith, is the definition of sin. Sin against your God, and sin against your parents whose trust you have betrayed. As a result of your choices, you will no longer have a telephone in your room, there will be no more overnights, and you will not be attending weekly movie shows. These conditions will last for six weeks, during which time we expect to see an improvement in your behavior and in your grades."

Babs stood silent, stewing in anger and shame. Before she could speak, her mother continued, in a gentler but stern tone.

"It was difficult to make the decision to rifle through your personal belongings, Babs, but I do not apologize for it. When Grandma told me of your late-night phone use, I began to think of other things. A decrease in homework time, an increase in lipstick. Once I did smell cigarette smoke on your clothes, but I rationalized that it was residue from Karen's house, since her mother I know is a heavy smoker. I decided to call the other mothers to see if they knew about two a.m. phone calls and other things."

At this, Babs gasped with embarrassment, saying, "Oh, you didn't!"

With no show of concern, her mother continued, "Indeed I did. And all three were aware of the behavior and all three showed no signs of disapproval. Linda's mother even told me she had caught Linda with a boyfriend, blouse all unbuttoned and what is called a 'hickey' on her neck."

Babs hopefully imagined a tornado blowing the whole house away, with only her in it, permanently planting her in Oz.

"These mothers," Barbara went on, "who I am certain are lovely women, dismissed these things as mere adolescent shenanigans. Obviously, your father and I do not share this lighthearted opinion. We are not so old or out of touch that we do not remember the temptations of youth, but we thought that you were strong enough and smart enough to resist them. Holding hands is one thing, but at twelve years old extensive kissing, and in a public place, is something we never dreamed you would engage in. Trying a puff of a cigarette is normal curiosity, but making it habit, especially at your age, is despicable."

A silence engulfed the room, and Babs realized it was now her turn to speak. She wanted to scream at them and tell them she was just having fun and that it felt wonderful to be with girls who did not have nervous breakdowns over report cards. And it was heaven to have boys appreciate her new curves. But she controlled herself and took a somewhat repentant tone.

"I am sorry I disappointed you. Yes, I knew I was breaking unwritten rules, but I figured if you never found out, it wouldn't hurt you."

Her father interrupted: "You must see, Babs, that this is not about us—it is about you. Sneaking, lying, petting, smoking—these are things that will land you on the wrong side of the road of self-worth."

"Okay, okay!" Babs responded. "But Karen and Linda, and my other friends, are not bad. They just don't feel tied to the same rules."

"We are not judging their souls," said Barbara. "Of course they are not bad people. But at twelve years old you have not earned the right to disobey the rules, and at no age will you earn the right to lie to others or to abuse your body. It is our responsibility to guide you on a path that we feel will be best for your integrity and your potential. When you grow older, if you decide to take another path we will respect that—but for now we will see to it that our rules are followed."

"Everything you do comes as a choice," her father said, now in philosophical mode. "You may choose immediate physical satisfaction, as animals do, or you may choose spiritual satisfaction that raises you to a higher, deeper level of growth, as we believe humans are supposed to do. As your parents, we will do everything we can to push you to decide to take the higher road."

Babs refrained from a nearly overwhelming urge to roll her eyes, and instead made one more comment. "About my grades," she stammered.

"I do hope you noticed that there were five As on my report card, so it's not like I just ignored my schoolwork. The C in Religion is because I did not turn in two assignments, and the teacher did not let me hand the assignments in late. That left two zeros in the record book, which made it impossible to raise my grade. My B in English is a result of sloppy work I did on our required reading, a novel called *Lord of the Flies,* which I thought was a horrible book and a waste of time. I don't like not getting As, so I will not let that happen again." She paused, then added, "May I be excused?"

Her father replied, "The grades are not important to us, Babs—the effort that goes into your schoolwork and your attitude toward study are. We only ask that you do your best. Don't ever blame anyone or anything else for your lack of achievement. Your C is because of your failure to turn in your work on time. Your B is because of your arrogant choice to ignore the work of a fine author."

He walked over to his daughter and hugged her warmly and spoke softly: "There are so many mistakes you can make at this age that will affect your entire life—we just want to help you live through them. We love you beyond words, Babs. No matter what you do or say, we love you. You are excused."

•

The remainder of Babs's seventh-grade year passed quickly with her parents closely observing her activities and habits. She filled the late-autumn and winter weekends watching Louie Pentello play football for the Lions on Friday nights, and Jimmy Brown for the Browns on Sunday afternoons. Springtime provided the opportunity to enjoy the freedom of her legs and the development of her body in a new way. The weights and workouts at the Pentellos' had shaped her physique into a running machine, immediately noticed by the school's track coach. Babs Turyev, who one year before had limped down the halls in braces, now sped along cinder tracks, and in May earned the title

"Catholic Youth Organization, Diocese of Cleveland, Ohio, First Place Champion, 100-Yard Dash."

On her thirteenth birthday, Barbara and Richard surprised Babs with a dinner party at Gruber's, where Grandma and Grandpa Schneider, the Pentello family, Father Templeton, Karen Grovac, and seven of her friends from the track team, along with all their parents, sang "Happy Birthday" when she entered the private room. This was her grand entrance into being a teenager.

After dinner, as they were leaving the restaurant, Karen, who'd had the place of honor next to Babs at the dinner table, handed her a small gift and whispered, "Open this when there's no one around."

Later that night, alone in her room, Babs opened the gift. It was a pack of Tareyton cigarettes, with the slogan written on the card: "I'd rather fight than switch."

Babs laughed, put the card in her box of mementos, and threw the cigarettes in the trash.

•

The world around her exploded in momentous happenings after the summer of 1963, but Babs's personal world remained relatively unchanged. The Cleveland Browns began a new era without coach Paul Brown, and owner Art Modell, who fired him, was now unaffectionately known in the Turyev and Pentello households as the Jackass. For the Turyevs, the assassination of President Kennedy was a shocking awakening to the violence that lurked underneath the tranquil façade of the nation. But, although they shared the grief over the tragedy with all Americans, Richard had long ago become aware of adulterous and ruthless actions of politicians, including those of the president, so his mourning was tempered with an unforgiving sense of karma. Babs detected her father's attitude, but her own grief did not allow for any bad feelings toward the slain president. She was keenly aware, however, from listening to the dinner-table conversations of the steady stream of

NASA guests, that the new President, Lyndon Baines Johnson, had a strong and genuine commitment to and understanding of the NASA program.

The winter holidays passed with quiet family celebrations, but the universal blast of Beatlemania in January and February was the opening act of a new era in American culture, and Babs could feel it: a sweeping change, still slightly out of reach, but coming her way.

In June, she finished her time at Our Lady of Peace with straight A pluses on her final report card. She had also achieved a perfect score on her high-school-entrance exams. She believed her choice of high school to be predestined. Ever since her healing at the National Shrine of Our Lady of Lourdes, she had known that she would attend a school on the west side of Cleveland called Lourdes Academy.

*

Chapter 5

Lourdes Academy
Cleveland, Ohio, 1964-1968

Lourdes Academy, an all-girl Catholic high school housed in a hundred-year-old brick building, blended seamlessly into the landscape of the near west side of Cleveland. Founded in 1892 by the Holy Humility of Mary Sisters, it developed a solid reputation for educating young women in a rich tradition of liberal arts and public service. Staffed primarily by the sisters, with a smattering of female secular, or lay, teachers, the school boasted a well-educated faculty, all women, most of whom had earned master's degrees or higher.

The graduation curriculum required: four credits of religion, four credits of English, three credits of history, three credits of foreign language, two credits of math (algebra and geometry were mandatory), two credits of science, two credits of art and/or music, and two credits of general electives. There were no honors, advanced placement, or remedial classes. The expectations were high for all students, and it was understood that exceptional performances earned As, above-average performances earned Bs, average performances earned Cs, below-average performances earned Ds. Students who failed to meet the class criteria received Fs and took the class over until they passed. In their junior year, students could choose among three tracks: college preparatory, business studies, or general education. The focus differed for each track, but the academic expectation of excellence remained the same for all.

By 1964, Lourdes enrollment had reached over five hundred, with many students now traveling from suburbs, in addition to students from the local west side Cleveland neighborhoods, and a few from the east side. The school was within twenty blocks of the West Side Market, St. Patrick's Church, the West Side Community Center, and the all-boys high school St. Ignatius. It was also a short bus ride from the Public Square of downtown Cleveland. A diverse population of Hungarian, Puerto Rican, Mexican, Middle Eastern, and European immigrants permeated the streets around it with a vibrant buzz of languages, aromas, and activities that seasoned the ethnic ingredients of Cleveland's melting pot. Each culture maintained and valued its own history and traditions, while treasuring American history and traditions.

The girls of Lourdes Academy played an important role in this vibrancy. They provided tutoring, yard cleanup, babysitting, care for the elderly, and other services that defined them not merely as girls who attended school in the neighborhood but as genuine neighbors. They did not receive academic credit for these activities; they did not receive external awards for these activities; they did not receive college scholarships for these activities. They simply performed these things because they understood the expectations of Christian service and community.

Deus meta intellectus—God is the goal of all understanding—was the school motto, the cornerstone of an educational environment unlike anywhere else.

This educational oasis planted and nurtured the friendships that would last a lifetime for the fourteen-year-old Brigid, Rosie, and Babs.

•

One early September morning in 1964, Brigid Nagy, dressed in a crisply pleated plaid skirt and a shiny new blue blazer with a fleur-de-lis patch on the pocket, boarded the No. 79 City Transportation Service (CTS) bus and joined some friends who were also on their way to their first day at Lourdes Academy. Several young men from St. Ignatius, Cathedral Latin, and Benedictine, all-boy high schools, also rode that bus, and together they left the lily-white peace of Parma and ventured into the multicolored commotion of the big city. The Lourdes girls and Saint Ignatius boys stepped off the 79 onto Abbey Avenue, walked pass the thick smell of the Fish Market, crossed West 25th Street by the West Side Market, and caught the No. 22 C.T.S. bus going west. The Benedictine and Latin boys crossed the gargoyled Lorain-Carnegie Bridge and entered the subterranean rail world of the Rapid Transit, where they would ride east.

That same morning, at nearly the same time, Babs Turyev climbed aboard the Shaker Rapid train and in a few minutes, rolled into Cleveland's Terminal Tower, where she transferred to a No. 22 C.T.S. bus that took her to 41st and Lorain, a few steps from Bridge Avenue, where stood the old, ivy-covered building of Lourdes Academy

A little later that morning, Rosie Vanetti squeezed into her cousin Beth's 1962 Corvair, along with four other Lourdes upperclassmen, and zoomed down Detroit Avenue, heading for the school parking lot, hoping to avoid their first tardy of the year.

Brigid, Babs, and Rosie were assigned the same homeroom, Room 301. A tiny, ancient nun with rimless eyeglasses, pouchy stomach, turkey-skin neck, and saggy jowls, greeted them with a gruff "Good morning. My name is Sister Roberts," and told them to sit wherever they chose; they would be assigned seats after the bell. The girls started chatting among themselves. Brigid limited her conversation to Gayle, a friend from St. Charles, also assigned to 301. Babs introduced herself to Carol, one of the few black girls in the school, who also traveled from the east side. Rosie bounced around from girl to girl, gregariously introducing herself to everyone.

Despite the uniformity of plaid skirts, saddle shoes, and white blouses, it was obvious which girls fell into the three dominant styles of the day.

The "greasers/racks" teased or ratted their hair, and rolled their skirts a bit higher above their knees. They darkened their eyes with mascara and liner.

The "collegiates" smoothed their hair into its natural flow of dangling curls or sleek straightness, and dabbed their cheeks with just enough blush to appear innocently attractive.

The "mods" (but not yet "hippies") combed their hair straight with a prominent part or a headband. Shorter-haired girls wore pixie cuts.

There were many girls whose style did not fall into one of these specific types, but on weekends, out of uniform, everyone's attire would mark distinct differences between the leather-jacket, tight-stirrup-pants, pointed-shoes group and the cranberry-skirts, madras-blouses, penny-loafers group.

There existed, however, a spirit that suffused the classroom from that very first day: a spirit of unity that ignored the differences and united the similarities. It was this spirit that beckoned many of these young women to travel to an old inner-city school, passing up newer suburban schools along the way.

It was a spirit that said, "You are part of something higher than yourself. You are important. You have value. You will succeed." It was the spirit of Lourdes Academy.

•

Before the bell, a prayer written in elegant cursive script beckoned from the chalkboard. This prayer, Sister Roberts explained, would be recited before this class and every class throughout the day. Brigid wrote the prayer in her notebook, under the heading "Homeroom Notes":

All for the greater honor and glory of God,
In union with Jesus Christ,
And Mary, our dearest Mother.

When the bell rang that officially started the school day, the girls automatically stood, and for the first of many times, recited the prayer in unison. This was the beginning of their high-school journey together. After the prayer, the principal, Sister Mary Teresa, spoke over the public-address system and welcomed the "women of Lourdes to a new year of love, learning, and laughter."

After the PA announcement, Sister Roberts informed the class that, in homeroom, their seating assignment would be by birth dates.

"I do it this way as a reminder to you of your place in history," she said, "because most of you were born in 1950 and all of you between 1949 and 1951. These were years of great population growth in our country. Your fathers were eager to wed your mothers when they returned from battle, and your mothers were eager to have children and enjoy a new America. Never forget that your parents' generation sacrificed everything so that your generation could have everything. Much has been given to you and much will be expected of you."

Brigid, touched by the sentiment, nodded her head in agreement. Babs tried to calculate the odds of how many girls in the class were born in June. Rosie wondered why a cat outside was meowing so incessantly.

The nun's rapid-fire directions interrupted their thoughts.

"Sit in the vertical rows. All January and February birthdays, row one. March and April, row two. May and June, row three. July and August, row four. September and October, row five. November and December, row six. Talk to each other to find out the exact dates and put yourselves in chronological order. Hurry up, hurry up."

The girls scurried to their assigned rows, met their birth-month mates, and seated themselves accordingly. As Brigid moved to row three, she observed that this was an effective way to provide the students an opportunity to meet and talk with each other. She decided to keep a journal of good teaching techniques that perhaps she could use someday in a classroom of her own. Babs smirked internally, proud of herself for predicting that row four would have the most students. She had read somewhere that May and June consistently had the highest birth rates.

Rosie dawdled by the window, trying to spot the screeching cat, but

Sister cut her search short, growling, "Get to your seat, Miss Vanetti."

As the classmates chatted amiably, deciphering the order of their seating arrangement, Brigid, Babs, and Rosie were in a stalemate once they discovered that they were all born on June 1, 1950.

"Okay.Okay," said Brigid. "Well, I was born in the afternoon. Who was born in the morning or evening? We'll do it that way."

"Afternoon for me," said Rosie.

"Me, too," Babs said.

Brigid laughed and responded, "Okay, how about hospitals? Closest hospital gets first seat, farthest seat three."

"St. John's," they said in unison.

Wow, Babs thought. What are the odds?

"Well, looks like alphabetical order by last name," Brigid said decisively, and they took their seats.

They had little freedom even to whisper among themselves once Sister began talking. When the bell rang for first period, the three girls born on the same day, at the same time, and in the same place compared their schedules and saw that they were all in the same classes as well. Giggling at the coincidences in their lives, they all walked together, more confident now that they were not alone, to their first high-school class.

The other teachers had prepared seating charts on which the girls were placed alphabetically, so Babs Turyev and Rosie Vanetti sat by each other in every class. Brigid Nagy was placed in between the Ms and the Os and was relieved to see familiar faces from St. Charles among them.

During the breaks between classes, Brigid, Babs, and Rosie caught up with one another and decided to sit together at lunch. First, they stopped by the gym, because Rosie wanted to see her cousin Beth to remind her to wait for her after school. None of the girls realized that the gym was designated "Seniors Only" during lunch periods. Brigid was the first to feel the haze.

"Oh, my God!" shouted one of the seniors, Kathy Pannini, a slim, olive skinned Italian girl with deep-brown eyes and a wicked smile. "We have freshmen invaders! Eeeek! Look at the one with saddle shoes and red nylons! And look at the crooked seams!" She proceeded to fall to the ground, holding her stomach in a fierce belly laugh.

Although Brigid's hose were cinnamon-colored, not really red, she knew the girl was pointing at her. She felt the heat start at her neck and grow stronger as it reached her scalp, and she was sure her face now matched the color of her hose.

Rosie whispered to Brigid, "Don't let her bother you—that girl is a mean jerk. Beth can't stand her—nobody pays any attention to her."

Despite Rosie's support, Brigid was embarrassed to the core and she left the gym, Babs following close behind. Rosie, lone freshman in the seniors-only gym, was determined to find Beth. But Beth was not there, and Kathy Pannini was not finished. She swaggered over to Rosie and, in an instant, stripped Rosie's skirt off and threw it up so it stuck on the rim of the basketball hoop. Howling insults about Rosie's polka-dot pantaloon undergarment, she was about to go for Rosie's blouse. Another senior stepped in and stopped her.

"Stop it, Kathy. You've had your fun. This is just too mean. And Beth is going to kill you."

Kathy backed off, but tripped Rosie with an outstretched foot and laughed as Rosie stumbled to the hard gym floor. Another group of seniors retrieved the skirt with a long-poled hook used to open the windows. Rosie ran to the lunchroom, holding in her tears, and proceeded to tell her newfound pals the gory details. Buoyed by their attention and sympathy, Rosie embellished the story with a dramatic scene of being held on the ground against her will and threatened with the window pole. The freshmen sat in awe and fear as Rosie's torment grew with every word.

Brigid, quite disconcerted by the event, sighed. "I thought these types of things only happened in public schools."

The remainder of the first day of high school passed pleasantly, and at 3:15 Brigid took the bus south, Babs rode the train east, and Rosie piled into Beth's car and headed west.

During dinner, the girls told their mothers about their new friends, particularly the classmates who shared their birthdays. By the end of the evening, Mrs. Nagy, Mrs. Vanetti, and Mrs. Turyev had reunited through telephone calls and made plans to meet for lunch the following week.

Brigid finished her homework and got a phone call from Martin Gorman. They chatted for the full twenty minutes of her allotted phone time.

Babs completed her homework, and the following two chapters in her algebra book as well. She and Karen, who now attended Shaker Heights High School, swapped first-day-of-school stories over a milkshake at the nearby soda fountain of the local drug store.

Rosie spent the evening on her front porch with her cousin Beth, plotting revenge.

As the three young teenagers said their evening prayers that night, they thanked God for their many blessings, and begged forgiveness for any sins through a heartfelt Act of Contrition.

Before getting into bed, Babs tried to calculate the odds of three babies who'd been born on the same day, at the same time, at the same place, all attending the same school fourteen years later. She did not have enough data to calculate the odds accurately, but she knew they would be significantly high.

Before saying a final goodnight to her parents, Rosie gathered as many eggs and rolls of toilet paper as would fit in her gym bag. Kathy Pannini's car would never be the same.

Finally, before she slipped into slumber, Brigid emptied her dresser drawers of all cinnamon-colored seamed nylons. From now on when she wore saddle shoes, she would be a bobby-soxer.

•

In homeroom the next day, the students were greeted by a special PA announcement from Sister Mary Teresa, who spoke in a monotone yet somehow threatening voice.

"Yesterday there was an incident of unchristian behavior in the gymnasium, during which one of our students was physically accosted and another verbally accosted."

A slight murmur vibrated across the room, quickly shushed by a fierce look from Sister Roberts. The announcement continued: "The student responsible for the incident has been permanently expelled from Lourdes Academy." Brigid and Rosie stifled startled gasps. "Let this be a lesson and a warning that no such behavior will be tolerated. We are a family of women dedicated to serving God in the spirit of obedience and holiness as exhibited by Mary, the Mother of God. We are here for each other, to help each other reach our full potential in mind, body, and spirit. If you do not abide by this philosophy, you will be removed from our community. No more will be said about the incident that occurred yesterday. Have a blessed day."

Beth was waiting for Rosie at the door of the classroom when the bell rang to end homeroom period.

Before Rosie could speak, Beth whispered, "Don't say a thing to anyone about the eggs and the toilet paper, just shut up about the whole thing. Not another word. Pannini was in trouble already. This was the last straw for the nuns—so don't think you got her expelled; it was bound to happen."

Rosie gave Beth a look of relief, while Beth eyed Brigid, who had just joined them.

"Good move gettin' rid of the red nylons," she said as she turned and swaggered away.

•

The first few months at Lourdes swept by in a flurry of new friends, new knowledge, and new social lives. Brigid, Rosie, and Babs fell into a secure routine during school hours, meeting at Rosie's locker in the morning, primping in the restroom between classes, and exchanging homework, home news, and adolescent gossip about boys, music, and new television shows at lunchtime. They ate together at lunch, sitting at a long table where twenty other girls plunked down their brown bags or purchased the daily fare of spaghetti, creamed chicken and rice, or hamburgers—whatever the Lourdes cafeteria cooks had prepared for the day. There were groups of girls, but no visible cliques. Students sat with friends, but anyone at any given time could sit in any given seat. When "first bell" rang, the girls would clean up all remnants of crumbs and containers, and dispose of them in the trash. At "second bell," they walked in silence to their classes. Such was the way of the world in Catholic girls' schools in 1964.

Brigid's favorite classes were English and Latin, although she did not like the English teacher, Sister Madeline. Sister Madeline was a beautiful woman with the proverbial creamy complexion and a hint of blush on high cheekbones. She spoke in what sounded to Brigid like a faux-British accent. There was a friction between that nun and Brigid, though Brigid could never understand why. Despite the friction, however, the content of the English class was too enjoyable for Sister Madeline to taint Brigid's appreciation of literature and language.

The etymological roots of the ancient Latin language fascinated her, and she relished the connections between the so-called "dead language" and dynamic, ever-changing English. The Latin teacher seemed as ancient as the language itself, but her intelligence and vast knowledge of the subject broke down that barrier of age, and she was respected by all the students, even those who counted the minutes until the class period ended.

Except for the English teacher, Brigid liked and respected all of her teachers. The cranky but kind world-history teacher, the fossilized but sharp religion teacher, and the feisty but slow-paced algebra teacher all had two things in common: they possessed superior knowledge and intelligence in their fields of study, and they were of high moral character. By the end of October, Brigid's education journal, which she'd titled "Things That Make a Great School and a Great Teacher," had more than several entries.

1. Use birthdays to arrange seating charts—this is a good ice-breaker and gets the students talking to each other.
2. Make sure all students know the consequences of breaking rules.
3. Never allow disrespectful or unkind words or behavior to be tolerated.
4. Deal with behavior problems quickly and decisively.
5. Never let a student feel that you dislike her.
6. Expect the best from every student.
7. Know your subject matter inside and out.
8. Respect your students and they will respect you.
9. Be a good person.
10. Honor God in all you do.

Unlike Brigid, Babs hardly thought about her teachers or the way the school was administered. She was thoroughly enjoying the camaraderie of her classmates and the urban landscape of the west side. Both Babs and Brigid shared a sense of excitement in leaving their green, clean, suburban communities and venturing on their daily trek into the grit and greatness of the inner city.

The curriculum came easy to Babs, and she felt both a personal and academic satisfaction when the head of the math department asked her if she would be willing to tutor students in algebra. After a few weeks in algebra class, it was obvious that Babs belonged in a higher-level math, but, when she was offered the opportunity, her parents decided against it. They wanted to keep her with peers her own age. Instead, her mother and father made a point of discussing NASA situations with her at least three times a week. After dinner, Barbara would steer the conversation toward the buzz of nuclear physics, quarks, and quasars in the NASA world. Barbara's research in aeronautics put her on the front line regarding the photographs and data received from NASA's Ranger 7 craft and a multitude of other satellite and missile analyses. Babs became joyfully lost in the worlds of NASA's Saturn, Gemini, and Apollo projects, which made the world of Algebra I seem small and insignificant as well as too easy.

Richard would remind Babs, though, that basic mathematics is the foundation of the universe, and he would occasionally work with her on solving the kinds of equations that he encountered daily, feeling silent pride at his daughter's aptitude for keeping up with some of the most majestic profundities of numbers.

Babs would often discuss, or attempt to discuss, the NASA ideas with Brigid and Rosie. At lunch one day, she was particularly excited: "Seriously, NASA can now transport a payload of over forty-three hundred pounds into orbit, and astronauts are actually functioning in zero gravity without space suits! And eventually supersonic transports and turbo thrust engines will take man to the lunar surface!"

Brigid and Rosie stopped chewing, looked at each other, looked back at Babs, and in their most interested, intellectual voices said in unison: "Huh?"

Of the three, Rosie was the least interested in academics, and as a result she maintained average or lower-than-average grades. Her interests were earthy, and neither the abstract world of English poetry nor the laborious deep thinking behind Einstein's relativity could tempt her from her real world of dating and dancing. She moved through her day in a slow stride, enjoying every tidbit of gossip, every discussion of weekend sock hops, every song played from the jukebox that blared in the Lourdes lunchroom, and every shortcut she could take in assignments and projects.

Her love of—passion for—animals continued to intensify. When teachers assigned a free-choice-topic option on an essay, Rosie always turned to aspects of animal behavior and treatment. Her first research presentation, in English class, focused on an American Association for the Advancement of Science (AAAS) conference held the previous year in Cleveland. MV had served on the welcoming committee for the conference, and Rosie had been able to go to many of the lectures and discussions on animal behavior, given by leading experts on the subject. One of the most exciting outcomes of the conference, Rosie explained, was the decision to form a society, distinct and separate from the AAAS, specifically focused on animal behavior. Rosie concluded her presentation by suggesting that Lourdes Academy form a club similar to Future Teachers of America (FTA) and Future Nurses of America (FNA), called Future Animal Behavior Scientists (FABS). No one else seemed interested in pursuing such a club, but the idea lingered in Rosie's psyche.

When the school day ended, Rosie would go home, wrestle with Muscles on the front porch, change into a comfortable work dress, and walk to the store, where she spoke briefly with her mother before Mama Rose dashed home to care for Rebecca, Renaldo, and Robert. Rosie spent the next two hours sweeping the floors of the store and neatly arranging cans and boxes of food. On most days, she would walk home with her father, who would share with her the news of the neighborhood. Occasionally he would listen to the latest stories of Lourdes life, but it was obvious to Rosie that his interest in her activities was feigned; he carried the neighborhood's woes on his shoulders and the family's needs in his wallet.

In the evenings, Rosie would rush through homework, chat with Grandma Rose, listen to her favorite radio station, WHK, and its "Good Guys" group of deejays. The best part of her evening was watching television with her family. *The Dick Van Dyke Show, The Lucy Show,* and a new show called *Bewitched* earned top marks in the Vanetti family. Rebecca took a liking to *The Flintstones,* so Rosie forced herself to sit with her sister and pretend to laugh at the antics of the characters of Fred and Barney. Some nights, when she was supposed to be in bed, Rosie would sneak down, sit on the staircase that bordered the TV room, and clandestinely view the adult soap opera *Peyton Place.* She proudly discussed the illegitimate offspring and adulterous characters with Beth and the other upperclassmen on their way to school in the morning, as they helped her fill in the answers to her algebra homework.

•

Unbeknownst to Brigid, Rosie, and Babs, their mothers had been meeting for lunch twice a month since September. The girls had been aware of the first meeting, but the mothers decided not to tell them about their other lunch dates. They figured the teenagers would be much likelier to share school stories if they thought their mothers were isolated from one another. Through this arrangement, Dar learned that Brigid sometimes expressed resentment that so much of her time was spent babysitting her five sisters; Barbara discovered that Babs had started smoking again, usually in a greasy-spoon restaurant called Johnson's, where the girls often gathered before and after school; and Mama Rose confirmed what she had already suspected, that Rosie was performing miserably in school. It was a surprise, however, to hear that Rosie could not care less about her grades or schoolwork, and that she preferred *Peyton Place* to study time.

Armed with these tidbits, the mothers took loving but firm action. Dar ignored the resentment, though it pained her to think of Brigid having such negative attitudes toward her siblings. She decided to ease the babysitting responsibilities and allow Brigid more telephone time and movie privileges. She broached the topic one evening to an unsuspecting Brigid.

"Brigid, we are so proud of the way you have adapted to high school. Your behavior is still admirable, and your grades are excellent. It's time you had a bit more freedom and privileges. Grandma Nagy can watch the girls more often and you may attend a movie two Sundays a month instead of one. And your telephone time will be extended until nine p.m."

"Wow, Mom!" Brigid exclaimed in excited appreciation. "Thank you!"

Although the new benefits were administered by her parents and not by her school, Brigid acknowledged the event in her education journal:

11. Reward good behavior.

Barbara, a bit hurt by what she viewed as a disobedient betrayal, nonetheless decided to approach the smoking problem positively. During a family dinner conversation, she randomly interjected the results of a NASA study on the dangers of cigarette smoke, while announcing that she had enrolled the family in a community fitness program, where they could all participate in exercise regimens and nutrition classes. Babs mildly protested that she was already keeping up her exercises with Joe Pentello, but Barbara explained that the recreation center had an inside track, where Babs could run. Babs grudgingly agreed, and cast a suspicious eye at her mother's smirk.

At the Vanetti household, Mama Rose visited Rosie's bedroom one evening, carefully timed, fifteen minutes before *Peyton Place* was scheduled to air. She engaged in a lengthy conversation with Rosie about her academic achievement during the first few months of high school. Before she reached midway in her planned remarks, Rosie began to cry. She downright blubbered. Shocked at this reaction, Mama Rose put her arm around Rosie's shaking shoulder and quietly held her. Mama knew this was a genuine expression of emotion and not a phony display of waterworks aimed at sympathy, to escape punishment.

When the shaking finally diminished, and the tears ebbed, Mama softened her tone and asked, "What the hell is the matter?"

Rosie burst out her reply in staccato sentences, punctuated with leftover emotion.

"The work is so hard [*gulp*]. I really hate school [groan]. I tried at first [*pant*]. But I just don't get it [*sigh*]. Algebra is like a foreign language [*cough*]. Latin might as well be Martian [*whine*]. I don't care about the ancient Greeks [*moan*]. My English teacher thinks she's a beauty queen [*sniff*]. The religion teacher hates animals [*wail*]. My friends think I'm a clown [*blubber*]. My two best friends are the smartest kids in the class [*wheeze*]. I feel stupid. I am stupid [*whisper*]."

Mama Rose brushed her hands gently over Rosie's tear-drenched cheeks and looked straight into her daughter's reddened, swollen eyes, sighed softly, and said, "So, other than that, how are things going?" She smiled and went on, "I am so sorry you have been so unhappy. It is a hard adjustment entering high school, and I know you didn't get off to a good start. Fourteen years old is a damn tough age anyhow, and I know Lourdes has high standards. So, first things first: You are not stupid. Sometimes you do stupid things, really stupid things, but you are not stupid. You may be average in some school subjects, and there is nothing wrong with that, and there is nothing stupid about that. If a C is your best work, I don't give a damn, as long as you have tried."

Rosie interrupted: "But Brigid and Babs are so smart. They—"

"You should be glad to have such smart friends. And they should be glad to have a warmhearted friend like you. You all have something to offer each other. Be comfortable with that, and be happy for them when they succeed," Mama advised.

"Well, what are we going to do about my grades? In some classes I'm not even getting Cs."

"Have you tried your hardest?"

"No. Mostly because I just gave up."

"Okay--we will get you a tutor, and instead of television every night, you will spend three evenings with the tutor. In the meantime, beef up your effort and pay more attention to your own schoolwork than Brigid's and Babs's."

Exhausted by the tears and realizing that *Peyton Place* had ended, Rosie hugged her mother and went to bed, relieved to have finally confided that things were not going well, but uneasy about whether or not things were going to get better. That night she dreamed of elephants crying in the jungle.

•

A few weeks later, the mothers met for lunch and gloated over their perceived successes.

"We should write an advice column," said Rose.

"Masters of Motherhood," Dar added.

"Dedicated to our Daughters," Barbara pronounced.

They laughed as they shared their stories, and went on mulling over their worries and their hopes for their "little girls." By the end of the lunch, they had decided that it would be a wonderful idea to get the three families together during the holidays. The men all shared a passion for football and a disdain for "the jackass," Art Modell. The Browns were headed for a Western Conference championship. There would be plenty for the men to talk about. The grandmothers would surely enjoy spending time with women of their own era, and the plethora of children could certainly entertain themselves. Rosie would make pasta, meatballs, and bread; Dar her chicken paprikash and Irish stew; and Babs her kuchen, Black Forest cake, and baklava for dessert.

When the women informed their husbands of the plans, the men were less enthusiastic. Miklos, usually very willing to socialize and to converse with anyone about anything, said he'd been looking forward to staying home on his only Saturday off from work in December. MV collapsed in exhaustion on the living-room davenport and complained to Rose that he didn't feel the need to fit yet another activity into his already overloaded schedule. Richard, who was now sixty-four, told

Barbara that for him weekends were precious times of rest and though he respected the wonderful relationship she had developed with these mothers, he had no interest in rekindling a chance acquaintance from fourteen years before. The wives showed sympathy and understanding, then proceeded with their plans.

Meanwhile, the girls' lunch table at Lourdes Academy buzzed with holiday spirit as Christmas and the upcoming vacation dominated the chatter. Rosie, Brigid, and Babs detached from the general holiday chit-chat to collaborate on a plan of action for the family get-together. They were excited about the festivities, but with a smidgen of trepidation.

"Don't say anything about how Sister Madeline yelled at me for sleeping in class," Rosie warned.

"And please don't mention my Johnson's habit," said Babs as she pantomimed holding a cigarette and blowing smoke.

"Well, fortunately I am a perfect young lady and have nothing to hide," Brigid bragged, and was immediately bombarded by pieces of baloney sandwich and chocolate-chip-cookie crumbs.

•

On Saturday, December 12, 1964, the Vanetti, Nagy, and Turyev families converged on the Vanetti house, bringing a lively, loving multicultural and multigenerational celebration of faith, family, and friendship. The Vanettis had decorated their home with holly and shimmering tinsel. Fiery red full-bloomed poinsettias wrapped in green velvet bows greeted the guests at every turn. The three buffet tables, trimmed in fresh pine boughs and cones, offered an array of delicacies and home-cooked dishes that filled the air with the mouth-watering aromas of meats and spices and sweets.

Proud of her home and her family, Rosie greeted the guests with warm hugs and a genuine smile. Before long, Rebecca, Renaldo, and Robert Vanetti, Michele, Sally, Joan, Cindy and Suzy Nagy, and David Turyev were led off to the play area, where a variety of toys and activities had been assembled that would keep them amused until dinnertime. The older children took charge of the younger ones, and the gleeful sounds of children at play added splendidly to the cacophony of laughter, conversation, and the televised voice of Ken Coleman announcing the Browns last game of the season, against the New York Giants.

The men had settled immediately in front of the television set. There was intense reaction regarding Coach Blanton Collier's play calling as the firefighter, the councilman, and the astrophysicist managed to engage in personal and professional exchange. Beer and Scotch helped keep the exchange moving at a congenial pace, and any misgivings the men had had about the gathering quickly dissolved into camaraderie and male bonding.

Realizing that it would be futile to suggest coming to dinner before the game ended, the ladies relaxed at the kitchen table and enjoyed wine and cheese. Barbara shared with the women some of her research from NASA. Rose and Dar found the information fascinating, and asked Barbara to keep them informed whenever they met for lunch. Rose talked of grocery-store prices and food imports, and Dar felt free to discuss the traumas and delights of staying home as cook, nurse, housekeeper, fiscal manager, and the numerous other roles of a housewife.

"Don't you just lo-o-o-ove the term housewife?" Barbara asked in a sardonic tone.

"I know some women take offense at it," Dar said, "but really, sometimes I do feel I'm married to the house! You can call me a housewife, a homemaker, anything—when I hear my kids laughing and my husband cussing at Art Modell, I am the happiest woman in the world."

"Amen, sister. Here's to the women of the world," said Rose, lifting her wineglass to clink with the others'.

"And to their men," added Barbara, with another clink of the glasses.

"And to their daughters," said Dar, with a smile now flanked by wine-flushed cheeks.

"And to their sons," Barbara and Rose chimed in together.

Grandmas Clemente, Nagy, and Schneider sat comfortably on the enclosed back porch and listened to the clinking of the glasses. Their drink of choice was tea, and they had each decided to begin their dinner with dessert. Such is the privilege of old age, whereby order and etiquette go by the wayside in favor of, as Grandma Schneider called it, "doing whatever the hell we want, whenever the hell we want to."

That statement opened the door for amiable chats about stories from yesteryear. The ladies, from vastly different backgrounds and cultures, listened and laughed and, by the end of this conversation, loved. A light, airy snow had begun to fall, and the old women sat in quiet contemplation as the flakes dissolved on the warm panes of glass that enclosed the porch.

Grandma Clemente softly broke the silence with an invitation: "Would you girls like to go outside and see my shrine to St. Riccardo, imported from Italy?"

Grandmas Nagy and Schneider did not need to be asked twice. They donned their coats, hats, and the small rubber boots that they carried in their handbags, always prepared for Cleveland weather. The men did not look up as the old women walked past them on their way out to the frozen garden, but they did not escape unnoticed by their granddaughters.

"Where are they going in this snow?" Babs whispered.

"Only one way to find out," said Rosie. "Let's follow them."

The girls had been sitting on the staircase, with a clear view of the television, the kitchen, and the back porch. Although their main focus was the game, they couldn't help being aware of the pleasant and jovial atmosphere created by the various groups.

"Hope I don't sound queer," said Brigid, "but, looking around at our families and hearing the wonderful sounds of happiness—well, I just think it's really cool."

The other two agreed as they followed their grandmas out the door.

The women had traipsed through the falling flakes and were standing before the small shrine that housed the beautiful Italian-made statue of St. Riccardo.

Grandma Nagy asked, "Why St. Riccardo?"

By this time, Rosie, Brigid, and Babs had joined the women, and slipped their arms under the oversized sleeves of their grandmas' coats. The girls had not bothered to put on coats, succumbing to the teenage notion that they would never get sick and would live forever.

The grandmas welcomed the girls with smiles and warm embraces. They put their arms around the girls' shoulders to shield them from the cold. Grandma Clemente then told the story of Baby Ricky. By the time she had finished, everyone's face, young and old, felt the warmth of tears against the cold falling snow landing on their cheeks.

The spirit of the moment was broken when Mama Rose shouted from the back door, "It's time to eat—get in here! You'll all catch pneumonia, and we don't have time to be your nurses!"

The old women and the teenagers all rolled their eyes and laughed as they went back to the party. Rose, Dar, and Barbara met them at the door, helped them brush off the wet snow, and handed each of them a cup of tea and honey. A roar came from the living room and the ladies knew this to be a signal that the game was over and the Browns had won. The feast would now officially begin.

Twenty chairs and a high chair crowded the dining table, but no one complained. The men and women smiled, the teenagers talked, and the children behaved. Falling snow could still be seen through the frosted window panes, and red and green twinkling lights glowed from the porch, accenting the inside decor. Norman Rockwell could not have created a more pleasant scene.

After dinner, Brigid accompanied Christmas carols on her saxophone (which her mother had commanded her to bring). Just when it seemed that the night could not get any better, Richard came in from the kitchen with an uncustomary wide smile on his face. Barbara had been slightly irritated, because he had insisted on making a telephone call during the caroling. She could now see that, whatever the reason for the call, it provided him with great satisfaction.

After a chorus of "Silent Night" — which ended abruptly once Renaldo began to hiccup and couldn't stop, causing the others to burst into with laughter, Richard stood in the middle of the group and asked for their attention.

"To my delightful new friends, Miklos and Massimo, and my loving daughter Babs and her friends Rosie and Brigid: I have just received word that my friend Joe Pentello is giving me six tickets to the Browns championship game on December 27. I would be honored if you would be my guests."

Rosie, Babs, and Brigid shrieked their delight and locked arms in a circle of jumping and screaming. Miklos and MV went over to Richard, shook his hand, and nearly toppled him with hearty slaps on the back. The children, not quite certain of the reason for all the jubilation, nevertheless ran around and screamed and jumped up and down, not to be outdone by their elders. The women looked on in peaceful contentment. Faith, family, and friendship: they could ask for nothing more—except possibly a win on December 27.

•

Even in the most Catholic of households, talk of the quarterback Frank Ryan and the running back Jimmy Brown had dominated the setting up of Nativity scenes and Advent wreaths. The Browns did win the N.F.L. championship. The Nagy, Vanetti, and Turyev fathers and daughters enjoyed a second-half gridiron spectacle of Browns offense and ironclad defense. Their seats offered the girls a close-up glimpse of Baltimore Colts greats Johnny Unitas and Don Shula as well as of their favorite Browns, Leroy Kelly and Ernie Green. Joe and Louie Pentello sat close by. After the game, a grand celebratory crowd of frenzied fans streamed from the lakeside all the way up to Ninth and Euclid Avenue.

A large group also gathered in the Public Square across from the Higbee Company department store, whose intricate, animated Christmas windows were for once overshadowed, by a sea of orange and brown clad revelers.

Rosie shouted above the cheers, "My grandma says everything connects. There's somethin' really special goin' on when a bunch of people are feelin' the same spirit. And there's another somethin' special goin' on right there."

She pointed to Louie Pentello's arm wrapped firmly around Babs's waist.

"Woo-hoo!" squealed Brigid.

When the excitement of the crowd degenerated to a drunken howling, the families went their separate ways, fathers and daughters feeling a love for Cleveland and its people, and a confidence that this would be one of many championships soon to come.

•

In 1965, the Cleveland winter served its annual helpings of slushy snow and gusty winds, but Lourdes Academy provided a haven where the girls could enjoy warm and calm conditions of scholarship and friendship. The absence of males gave them a certain freedom in their thoughts and actions. It eliminated the gender expectations imposed upon them by the world outside. Students at Lourdes Academy were not being instructed in how to be girls; they were being enlightened on how to be.

Freshmen participated in almost all school activities, including Friendship Week, pep assemblies, community food drives, and Big Sister/Little Sister luncheons. The school administration provided the structure for all of these, but the creative power belonged to the students. The toughest greasers and the softest preppies worked together in an environment of cooperation, and that experience established and nurtured a sense of school pride that would last forever.

One of the biggest events of the year was the senior-class play, in which every senior was expected to participate. The Class of 1965 performed The *Sound of Music*, and for months the halls were alive with "Edelweiss" and "Climb Every Mountain", as rehearsals echoed through Glee Club, Orchestra, and lunchtimes. The sound of female voices raised in song throughout the school added an ethereal spirit to the daily movement of life at Lourdes.

Teachers integrated the play into the curriculum: social-studies classes studied Nazi Germany; language classes studied the spread of Indo-European languages; math classes studied the biographies of Austrian mathematicians; science classes studied the biological and chemical advances during the era; and English classes researched the Holocaust, reading literature such as *Diary of a Young Girl*, by Anne Frank, and *Night,* by Elie Wiesel.

Sister Madeline assigned a 250-word personal essay and gave the girls a free choice of any topic related to the era. All essays were required to include: historical facts or events, possible effects on future societies, and a personal reflection. Grades would be twofold: twenty-five points for content, and twenty-five points for grammar/ writing technique.

Brigid, Rosie, and Babs each chose a topic that forecast the focus of her life.

9TH-GRADE ESSAY ASSIGNMENT
WOMEN OF THE NAZI WORLD
BY BRIGID NAGY

The forced role of women in Nazi Germany is a topic that is not often discussed, because the horror of the Jewish Holocaust overshadows the era. But it is an important topic because it shows the influence Hitler had in all corners of society, and it also slightly foreshadows the issue of women at work in our own society.

"Take hold of kettle, broom, and pan,
Then you'll surely get a man!
Shop and office leave alone,
Your true life work lies at home."

The above rhyme was a commonly quoted saying during the time that Hitler ruled Germany. This rhyme tells women and the culture in general that women's role in society should be focused on cooking, cleaning, and marriage. In 1933, "The Law for the Encouragement of Marriage" was passed. One of the main provisions of the law was that married couples could get loans from the government, and if they had children, a portion, or even all, of the loan could be paid off. One child reduced the loan by 25%; two children, 50%; and so on. It was required that in marriages where the loans were received the woman must not be employed outside of the home.

As a result of this law, many women left their jobs, and the number of female doctors and other female professionals diminished significantly. Also, the number of births in Germany increased from less than one million in 1933 to over one and one-half million by 1939, giving Hitler a boost in the number of potential soldiers to fight his war. Although many women disagreed with these conditions and joined groups that expressed opposition, the majority of women succumbed to forced motherhood and total lack of freedoms.

I think that motherhood and being a housewife is one of the noblest roles a woman can have. However, the role should be of her own choosing.

TEACHER'S COMMENTS: EXCELLENT CHOICE OF CONTENT. ADEQUATE RESEARCH. GOOD WRITING SKILLS. ROOM FOR IMPROVEMENT IN SCHOLARLY DICTION. 24/25 = 49/50

9th-GRADE ESSAY ASSIGNMENT ANIMALS OF THE THIRD REICH BY ROSIE VANETTI

Jewish humans were being slaughtered and tortured and burned alive during World War II, but guess what, animals were protected and there were even laws supported by Hitler and his criminal helpers that made it illegal to harm animals. It is hard to believe, but on November 24, 1933, Chancellor Adolph Hitler signed the "Law of Animal Protection," and this law made it illegal to torture animals, or not take care of animals properly, and also made it illegal to experiment on live animals. This was a very good thing and it is almost funny because the things the nazis were doing to humans were horrible and yet they cared about animals. Of course it was terrible how the Jews were treated it makes me cry. But this law is important because it shows that animals are considered important and good even though people can be considered not important and bad. My personal thoughts are that people in every era should treat animals well and I am going to find a way to save and help animals that are not being treated well.

TEACHER'S COMMENTS :EXCELLENT CHOICE OF CONTENT, BUT MUCH MORE DEVELOPMENT IS NEEDED. MINIMAL RESEARCH IS INDICATED. WRITING STYLE IS TOO CASUAL. SEVERAL GRAMMAR AND SPELLING ERRORS. POOR ORGANIZATION.15/15 = 30/50

9th-GRADE ESSAY ASSIGNMENT MUSICAL NUMBERS IN THE SOUND OF MUSIC BY BABS TURYEV

"Raindrops on roses and whiskers on kittens ... these are a few of my favorite things." So sings the character from the play as she lulls away the

troubles of the Von Trapp children. But here are some numbers that the sounds of music cannot sing away.

From 1933-1945, the Nazi regime under Adolph Hitler murdered over 11,000,000 citizens of Europe. At least 6,000,000 were Jews. Others who were murdered were Romanian Gypsies, homosexuals, the disabled, and political opponents to Hitler. 67% of the Jewish population of Europe was exterminated, and in Poland 90% of their Jewish population was killed by the Nazis. These numbers include millions of children, who were specifically chosen to die so they would not grow up and create more Jews. In the concentration camps where most of the murders occurred, the prisoners often had their identification numbers tattooed on their arms.

I did not look these things up in any books or encyclopedias. My father, a German Jew, knew the statistics by heart. For the first time ever, he shared with me his sorrow and guilt for leaving Germany in 1936, only to learn later that his parents, my grandparents, were slaughtered in Auschwitz in 1942. Through his connections with our government, he learned his parents' fate. He has their numbers tattooed on his hip.

I cried when he told me all of this, and I wondered, what were the favorite things of Isaac and Esther Turyev?

TEACHER'S COMMENTS : EXCELLENT CHOICE OF CONTENT. ALTHOUGH THE PERSONAL ASPECT IS GRIPPING, THE TONE IS TOO REFLECTIVE FOR A FORMAL ESSAY ASSIGNMENT. GOOD INTERNAL RESEARCH; EXTERNAL SCHOLARLY SOURCES WOULD HAVE ADDED MORE DEPTH. VERY GOOD WRITING SKILLS. EXCELLENT CONCLUSION 20/25 = 45/50

When Sister Madeline returned the papers, she lauded the students for their unique, thoughtful insights.

"Whatever the marks on your papers," she said, "it is your insight into the human condition that reveals who you are. And each of you is a very special, caring young woman."

Later that night, Brigid added No.12 to her list of Things That Make a Great School and a Great Teacher: Grace matters more than grades.

•

The summer of 1965 oozed by, with the sweltering heat of Cleveland sunshine alternating with the cooling storms of Lake Erie rain. Brigid, Rosie, and Babs started their lifelong tradition of spending their birthday together, this time at the Parma Theater watching the movie Cat Ballou, a kooky Western comedy at which the girls would have laughed boisterously if they had not been accompanied by Martin Gorman, Anthony Spermulli, and Louie Pentello. The boys' presence kept the girls' giddiness in check.

Brigid and Martin were still "just good friends"; Babs and Louie had crossed the line to romance and were now "going steady"; and Rosie and Anthony "liked to neck."

For Brigid and Babs, the relationships provided stable chastity throughout the fifteen-year-olds' awkwardness of awakening hormones in the summer sultriness. For Rosie, the summer hit "I Can't Get No Satisfaction" did not apply.

•

Despite the summer fun of rocking, rolling, and romancing, the girls welcomed the beginning of the new school year. In August, Brigid had been invited by four boys from Parma High School to play saxophone in their dance band. She could also sing a respectable tune, adding vocals to her contribution. This new adventure was going to be a surprise to her friends, and she looked forward to the encouragement and kudos she knew they would offer.

Brigid had missed the structure of the school day, and the monthly school Masses that brought her such solemn peace. When she was a little girl, she secretly thought she might have a vocational calling to be a nun. Their humble apparel and their spiritual fortitude appealed to her on a deep level of her psyche. At Lourdes she also observed the intelligence and the understanding of the language and the arts that so many of the sisters possessed, and she planned to emulate their ability to teach and influence young people to appreciate these things.

Over the summer, Babs had been consumed by discussions of the Mariner 4 Mars mission, which took photographs of the planet. Her father was on the team that was analyzing the data, and he shared both the findings and the excitement of seeing a close-up view of the surface of another planet. After the dismal recollections of the Holocaust dredged up in the spring, Babs was happy to see her father concentrating on the joy of space exploration. Forgetting about the hell of the earth was easier when gazing at the wonders of the heavens. She was eager to show her friends the pictures that few at the time had been privy to.

Rosie passed algebra during summer school and got a head start with geometry, for once anticipating a successful grade in math. But it was the stories of her body mates that she was eager to share with her soul mates.

All three girls had these little bubbles of excitement in their lives, and, one by one, each of the bubbles burst during their sophomore year. Brigid's was the first to pop, and it happened on the first day of school, when she walked into the building to see strange women in ill-fitting blue suits with white blouses. Their hair was plainly set, in no particular style, and their shoes looked like the ones Brigid's Hungarian great-aunts wore: black leather with tiny holes on the sides, thick heels, and thick shoelaces. The women gave off an air of familiarity that was incongruent with their unfamiliar appearance. When Brigid took a closer look, her spirit gave a silent shriek: they were nuns. Rumors had been circulating throughout the diocese that, with the end of the Ecumenical Council in 1964, big changes would be coming in

Catholicism. Obviously, one of those changes involved religious garb. Another was the celebration of the Eucharist, Brigid's beloved Mass.

All the students met in the auditorium to attend opening-day Mass. The priest, Father Trick, walked up to the makeshift altar and announced that, following the recommendations set forth by the Ecumenical Council, Lourdes Academy would be celebrating Mass in the English vernacular. A hushed gasp filled the room as the priest faced the girls and said, "In the name of the Father, and of the Son, and of the Holy Ghost . . ." Gone were the holy words "In nomine patri"; gone were Kyrie, Gloria, Pater Noster, Sanctus, and Agnus Dei.

A few of the girls attended parishes where these changes were already in place, but most of the girls were dumbfounded. Latin and the St. Joseph Missal prayer books were the mainstays of liturgical worship and these were no longer used. These changes were stunning. Brigid tried to be attentive, but her mind would not be still.

"The mystery is gone. The sanctity is gone. The majesty is gone. What made them do this? And the nuns: their humility is gone; their modesty is gone. Everything I loved is gone."

Brigid, Babs, and Rosie were not scheduled together for any classes except lunch, which they anticipated with relief. The cafeteria vibrated with chatter about the new look of the nuns and the English Mass. After a few minutes, however, those topics gave way to catching up on summer romances, rock and roll, and the distant rumblings of Viet Nam. Brigid, however, did not want their conversation to turn so easily.

"Don't you feel like everything's changed overnight? Like all of the holiness has been sapped? How can you think these changes are not important? They've taken away our identity and the identity of the nuns."

Babs looked at Brigid with a sullen smirk. "I lost my identity as a Catholic when I found out that the Church turned its back on my father's heritage," she said. "The Mass is better in English, because it's a break from the connections with the Nazis, and frankly I couldn't care less what the nuns look like. The smart ones will still be smart, and the dumb ones will still be dumb. Now . . . look at these pictures I brought of Mars."

Rosie could no longer contain herself. "Okay, does anyone want to hear about what it's like to 'do it'?" She took over the conversation and graphically reported the joys and joustings of her summer's sexual explorations. Despite their preoccupation with their own news, curiosity overcame them, and they listened attentively—and in awe—to Rosie's exploits. When the bell interrupted her monologue, they agreed to meet at Johnson's after school to finish the conversation. But before they left for class Babs grabbed Rosie's shoulder and said, "I am worried about you, Rosie. We need to talk about what all this may do to you."

Brigid nodded in agreement, but Rosie rolled her eyes and said, "You need to be my friend, not my mother."

A few months later, Rosie's bubble did indeed burst: she confided to her friends that she herself would soon become a mother.

•

Brigid and Babs told their mothers about the pregnancy after Rosie refused to tell hers. Rosie was depressed, refusing to eat, and her friends were worried about her health.

"My mom will kill me," Rosie whimpered to her friends at a weekend overnight in Parma. "She will kill me."

Barbara hosted a mothers' luncheon at her home, thinking it would provide a better atmosphere for what most likely would be an emotional event. But when Dar and Barbara broke the news to Rose, it turned out not to be news at all.

"I know, I know!" Mama Rose cried. "I've been waiting for her to tell me, but of course I knew. I always keep track of her menstrual cycle and of course I saw the fatigue and the terror in her eyes every time we spoke. But I wanted her to tell me, I wanted her to trust me."

"She thinks you are going to kill her," Dar said.

"Well, hell, yeah, I'm gonna kill her. But I still want her to trust me."

•

The families shared their second annual holiday meal at the Vanettis' home on Sunday, December 19. Once again, the Browns were a favorite topic of the men, since the team was playing for another national championship, this time in January. There was no open discussion of Rosie's pregnancy or any mention of the bump that now showed slightly through her stretch pants. The gathering went on, and though the mood was not as Norman Rockwellian as the previous year's, love and the spirit of the season prevailed. Food, fun, and football, when added to faith, family, and friendship, never fail to provide fulfillment.

Those realities helped the girls sustain their sanity and their perseverance through the cold losses of January. The first disappointment was the Browns' loss to the Cardinals in the NFL championship on January 2, but that was trivial compared with what followed.

Rosie miscarried on January 3, as a result of a hard fall on an icy sidewalk on Detroit Avenue. Physically, the damage was minimal. Rosie's body recovered fully, and a three-day convalescence at home during the remaining Christmas vacation had no effect on school or work. Grandma Clemente served her tea every day and created a peaceful, healing environment. Rosie, however, fell into a deep funk, not because of the loss of her baby but because of the guilt in her heart—guilt that she was relieved the pregnancy was over, that she rejoiced in the freedom of not having a baby to consume her life.

Rosie's depression did not go unnoticed by her friends. Two weeks after the miscarriage, she was sitting in Johnson's having a smoke and a Coke before school. Brigid took up the subject.

"Rosie," she said, "it's normal to feel bad after you lose a life that was growing inside of you. But you'll have other kids. There will be a right time for a child to be in your life—this was just not the right time. God knows what's best for you."

'No, no," said Rosie. "That's not it. I . . . I hate myself. I hate myself—not because I lost the baby but because, because I'm happy about it! I didn't want to have a baby."

"My God, that was a human being, Rosie! How can you be so cold?" Brigid spouted these words spontaneously and then immediately regretted them, but before she could apologize, Babs interrupted.

"Shut up, St. Brigid!"

Turning to Rosie, she went on, "Of course you didn't want to have the baby. Your whole life would have been turned upside down. It's okay to feel the way you do. The point is that if you did have the baby, you would have been a great mother and you would have loved it and taken care of it—we all know that. Be proud of yourself for that and just accept these other feelings as a sign that, for once in your life, you're normal."

Brigid and Babs hugged Rosie with genuine warmth. The smoke-filled coffee shop on 41st and Lorain burst with the laughter, love, and learning of these three girls from Lourdes Academy.

•

The 1966 senior-class play, *Carnival,* did not generate much buzz throughout the school, and sophomore year seemed to fizzle into a cool, wet spring. Babs earned her friends' enthusiasm with a prom invitation from Louie Pentello. An invite from a Cathedral Latin Lion was a badge of coolness that only a few Lourdes girls received. Brigid and Rosie were excited to join in doing Babs's hair in a soft flip, and the preparations of her nail polish, shoes, dress, and jewelry—all in the hue called "blushing pink." When Louie arrived, in a blushing-pink bow tie and cummerbund, the audience at the Turyevs'—Barbara, Richard, David, Joe, Madge, Rosie, and Brigid—applauded the couple in unanimous approval. Babs's old friend Karen Grovac snapped the moment with her Polaroid camera.

Barbara's and Richard's eyes and hearts filled as they watched their little girl, soon to be sixteen years old but looking tonight like a grown woman, ride off into a night that had the potential to be a milestone.

"I bet they do it," Rosie whispered to Karen and Brigid. Karen nodded in agreement while Brigid pouted in disgust.

After the prom, Babs and Louie parked at Shaker Lakes. The setting of blue waters and weeping willows, where Barbara had first noticed Babs's limp and frightening fever, was now a scene where young people came to catch a fever of a different sort. As the radio played The Temptations' "My Girl," Louie Pentello's windows steamed up, and Babs lost herself in the wallow of first love. It was Louie who stopped the action.

"You're fifteen," he whispered.

"I'll be sixteen in a couple of weeks," Babs moaned.

"Babs, I am leaving for college in a couple weeks."

"Louie, I think I love you."

"Babs, I know I love you."

Louie sat up, rolled down the windows, and the two friends spent the next hour in gentle snuggling and a cosmic conversation about the future of life and love. Louie's sentiment inspired a life-changing decision in Babs's conscience. She would wait for marriage to share the intimacy of lovemaking.

When Babs got home, Richard and Barbara were waiting for her in the garden, stargazing at the same sky that just a while ago had filled Babs's and Louie's hearts with wondrous, grand thoughts of fulfillment. Babs told them most of the occurrences of the evening.

As she kissed her father gently on the forehead, she whispered in his ear, "You always talk about the war between flesh and spirit, Papa. Tonight, Louie's spirit won a battle."

•

The summer of 1966 began with a Sweet Sixteen pajama party at

Brigid's house on Saturday, June 4. After dancing at Parmatown Lanes to the tunes of Brigid's band, Brigid, Babs, Rosie, and thirteen of their friends spent the night in the Nagys' bungalow. Rosie's cousin Beth, now nineteen and a sophomore at Cleveland State University, slipped some six-packs of beer to the girls through a basement window, and several of them drank themselves silly. Brigid was sick with worry that her parents would discover the illicit activity, but Babs and Rosie made sure the girls were quiet and the evidence well hidden. Only a few of the guests took part in the drinking: the rest were satisfied with the Coke, Charlie's Chips, and Sloppy Joe sandwiches provided by the Nagys. When sleep finally took hold, at 4:00 a.m., the girls had dispersed through the house, with some in the basement, some on the couch upstairs, and a few on the cushioned swing on the front porch.

At seven, Dar woke everyone, shouting in a steely, sharp voice that made Brigid tremble. "Get up, ladies. This isn't the chorus-girl life. Get the contraband out of the basement, come up and have breakfast, and then clean up my yard."

The girls groggily staggered to their feet, scrambled for a space at the lone bathroom sink to brush their teeth and comb their hair, and sank into the chairs crowded around the kitchen table and at card tables that Miklos had set up in the front room.

Brigid, flushed with embarrassment at her mother's inhospitable tone, whispered in a huff, "Mom! What are you doing? We just got to sleep. Why are you waking us up so early and being so mean about it?"

"Don't you dare question me as I stand here making three dozen eggs and three pounds of bacon for a bunch of rude guests who kept us up all night and floated around the house in their underwear like this was a brothel. Such an example to set for your sisters! And don't think I don't know about the beer. We caught Beth toilet-papering the yard at two in the morning, and she confessed to everything. She at least had the decency to pretend to apologize."

Brigid was too exhausted and shocked to respond, so she asked Babs and Rosie to help her start cleaning. A few of the other girls thanked Mrs. Nagy and drove away without eating breakfast, and those without cars ate and then called their parents to come and get them. Mama Rose and Barbara arrived at nine, made sure that any mess was cleared up, including the twenty rolls of toilet paper that blanketed the trees and lawn of the Nagy yard, then took their daughters home.

Brigid's sister Michele provided some more information, explaining how Dar and Miklos heard a commotion in the yard at 3:00 a.m. and found Beth and a friend of hers slinging toilet paper around the bedroom window.

"I snuck and listened on the steps. I have never seen Mom so mad as when Beth spilled the beans about the beer. Dad took a headcount and made sure everyone was accounted for, and both of them were actually kind of in shock that they were so stupid not to have expected anything like this. I think you're really in for it."

When everyone had left, Dar icily told Brigid to take her sisters to the noon Mass and that they would discuss the events of the night before at another time. Brigid wearily obeyed. Nodding off during the sermon at Mass, Brigid barely heard the priest's spiritual analysis of something called "the generation gap."

•

Turning sixteen was a milestone for the girls in many ways. For Brigid, after a brief grounding period for the pajama party episode, it was the increased freedom of being permitted to have single dates in a car, after being confined to group dates for the past two years. Her gigs with the band also provided her with spending money and opportunities to meet people outside of the realm of Catholic dances and sports events. These freedoms culminated in a relationship she developed with a young man, Charlie, who lived on the east side of Cleveland, with whom she hoped to share the remaining proms, semi-formals, and any other activity that mandated an escort. But a west sider dating an east-sider was not an easy alliance in 1966 Cleveland. The west side was dominated by a population of white people; the east side dominated by a population of black people—"and never the twain shall meet."

The racial battles over Cleveland City Schools' segregation and desegregation policies had been simmering and exploding, simmering and exploding, in dangerous cycles of violence since 1963. Although her new friend, Charlie, was white, he allied himself with the black students who were protesting and fighting for schools with the same standards and quality of teachers as those that served the predominantly white schools. Being a white person in a black-populated school, Charlie saw firsthand the injustices and inequalities suffered by the action of city planners and school-board policies. Charlie informed Brigid that when one compared the data on overcrowding, textbook purchases, teachers' education level, facilities, it was obvious where the commitment to education failed.

The conversations about Negroes and white people fascinated Brigid. She had never heard disparaging words about Negroes, except for the Thomas Smith incident, but somewhere in her life experience she had developed the assumption that people just "stick to their own kind." Parma was where white people lived; it was just understood; she had never wondered why.

One conversation she had with Charlie, the last conversation she would ever have with Charlie, awakened her to a deep evil that she could not comprehend.

One evening, while they were slouching in the car at Manners Big Boy, sipping a Coke and enjoying a piece of strawberry pie, Charlie casually commented, "So, yeah, I'll be marching with the niggers down to the Board of Education, and we won't back down until they make the east-side and west-side schools equal."

Brigid, choking on the crust, blurted out, "Charlie! How can you use that word? Those people are your friends!"

He laughed. "Well, yeah, but a nigger is still a nigger."

"But my God, Charlie, that's such a horrible thing to say, and so disrespectful. Please don't refer to Negroes by that name when you talk to me. Really, you should never use that word. It's so vulgar and wrong."

Charlie grabbed Brigid's chin and looked unblinkingly into her eyes. "Look, Brigid. I don't know where you've been all your life, but here's a news flash: those people ain't like us. Sure, I fight for them, because I think they are getting screwed—and I am getting screwed, too. And, yeah, some of them are my friends, but damn, they're still nig— Um, Negroes."

Brigid looked back into his eyes, searchingly. She thought she would see something different, something that could explain this incomprehensible attitude. But she didn't see anything different. He was the same Charlie she had known for months: intelligent, handsome, and, yes, she even saw the same kindness that had always been there. Yet now she realized that there was an ignorance at the center of his being that she would never understand. She also realized that it was an ignorance she could never erase. She wondered if this ignorance resided in the hearts of all men.

That night, Brigid gave a late call to Babs and told her what had happened and that she had decided not to see Charlie anymore.

"Oh, Brigid," Babs sighed. "Didn't you pay attention in history class when we talked about slavery, or segregation, or Jim Crow? Didn't you listen to my father's story about the holocaust? For God's sake, didn't you read Ralph Ellison's *The Invisible Man*? That stuff is real: there is hate in people's hearts for others who don't look or act like them."

Brigid was shaken. "But I thought those ideas were held by just a few evil people and eventually we rid ourselves of those kinds of terrible things. I mean, I thought I knew Charlie. I've watched him defend Negroes and argue with white people about how unfair the system is. I just thought that people with at least half a brain would be on the side of justice ... and humanity."

"Jeez, you need to get out of Parma."

"I do get out of Parma. Charlie and I talked about that. I just don't know what's wrong with me that I never cared to wonder why no Negroes live here."

"Why would you wonder about that, when your life is safe and orderly, with good schools, low crime, nice restaurants, and happy neighborhoods? It doesn't matter who lives in your city as long as your city has all the good things that make you feel happy and secure."

"Are you making fun of me?" Brigid felt emotions rising in her chest. "I do have all of those things and I am proud of the people who have made this city a place where I can have all those things. I guess I'm just confused."

"The world is a confusing place, Brigid. Don't worry about what you can't change. I'm going to bed. Go play your saxophone or something. G'night."

When Brigid hung up the phone, she picked up a *Time* magazine. Her mind was unsettled, and reading always soothed the chaos. She grabbed a glass of milk and some Oreo cookies, and started reading the cover story. It was about a place called Viet Nam.

•

Rosie's summer was filled with babysitting, stuffing envelopes, interning, and dancing. Her father was in a campaign for re-election, and although he faced no serious opposition, he wanted to get enough votes to impress the Democratic Party machine, because he was contemplating running for mayor of Cleveland. When it was an election year, the entire Vanetti family, from babies to cousins, aunts and uncles, and on to extended families of friends, contributed in one way or another to the campaign effort. Rosie loved the give-and-take of politics when she closely observed her father as he traded, persuaded, and abated the fears of his constituents. MV's most alluring trait was his authenticity. He genuinely loved his neighborhood and the people in it. No one, not even his most ardent opponents, ever questioned his integrity or the motivations for his political zeal. He was a champion of the people's needs, not his own.

When the Vanetti household started down a campaign trail, Rosie marched steadfastly on its path. The post-miscarriage depression had subsided, and Rosie slowly regained her self-respect.

Since August, Thursdays had brought a respite from political and familial duties. On Thursdays, she worked as an intern at the world-acclaimed Cleveland Zoo, in the elephant exhibit. Rosie spent most of her time there with a baby Asian elephant named Aspara, which the zoo had obtained the past winter. The zookeepers treated Aspara tenderly, but Rosie was amazed at the maternal care and guidance that the adult female elephants provided. She called the females in the herd Aspara's Aunties. There was constant touching and teaching. The Aunties taught Aspara how to use her trunk to get food, to greet other elephants, and to play with the young calves.

During her babysitting hours, Rosie shared elephant stories with her brothers and sister.

"They love each other like we love each other. They help each other, and each sound they make expresses some sort of emotion to each other. They are so much like us."

Robert asked, "Do they get sad?"

"Yes," Rosie replied.

"Do they cry?" Renaldo said, with a slight laugh because he thought it might be a dumb question.

"Yes, elephants cry, too," Rosie answered and then slipped into deep thought.

Even as a child, Rosie had wondered about the behavior of animals, especially elephants. It bothered her that humans had such a smug attitude toward nature. The conservationists at the zoo had taught her about the extinction of so many species, caused by human folly or sometimes by human wickedness. In between her other responsibilities,

Rosie would read books about endangered or extinct animals. Her favorite was also the saddest: the pathetic and sorrowful story of the dodo, a bird that lived on the island of Mauritius before humans arrived and hunted it to extinction. She filed the tale in her memory and promised herself that someday she would make use of that memory for a good cause.

Working for a good cause had become engrained in Rosie's psyche. Her daily political interactions and her work with the elephants had firmly planted the spirit of an activist in her. She became restless to release that spirit. That day would come later in the 1960s, when it seemed everyone under the age of thirty had restless spirits. For now, Rosie soaked up the essence of politics and pachyderms and enjoyed the freedom of being sixteen in a summer that rocked to the sounds of the Beatles, the Beach Boys, and the Byrds.

Music drove the highs, the lows, the hormones, and the learning of her generation. That summer offered an array of ballads, blues songs, rock and roll, and the entrance of psychedelic. Rosie faced the music as she faced life: head on, loving every genre, every beat, every lyric, and every artist. She swayed to "Somewhere My Love," stomped to "Hanky Panky," grooved to "A Groovy Kind of Love," popped to "Mother's Little Helper," and gravitated to every song that Dusty Springfield crooned. Each song made her want to experience everything in life. She and Babs tried to go to every gig that Brigid's band played. When it was in a preppie dance hall, Rosie would wear her madras; when it was in a greaser dance hall, she wore her pointy shoes and leather jacket; for the surfer barn on the west side, she donned her cutoff jeans and sandals. Rosie never worried about the dichotomy of nature versus nurture that Brigid and Babs were obsessing over. She embraced both the animal and the divine. The only lines she ever memorized from an English class were from Alexander Pope's "Essay on Man":

Know, then, thyself, presume not God to scan;
The proper study of mankind is man.
Placed on this isthmus of a middle state,
A being darkly wise, and rudely great:
With too much knowledge for the sceptic side,
With too much weakness for the stoic's pride,
He hangs between; in doubt to act, or rest;
In doubt to deem himself a god, or beast;
In doubt his mind or body to prefer;
Born but to die, and reasoning but to err;
Alike in ignorance, his reason such,
Whether he thinks too little, or too much:
Chaos of thought and passion, all confused;
Still by himself abused, or disabused;
Created half to rise, and half to fall;
Great lord of all things, yet a prey to all;
Sole judge of truth, in endless error hurled:
The glory, jest, and riddle of the world!

Rosie loved the "middle state." During that summer of her sixteenth year, she fluctuated gleefully between "thought and passion," God and beast.

•

After the prom, Babs thought and hoped that she and Louie would grow closer, in love and friendship. This was not what happened. Louie left Shaker Heights two weeks after prom night to attend Notre Dame and play football.

Before he left for college, Louie took Babs to the Kon Tiki Restaurant, in downtown Cleveland, and then down to Leo's Casino, on Euclid Avenue, to see The Temptations perform. Babs was uncharacteristically ecstatic. The evening had been a perfect blend of great food, great music, and great conversation.

Then the good night turned into a goodbye.

While parked at their favorite spot at Shaker Lakes, Babs softly promised Louie, "I will be true to you, Louie. No other guy has ever interested me like you do. There will be no temptations for me to be anything but your girl."

Louie's shoulders stiffened, and his gaze turned toward the windshield, his eyes avoiding Babs's. He gave an unexpected, crushing response.

"I have told you that I love you, Babs, and I do. And that is why I cannot have you wait for me. I cannot promise that I will be true to you. And I cannot ask you to be my girl. You are sixteen, way too young to be passing up dates with guys. And I will be a college freshman, way too free to be passing up opportunities to be with girls in any or all circumstances. I don't want either of us to feel guilty or feel like we're cheating if we start enjoying other people. In the long run, it's better for us not to make any commitments."

Babs sat quietly, and when Louie finally gathered his nerve to look at her, he saw the silent, flowing tears.

She looked back at him, and said, "Take me home."

They rode home in silence, and Louie parked the car in the driveway of Babs's house. She pecked Louie on the cheek, and said, "You know I wish you the best."

Louie hugged her, then watched as she quickly climbed the steps that led to her door. Memories of the little girl who several years ago could barely walk flashed through his mind and into his heart. If she had turned around, she would have seen his tears silently flowing, too.

The hole in Babs's heart would take time to heal, and it was her mother and grandmother who salved the wound.

Grandma told her, "He did a very noble thing. He was honest, and even though it might not feel like it, he was loving. Good for him, and good for you."

Barbara agreed. "You know, Babs, Louie is a fine young man, and I do hope you two can someday build a life together. But your identity rests within yourself. He may have complemented your spirit, but the essence of who you are is independent of any man—or anyone else, for that matter. Remember that as your heart mends."

Rosie and Brigid offered different perspectives.

"Screw him," snarled Rosie. "You were way too smart for him anyhow."

Brigid said that she had been worried about Babs and Louie's getting "too close." She confessed, "Well, I didn't want to be the only virgin in the group."

•

There were other worries simmering during the summer of 1966 that concerned the Turyevs. Racial tensions across the country had been festering since the Watts riots in California, the previous summer. Although Shaker Heights was an island of affluence, it was surrounded by poverty-ridden black neighborhoods that stewed with unrest.

Richard came home one evening in early July and told Barbara that he had been assigned to work on a project in Berkeley, California, and would be gone for the rest of the summer.

"I want you to take the family and spend the next two months at the Cape," he said. "I have heard rumors from people in the government that communists are coming into Cleveland to rile up the Negroes and create the same type of chaos that destroyed Watts last year. Shaker may be a target, because it seems like these people resent the wealth that we have worked so hard for. Since I will not be close by, I would feel better if you took the children far from whatever violence may occur."

"We have never had trouble here before," Barbara responded. "Two months is a long time to be away from home, for all of us."

Richard frowned. "I will visit the Cape a few times, so we will not be separated for too many weeks at a time. The potential for a massive uprising is strong, and I saw what these animals did in Watts."

"Richard!" Barbara raised her voice in shock and anger. "Surely you are not referring to that community of people as animals! I was just speaking with Mollie, a waitress at the coffee shop, and she told me how just ten years ago her father was found hanging from a tree down in Mississippi because he smiled at a white girl. Think about what they have gone through, Richard. Many of the Negroes have come up from the South, where they couldn't drink from the same water fountains, or shop at the same stores as white people, or saw their children spit on and beaten. Are you going to deny them their anger?"

"You dare to preach to me about people who have been abused? You don't see Jews looting German stores and burning down German stores with their anger, do you? People have a choice, Barbara—a choice. Do we choose the saint or the savage? When anger turns to destruction, it is the beast that emerges. I don't want you or the children anywhere near those beasts."

"When people are treated like beasts, they respond accordingly," Barbara retorted, not backing down from what was developing into a full-blown quarrel.

"I sailed away as my heritage was burned in the ovens of Auschwitz. I am fully aware of what happens when people act like beasts and when people are treated like beasts."

"Negroes sailed away from their heritage in chains—and are still fighting to break those chains," Barbara replied, now speaking through tears.

Richard opened his mouth to speak, but instead reached for Barbara and held her, speaking through hidden tears.

"I am getting old, Barbara—the world is changing too fast for me. I just want you safe. The communists are going to stir things up and the anger of oppression will take an ugly turn in the Negro neighborhoods and perhaps the entire city. Please, go to the Cape."

Barbara gazed into his weary eyes and felt the weight of his woe.

"I will go, Richard. And hopefully you will soften your heart long enough to try to understand the black man's plight."

Richard remained silent.

Babs had been eavesdropping in the hallway, hearing every word of the conversation that had grown louder, filtering through the door of her parents' room.

She knew that the racial conflicts were things she should be informed and concerned about. But she was a sixteen-year-old with a broken heart, and all she could think of was two months, on a beautiful beach, far away from the sights and smells and sounds that reminded her of Louie Pentello.

And so the Turyevs escaped the turmoil on the east side of Cleveland that exploded into fire and looting on Hough Avenue for three days in mid-July. But the cool breezes of Cape Cod did not reach into the heat of the ghettos to calm the smoldering embers of lawless discontent that would flare up again, and again.

•

Lourdes Academy opened its doors in the autumn of 1966 for the seventy-fourth time, and began preparations for the seventy-fifth anniversary which would begin in January of 1967. Faculty and students shared the pride and excitement of this diamond jubilee, and soon the doldrums of a waning summer disappeared into a vibrant academic wave of enthusiasm. Brigid, Rosie, and Babs entered their junior year with fresh perspectives on their own worlds and the worlds that surrounded them: Babs carried the lessons of young love; Brigid, the awakening to an imperfect world; and Rosie, the confidence of a girl with a mission. Their choice of curriculum, in the college-preparatory track, complemented their strengths and interests. Brigid enrolled in American Literature and Creative Writing, Glee Club, Latin 3, Theology, American History, and Chemistry. Babs selected Trignometry, Physics 2, Astronomy, American History, American Literature, Theology, and French 1. Rosie chose Psychology, Sociology, American History, American Literature, Business Math, Spanish 1, and a study hall. All three girls opted out of the required physical-education class, hoping to pass an abbreviated version of the class in summer school. Lourdes continued to serve as an oasis of intellectual serenity in the desert of worldly chaos.

Although the friends showed no aspirations to leadership, teachers and classmates appreciated their skills. As a result, peers elected Rosie president of Junior Council on World Affairs; teachers selected Brigid as assistant editor of the literary magazine; and teachers and students alike chose Babs to be the first junior ever to serve as president of the Math Club. The girls immersed themselves in the traditions of their high school, treasuring the class-ring ceremony, the junior retreat, and the camaraderie of Friendship Week.

During a morning at Johnson's, two days before taking the Preliminary Scholastic Aptitude Test—a test that would indicate their ranking among other juniors across the country, and possibly lead to funding for their college educations—the girls discussed the beginning of their new school year.

"If anyone would have told me that I'd ever be staying after school cutting out stencils for a Friendship Week bulletin board, I would have laughed in their face," Rosie said, inhaling a deep drag of Taryton charcoal-filtered tobacco.

"I really love Lourdes," Brigid said. "I love getting out of the suburbs and coming down to this old neighborhood and this old building, a hop, skip, and a jump from downtown. I love the feel of it—I love the smell of it, and I love ...."

Babs snapped at Brigid, "Okay, okay--we get it. Christ, we get it. You love it. You love everything. Yay for you."

"Well, Miss Sunshine, I am going to ignore your rudeness and kindly ask you: What crawled up your derriere and died?"

Rosie laughed at Brigid's attempt to be harsh. "It's ass. You should say, 'What crawled up your ass and died.'"

That comment provoked a giggle from the girls that evolved into hearty laughter which led to uncontrollable snorts and ended with coffee spewing from their noses.

When that subsided, Babs informed the others that her father had put a lot of pressure on her to perform well on the PSAT.

"We don't need the money for my college, but it's a matter of prestige for him. He's involved in some significant work with this Mars project, and he wants to boast about his daughter's academic achievements. He has made it clear to me that a top national score would put his career and our family's status in the NASA spotlight."

Brigid asked, "Well, you're not concerned about your score, are you? Good Lord, you ace everything."

Babs sighed. "You never know when you're going to choke. It's just that, even though his expectations have always been high for me, he has never made me feel this type of stress."

"Well," Rosie said. "I'm going to have a hot date the night before the test, get the adrenaline going, and get a perfect 'score.'"

Two days later, after the test was over, all three girls felt that they'd done well, and Babs became more relaxed. The next academic projects related to the Seniors' drama production, which this year was *South Pacific*. The halls of Lourdes Academy were transformed into another land—this time, a land of exotic birds, military scenery, and grass skirts. The annual essay for all English classes again allowed for a wide range of exploration: "Write a 300-word essay on any aspect of the themes, settings, or characters of the play. The essay will be worth 100 points, 50 points awarded for development of relevant content, and 50 points for writing style and mechanics."

The Pigeons of the South Pacific in World War 2
By Rosie Vanetti

Many men who served in the war in the South Pacific received medals for bravery and special duty achievements. You have no doubt heard of the

Medal of Honor, or the Purple Heart, or a Good Conduct Medal. But have you ever heard of the Dickin Medal? Probably not.

The medal started being awarded in 1943 and originated in the mind and soul of Maria Dickin who was an English woman who felt sorry for animals and started a hospital for sick or wounded animals. It was called "People's Dispensary for Sick Animals of the Poor." They didn't let women into the Royal Veterinary College, so mrs. Dickin had to use her own knowledge and train people to run the hospital.

When Mrs. Dickin started hearing stories about how animals were saving lives in the war, she decided to honor these animals with an award and that was called the Dickin Medal, named, obviously, after her.

Between 1943 and 1949, 54 of those medals were awarded, and of those 54, 32 of them were awarded to pigeons. Yes, pigeons. Those dirty birds that leave their droppings all over Public Square could be the offspring of a bird that saved your father's or uncle's life.

Pigeons actually had a military rank and if they died on a rescue mission, they would be buried with military honors. Many pigeons serving our country were shot at by the Japanese as the pigeons carried messages or were used to find men shot down in the South Pacific Ocean. Very often pigeons lost a leg or eye or were wounded, but most of the time they still bravely made it back to their destinations and delivered their information. So when you watch this play and see the sailors and nurses, remember that humans weren't the only ones who Bali Hai was calling.

TEACHER'S COMMENTS:

- Miss Vanetti, very good and interesting choice of topic.
- Your paper should include more specific description of what types of duties the pigeons performed.
- The style of your writing is much too informal for an objective

essay, and, as I have repeatedly said in class, use of second person is not acceptable in formal writing.

- Be careful to revise and double-check your writing before submitting it. There are a few spelling and grammar errors as well as usage inconsistencies.

38/38 = 76 = C

Nobel Prize for Physics Defeats the Racism of World War II—20 Years Later
By: Babs Turyev

One of the major themes in the play South Pacific is the racism that exists in human relationships. Nellie could not accept the Captain's children until late in the play because of their Polynesian ancestry, and the romance between Lt. Cable and the Polynesian girl Liat is foiled because of Cable's family's prejudices.

But the racist and prejudicial biases extended far beyond personal relationships and even spread into the atomic world of quantum physics. Because of the obvious break in communications between Japan and the United States, three major physicists of the time, Julian Schwinger and Richard Feynman of the United States, and Sin Itiro Tomonaga of Japan, worked in isolation from each other and could not communicate the findings of their work until several years later.

The importance of their work is extremely significant in the scheme of understanding the physical matter of our universe, and at the time, the findings from their experiments and research opened up a whole new world of quantum electrodynamics. Noted physicist F. J. Dyson wrote in Science Magazine last year, that "Tomonaga, Schwinger, and Feynman, rescued the [quantum] theory without making any radical innovations. . . . By polishing and refining with great skill the mathematical formalism, they were able to show that the theory does in fact give meaningful predictions for all observable quantities."

The American physicists used experiments to advance the understanding of quantum theory, and the Japanese physicist made his discoveries on a purely theoretical basis. Yet they both arrived at the same place, a place that advanced the concept of relativity and moved science closer to finding a theory that may unify all of the theories.

I can only imagine what knowledge could have emerged from that great era of discovery if nations could share information and work together; if Tomonaga and Schwinger and Feynman could have talked and read each other's research and focused on atomic exploration and not atomic explosions.

The Nobel Prize Committee recognized the contribution of these three men and refused to let race intervene in the wonder of their work. In 1965, Japanese and Americans united in pride and victory as Julian Schwinger, Richard Feynman, and Sin Itiro Tomonaga shared the Nobel Prize in Physics.

TEACHER'S COMMENTS:

- Barbara, the topic of racism is appropriate and relevant to the assignment, but comparing the lack of communication between physicists whose countries were at war to personal relationships between people of different ethnicities is an invalid stretch.
- Your paper would have been more relevant if you focused on the treatment of Japanese Americans living in the United States or some more specific references to racism.
- Grammar and writing style are very good, and essay is very well organized. Points deducted for a use of first person and some informal sentence structure.

38/47 = 85 = B

The Power of Lyrics in the Broadway Musical South Pacific
By: Brigid Nagy

Music has been a powerful and meaningful tool of expression and communication since the very origins of our species. Archaeological findings of holed stones and bird bones provide evidence of man-made music, dating back to prehistoric times. Whether it was to imitate the sounds and rhythms of nature, or communicate the thoughts and warnings of ancestral hominids, stone age flutes and pipes have suggested that primitive instruments were in use from as long ago as 40,000 years, and the musical sound of human voice long before that.

It is no wonder that even today, music dominates our souls, and Broadway Musicals dominate the genre of drama. When music added lyrics (or lyrics added music), a whole new dimension of meaning opened up. No longer was music just the sounds of air and vibration; music with words added a message. An astute audience will listen carefully, not only to lively rhythms and melodic tunes of the play South Pacific, but also to the lyrics that bounce and flow in these rhythms and tunes.

In the song, "101 Pounds of Fun," Nellie, dressed as a male sailor, sings the accolades of what is implied is a perfect woman: A blonde, curly-haired woman, with a broad chest, narrow waist, seductive hips, and attractive lips, all used to "trap" a man. The message of a woman's worth is clearly stated in these lyrics. Add to these lyrics those of a bunch of "unrelieved" sailors singing, "There Is Nothing Like a Dame," and the head nurse singing "I'm Gonna Wash That Man Right Outta My Hair," not because of her self-esteem, but because of her prejudices, and there exists a very troubling, powerful view of women and male/female relationships.

It makes one wonder what those primitive holed stones and bird bones would have communicated if they were accompanied with lyrics ... possibly the same message as Rodgers and Hammerstein.

TEACHER COMMENTS:

- Brigid, Analysis of lyrics is an excellent topic choice and your insights and conclusions regarding Honey Bun are very good.
- The introduction regarding prehistoric music is too long, and as a result your content focuses too much on history and not enough on the era of the play.
- Diction and writing skills are excellent, with some minor syntax and cohesion difficulties.

45/48 = 93 =A-

Brigid was not satisfied with the score; she seldom received less than 95s on her writings. She made an appointment to see her English teacher, Sister Abraham, who had the reputation of being the hardest grader in the school, to discuss the points that were deducted.

"Sister, I would like to know specifically what the 'minor syntax and cohesion difficulties' are in my paper," said Brigid, in a haughty tone.

A stern and professional reply came from Sister Abraham: "The word 'bunch' does not indicate the use of superior diction, and your last sentence is clumsily put together in a manner that almost obscures the message. The five points deducted for content are a result of too much text being given to material that should have been more relevant to the era being studied. On a personal note, it appears that you have not yet acquired the appropriate manner in which to address a marking you do not agree with. A better approach would have been 'Sister, can you help me improve my writing skills?'"

Flushed with an awkward sensation of having been humbled, Brigid murmured, "Thank you," and left the room.

The evening phone conversations among the girls didn't focus on the essays, although Brigid would have liked to have her friends ease the sting. Instead, Rosie talked about the election next month, and Babs bemoaned the absence of her father, who was still in Berkeley. Neither Rosie nor Babs could conjure up sympathy for an A minus on an essay that had no great effect on anything except Brigid's pride.

A clear separation was growing between the paths of the friends. The lack of a common lunch period meant that the brief coffee at Johnson's, and hurried evening phone conversations provided limited bonding and sharing. Weekends seemed to speed by in warp speed. The intensity of the relationships remained intact, but the limits on frequent conversation allowed the girls to develop other friendships.

With a landslide victory guaranteed for her father, Rosie spent many of her Saturdays at Junior Council on World Affairs activities, learning about the policies and programs of the United Nations and opportunities to work abroad. She became friends with classmates who shared her love of animals, and together they sought ways to offer hypothetical proposals for protecting endangered species at mock UN conferences. Babs, too, developed new connections, particularly with the girls in the upper-level science and math classes. Her interests went beyond the globe and reached out to the solar system, where her parents' research continued to push her toward the inquisitive heights of current theory. As November approached, Babs's father was still spending half his time in California. During his absences, Babs's mother shared with Babs the data that she herself was collecting, and when her father returned, a lively dinner-table discussion of Mars exploration and cosmic revelations in the world of physics and biology ensued.

Richard's presentation at the American Institute of Astronautics and the American Astronautical Society conference in Maryland last Spring, called "Stepping Stones to Mars," increased his international status as an astronautical expert, and as an integral player in the plan to explore Mars. His expertise in the intricacies of the lunar mission included everything from layered space suits to landing gear, and this expertise directly carried over to a Mars landing.

Both of Babs's parents visited the higher-level physics and biology classes at Lourdes, to discuss the discoveries and theories about the atmosphere on Mars and the developments in rocketry that scientists were now confident would take mankind on lunar and interplanetary voyages.

Barbara's latest research project consisted of analyzing data from the Gemini missions, which included studying a theory that the seeds of life on Earth might have been planted by Martian meteorites. She discussed this theory of panspermia with the captivated young women.

She explained, "Panspermia comes from the Greek words pan, meaning all, and sperm, meaning seed, and can be literally translated seeds everywhere. This theory, which tells us that organisms float or blast across the universe, sharing their life with infinite numbers of their neighbors, originated in ancient Greece. Data coming in from space travel have suggested that indeed it may be scientifically possible that seeds of life on Earth were extraterrestrial."

Barbara paused, perceiving a sudden chill of anxiety, and stony silence.

A quiet young lady raised her hand and spoke softly from the back corner of the room. "Dr. Turyev, we know that life was planted from an extraterrestrial. We call Him God."

Nervous laughter tittered through the room, and Barbara's broad grin immediately lessened the tension.

"Oh, good Lord," she said, "that is the best line I have heard to sum up this theory theologically. May I steal that from you and use it in my report for NASA?"

The nervous laughter turned into spontaneous smiles. Visible relief came over the face of Dr. Evelyn Krase, one of the few lay teachers at Lourdes, who was head of the Science Department.

Dr. Krase addressed the students: "Ladies, it is important to note that although many Catholics believe in the literal meanings of Genesis—for example, that the world was created in seven days—Holy

Father Pope Pius XII, in his encyclical, "Humani Generis," clearly told the faithful that the theory of evolution did not contradict Catholic doctrine, and as Catholics we are free to embrace the theory. We will discuss this during another class, but please be aware that the information Dr. Turyev has shared with us today in no way contradicts or diminishes our cherished belief in the creation of the human soul by our Divine Creator."

Barbara concluded the discussion by saying, "I have been a Catholic all of my life and I am proud to be a part of the Catholic community. I am also proud to be engaged with some of the greatest scientific minds of this century, and to follow in the tradition of great Catholic scientists who preceded us throughout the centuries. Many of us in the scientific community have a strong faith in God and we view our pursuit of knowledge as a study of creation. We know God did it—we want to try to understand, from the perspective of physics, how He did it."

Brigid liked these discussions, but, unlike Rosie and Babs, she had no penchant for viewing the Bible as myth and fable. In fact, she believed that the world could indeed have been created in seven days. But she did not argue or debate the theories of science any more than the changes in liturgy. She relished the information about the journeys into space and she also observed how some of her classmates, who had been emotionally detached during the chanting of the Latin Mass, were now enthusiastically singing the vibrant chords of "To Be Alive." She preferred the chants, but she could not ignore the benefits of the modern music for some worshippers.

Her own musical life had changed in other ways. The band was becoming very popular, increasing the demands on her time to a degree that she found unacceptable. She left the band and put her saxophone away, returning to her playing only when she needed to relieve stress or to connect with the cosmic musical spheres.

In addition to the divergence of Rosie's, Babs's, and Brigid's interests, the economic disparity in their households was also becoming more evident. While it did not affect their bond, it did affect certain aspects of their lives. Brigid started work at the Higbee's Department Store on Public Square in downtown Cleveland. It was imperative for her to earn enough money to pay for her Lourdes tuition and transportation. She was amazed at a family decision regarding the remainder of the Nagy sisters: they were not going to attend Catholic high schools. Dar and Miklos had donated hundreds of dollars to the Cleveland Diocesan Catholic High School Foundation, and received specific promises from the diocese that enough money had been pledged to keep Lourdes Academy open. This year, though, word trickled down through rumors and newspaper articles that several Catholic high schools would be closed, Lourdes Academy among them. Dar and Miklos felt betrayed, lied to, and swindled. Although their faith in the Catholic catechism remained strong, their faith in the leaders of the Cleveland Diocese was now nil. This betrayal, coupled with rising tuition costs, spurred their decision to send Michele to Valley Forge, the new public high school in Parma. Michele, already labeled the rebellious Nagy, was overjoyed to be free of nuns and novenas, and happy to be out of the shadow of her straight-A-earning, sodality praying, and doubtless future Pulitzer Prize-winning sister. Brigid, however, was heartbroken that her sisters would not know the joys and spirit of Lourdes Academy.

Rosie, too, started working more hours. Although she did not get paid, her work was valuable for the financial stability of the family's store. Neither Brigid nor Rosie ever remarked on Babs's designer clothes or excursions to the Cape, or her lack of a need to work. The girls appreciated their differences and treasured their bonds. Yet the rifts in activities and interests and lifestyles began to take a toll. When the annual Christmas gathering was being planned, it became difficult to find a date when everyone would be available.

One morning, Mama Rose appeared at Johnson's, to the shock and dismay of all present. After she slapped the cigarettes out of Rosie's and

Babs's lips, she pounded her hand on the old wooden tabletop, looked at the three stunned girls, and said, "Our families' Christmas gathering is Tuesday, December 13. Dates, jobs, meetings—whatever other things you think you have to do as sixteen-year-old prima donnas, come second to this tradition. You will attend for the entire evening. You will sing Christmas carols. You will pray with your grandmothers. And you will stay until your parents say it is time to go. You will be at my house at five o'clock sharp and you will have a good time."

And they were; and they did.

•

The Turyevs welcomed 1967 with the Pentellos, at a grand New Year's party in the ballroom of the Sheraton Hotel on Public Square. Although the setting was festive, the mood was bittersweet. The Browns had finished the season with a 9–5 record and for the first time in several years did not earn a playoff berth. The team, wrenched by the sudden resignation of the star running back Jimmy Brown during the summer, could not find the right rhythm or resilience to defeat the defenses of the N.F.L.

Joe Pentello's animosity toward Art Modell had simmered to a boiling point of overt hostility, so when a newly formed expansion team, the Atlanta Falcons, offered him a lucrative contract to join their training staff, he readily accepted. Autumn had been difficult for the Pentellos. In addition to the Browns' troubles, Louie had broken his leg during August training at Notre Dame, and that kept him off the gridiron for his freshman year. He and Babs had not communicated since their summer breakup, but since the Pentellos and Turyevs had long been close friends, a farewell New Year's Eve party was welcomed by all. Richard, Barbara, Babs, Joe, Madge, and Louie clinked their champagne glasses at midnight, toasting to the past and to the future of their old worlds and their new. The kiss Babs and Louie shared at the stroke of midnight revealed that the flame of their young love had already flickered out and that both of them were ready for the blaze of new romances.

In Parma, Rosie and Brigid blazed new romantic trails of their own. Frank McCoy, a freshman business major at John Carroll University, asked Brigid to be his date for a New Year's party at a friend's house in Parma. Brigid had met Frank at Higbee's, where they were both assigned to the Men's Notions department as sales clerks. Frank had been working at Higbee's for two years, and Brigid turned to him for advice when the new job responsibilities sometimes had her confused. She especially had problems balancing the cash register.

"Thank goodness you are going to be an English teacher and not a math teacher," Frank joked one day as he watched Brigid frantically searching for eighty-eight cents on her balance sheet.

Usually Brigid could flip off witty, charming sarcasms, but Frank's playful smile, masculine jaw, and contoured, muscled arms, weakened her response potential.

So, with no wit and no charm, she responded, "Oh, shut up."

He asked her to go out to dinner and that began a courtship and, it turned out, a guaranteed New Year's Eve date.

When Rosie confided that she had nothing special to do on New Year's Eve, Brigid asked Frank if he had any friends who might like to spend the evening with a vibrant, fun-loving Italian girl from West 61st Street.

Rosie thus began a courtship with Amir Singh, a foreign-exchange student from Calcutta, India, whose college major was zoology.

•

Despite the exciting beginning to the year, January brought sad and troubling events. Grandma Nagy died suddenly, of congestive heart failure, and once again the Hungarian clan gathered for a raucous combination of the celebration of life and the mourning of death. The kurva did not attend the services, but when Miklos and his sister

Yolanda had met with the funeral director to make arrangements for their mother's burial, they were stunned to learn that the kurva had bought the plot on the right side of their father's grave. Their mother would rest on one side of their father's grave, and the kurva would rest on the other. Miklos stormed out of the meeting, drove to the house of the kurva's son, and threatened every physical harm he could think of if the plot was not sold that day to the Nagy family.

Yolanda was still at the funeral home when the director received a call informing him that the plot was now in the Nagy family's name. The family did not yet know, that sadly, Yolanda would be buried there next year, and never did know of Miklos's strong-arm tactics that secured to her that final resting place.

On January 27, as the Nagys were receiving comfort and support from their friends, tragedy also invaded the Turyev household, and the entire nation as well. Three American Apollo astronauts were killed when a fire broke out in their capsule during a prelaunch test. Astronauts Gus Grissom, Roger Chaffee, and Edward White were friends of Richard Turyev. Barbara, Babs, and David had met them on several occasions. The horror of the fiery deaths cast a pall on the entire NASA family.

•

Faith, family, and friendship slowly began to fill the voids left by the deaths, and the girls turned to each other and social events for comfort and diversion. Babs, who was emerging as the intellectual wizardess of Lourdes Academy, was elected Snow Queen for the winter Snow Ball, an event hosted every year by the junior class.

The Saturday after the announcement, Rosie went dress shopping with Babs at Higbee's, where Brigid met them in the Crystal Room for lunch.

"I am so excited for you, Babs!" Brigid said. "It's such an honor to know that the girls respect you so much. I mean they voted for you, even though you don't meet the physical norms of beauty established by, ya know, Playboy or other male preferences."

"Who the hell says things like that?" snapped Rosie.

Brigid retorted, "I'm just saying that one of the things I love about Lourdes is that we don't let male-dominated standards dictate our self-worth. For someone so smart to be selected as the queen of a dance over all the really pretty girls in the school says a lot about what we value."

Rosie repeated, "Again, who the hell says things like that? Seriously, Brigid, think before you open your mouth. Babs is as pretty as any girl in the school. She—"

"Christ!" Babs interrupted. "Thank you both for what I think are compliments somewhere. Right now, my only concern is that I have a dress, I have shoes, I have a hair appointment—but I don't have a damn date!"

"I really don't like it when you use Christ's name in vain," Brigid said to Babs.

"Shut up!" Rosie screeched at Brigid.

"Just find me a damn date," Babs said to them both.

After forty-five minutes of intense consideration of every boy any of them had ever met, they came up with what seemed like a perfect solution: Brigid's old and dear friend, Martin Gorman.

Later that month, Babs and Martin, Brigid and Frank, and Rosie and Amir squeezed into Martin's Corvair and sloshed through the dirty-snowed streets of downtown Cleveland to the Hollenden House Hotel. The Snow Queen of the Snow Ball began to melt with heated hormones as she and Martin danced to the tunes of the Beatles, the Monkees, and the Rolling Stones.

From that night on, all three couples dated steadily, and at the Junior prom in April, they triple-dated, having donned their formal attire: Brigid in a rippled chiffon gown in green; Babs in flowing pastel-blue silk; and Rosie in a tight-fitting, fiery-red knit. This time they lounged after the dance in the Turyev Cadillac, which Richard had lent them for the evening. Except for cigarettes, they did not succumb to the vices that often plague prom nights. A romantic stroll at Edgewater Park on the shore of Lake Erie, a few French kisses, and an occasional hands-in-motion embrace supplied the evening with innocent passion.

•

The month of May had a special charm for the upper classes of Lourdes Academy. Juniors and seniors strolled the short walk to St. Patrick's Church on Bridge Avenue, where they all celebrated the seniors' last Mass as Lourdites. The seniors paired with the juniors to turn the juniors' class rings around, so that the date faced outward, signifying a look to the future, a path to their last year at Lourdes. This year, the ceremony demanded deeper layers of tradition and grandeur, because of the seventy-fifth anniversary of the founding of the school. Both Cleveland newspapers, The Press and Plain Dealer, covered the celebration. The bishop and the mayor of Cleveland attended, along with numerous Sisters of the Humility of Mary (the order dropped the word "Holy" from its name when the nuns changed garb) who had taught at the school in the decades before.

One of the distinctions of Lourdes Academy had always been the unique demographics of the students. Though situated in the heart of Cleveland's near-west-side inner city, it attracted girls from all corners of the city and the suburbs. The theme of the seventy-fifth anniversary was "convergence," a term that conveyed the intersection of ideas, cultures, and neighborhoods, that the women of Lourdes Academy embodied.

The sisters chose Brigid to write the text for the official jubilee brochure. Her words would appear on all jubilee publications, and later, in the 1968 yearbook, *Memorare,* as well as the school newspaper, the *Lourdes Light.* The newspaper writing would win an award for excellence in copywriting from the Quill and Scroll Scholastic Journalism Honor Society.

Convergence, by Brigid Nagy

In a world of wandering and wondering,
busyness and blundering,
Lourdes resonates a thundering ...
The sound of hearts beating, friends greeting,
young people meeting.
Plaid skirts crowded into buses from the
North, South, East and West.
Girls from across the city,
converging.
Their thoughts, their ideas,
merging ... emerging.
At night they travel their separate ways,
increasing and renewing the spirit
of human understanding
begun at home, developed at L.A.
through
a curriculum which influences and provokes ...
a curriculum that removes the barriers of formal education ...
a curriculum that merges science and humanities ...
An atmosphere of converging.
Sisters don contemporary garb -- religious yet real,
the sacred and secular meet.
All contributing to a convergence ...
of love ... of laughter ... of learning ...
at Lourdes.

Junior year ended in an array of optimistic revelry, culminating on June 1 with a celebration of the Nagy, Vanetti, and Turyev families at the Brown Derby restaurant. The parents knew that college choices loomed in the near future, and that their oldest daughters would soon be entering worlds beyond their control. Rosie's father developed political connections in Columbus, Ohio, in the hope that Rosie would be accepted at Ohio State University.

Brigid had been exploring the Catholic college Marquette University, in Milwaukee, Wisconsin, after reading an obscure volume of poetry by Jessica Powers, a Carmelite nun who attended Marquette in the 1920s. Miklos had agreed to take Brigid to see the school over the coming summer, but he made it clear that, unless she received hefty scholarships, they could not afford the tuition.

Babs was already planning a trip to Berkeley to visit the University of California campus close to the NASA complex where her father worked.

The families sang "Happy Birthday" to the three guests of honor, as Brigid, Rosie, and Babs blew out the candles and, unbeknownst to themselves, blew in the surreal happenings of the Summer of Love.

•

Babs was the first to inhale the smoky counterculture of the summer of 1967. Her trip to Berkeley, later in June, placed her at the epicenter of the earthquake that came to be known as the hippie movement. From the Berkeley campus it was only a short drive to the Haight-Ashbury district of San Francisco, where drugs, psychedelic music, and radical alternatives to all societal norms dominated the scene.

Richard had entrusted Babs's well-being to one of his assistants, Rosemary Pines, a promising graduate student assigned to the Mars research team he presided over. Rosemary convinced him that a jaunt to Haight-Ashbury would be an excellent way to introduce Babs to a world with which Cleveland had not yet become acquainted.

"Dr. Turyev, your daughter has no idea of how different the West Coast is from the Midwest," Rosemary said. "Babs needs to get a real feel for what is going on here, so she can make an informed decision whether or not Berkeley is the place she wants to go to school."

At first Richard protested. "Babs is a mathematical genius. She does not need to be exposed to all the base tendencies of this youthful rebellion. She should remain on campus and visit the labs and dorms and libraries where she will be spending most of her time."

Rosemary suppressed a mocking laugh at the naiveté of this parental response but replied in a serious tone: "Of course we will visit those, but I do think it would broaden her perspective to get a taste of one of the most significant cultural phenomena of her generation."

"Okay," Richard finally agreed. "But keep her away from any illegal activities or rowdiness."

Rosemary gave what turned out to be a hollow assurance, and the next day she and Babs drove to San Francisco.

Walking through the intersection of Haight and Ashbury Streets, Babs was astounded by, though not attracted to, what she witnessed. Women with nothing but beads over their breasts danced wildly to psychedelic music that washed through the streets from a seemingly unknown source.

"Aren't they beautiful?" Rosemary asked. "The freedom of women to expose their bodies and express their spirits—it's just beautiful."

"I'm not sure if I think it's beautiful," Babs said, shyly.

As they continued their tour, they were approached by numerous people offering them hand-rolled marijuana cigarettes and multicolored pills, among other things. She also observed glimpses of sexual acts taking place in the midst of the dense crowd. When a splash of urine landed on her shoe as they were approaching a T-shirt vendor, she turned to Rosemary.

"I really have seen enough. Let's go back to campus."

"Sure," Rosemary replied. "Let me buy a couple of shirts, and then I will take you back to Daddy."

There was little conversation on the drive back. Both of the young women were lost in their own thoughts as they listened to the radio blaring Janis Joplin, The Mamas & the Papas, and a new group, Pink Floyd.

Babs broke the conversational lull when she asked Rosemary, "Why did you take me to San Francisco?"

Rosemary turned the volume down and said, "I thought you should see what life would be like for you three thousand miles away from your secluded Ohio. Berkeley is very much touched by what you saw today. I thought you should be aware. Are you upset?"

"It all seemed so unnatural and unreal. I guess it is good that I'm aware that all of that kind of stuff exists. I'm not really upset, but I'm glad we left," Babs said.

Rosemary placed her hand on Babs's thigh.

"I didn't mean to upset you. Ideas and people are much freer out here than where you grew up. Things that seem unnatural grow more acceptable the more freedom you have."

There was no further discussion about the day between Babs and Rosemary. Later that evening, at dinner, Babs told her father about some of the sights and sounds of their trip, but focused on the beautiful scenery of the California countryside. Richard informed Babs that in the morning they would tour the campus and she could see the NASA and university labs. In the evening they would go over to Lafayette, California, to engage in some sky watching at the Leuschner Observatory. Tonight, Richard planned to return to his office for some late-night research. He asked Babs to stay in his apartment for the night, to which she readily agreed.

Babs had just donned her pajamas when, at ten o'clock, the buzzer of the apartment intercom droned.

"It's Rosemary. I forgot to give you something this afternoon. May I come up for a second?"

Babs, wishing she had packed a robe, responded meekly, while feeling unexplainably squeamish, "Yes."

When Rosemary entered the room, she gave Babs a T-shirt she had bought earlier, and touched the sleeve of Babs's pajamas. "Ahhh," she said. "Silk. I love silk."

"So do I," said Babs, mindlessly.

Rosemary walked toward the open sofa bed where Babs was to sleep, and exclaimed, "Well, since you're in pajamas, that calls for only one thing—a pillow fight!"

Babs thought it incredible that a serious graduate student employed by NASA would want to engage in a pillow fight with the daughter of the head researcher. She backed away but could not dodge the swat of a pillow across her face. It was not forceful, but it caught her off balance enough that she fell onto the edge of the bed. Rosemary, who Babs now noticed was not wearing a bra under her blouse, which was unopened to the third button, was gleefully tapping Babs with the pillow, bending over her with deliberate movements of soft contact.

When Babs finally successfully resisted the pillow, the tapping, and the contact, she told Rosemary that she was tired and asked her to leave.

"Okay, party pooper," Rosemary sighed. "Give me a kiss goodbye. I'm not scheduled to see you anymore, but hopefully I will see you when you come back for college."

Before Babs could back away, Rosemary pulled her close and kissed her on the mouth. It was too long to be innocent and too short to be passionate. Babs stood in frozen confusion as Rosemary left the apartment.

The images and sensations of the entire day welled up inside her and she barely made it to the bathroom, where she vomited. She needed time to absorb and sort out the events of the past ten hours, especially the past ten minutes. Exhausted, she lay down on the bed. Instead of the fitful, sleepless night she feared, she fell into a blissful dream of Martin Gorman.

•

The next morning, Babs made a conscious effort to banish yesterday's incidents to the deep recesses of her mind. She and her father toured the Berkeley campus, and she relished the flair of Sproul Hall and the sight of dozens of students congregating before it, sometimes shouting diatribes and slogans. Although it was summer break, enough students remained on campus to gather and protest against the Viet Nam War and for free speech. Babs watched these groups and sensed a spirit of idealism that she had not witnessed in the Haight-Ashbury crowds. The Berkeley students rebelled for a cause, not just for the sake of rebellion. While her father stopped to talk to a colleague, Babs walked over to a group of students and began a conversation with a young man whose ponytail streamed far below his shoulders; he had the beginnings of a stubbly beard and a voice as mellow and mesmerizing as a nightingale's.

"Good morning," Babs said in a friendly but slightly intimidated tone.

"Well, good morning," the young man replied. "You look rather young to be walking around this campus. Are you here to check us out?"

"Yes, actually, that is exactly what I am doing here. I plan on attending college here next year."

He looked Babs up and down and smiled.

"Ha!" he said. "Well, you should have come last month, when the Reverend Dr. King was here. We were out in full force then. Thousands of us, man, marching for peace and speech and everything in between. You would have gotten a real taste of Berkeley then. What's your name?"

"My name is Babs. What's yours?"

"They call me Papa," he said, and winked at her. "All hell is going to break loose here in the fall, Babs. Don't let your parents watch the news or they will never let you come here."

"What's going to happen in the fall?" Babs asked.

"Any shit you can think of. We want to shut the place down. The governor's been trying to shut us up, the president's been trying to blow us up, but all they've done is rile us up. In October things are gonna pop. Hey, do you like music, honey? 'Cause if you do, down in Golden Gate Park is where it's happening. Jimi Hendrix, the Dead—they all show up there to jam."

Babs tried to act as if she were familiar with these singers.

"Oh, cool," she said, sounding much like the naive Lourdes Academy high-school girl she was. When she saw her father approaching, she ventured one more question.

"Tell me, what do you do when you are not trying to shut the place down?"

Papa smiled and said, "I'm a psych major."

Richard was nearly upon them, and Babs walked toward him, not wanting Paternal Papa to engage in any discourse with Protester Papa.

They proceeded to tour the campus and to meet with a few professors from the Math Department. The beauty of the views from every angle on the grounds enthralled Babs. The majesty of eucalyptus and redwood trees coupled with the distant sunlit mountains, and the traditional academic grandeur of Sproul Hall, convinced her that this was a place she wanted to be.

When Babs and Richard stopped to rest on a bench by Strawberry Creek, she asked, "Papa, why have you never spoken about how absolutely beautiful this place is? I love everything about it!"

Richard sat silent for a moment, then looked at Babs and said, in a matter-of-fact voice, "I have honestly never taken the time to notice."

"There's a lot of things you may have not noticed," Babs said. "You never mentioned the tremendous amount of radical energy that has apparently overtaken this place. How did you react to the student protests? The free-speech stuff? Did you see Martin Luther King, Jr., when he was here?"

Richard looked straight ahead, avoiding Babs's anxious eyes. "A sense of wild chaos undermines how these students behave. I appreciate the idealism of a revolution to produce change and I wholeheartedly support the notion that opportunity to speak freely should not end at the campus gates. But when protest interferes with the academic progress of the university, then it is counterproductive and criminal. I trust that you will not get involved in the more radical components of this youthful folly."

Babs, not wanting to damage her chances of attending this haven of free thought, answered cautiously, but honestly.

"I am very interested in knowing about the injustices these students rebel against. The hippies at Haight-Ashbury interest me only as a curiosity. They try to expand their minds with drugs, which I think in the end will in fact destroy their minds. But here at Berkeley they expand their minds with ideas."

Richard smiled and gave an uncharacteristically modern and insightful response.

"And it also gives them a reason to party."

Babs laughed aloud and patted her father's hand, saying, "Agreed."

Later, they dined with NASA associates of Richard's and then went to the observatory, with a small group of visiting students. The featured sighting of the evening was the full moon. The visitors were given ten minutes each to gaze at the moon through the observatory's powerful telescope. The moon was Babs's favorite celestial body, and to have the chance to view it through such an accurate instrument was a gift of measureless worth. When her turn was finished, she and Richard walked out to the viewing deck and stared at the dark night sky and, as they had so many times in their backyard in Shaker, repeated the stories of their favorite constellations.

They went back to the apartment and, while packing for their return home, Babs said to her father, "I noticed there were no Negroes or females, except for Miss Pines, in your NASA group. Please don't tell me it's because they lack the intelligence, because if you tell me that, I will . . . "

"My goodness," Richard said. "You are already developing a spirit of rebelliousness. No, my dear, lack of intelligence would be the easy, and false, excuse as to why there are no women or Negroes amongst us. The reason has nothing to do with lack of intelligence, and everything to do with lack of opportunity."

Father and daughter then went to bed, slept soundly, and caught an early flight home to Ohio, which now, to Babs seemed like a planet in a distant universe.

•

When Babs returned home, she became very withdrawn and quiet. Martin feared that perhaps the trip to California generated a gulf between them and he thought Babs was trying to slowly distance herself from him. He shared his feelings with Brigid who indicated she noticed it too. One Saturday, when the girls met for lunch at Higbee's Crystal room, it was Rosie who, in her soothing, sympathetic manner began the conversation.

"What the hell is wrong with you, Babs? You've been like a clam since you got back from Berkeley. Do you think you're too good for us now that you've hobnobbed with groovy hippies and in-the-know protesters?"

"Aauuuugh!" said Brigid. "Rosie, you are so blunt. Babs, we're just worried that maybe you, well, took some drug, or did something you feel bad about and can't confide in us. You know we love you whatever the situation. We just want you to come out of your shell and talk to us."

Rosie just looked at Brigid with impatient disbelief, but after a long moment, it was Babs who responded.

With a weary demeanor, she told them the details of what she saw in San Francisco, and the students she talked to at Berkeley. She did not mention Rosemary Pines.

"I'm just a bit disoriented and am sorting out the sheltered life we have lived, away from the wilderness beyond our shelter. I'm relying on our old-fashioned picnic on July 4th to shake me out of this fog."

Rosie and Brigid thoughtfully assimilated the drugs and sex and protesting that Babs referred to.

Brigid said, "Well, we have to make a pact that when the world gets too confusing we will turn to each other for solidarity and support."

"Or we can turn to Babs to get us some of those drugs," Rosie said half-jokingly.

The lunch ended, as all of their lunches did, with laughter and love, but this time with a sense that things were changing, and time was weaving a tapestry of colors that might not blend with the fabric of their current lives.

On the following Tuesday, red, white, and blue were the colors of the moment, as Rosie and Amir, Brigid and Frank, and Babs and Martin spread their blankets at Edgewater Park to watch July 4th fireworks. Resentment towards the Viet Nam War and the growing feelings of alienation and anger in young Negroes were slowly having their effect on the patriotic fervor of the country, but so far not enough to change the mood of this evening.

The next morning, Richard and Barbara sat at the breakfast table and called Babs to join them. Barbara told Babs that they were anxious to share some news with her.

"Babs," she said, "your father and I have decided to invite Rosemary Pines to spend August with us at the Cape. She is helping me with some research, and she can also provide you with tutoring on some astronomical studies you have been interested in."

Babs felt faint, her face filling with a crimson fire of heat and nausea. She abruptly laid her head onto her folded arms crossed on the table.

"Babs!" shouted Barbara. "Whatever is the matter?"

Babs controlled her breath, and in a monotone, restrained manner, told her parents that she was very uncomfortable with Rosemary's presence in her life. She then described the events of the trip to Haight-Ashbury, and the incident at the apartment.

Richard and Barbara's tension tightened with each detail. When Babs finished, she was crying.

"I am not accusing her of anything, Papa, but nothing about her felt right. She made me extremely uncomfortable and it just wasn't right. I'm so sorry."

Richard, his face now equally crimson, rested his hand upon Babs's arm.

"Her behavior was unacceptable, Babs. Totally unacceptable. I wish you would have told me sooner. You are not to be sorry for anything. It is I who am sorry for trusting someone I knew so little about. Excuse me, I need to make a phone call."

Barbara went over to Babs and hugged her.

"Are you telling us everything, dear? It's important for us to know if anything else happened."

"No, nothing else," Babs replied.

"Well, we will leave the discussion with the thought that this made you uncomfortable. Your discomfort is a completely normal and legitimate feeling. First, being exposed to the behavior in San Francisco, and most importantly, being subjected to suggestive behavior in the apartment from someone invading your private space and a stranger giving you an intimate kiss. Do not hesitate ever to tell us if an occasion happens when you feel you have been touched or even spoken to in a way that makes you feel uneasy. Your world is about to be open to many different types of people and interpersonal communications. Always follow your head and your heart and never be afraid to walk or run out of a situation that feels wrong."

Babs felt an overwhelming relief and never again felt the need to mention anything about Rosemary Pines.

Richard flew to Berkeley that evening, and in the private offices of the Dean of the Graduate School permitted Rosemary to tell her side of the story. He asked her if she took Babs to the heart of the drugs and sex scene at Haight-Ashbury, if she placed her hand on Babs's thigh, if she returned late to the apartment when Babs was alone, if her blouse was unbuttoned, if she made physical contact with Babs while sitting on the bed; and if she grabbed Babs to kiss her on the lips.

She answered, "Your daughter has created a melodrama. It was all very innocent."

To which the dean replied, "Your actions were extremely inappropriate, bordering on molestation of a minor. This will be your last semester at Berkeley, and you are removed from Doctor Turyev's staff."

Rosemary smirked and left the room, her only communication, a raised middle finger.

*

Mid-July brought another college visit, this time a trip to Milwaukee, Wisconsin where the Nagy family explored the shores of Lake Michigan and the campus of Marquette University. Except for a brief vacation to Niagara Falls several years ago, the Nagy family had not ventured out of state, so Miklos and Dar decided to use Brigid's desire to attend Marquette as a reason to tour some sites of the Midwest on their way to Wisconsin.

Brigid, Michele, Sally, Joan, Suzy, Cindy, Dar, and Miklos, piled into the nine passenger station wagon, cramped with suitcases, cans of Charlie Chips, Necco Wafers, and Tootsie Rolls to hold them through the 400-mile trek through Ohio, Indiana, Illinois, and Wisconsin. Their first stop, a fulfillment of a lifelong dream of Miklos's: a visit to Notre Dame.

Brigid secretly did not want to participate in this excursion. While researching colleges, she became keenly aware of the doors that were shut to women. Most of the Ivy League colleges admitted men only, and the major prestigious Catholic colleges such as Notre Dame were available to women only on evenings and summers, and predominantly to celibate nuns. One of the reasons she chose Marquette was its distinction as the first Catholic college in the world to embrace the vision of coeducation.

A tour of the grand testosterone-laden campus of Notre Dame did not appeal to Brigid, but because of her respect for her father, and her appreciation that her future revolved around this trip, she remained silent. She and her sister Michele broke away from the family and walked the campus alone. While Brigid could not help but be impressed by the sheer elegance of the architecture and spirituality of the ambience, Michele eyed every summer school male who sauntered past them. The men often responded with a wink or a whistle for the attractive sisters who were enjoying both the beauty and the beaus of Notre Dame.

They met up with the rest of the family at the Knute Rockne Memorial Building. Brigid noticed that her father's face had an unusual, satisfied sensation resonating from it, much like the look her mother had at the Judy Garland concert. She hadn't realized how much this trip meant to him, and she was happy they had come.

"Dad," Brigid said, "this was a great idea to stop here. I'm so happy you got to see all of this."

Miklos answered, "Knute Rockne has always been a hero of mine--just to walk where he walked is a thrill."

They concluded the tour with a lunch at an off-campus diner where Brigid noticed young women enrolled in summer classes at St. Mary's. She wondered how these women felt being in the shadows of the great Notre Dame. They looked happy enough, away from home, enjoying their freedom, regardless of the slights of their world ruled by men. As the Nagys headed toward Chicago, Brigid fell asleep with thoughts of life away from Cleveland.

She awoke to the unfamiliar sound of her father's cussing and her mother's scolding.

"Miklos, for goodness sakes, calm down. Just drive slowly and be careful," Dar reprimanded.

"For Christ's sake," Miklos bellowed, "these people don't use turning blinkers, they are driving up my butt, at least twenty miles over the speed limit, they cut me off like I'm invisible, I'm about to ...."

"Calm down!" Dar's voice crackled with a nervous edge.

"Segglyuk!" Miklos whispered in Hungarian after another car zoomed in front of him.

Nerves were frayed and Cindy and Suzy were crying with fatigue when they pulled into the valet service at the Palmer House Hotel. Their two adjoining rooms were ready, and the Ohio Nagys settled in for a two-hour nap from which they arose rested and ready to walk the streets of the Windy City.

In two days they managed to see Navy Pier, University of Chicago, Lincoln Park Conservatory, Union Station, and Marshall Fields, as well as the construction site of what was to be one of the tallest buildings in the world, John Hancock Center.

Brigid was a city girl, and the ever-present hum of activity soothed her soul. Chicago was a massive metropolis, and the thought that it was an hour train ride from Milwaukee filled her with excitement and anticipation. The next day, they arrived at Marquette. Brigid was delighted to see the "concrete campus." Marquette did not have the greenery of Notre Dame, and that was fine with her. She liked the urban flair and the feel of the city that reverberated up Wisconsin Avenue on to the grounds of the university.

The tour, guided by a senior majoring in engineering, started with Gesu Catholic Church and proceeded through the various buildings of Johnston Hall, the women's residence halls, Marquette Hall, the Todd Wehr Science building, and the Student Union. They ended at the Joan of Arc Chapel where the Nagys stopped to pray. The guide explained that the chapel was originally built in France in the 1500s, then dismantled and sent to Milwaukee where it was rebuilt piece by piece a few years ago on the Marquette campus.

The chapel and Gesu church were the most visually appealing edifices on the campus. Once those buildings were seen, there was not too much more to look at.

Along the way, they passed numerous nuns and priests and several students enrolled in summer classes and programs. Dar had spoken with Barbara Turyev about Babs's visit to Berkeley and was relieved to see Marquette's environment was, as Dar called it, "normal."

One of the many questions Miklos asked the guide was focused on student unrest.

"The news shows a lot of students across the country acting up and protesting and fighting with cops and that type of thing. Is there much of that going on up here?" He asked.

Brigid's stomach tightened, because the answer could mean the difference between her attending here or not. The student, savvy to the interpersonal skills of parent-student communication, calmly answered.

"There are small pockets of discontent, but we have a quiet campus, and any protests that have occurred have been comparatively mild."

Dar then commented, "One of my friends told me that Catholic colleges are filled with nontraditional teachings and liberal philosophies. Have you found that to be true?"

The student answered honestly. "The faculty tend to be quite liberal, and the students tend to be quite traditional. It provides an interesting exchange of ideas. In my opinion, that's what a college should be."

"Where do you stand personally in the debate?" Brigid asked coyly, more interested in his wavy black hair and deep brown eyes, than his theological leanings.

"Well, I am President of the Young Republicans. I tend to lean toward the traditional."

Miklos, President of the Parma Firefighters Union, told the young man that he was quite nice for a Republican. He thanked him and returned to the Holiday Inn where the family enjoyed an evening of swimming and discussion.

"I love it. I love everything about it. It gives me the same feeling I had when I first visited Lourdes. It's just what I want," Brigid bubbled.

"Well, it's certainly not as beautiful as Notre Dame or as hallowed as the University of Chicago," Dar commented.

"Those were really cool campuses, but you know me, Mom, I rely on feelings a lot. This place just feels right. And Notre Dame only accepts testosterone," said Brigid in what sounded like a plea.

Later that evening, Brigid listened intently through a crack in the door between their adjoining rooms, as her parents discussed her fate.

Miklos began the conversation. "She deserves a chance, Dar. We've never had any trouble with her, she's smart as a whip, and I just think she should have a chance."

"We can't afford it. If she doesn't get a scholarship, I just can't see spending that kind of money when she could go to a public college in Ohio for less than half the price.

Even if they finish, girls end up getting married and having children, and their whole education is a waste anyhow. We have five other children to consider before we dole out twenty-four hundred dollars a year every year for four years, on one child." Dar seemed adamant.

Brigid gasped at the discussion. She never dreamed that it would be her mother who would object to the choice. She quietly joined Michele and Sally, watching the new show, *Star Trek,* hoping that soon she could explore her own frontiers.

The next morning, they strolled down by Lake Michigan, shopped at The Boston Store, and then headed back to Ohio. Brigid had fallen in love with Milwaukee, and settled her whole being into attending Marquette. She hated that after twelve years of superior academic achievement, money would be the deciding factor of where she went to college. Even more, she hated that if she were a tall boy who played basketball, she probably would not have to worry about money for college. Such were her thoughts as she closed her eyes and slept through the eight-hour return trip to Parma.

Although it was past ten when they arrived home, Dar permitted Brigid to call Frank and invite him over to sit on the porch and chat. Frank lived on the John Carroll campus, a half hour drive away, and was sitting on the front porch by 10:35. A gentle kiss and embrace was followed by a not-so-gentle conversation.

As Brigid rambled excitedly about the trip and especially about Marquette, Frank appeared quietly annoyed. Finally, he spoke.

"Don't you think it's kind of stupid for a girl to go away to college? You won't have anyone to look after you. I've seen quite a few girls break down at school because they are so far away from their parents and boyfriends. And don't you want to get married and have a home and kids? How is Marquette going to help you accomplish that?"

Brigid had just gotten over the shock of her mother's lack of support, but this comment stunned her.

"Ha! You're kidding, right?" she said with an air of hope.

"No, I'm not kidding," Frank quickly responded. "I thought all this Marquette talk was a pipe dream, and that you would come back, attend Community College and settle down--with me."

"Frank, you know my passions are reading and writing and all sorts of things. Why, on earth would you think I wouldn't want to get a degree first, before I settle for anything else?"

"Or anyone else."

"Good God Frank, there is so much wrong with the things you are saying, I don't know where to begin."

"Forget it, Brigid. We can talk about this another time. I came here because I missed you and wanted to see you. Not really keen on hearing about a place that's obviously going to take you away from me."

He kissed her again, with a bit more passion, and told her he would call her tomorrow.

Exhausted, but not quite ready for bed, Brigid called Babs, then Rosie, and arranged to meet them downtown for lunch on the following day. Although her heart was panging with the ache of disappointing love, she had no intention of sitting around, waiting for Frank's call.

The girls met for lunch and shared their hopes and excitement about what their college lives would look like. None of them mentioned the men in their lives and all of them were eager to begin and enjoy their remaining time at Lourdes. There was an undercurrent of money worries and what-ifs, but for the most part, they were optimistic and idealistic.

Rosie did not make a college visit to Ohio State since she had been on campus numerous times when she travelled to Columbus with her father. She was already anxious to don Buckeye gear and gallivant around High Street and Lane Avenue. Her father had secured a position for her in the dean's office, so all there was left for her to do was keep her grades at C level, and earn some money to help defray costs. The fact that none of the three friends had yet applied to the colleges of their choice seemed not to matter, they would get that done within the week.

August flashed by in a flurry of dates and dances, and working. The young women enjoyed the romances of social life and responsibilities of work. Babs spent the month at Cape Cod, thrilled that her parents allowed Martin to visit for a few days, under close parental supervision. Brigid and Rosie worked twenty hours per week, and shared their weekends with Amir and Frank, movies and music. By the time Labor Day arrived, the girls were ready to return to Bridge Avenue, where they were greeted with a fleur de lis banner that said, "We are fine. We are great. We're the class of '68! Go Seniors!"

*

In late September, Babs and Brigid received notification that their National Merit Test scores qualified them as semi-finalists, and they would be moving on in scholarship competition. Rosie received her admission acceptance to Ohio State University. The girls swirled between past, present, and future, as their lives unfolded in a whirlwind of memories, moments, and maybes. Seasoned by a summer of college reality, Rosie, Brigid, and Babs anticipated being bored by a year of high school reality. However, senior year brought pleasant, sentimental surprises as they flowed through the rhythm of their last Friendship Week, their last Kickoff Dance, and their last preparation for the senior class play. Their senior class play.

The class chose *Show Boat,* a musical that called for extraordinary talent, and extraordinary insight. Among other things, the script addressed the social and legal issues of the anti-miscegenation laws. Most Lourdes students were unaware of the landmark Supreme Court decision of the previous summer that declared laws forbidding marriages between "whites" and "coloreds" were unconstitutional. Most Lourdes students were unaware that those laws existed in the first place. Although seniors were exempt from the essays related to the annual production, the play was rich in human drama and historical nuances, and enriched the seniors' education in an array of interdisciplinary studies.

Rehearsals for the production were long, and often lasted late into the evening. The three friends each earned a spot in the chorus, and Brigid received an extra part as a saxophone player in one of the night club scenes. One night, when practice edged into the late hour of ten o'clock, they noticed a silver-haired woman walk quietly into the dimly lit auditorium where Ellen Bodnar, one of their classmates, who played the character of Julie Laverne in the play, was practicing the song "Bill." Ellen, the president of the student council, was a young woman of confidence and self-assurance. There were only a few people left in the room, and they noticed that as the introductory music began to play, Ellen gave a slight nod to the woman with the silver hair. As she climbed and sat on the upright piano to sing the song, the small group in the auditorium sensed a gentle current of electricity in the air and noticed Ellen's eyes shine glassy with tears. Although Ellen projected a mediocre voice and slightly off-key pitch, she could occasionally sell a song. Tonight was more than that. Tonight, she sang with a depth of emotion and quality that filled the room with a hushed, gentle warmth. When the song was finished, Ellen walked out of the auditorium and the lady with the silver hair, sat in the last row heaving silent sobs.

The director, herself overcome with a sense of emotion, approached Ellen and said, "If you give that passionate feeling to that song during the performance, you will have the audience eating out of your hand."

Ellen smiled, walked over to her mother, embraced her, and left the rehearsal.

Later that week, Rosie was walking to class with Ellen. She asked about the interaction between Ellen and her mother.

"Hey El, what was going on between you and your mom at play practice? First of all, you sang that song like there was no tomorrow. Best ever. Hope you can pull it off like that on opening night. And second of all, your mom was crying so hard, she had us all bawling."

Ellen stopped at her locker and Rosie stayed with her.

"Long story short," Ellen replied, stuffing books into her locker. "My mom is never satisfied with anything I do. When I made first chair clarinet, she said she always wanted me to play the violin; when I got a scholarship to Lourdes, she said she wanted me to go to Nazareth; when I was elected President of Student Council, she said President of the Class is more prestigious. Get the picture? Well, she made it clear that she was worried that I got such a big part in the play, and she questioned whether or not I was good enough. That night, she came in unexpectedly, and I was preparing myself for failure. But all my emotion came out in that song, and well, I'll probably never sing it that well again. I saw her start to cry and I knew she was proud of me, finally. And that was that."

"Damn, it's amazing the power our moms have over us," Rosie said.

"Yep. Now, yesterday? I received my acceptance and a nice offer of financial aid from Marquette University, where I have always wanted to go to college. My mom's response? 'I really wanted you to go to Saint Mary's.'"

Ellen gave Rosie a pat on the back and scurried to class.

Rosie shared the story with Brigid and Babs during play practice later that night. They laughed and commiserated about the power of mothers, but Brigid was more interested and excited about Ellen's being accepted to Marquette. She worried why she had not yet received her letter of acceptance.

When she went home that evening, a large gold and blue hand-drawn "M" was taped onto the inside kitchen door. A big congratulations sign was spread over the table, under an opened letter postmarked Milwaukee, Wisconsin.

Brigid walked into the front room where her mother, father, and five sisters gave her what was known as the "family applause."

"You're going to Marquette," her father said as he hugged her.

"We'll find a way," her mother blubbered through an enthusiastic bubble of tears.

"Don't screw this up for the rest of us," Michele whispered wryly.

*

Showboat steamed across Lakewood Theater and the Class of 1968 earned outstanding reviews, as the greasers, preps, collegiates, and surfer girls sang and danced to Captain Andy's floating show. When the Broadway tunes were finished, the cast met for a party. It was a carefree time of high school innocence that the girls would forever treasure.

The annual holiday party of the Nagys, Turyevs, and Vannettis offered a pleasant conclusion to 1967, with melancholy memories of Grandma Nagy and celebratory congratulations to the college-bound Lourdites. Babs, Rosie, and Brigid spent New Year's Eve with Martin, Amir, and Frank respectively. No triple date, just partners, having private time and romantic dinners, some more romantic than others.

Love faded to lamentation as Aunt Yolanda's death in January brought the Hungarian clan together once again for a deep winter mourning. But good news swiftly followed bad news. When Valentine's Day came upon them, the usual follies and fables of romance were not the main topic. Babs and Brigid received word that they were National Merit Finalists. Babs received a full scholarship, and Brigid received a partial, but significant scholarship. For Babs, the money was not needed, but the honor was a source of great pride for her father. For Brigid, the award solidified her enrollment at Marquette and quelled the financial burdens and worries of her parents. Rosie was giddy with joy and excitement for her friends.

The remainder of senior year whirred by in a buzz of award ceremonies, term papers, and farewell banquets.

On April 4, 1968, the gates of hell began to reopen, as news of the assassination of Martin Luther King Jr.cast a melancholy lull on the plans of spring.

Lourdes Academy students grappled with the loss of the leader in their own way, most of them uncertain of the enormous consequences to the country. The black students stayed home and shared their grief and anger within their community.

A few of the nuns at Lourdes lambasted the seniors for their seemingly lackadaisical response to the tragedy. After the third class period of getting scolded for being ignorant, self-serving, and even racist, Ellen Bodnar spoke up for her classmates. It was in Religion class, during the rant of the beautiful, coiffed Sister Anna.

Sister began class without reciting the traditional prayer.

"You girls should be ashamed of yourselves," she said. "I haven't seen a tear shed, or heard a word said about what your black sisters are going through. You're marching through your day like it's any other day, like the nation hasn't lost a hero. You come to this dirty neighborhood, then go back to your white suburbs, wash your hands, and pretend what happens in the outside world doesn't matter. You--"

Ellen stood up and quivered. "Sister, please stop. I am sick of hearing how insensitive we are. You, Sister, you are the hypocrite. Your so-called community activism has replaced Christ-centered activism and you are so out of touch with the people you are supposed to be serving. Us."

Sister Anna's jaw stiffened and she was about to speak, but Ellen continued as she turned to the class.

"How many of you go home and wash the dirt from this neighborhood off your hands?"

No one raised her hand.

"You see, Sister, you are the only one who feels the need to wash the dirt. We are one with this community. Their dirt is our dirt. We don't need to wash anything away. Now, how many of you called our classmates last night and reached out in sympathy and grief and offered help and condolences? How many of you went to church early this morning and lit candles and prayed for our country?"

Several hands were raised.

"And what did you do, Sister? Stand arm in arm with the white priests and nuns and sing 'Kumbaya' on the corner of West 25th Street? Stop telling us what is in our souls and take a good look into your own."

The silence in the classroom was deeper than quiet. It was a thick, tangible, atmosphere of void. The girls sat motionless, with heartbeats that barely pumped. Ellen grabbed her books and stormed out of the room, angry tears streaming from swollen eyes. Brigid followed her. Sister Anna's face burst with a fiery red hue and she walked calmly out of the room, straight to the main office.

When Ellen and Sister were completely out of sight, the room erupted in conversation and comments and exclamations.

"Holy hell, where did that come from?"

"We've been hearing it all day. We weren't acting sad enough. Don't we care? How can we be laughing on a day like today? I was sick of it, too. Good for Ellen!"

"She should have never talked to a nun that way. She humiliated Sister. It's not right."

"I talked to Carol last night. She knows we care."

"Ellen has never acted up like that in four years. She must be really pissed."

Thirty minutes later, Brigid returned to the classroom with a warning look that indicated to the girls to shut up.

Sisters Anna and Teresa followed, with a flushed, head-bowed Ellen close behind.

Sister Anna spoke first.

"These are very difficult times for people of faith to choose the right words and the right actions. If I have seemed to judge you harshly, it is only because I want to prepare you for what lies ahead. We all deal with grief and shock in our own way, please let me know how I can help you with your grief and shock. There are sad days ahead of us."

Ellen lifted her head, and confidently added, "I sincerely apologize to Sister Anna and to you my classmates. I was disrespectful and mean and in my anger and frustration, I lost control of my sense of civility and Christian responsibility. Sister, please forgive me, and class, please forgive me for being rude and impertinent."

Sister Anna looked like she wanted more, but Sister Teresa then took over.

"There is a way to discuss without being accusatory or impolite. Ellen mistakenly chose another way, but she has learned from it. Sister Anna will lead a discussion of the situation where all may speak freely and courteously."

The discussion began.

"My parents didn't like him. They said even though he preached non-violence, violence followed him wherever he went."

"A lot of people were mad because he started all of this anti-war stuff. Didn't even have anything to do with the coloreds."

"For heaven's sake. He was killed in cold blood. He was fighting for equality and peace. How would you like it if you were told you couldn't eat in certain restaurants or go to certain movie shows. And what the heck are we fighting for over in Viet Nam, anyhow?"

These were the ensuing exchanges, when Sister Teresa's voice came over the public address system into all of the classrooms.

"Women of Lourdes Academy, our country has suffered a terrible loss of a great man, and a powerful voice for those whose voices have not been heard. We will close this day with a recitation of the rosary in supplication for peace in our country, comfort for the family of the Reverend Martin Luther King Jr. and members of our community who have suffered most from this tragedy."

*

Time eased tempers, and soon prom plans and graduation parties took precedence over world affairs. Rosie and Amir, and Babs and Martin double dated to the prom at the Riviera Country Club, and Brigid and Frank double dated with Ellen and her boyfriend. It was uneventful and pleasant, and culminated in a quiet after-prom party at the east side home of Crystal Perkins, one of the black students at Lourdes. There was much talk of Dr. King, and some talk about the hopeful voice that Senator Bobby Kennedy was bringing to the country.

The remainder of the Senior year for the Class of 1968 saw Babs selected as class valedictorian, Rosie selected for the honor of carving the class numbers in the ancient school rock, and Brigid selected to crown Mary at the final May Crowning.

The girls spent part of their eighteenth birthdays at the Shaker Heights Library, where they gathered with several other Lourdes Academy seniors to help Babs write her speech for graduation. Babs wanted to represent the memories and plans of a wide variety of her classmates, so in addition to Rosie and Brigid, she invited the presidents of all of the major clubs, including Athletics, Drama, Foreign Languages, Student Council, National Honor Society, Class Officers, and a few other assorted classmates. For three hours, these leaders of 41st Street and Bridge Avenue shared their triumphs, defeats, joys, and sorrows of their times in high school.

Afterwards, Rosie, Babs, and Brigid stopped at a local pub and ordered bottles of 3.2 beer, proudly displaying their driver's licenses to the bartender, who bought their first round. It was Brigid's first acquaintance with alcohol, and Babs and Rosie squawked with laughter at Brigid's newly acquired fondness as she gulped down two bottles to their one. When Rosie's cousin Beth walked in to join them, the evening evolved into a release of bawdy laughter, a fitting transition from adolescence to adulthood.

Four days later, on June 5, 1968, Barbara "Babs" Turyev, addressed the attendees at the solemn graduation commencement ceremony of Lourdes Academy.

"Bishop Issenmann Principal Sister Teresa, faculty, parents, dearest families, friends, and classmates from the class of 1968. My remarks this evening will be brief, not only because I know we all hate long speeches, but because time itself is brief.

"Although our four years at Lourdes have been filled with learning, and laughter, and love, they have gone by with the speed of a blink of an eye. For four years, we have come together as a class to support each other in troublesome times, and to celebrate with each other in joyous times.

"When I recently met with several of my classmates, the one realization we all shared was how fast the time has gone. As a daughter of a physicist whose work consists of conquering time and space, I can say that time is a universal mystery. Next year, one of our countrymen may walk on the moon, yet not even the brightest minds in the world can truly grasp the essence of time.

"But one aspect we can grasp is what we do with our time. At Lourdes, we have used our time to seek and gain academic knowledge, to forge friendships, to accept those who are different from ourselves while strengthening our own identity, to explore the frontiers of change in our faith, in our bodies, in our world.

"Seeking, forging, accepting, strengthening, exploring; these are the gifts we have received from our time at Lourdes.

"Now, we move ahead to a time of career, or college, or commitment, and we must ask ourselves, how will we use those gifts?

"I have been taught from an early age that we, as human beings, have an obligation to choose to rise above animal instincts and evolve upwards in spirit, aspiring to the divine nature in whose image we are created. We must understand our spiritual and cultural traditions, breaking those that break people's spirits, and espousing those that espouse people's aspirations.

"Lourdes has taught us that no creatures nor persons, female, male, black, or white should be imprisoned in the shackles of hate and ignorance. It is our time, classmates, to help break these shackles. To take what we learned from our classes and experiences and from each other and choose to use our time to move humanity away from our baser instincts and toward our mystical, cerebral destiny.

"And as we ponder these deep reflections, I trust that we will do them, as we promised every day before every class, 'all for the greater glory of God, in union with Jesus Christ, and Mary, our dearest mother.'

"Now, as we leave Lourdes Academy, my wish for all of you is ... to have a good time."

The applause was thunderous, and the awarding of scholarships and diplomas ensued with solemn dignity. The Class of 1968 returned to their homes with a sense of accomplishment, idealism, and hope.

They awoke the next morning to learn that Robert F. Kennedy had been assassinated.

*

Assassinations had become a numbing regularity in the lives of '60s youths, but the girls carried on. In the summer of 1968 they were not yet fully sensitive to the world that was blowing up around them. They spent the month of June dancing and dating like they always had, only this time with a bit more freedom, longer curfews, and tastier libations. A jolt to their festivities came with a revelation from Martin Gorman.

On a triple date night at Jim Swingo's Restaurant in downtown Cleveland, Martin calmly informed the group that he was enlisting in the Marine Corps.

"Pshh, that is not funny," Babs said, not taking the announcement seriously.

Amir knew it was real, and reached over to put an arm on Martin's shoulder.

"Why man? Why would you want to go to that Viet Nam hell hole?"

The reality started to settle in Babs's mind.

"Wait a minute…wait a minute. Martin. You're not serious. Please say you are not serious. We never even talked about this possibility."

Rosie and Brigid were frozen in surprise. Martin, an intelligent young man, had been accepted to several good colleges, and had mapped out a path to become a chemical engineer. Brigid had loved him as a friend since fourth grade, Rosie considered him a loyal pal, and Babs's feeling for him had grown from respect to romance to relationship. When they envisioned their future, meeting in Cleveland pubs and clubs while they all finished college, Martin always appeared in the picture. Apparently, Martin had a different vision. As he held Babs's hand close to his chest, he spoke with dignity and conviction.

"I know this comes as a shock. Babs, I wanted you to be close to your friends when I told you. The truth is, I don't love the books and academic crap like you all do."

"Not all," Rosie popped in.

Martin smiled. "Okay, like most of you do. Four years of college just doesn't appeal to me just now. I have had friends die in Viet Nam. Too many. I just feel a need to avenge them, or, at least just do my part."

"That's nuts," Frank said. "Guys are getting out of that stuff as fast as they can. College, Canada, any way they can. It's just nuts that you would run to something that everyone else is running away from. It's a crazy war, Marty; no one knows what the hell they're doing over there."

"When do you leave for training?" Babs asked, swallowing a sob.

"Probably in a few weeks," Martin replied, still holding Babs's hand.

"I want to leave. I can't eat; I want to get out of here," Babs said as she looked at Martin with confusion and despair. They got up and left the restaurant.

Rosie and Amir followed them out, because they had driven the car that brought the four of them.

Frank said to Brigid, "Let's stay. They will want to be alone, and I am hungry, you're all dressed up, let's just stay."

Brigid agreed, but a growing irritation with Frank's callousness and myopic worldview had dampened her attraction to him. He was the handsomest boy she had ever dated, and in her opinion, probably the handsomest boy she had ever seen. Exterior good looks can mask a multitude of sins, and once a woman is hooked on a white-hot smile, it is difficult to break loose from the black, cold heart that lurks beneath. Tonight, however, Brigid did break loose.

"So," said Frank, "you're really going to Marquette?"

"Of course, I am, what could have possibly changed my mind since last month?" Brigid responded.

"I just can't get it that you would leave me. That you think college can help a woman be a good wife and mother."

" I have already told you that being a good wife and mother are not my immediate goals, Frank. I want to write. I want to teach. I want to live in another city and experience different people and things."

"I want, I want, I want. You sound like one of those selfish feminist bitches."

"Oh my God, don't you dare talk like that to me," Brigid was almost shouting.

"Oh my God, don't you dare talk like that to me," Frank mimicked Brigid's words. "Yeah, you sound exactly like one of those feminist bitches. As a matter of fact, you are one of those damn feminist bitches."

Frank laughed as if he just said the funniest thing he ever heard, as he cut into his bloody, rare filet mignon.

Brigid excused herself, found a pay phone, and called Beth to ask if she could pick her up. Beth had become a big sister friend whom the girls could call on when they needed a ride, or an escape. After Brigid explained the situation, Beth said, "Sure, do you want me to bring my boyfriend along to beat the snot out of Frank?"

"No." Brigid laughed. "Just get me out of here."

She went back to the table where Frank, obviously annoyed, said, "Look, Brigid, I think you are a gorgeous, wonderful girl. I just don't want to see you become one of those bra-burning, man-hating women. I'll make enough money someday and you won't have to work. I'll take care of you, babe."

"You're assuming we are getting married? You're assuming that women who want to be independent are man-haters? And good Lord, don't call me babe. Oh, Frank."

She silently wondered why it took her so long to see the cold heart. Shakespeare's words of Hamlet awakened in her head: "That one may smile, and smile, and be a villain."

"Bitches," Frank said, still laughing.

Brigid had been rumbling a speech around in her mind, to lecture Frank on the causes and injustices that she espoused and planned to conquer. She wanted to tell him that he was the worst kind of man, belittling women's minds while flirting with their hearts. Buying their dinner, while wanting to keep them in the kitchen. Praising their brains, while grabbing their breasts.

Instead, she stood up, bent over and draped her arms around his shoulders, gave him a prolonged, sensual kiss that was akin to a tonsil tickle with her tongue, and then told him to "drop dead."

Beth was waiting in the parking lot.

Brigid never heard from Frank again, except to read about him, many years later. He became well known as an adulterous philanderer, and an opportunistic Congressman leading the fight for women's rights.

*

Racial violence once again exploded during the summer of 1968, this time in the Glenville area of east Cleveland. Carl Stokes was sworn in as the first Negro mayor of a major city in January. Many city leaders harbored profound hope that the residue of discontent and hate that still lingered from the Hough riots would be quelled with his election. For a while, things appeared to be getting better, but unemployment was still high, and radical groups still instigated violence. In late July, a deadly, violent shootout occurred between the Cleveland police and black nationalists, which triggered days and nights of looting and rioting. (A trial later found the leader of the nationalists guilty of first-degree murder as dozens of witnesses, black and white, testified to his planning the ambush of white police officers.) Mayor Stokes decided to keep white officers and National Guard troops on the outskirts of the area. The rioting continued, but no one else was killed. The violence tainted the legacy of Mayor Stokes, but one of his most avid supporters was Rosie's father. Talking to his family one night at dinner, MV discussed the situation.

"The mayor saved lives. He kept white people out of harm's way, and drove his car through the streets of the Glenville neighborhood trying to keep peace. A leader has to make rough decisions. He made the decisions. He accepted the consequences. Now, again, we have to rebuild."

Rebuilding trust after incidents like the riots in Glenville and Hough neighborhoods was not an easy task. A reality existed in which white people were more afraid to see a black person walk down the street than a white person, and black people were weary of the stereotype that led to that fear.

The girls were not immune to this unstable racial chemistry. A week after the riots settled, Rosie and Amir went to the east side to Leo's Casino where big- name black singers, comedians, and bands performed. Leo's had been a place where racial tensions were eased with the universal heartbeat of music that transcends human ignorance. During the most heated strain of Cleveland unrest, black and white people sat in the smoke-filled club, close together in an intimate gathering of humanity and art.

As they stopped at a traffic light and approached East 75th Street and Euclid Avenue, Rosie reached over and locked Amir's door (a useless gesture since the windows were rolled down, but such is the stupidity of youth). A group of young black men walking on the sidewalk saw the action, and shouted to Rosie.

"You don't have to be afraid of us, baby. Don't you be lockin your doors. We don't want your skinny white ass."

Amir nervously considered that the manly thing to do would be to defend his woman and confront the men. He breathed a relieved sigh when he looked at Rosie, who was laughing heartily. "I guess he told me," Rosie said, loud enough for the men on the street to hear. They laughed too.

Later, inside Leo's, as they swayed to the mellow blues of Nina Simone, the black man from the street, seated two tables away from Rosie and Amir, sent over two complimentary drinks with a wink and a blown kiss.

*

Martin's departure for Parris Island Marine training cast a pall of loss over the group. Cognizant that their lives were changing drastically, they decided to enjoy their last few weeks at home in a frenzy of final frolicking. The last week of July was spent on their personal home turfs.

Brigid's work schedule clocked in at twenty hours a week. During her free time, she swam at Ridgewood Pool where she spent many summer days in her childhood; shopped at Parmatown; played some blues with her old band; danced at the United Auto Workers Hall; and ended the week with her family, munching candied apples at the St. Charles Carnival.

In between daytime fun, she managed to have a few dates with old flames and saw the movies *Rosemary's Baby, Green Berets,* and *Inspector Clousseau,* none of which she enjoyed. She did however, enjoy the freedom of being "single" and promised herself to remain so, at least for a few months.

Rosie volunteered at the Mount Carmel Festival; worked at the family store; played some baseball in pickup games at Edgewater Park; shared a brown bag lunch with her father at City Hall; and visited every family member within a five-mile radius of West 61st and Detroit. Most of her evenings were spent with Amir, in his apartment on the John Carroll campus.

Babs wrote to Martin every day, but did not pine. She and Karen Grovac lunched and dined at all of their favorite restaurants, starting with Corky and Lenny's and ending at Gruber's. A group of Our Lady Of Peace class of 1964 met at Shaker Lakes for a picnic with much reminiscing and some discussion of Babs's "miracle legs." On the last day of the week, Babs, her mother, and Grandma Schneider visited the Our Lady of Lourdes shrine. It was an emotional moment when the three generations of Barbaras renewed their faith and maternal bonds under the shadow of the statue of St. Bernadette.

Rosie, Brigid, and Babs made sure to save time for each other before they left for school. Babs was leaving first, on August 17, Brigid on the 24th, and Rosie on the 29th. In the first week of August, the three friends spent a day at Euclid Beach Amusement Park, splashing Over the Falls, racing on the Merry-Go-Round, and screaming through the Laugh-in-the Dark. The park was a favorite and famous destination during the past eighteen years. Now, it had one more year of life, and the friends wanted to enjoy the nostalgic thrills of the Flying Turns and the delectable delicacies of the Frozen Whip ice cream, one last time before the park prepared for its demise, and they prepared for their departure. After their day at the park, they ate dinner at Manner's Big Boy on Pearl Road in Parma, where they had shared many meals and grand gossip sessions after dates and dances.

At last the time came to say goodbye.

Babs started the heart-to-heart with a complaint against her parents.

"Well, I would like to tell you girls what dorm I will be staying in, but my mom and dad have decided that I will be living with my father in his apartment on campus."

Rosie controlled herself from spitting out her food.

"You can't be serious. Why?"

"I was hoping that they were oblivious to the riots that took place on campus last fall, but apparently my dad was not only aware, but actually took motion pictures of the flag-burnings and building fires. My mom had decided I wouldn't be going there at all, but then they decided I could go and just stay with my father. I fought and cried and threatened to do it all on my own, but it wasn't worth it." Babs sighed.

"Gonna be hard to have guys spend the night with your father in the next room," Rosie laughed.

"Oh, Babs, just make it work," Brigid said. "When they see things have calmed down, they'll change their minds."

"Things aren't going to calm down, Brigid," Rosie said. "At Ohio State things are just heating up. I can't wait. Anyhow I'll be at Baker Hall. Send you the exact address after I get settled in."

"Let's all write to each other once a month, okay?" Brigid pleaded. "There's no way I can afford long-distance phone calls. My parents are giving me $70 to last till Christmas. But I do want to keep in touch. Deal? I will write at the beginning of the month, Rosie the middle, and Babs the end. "

"Okay," said Babs.

"You are such a sap," Rosie said. "But yeah, I'm in."

"Promise?" Brigid wanted to confirm. "We'll type on carbon paper so we all get the same letters."

Babs gave an affirmative nod, and Rosie said, "Christ, yes."

With that settled, the three friends from Lourdes Academy, born on the same day, at the same place, at the same hour, as if cued by an invisible director, said at the same time, "I'm gonna miss you both so much."

And off they went: the lover of literature, the master of mathematics, and the advocate of animals. On their way to be liberalized, radicalized, and criminalized.

*

Chapter 6

September 1968 - May 1972

Marquette University, Milwaukee, Wisconsin
Ohio State University, Columbus, Ohio
University of California at Berkeley, Berkeley California

Marquette University
O'Donnell Hall
September 5, 1968

Dear Rosie and Babs,

Oh my gosh, I love it here! It was hard saying goodbye to my family -- I cried really hard when they left, but got over it pretty quick. The roommate that I was assigned with, decided not to show up which was kinda devastating, but then Ellen Bodnar and I arranged it so we could room together, and that has been fantastic. We have gone to all of the orientation activities together and we get along just great. It's amazing that we went to school together for four years, and I hardly knew anything about her -- or about so many of our high school classmates. We'll talk about that when I get home.

So anyhow, classes just started and I already love those too. The best is English class of course. The Professor is a tall, skinny guy, who stands on one leg, with the other folded over the podium -- a bit eccentric but he's a genius, and a scholar who is witty and a bit sardonic in his approach to higher education. Theology is going to be kinda strange. We are using something called the Dutch Catechism, and whoa -- my parents would not be happy with the diversion from traditional Catholic teaching coming out of that! Not sure how I feel about that yet, but it's very engaging. History class is in a movie theater, the Varsity, that serves as a kinda grand auditorium. The Professor is an Irish guy and seems pretty interesting. I sit next to Ric, a giant black basketball player (Negroes call themselves black now ya know), and he is a lot of fun. Basketball is king of the campus up here and I am excited to start going to games. Speech is going to be easy, and Math and French are going to be a pain in the butt, but I have absolutely no complaints.

Socially, oh my God, there are way more boys than girls. I've had more dates in three weeks than I had all four years in high school. Ellen is still a greaser, ya know with the hair and all-- kinda funny -- but she still gets guys, so we have no problems with getting invites to parties and dinners and stuff.

There are kids from all over the country here. I have to say the Chicago kids are the coolest, and so far everyone has been nice. I guess last year the black students had a big protest because they weren't represented on the faculty and in the student body, but seriously, besides the basketball team, I have only seen one black girl and she is the prettiest girl on campus, but still strange that she is the only one.

In the Union where a lot of the kids hang out, meet, and eat, it's divided into freaks, geeks, jocks, ROTC guys, and other groups. Freaks is what they call the hippie types. So far, I haven't aligned with any group, but it's all good.

Well lots to talk about, but I gotta go. I do miss you two -- there's so many times I wish I could pick up the phone and call you. We're not allowed to make outgoing calls, and everything goes through the switchboard. The lines at the pay phones on each wing are always long, and expensive. Also -- we have an 11:00 curfew on school nights and midnight on weekends! Are you kidding? They are working on getting that changed. In a way, it makes me feel safer. Not much of a rebel ya know.

Can't wait to hear from you! xoxoxoxoxoxo Brigid

Ohio State University
West Baker Hall
Sept. 15, 1968

Hi girls ! Woohoooo college life is great!

So funny that Brigid talked about her classes. I haven't been to any yet. We start tomorrow, so I thought I would write my letter now. My dorm is West Baker and it's all girl, but the boys eat at our cafeteria, and when I say boys, I mean the football players and damn, even the ugly ones are hunks.

I have been having fun since the first day. My mom and dad and brother and sisters and cousins and grandma and Aunt Kookie and a few assorted other people all came down and helped me unpack and they also brought pasta and salad and tiramisu and a whole smorgasbord of food to put in my refrigerator. My roommate is from Indiana, and her folks left early, so she was really happy to have so many people around. I got teary eyed when they left but got over it real quick when some girls from the dorm invited me to go down by the river to mess around. They had some weed (that's marijuana Brigid) and I smoked some. Pot (also marijuana, Brigid) is EVERYWHERE. Whew how about where you're at? Anyways, there's been a lot of partying, or should I say pottying, hahahahahahahahaha, and all in all it's been a great few weeks.

I am also enjoying my job at the Dean's Office. I look all prim and proper in business clothes and it's fun working in the office. Some kids told me that the Administration office is targeted for protests a lot, so things should get interesting.

Amir came down last week to go to the Fall meeting of the Animal Behavior Society. We have a great zoology and Entomology department at OSU and me and Amir had fun after the meetings too. I am glad we decided it was ok to date other people. There are kids here who tried to be true to their hometown honeys but within the first week most of them cheated. Being eighteen and glued to one person just isn't a very good idea. Anyhow,

Babs, the next meeting of that group is in Dallas in December and the topic is animals in space. Maybe we could all meet there? Neh.

I miss our Johnson visits and I miss you guys. We don't have access to outside calls either and our stuff goes through a switchboard too. Maybe someday we'll have private phones we can carry around with us. Yeah right.

Your turn Babs. Be careful everyone and don't smoke any bad stuff.

Rosie

University of California at Berkeley
Bonita Avenue
September 25, 1968

Dear friends,

I am in hell. I am miserable. Your letters made me so homesick I could vomit. Am I cheering you up yet? Forgive me, but in one month I have become a hermit with no one to talk to, living on top of a powder keg, afraid to move, afraid to speak, afraid to even think.

Living with my father and not in a dorm, is both a blessing and a curse. A blessing, because I am somewhat shielded from the madness that surrounds me, and cursed because I have not been able to have a serious, lengthy, uninterrupted conversation with anyone whom I would consider a peer.

Everything here is under protest. Ironically, I agree with much of the philosophy of the protests. The war is stupid, the black people are discriminated against, women are treated like morons, and students are forced to enroll in classes in which they have no interest nor practical value. But do I think we should destroy our buildings, hire criminals to teach our classes, burn our bras with cameras ogling our breasts, and disrupt our lectures? No, I don't. When I tried to engage a sign carrying hippie, yippie, whatever, in conversation, she was close to spitting in my face and with a weirded out pot fueled stare looked me in the eyes and said, "Man, you just don't get it, baby."

Christ, shoot me, if I ever do get it, because if I ever do get it, I don't want it.

Next week we are having a "delightful" black man named Eldridge Cleaver speak at a rally. He is a Muslim who was recently released from prison after a shootout with police and previously he was arrested for selling drugs, rape, and theft. The new voice of black America? I hope not. I so wish I was here last year to hear Dr. King. Anyhow, students and several faculty have insisted that Cleaver become a lector in one of our newly approved black history courses. Governor Reagan, a politician of movie star fame, tried to prevent that from happening, but Allah be praised, free speech prevailed, and intellectual decency just took another hit.

I guess I am getting an education here aren't I? My salvation has been my running on the beach and my time at the telescope. Discussions with my father inevitably conclude with his never changing mantra: "the beasts will remain beasts; the divine will ascend."

Like Alexander Pope, I am stuck in the middle.

Till next month,

Babs

Marquette University
O'Donnell Hall
October 5, 1968

Rosie and Babs,

Oh Babs - your letter broke my heart. I get homesick here, four hundred miles from Cleveland, but I have a roommate and dorm friends to turn to. I can't imagine being so far away in such a strange environment with no friends around. I'm glad you at least aired some of your feelings to us -- I hope it helped.

Things here are still fun. I am now working at Gimbel's Department Store in Downtown Milwaukee (just like Higbees in Cleveland), two nights a week and all day Saturday. It's hard to work and carry a full school schedule *but it's really cool to be downtown and cooler yet to have extra money. I am making $1.45 an hour -- enough to keep me in cigarettes and snacks and a new blouse once in a while. Oh, yes, I started smoking. Kinda hate myself for giving in, but I just couldn't resist that Marlboro Man anymore. I also have given in to the beer temptations. I mean, in Milwaukee you wake up to the smell of hops from the brewery. The air is thick with it, so by 5:00 I am dying for a Pabst. There's also beer blasts just about every week, where different clubs, dorm wings, frats, etc. get on a bus and go to a lodge or somewhere and have a beer party. It's taken me two months to give in to these things I said I'd never do -- can't wait to see what November brings! Haha*

The biggest struggle for me besides homesickness, is my Theology class. Everything we were taught in Religion class is being untaught. This new catechism opens the door to believe that Mary had other children, the gospels were propaganda, there was no Assumption, we are all priests, on and on. Kind of earth shattering stuff for me and I am still not sure what I believe about all of this. Gesu Church still has traditional Masses, but the university Masses in the basement of the dorms are extremely modern. I alternate between the two.

Babs, have you heard from Martin? My mom said there was an article in the Parma Post that he was now in Viet Nam. Let us know if you hear from him. The protests against the war here are small and sporadic. Ellen is dating a ROTC guy and the war is talked about a lot, but no organized movement yet. Nothing like Berkeley. The hotter topic is black power. Like I said, I only see a handful of black students on campus, but there are rumblings of anger. There's a priest named Father Groppi who has organized large protests for black people's rights in the city. Apparently last summer there were riots in Milwaukee--thank God they were after we visited, because I probably wouldn't be here if my parents caught wind of it.

I hope things get better for you soon Babs. And Rosie! Pot!? Really!? Think of how your parents would feel if you get caught. Not to mention how it fries your brain! Be careful, I see so many messed up kids here just floating on marijuana highs and God knows what else.

Can't wait to hear from you. xoxoxoxoxo Brigid

Ohio State University
West Baker Hall
Oct. 15, 1968

Hey girls! Well damn damn and triple damn.

Babs that is awful that you are so miserable, really awful. It's crazy around here too but we have other stuff going on to get our attention. Guess what that other stuff is? Buckeye football!! These people are crazier than Browns fans and I love it. The whole campus is excited but the protesters who are pissed at everything don't get into it much. But last week we beat the #1 team Purdue and everyone went nuts.

We have Newman club here for Catholics and I go to Mass there sometimes. Not much talk about faith, family, and friends, but I'm still a believer. Of course if I go home for a weekend, I end up at Mount Carmel with the family and go to Communion and hope the priest doesn't smell weed on my breath. I am laughing thinking of Brigid reading that.

You would die at my English Professor. We are reading Catcher in the Rye which I think I was supposed to read in high school. Anyhow it's the professor's favorite book and I swear he thinks he is Holden Caulfield. Every other word out of his mouth is the F word. F this, F that, F'in great, F'in administration, F F F , it's hilarious. Our parents would have us all in a convent if they had any clue what's goin on here.

I am learning about the Animal Science Program here it looks really cool and I am excited about it.

Thinking of Martin every time I go through the Oval and try to get around the protesters, but I do like their scene I must say.

Hey halfway done with first quarter!!!! I am flunking Math, mostly because it's at 8:00 a.m. and I don't go to it. Stay tuned for that. Only about a month left for Thanksgiving break I can't believe it. Babs don't forget to take your turn writing we will be worried about you till we hear you are back to your old sassy self. And hey if you can't beat em join em!

Rosie

University of California at Berkeley
Bonita Avenue
October 25, 1968

Dear friends,

Much has happened in a month. I have so much to share.

My father decided to leave campus during the Eldridge rally ("I will not breathe the same air as that racist, rapist, hate mongering fool" were his exact words), and he took me with him. Ohio never will look and smell and feel as good as it did that week. Most classes had been cancelled or so effectively disrupted that I barely missed any teaching and learning. But oh my friends, here's the best part. By coincidence or divine intervention, Martin was on leave, his last visit home before being shipped to Viet Nam. I had known this, but never dreamed I could be there with him. He sends his love to both of you and Brigid, he said you will receive his first letter from Viet Nam. If you were not my dearest friend (tied with Rosie of course), I would punch you in the nose for getting so much attention from my love, but I understand.

Martin has changed. His boyish smile is now a strong, manly grin. His arms are the size of tree trunks, his language is brief and to the point, his chest is like a rock, and his eyes are deep. Unlike many of the skinny, silver spooned, irrational babblers I see on campus, Martin is real. He is solid. He is a soldier, and he is going to war in a God forsaken jungle. He won't let me think about that. He only says he is well trained and he is doing something he believes in. He will "avenge the death of his buddies, and serve his country." That's it; that's Martin.

He left at 6:00 in the morning last week. My family joined his family at Hopkins airport. He was stoic. I was blubbering. And then he left, rode like the Lone Ranger into the sunset.

Even though his departure weighed so heavily on my heart, there were other major happenings that kept my mind off of him. First of all, my father told us that he would be leaving Berkeley at the end of the quarter.

He had been summoned by NASA to Cape Kennedy (he stills calls it Cape Canaveral by the way), to work full time on the moon landing scheduled for next July. Moon landing! The hairs on my arms stand up when I say that. The fact that he hadn't mentioned that to me was rather unbelievable, but he had to tell wifey first. That's how they do things. My mother also has an opportunity to work on the mission, so they are dragging Richard to Florida to be a part of the most significant scientific achievement of mankind.

Now, what to do with me?

It may surprise you since my last letter was so dismal, but despite the abyss that is Berkeley, I want to stay. I met a couple people, one is a girl whose roommate is moving out because she cannot deal with the instability of gas masks and lawlessness that pervade the sacred halls of academia. So I have the opportunity to live in a dorm with someone who is relatively normal, and actually wants to learn in a classroom and listen to lectures by academics and not activists. She lost a brother in Viet Nam and although she opposes the war, she does not participate in any rallies/riots, because she feels it is a betrayal of his honor. And although my sense of idealism has been shattered by the people who scream "shut it down" one day and "open it up" the next, I am starting to identify with the causes. Black students want their story to be told in history classes, women want to be represented on college committees (interesting though, the protesters seem to belittle women as much as the establishment), and this war just doesn't make any sense to me. I despise the methods, but I appreciate the message. I persuaded my parents to allow me to stay for the remainder of the year, and between you and me, I have no intention of leaving before I get my degree. As one of the groovy ne'er do wells said to me as he blocked the entrance into my Math class, "it's what happening, man."

So that's my life. And I love reading about your lives.

See you both in a few weeks!

Babs

Marquette University
O'Donnell Hall
November 5, 1968

Dear Rosie and Babs,

Still loving it here, but am feeling very detached from family. Okay -- now for a shock. My sister, Michele is pregnant and is getting married over Thanksgiving break.

I called her collect last night and we could both barely talk we were crying so hard. She was so smart and had so much going for her. Now she's going to be a high school dropout and tied to a high school dropout living in a basement apartment by the Ridge Rd. car wash where her future husband is working. My parents insisted she get married, otherwise they were looking into homes for unwed mothers. She said she does love the guy, but I just find it so overwhelmingly sad. I think if I would have been there she could have confided things in me and I could have fulfilled my role as big sister and guided her in a better direction. My parents are devastated and feel shamed. The "wedding" will take place in the sacristy with only the immediate family present. Michele said she is not allowed to wear a white dress, so in her rebel state, she is wearing a red mini skirt and red blouse. She said Father Veiss has been very nice and supportive, and forgave their sin in confession. The Irish side of the family is supportive, while still letting Michele know the shame she has brought upon them. The Hungarians want to have a big wedding party, but my mom said in no way were they celebrating premarital sex. Aunt Muncie told Michele, "The secret is not to get caught, honey."

Ugh enough about that. Parties, semi-formals, beer, and oh yeah, classes, are nicely filling my days and nights. Ellen has a boyfriend with whom she spends most of her time. She is having fun, but it's left me with a new group of friends. Lots of pot smoking and pill popping in the group. I find it amazing. I am sticking to beer though.

I don't really need drugs -- Theology class is still blowing my mind. This week, a famous theologian, who happens to be the head of the Theology Dept., came and talked to our class. His name is Bernard Cooke. Whoa, he laid on some liberal perspective. The message I related to was the concept of universal priesthood, and the call for humans to be something more than physical beings. He quoted from our text, "In our happiness as in our pain we have a hint of something beyond our finite bounds." We are connected to something eternal, something or someone eternally good. And that something or someone is in all living things and thus it is our calling to love each other and everything else. He says we are all priests, that the people of God all share in the priesthood. And best of all, he vehemently includes women in that equal approach. He ended the class with the message that as Christians, we should immerse ourselves in the world and transform it into a world of love. That was Jesus's message and it should be the main goal of the Church, and we are the church. It's all so wonderfully profound and thought provoking, and is just another part of our world that is changing faster than we can grasp.

Babs, I am so happy you have come to grips with your surroundings -- I love that you identify with the causes. I feel the same way, but the protesting and lawlessness are things I just can't get involved in. And -- oh my God, Martin! I wish I could have hugged him before he left. I am so happy for both of you that you had time to spend together. And -- oh my God, a man on the moon! To think your parents are going to play a part in that.

Rosie, I love you. I hated Catcher in the Rye and will never understand how Holden Caulfield emerged as a cultural icon. I also can't imagine why an English teacher, who should treasure language above all else, would resort to such vulgar use of it while teaching his class. It is exciting about the Animal Behavior class though, you will be fantastic when you get into that program. And ugh, I can relate to your Math problems. Math class is my biggest hassle and I am in the lowest section! Thank God I only have to take it for one year.

See you in a couple weeks! xoxoxoxo Brigid

Ohio State University
West Baker Hall
Nov.15, 1968

Hey Girls!! Woohoo Go Bucks!!

We are 7 and 0 man, it's too cool. The campus is crazy with football and anti-war shouts, and black power. Man, I love it. Once in a while I will chime in, but my job at the Dean's office depends on my staying out of trouble, so I am playing it kinda straight right now, at least when it comes to that stuff.

I got some tutoring in Math which bailed me out of failing and my foul mouthed English teacher said to write down what grade we think we deserve. Seriously, I think I am going to get a B just cuz I asked for it. Tax dollars at work, man. So it looks like I am gonna make it through first quarter.

I went home last week and brought back some of my mom's pasta and I am getting to be the most popular girl in the dorm, mainly because I share good food, and know where to get good weed. The city of Columbus is a bit of a drag once you leave campus, so unless I go home to Cleveland, I stay on campus.

Babs I cannot tell you how happy I am that you are sticking it out at Berkeley. When I tell my friends that I know someone at Berkeley they think it's the coolest thing in the world. You are on Olympus when it comes to the gods of cultural revolutions. (Hey I guess I did learn something in Mythology class!) And your mom and dad involved in Apollo? Damn! Coolest thing ever! Are you keeping your house in Shaker? Can't wait to hear all about it next week.

Brigid I am sorry to hear about Michele. I know firsthand the fear and shame and confusion that comes with what she's going through. And by the way, if you really wanna be a cool big sister, you should wear a red mini skirt to the sacristy too.

Rosie

University of California at Berkeley
Bonita Avenue
November 20, 1968

Dear friends,

Just keeping my turn in order, even though I am going to see you in a few days. I want to say thank you to Rosie for her encouragement of my decision to remain at Berkeley. That was cool of you to say that, and yes, every day I realize I am on Olympus, and right or wrong, these gods of protests are changing the world. They are, at the very least, a constant reminder that I want Martin home.

Brigid, I also want to tell you that my new friend, and soon to be roommate (her name is Chris), is an English major and she took me on a bit of a tour down Telegraph Ave., a main drag here. We stopped in all of the neat bookstores on the street. You would be in heaven. She called them the "holders of quaint and curious volumes of forgotten lore"; she said you would understand. I think the coolest thing about them is that most of them are hangouts and havens for the free speech movement. I'll tell you all about when I see you IN A FEW DAYS! I am looking forward to seeing you both; it seems like a lifetime.

Babs

*

The end of year holidays of 1968 saw subtle changes in the three friends and how they fit in to their home environments. Grandma Schneider noticed a significant weight loss in Babs and also commented on what she considered a definite shift of fashion taste. She labeled it "an unkempt hair-do complemented with a tendency toward disheveled attire." Richard and Barbara fluffed it off as "West Coast." Babs felt a growing sense of unconcern for any opinions her family offered.

Brigid, too, had lost weight, but her fashion sense had become more sophisticated. Whereas Babs had adopted the trend of long straight pony-tailed hair, jeans, and t-shirts, Brigid chose a wavy pixie hairstyle, short skirts, and boots. Her job at Gimbels had afforded her extra cash that she never had before, and her position as Junior Miss sales clerk kept her abreast of the latest fashions. Marquette was a moderately liberal-thinking campus, but still independent of the thought and styles that permeated the radical landscape of state colleges. Nonetheless, Dar had noticed a change in Brigid, and she worried about a sense of despair that her intuition told her was creeping into her daughter's soul, a sense that perhaps only a mother could detect.

Rosie had grown more flamboyant in style and personality. She was always munching and seemed in constant motion. She dressed according to her surroundings: hippie jeans and a headband when with her Ohio State friends, fluorescent colors when going to the bars, and appropriately modest when with the family. She made a point of visiting Brigid's sister, Michele, to offer help and support. Dar and Miklos and Brigid deeply appreciated this gesture of kindness, and hosted a lunch for Brigid, Babs, and Rosie on the Saturday after Thanksgiving.

The girls returned to school for the first two weeks in December, took their exams, and returned home in mid-December for a four-week Christmas break. The families celebrated the annual holiday party at Rosie's, but an intangible harbinger of melancholy transcended the gaiety. Parents felt the growing tug of detachment from their college girls; the girls carried the unease of rebellion that smacked into their daily lives; and always, there lingered the oppressive reality of the war.

The friends managed only one night out alone together, to a bar where they laughed and shared college stories. Though separated for only three months, they could feel changes in themselves and in each other, but no one could articulate the observations.

On New Year's Eve, Rosie romped at the Rose Bowl in Pasadena, California with Asmir, watching the Ohio State football team cap off an undefeated season. Babs helped her family settle in to their temporary home in Florida, sharing meals with astronauts and astrophysicists.

Only Brigid remained in Ohio, ringing in the new year with Ellen Bodnar and two young men who had invited them to Leo's Casino to see Jackie Wilson. Detained in a snowstorm in New York City, Wilson did not make it to Cleveland. The disappointment climaxed an uneasy end to 1968 for Brigid, whose mind was churning with the dichotomies that were consuming her life.

Brigid could not reconcile with her changing world. Sitting in a night club while Martin was fighting in a jungle; watching the police do their jobs, while remembering images of the Chicago police beating protesters at the Democrat Convention; sharing the evening with Negroes, knowing that if they ventured into Parma, they would be detained; appreciating the sacrifices of her parents while reliving the cold, judgmental atmosphere of Michele's wedding; and worst of all, trying to pray to a God whom her Catholic professors were saying might be based on myth. These thoughts crushed through her spirit and frenzied her soul.

She travelled back to Marquette in January unsure of the foundations of faith, family, and friends that had sustained her thus far in her life.

*

Marquette University
O'Donnell Hall
January 10, 1969

Dear Rosie and Babs,

It was so wonderful to see you over Christmas break, but we really didn't have enough time together, did we? Being home awakened in me the stark differences between college life and Parma home life. The orderliness of Parma life contrasts so greatly with the questioning chaos of campus life. At home, right is right and wrong is wrong. The church is right; the government is right; the war is right; the police are right and all the people who question the war are ungrateful, hippie troublemakers. And of course, according to our new pastor, the women's liberation movement is spearheaded by "females whose mission it is to upturn the order of gender roles that God has deigned to be righteous and holy." In other words, if you're a woman who has desires other than to serve men, you are rebelling against the natural and divine order of things.

Most of the students here just take things in stride and enjoy the moments. I'm too confused to be at peace, and always, always, Martin is on my mind. Have you heard from him Babs?

Other than the world messing with my mind, I don't have any hassles. My semester grades were As. Thank God for the tutor who helped me get through Math. Our basketball team has won five straight and going to the games is a great way to get my mind off things. The black guys around here date white girls and I haven't heard any complaints from anyone - - can't imagine that happening in Parma. The coach, Al McGuire is the most popular figure at the school - - he is a cute, fiery Irish guy; I love watching him in action. My dad would love him, and hmmm I guess my mom would too haha.

I am dating a lot, one night a freak, another night a collegiate, and occasionally one of the few greasers left in the world. My favorite is a guy named Jack who takes me to jazz clubs and reminds me of how much I love the Duke. One great thing about dating is the guys pay. I hope the feminists don't change that!

Ellen and I still get along great although she is totally unaffected by the changing world. Her perspective on life hasn't changed and she is solid with her faith and worldview. She is totally into the Beatles and seriously if I here "Hey Jude" one more time I am going to puke. Give me some Motown Marvin Gaye's "Grapevine" any day!

There was a big change in curfews this semester. We are allowed to sign out for the library till 2:00 a.m. Of course no one actually goes to the library and it's great to be out late like a normal eighteen year old. I don't drink much during the week though, but weekends, well I am usually up all night and sleep all day. I think that's my normal circadian rhythm.

Brigid xoxoxoxoxo

Ohio State University
West Baker Hall
Jan.20, 1969

Hey Girls!! Ohio State Champions! Yeah baby!!

The Rose Bowl was so damn fun, I can't even tell you. I got to see the Heismann Trophy winner, OJ Simpson, run like a mad man, unbelievable. But he wasn't fast enough for the Bucks and it was great to watch him fumble haha. We had a big rally here for the team and for once it seemed like most of the school was united. Well, until someone threw a rock at the ROTC building.

Hey Brigid, don't take this wrong, but you really need to get laid. You should be free as a bird, but you're so uptight. Don't let all this stuff get to your head, we are living in great times. These protests are gonna end the war, man. Just think of it. And those women libbers? They're gonna make it easier for girls like us to follow our dreams. And Negroes? Are you kidding me? Coolest damn people in the world. Go smoke some weed and lighten up. And if I knew what the hell a circadian rhythm was I would say something about that too. I do know what you're saying about things being different at home though. It's hard to relate to a place that hasn't changed when it seems like we have changed so much. I did a lot of pretending when I was home.

My semester grades were okay. Holding on to 2.00. This semester I take my first animal behavior class and it's the first time ever I am excited about a class. My job is okay but there's a lot of protests around the admin building where I work. If they ever have a picket line or a line to cross, I don't think I could do it. We'll see.

Brigid, I am sorry your parents were cold hearted to Michele. I talked with her ya know. She'll be okay. She said you have been the most supportive. Way to go. She'll need you when the baby comes. Did she tell you I brought her over the Supremes "Love Child" song? We had a good laugh.

Not much more to report here. Babs, can't wait to hear about your new digs.

Rosie

University of California at Berkeley
Ida Sproul Hall
January 30, 1969

Dear friends,

Oh, what a difference an absent father and a dorm room make. I am now truly at Berkeley, walking into rallies, protests, and mini revolutions at every turn. Free speech revolutions, black power revolutions, anti war revolutions, feminist revolutions, and oh, something we haven't talked about yet, a sexual revolution. Brigid, I chuckled at your curfew comment. Not only are there no curfews here, there is copulation on the lawns, in the square, and even in some dorms. The underground newspaper had a large photo of a naked girl sitting on the lap of a pot smoking hippie. An absolutely different world. There are aspects that disgust me, but there are also spiritual vibrations that somehow connect me to the core of what these people are fighting for. I am welcoming the revolutions but also wondering what will replace the injustices and foundations that they are tearing down. I can't even pretend to be a Catholic anymore. I'm moving toward the groove of transcendentalism, connecting to the physical universe but on a spiritual plane. I'm feeling it.

This place is certainly far, far away from the rigid traditions and discipline of Cape Canaveral (Kennedy). I am sorry that we did not spend more time together, but oh my God, my experience with the NASA folks was other worldly, literally and figuratively. The big news of course is the moon landing next year, and my father is working on training devices for an exploration flight scheduled in May. My mother is working on Mars research, some sort of feasibility study on how to analyze organic soil on the surface of Mars. Yeah, basically trying to figure out if there is life on Mars! It's not a cool opinion to have these days, but I have to say despite all of the societal flaws, our parents are pretty damn cool. I feel like I am the walking reality of dad's view of life; we must choose whether to be like the beasts or divine creatures. Berkeley reminds me of the earthly human tendencies we wallow in. The lunar mission reminds me of the potential we have to conquer the universe. What a great time to be breathing.

No word from Martin yet. He is always in my heart as he is in yours. Every night I watch the news and the casualties piling up. I take comfort in knowing that he is where he chose to be.

Rosie, I see many references to pot in your letters and in your behavior at home. I don't know how OSU is, but the air here is sometimes so thick with cannabis, I get a contact buzz walking to class. Neither Chris nor I indulge.

My first semester grades held no surprises but there are so many disruptions to classes, I don't know how they can even give any grades. This semester, I am taking advanced math and astronomy courses plus some required bullshit courses. Ha! Yes, I said bullshit. Bullshit courses are a target for the student power protests. Why should a mathematician have to take a foreign language? Why should I have to sit through a class that I could teach? Power to the people! Hahaha. Just one of the many mantras I hear as I march through the maze of revolutionary cadences. I must say I am getting used to the vibes of this culture shock but I still linger in the ether between the world of NASA and the world of People's Park. I am hearing that things are going to blow up this Spring on all fronts. Holding my breath.

Love you girls.

Babs

Marquette University
O'Donnell Hall
February 10, 1969

Dearest Rosie and Babs,

I am writing this only to maintain the normalcy of my monthly routine, in an effort to give me some sort of sanity. I have no blood in my heart, no thoughts in my brain, and no hope in my soul. The news of Martin's death has paralyzed every fiber of my being. When Martin's sister called me, as I know she did both of you, I believe she was in a state of detached shock. She described the soldiers at her door, their compassionate but military tone, their attempt at comfort ... all

the while describing the honor of Martin getting his legs blown off and bleeding to death on a worthless patch of ground. I cannot bear it. Reality is madness.
Brigid

Ohio State University
West Baker Hall
Feb. 20, 1969

Screw this war and screw this country. There is no sanity. Oh my God I can still see his smiling face, telling me to be careful in college. He was telling ME to be careful. I went home last weekend just to be away from here and be with my parents. I stayed high all weekend.

Screw everyone.
Rosie

University of California at Berkeley
Ida Sproul Hall
February 28, 1969

Friends,

I am numb. Martin's mother is keeping a patriotic demeanor. Serving his country, dying with honor, doing what he thought was right.

Jesus, nothing matters. I want to force myself to care about things, but I can't care. I don't care about anything except the confused anger that consumes me. Being so far away in this surreal world of kids who think they know everything but know nothing has sapped any sense of stability I have. You two are my rocks in misery, but my room mate Chris knows the depths of pain in this loss since her brother was killed. She said the shock will diminish but the pain lingers in different forms.

I look at the night sky and I think how small and worthless we are. Martin gave it all some meaning. Now he is gone. And I feel I am gone too.
Babs

Marquette University
O'Donnell Hall
March 10, 1969

Dear Rosie and Babs,

Martin's body will be home next month. It aches all over to write that. Martin's body. The wake and funeral might be during Spring break. Either way I will be there. Oh my God Martin.

My mother flew up last week to see me. She had never flown before. I had been weeping and sobbing uncontrollably for days after the news and she wanted to see for herself what my condition was. I didn't know she was coming so the first few moments when she heard the Hair album playing from my room and saw the Jimi Hendrix poster and picture of Richard Nixon with his teeth blackened out and devil horns sticking from his head hanging on my wall, her first inclination was to scold. But when she looked at my swollen blotched face and inflamed red eyes, she embraced me and sat and cried with me, never losing hold. Connecting with someone from Parma refreshed the grief and brought to light old images and memories. My mom had always liked Martin, since kindergarten. He had stopped to see her before he left. I hadn't known that. Oh my God, Martin is dead.

She took Ellen and me to dinner at Marc's Big Boy and we actually managed a little laugh at the Thousand Island dressing that they call their special sauce. I've gotten used to it, but a newcomer from Cleveland is always sorely disappointed to the point of gagging at a Big Boy without the creamy tartar sauce. She asked about protests. I never watch the news, but apparently it is filled with film from campus unrest. Lots of Berkeley coverage Babs. We told her that the protests here are now focusing on ROTC. Their drills, building, classes, are all being disrupted. I had a commitment to attend their winter semi-formal last week, doubled with Ellen, and there was a bomb scare or threat and we had to evacuate. A hassle, but in my opinion an ineffective protest. The world of protest seems so far away from me even though I sometimes walk right through the crowds to get to class. I've seen like a hierarchy of people in the movement.

SDS are the hardcore instigators here, intent on overthrowing, well, everything. Some of them are very well informed, others just seem like straight up anarchists; their numbers are small, but have success in rallying people. I have been to some of their gatherings, even hung out with them. Interesting, radical conversations, but the only thing that made an impression on me is that while they preach equality and condemn every ounce of establishment policy, they treat their women and girlfriends like cow dung. Big turn off. There are those who I think just sincerely want the war to end and fall into line with any protest against it. Some kids march, just to be a part of it all, sometimes creating a party atmosphere and picking up guys or gals, and just going with the flow. The black kids are also small in number but are very vocal. They protest the war, but mostly participate in their own demonstrations for better treatment of Negro students. In the meantime, I'm like an outside observer, so near and yet so far. Before Martin's death, I was content to enjoy the normal things that college offered. Classes, partying, exchange of ideas, new places, etc. Now, all of it is tainted with his blood. Religion, family, and oh my God government (Nixon makes me puke) - I can find no peace in any of them. And now, even Spring break will not offer relief.

Brigid xoxoxoxo

Ohio State University
West Baker Hall
March 20, 1969

Well girls, I quit my job at the administration building today. I was all dressed up in my nice little work clothes, shoes matched my gloves which matched my nail polish, which matched the bow in my hair, walking to work and when I got within sight of the building, I saw a large group of kids protesting the teaching of military science and ROTC courses on campus, blocking the door and holding up signs and shouting "pigs" at the ever present cops. I ran to a nearby phone booth and called my boss who was already in the building. He said if I was scared, he would send a cop to escort me inside. I told him I wasn't afraid, but that I just didn't want to cross a protest line. He said if I wasn't at my desk within a half hour I was fired. I went back to the dorm, pulled on my jeans and peace t-shirt, picked up a black armband in the lobby, and went and joined the protest. All the while, my heart was pumping to the beat of "This one's for you my Martin dear, this one's for you my Martin dear."

I'm going to try to get another job quick and make up some lie to tell my parents. If Mama Rose finds out I joined the protests, I will be back on 61 and Detroit before you know it. It seems like everyone back home supports the war and everything the damn president says and does. It's hard to figure out what's really real, the evil of the war or the goodness of the heroism. So many of my neighborhood guys are there, I want them back, I want them home. And then that bastard Nixon promises "peace with honor," but never can tell me what the hell we're doing there in the first place. Why did Martin have to die?

I know what you mean about not finding peace Brigid. There's no peace when nothing makes sense. But besides pot, I do find great comfort volunteering in the veterinarian hospital. I've been going there more and more. So many poor, uncared for animals. It makes me feel good just to hold them. I'm thinking I just can't stand anyone anymore. Since I found out about Martin, I go to classes but I am in a daze. Damn, I can't wait to be with you two. I think I'm going to follow Timothy Leary's advice and just turn on, tune in, and drop out.

Rosie

University of California at Berkeley
Ida Sproul Hall
March 28, 1969

Dear friends,

Your letters bring me cheer even when I am depressed as hell. Brigid, your assessment of the different groups made me laugh, mostly because of the truth of what you said. I am finding that of all the changes and protests, the one that receives the least favorable attention among the students is the feminist voices. Anti-war, Civil rights for Negroes, student power; these are the righteous causes. Female power is linked to sexuality, even by many of the women. Not even sexuality, just sex.

Stinking world.

I have been mellowing out with pot lately. You are definitely on to something there Rosie, but I don't like the feeling of losing control of my emotions, so I don't think this will be a lasting habit. What little peace I have still comes from gazing through the telescope.

Martin, Martin, Martin.

See you girls in a few days,

Babs

P.S. Good going on your choice to protest instead of crossing that protest line, Rosie!

Marquette University
O'Donnell Hall
April 20,1969

Dear Rosie and Babs,

It is my first day back on campus after watching one of the most important people in my life lie cold and hard as stone in a coffin, looking eerily handsome and peaceful in his decorated uniform, a half closed casket hiding the absence of legs that had been ripped off by mortar, as I stared I could only see the elfin face of that little boy who stole my crayons in kindergarten, pulled my hair in 4th grade, and stood by me in every struggle I ever faced, I could only hear the soft sounds of his whispering "Goodbye, I have to do this," and imagining the horror of his last moments and wallowing in the military magnificence of rigid soldiers honoring their fallen brother as they blasted their salute with the sound of 21 shots ringing through the silence of sadness and marching to the ancient cadence of the heroes of war yet as I wept with his friends and family I could not feel the honor I could not feel the heroism I could not feel the divine calling of humanity, I could only feel the beast, the beast that torments the human soul and leads to killing and hatred and rape and unkindness and insanity, the beast that is gluttonous and lustful, and greedy, and envious, and slothful, and prideful, and wrathful, the beast that lurks in all souls, the beast that is eating my soul.

And now friends, I must go to Theology class.

Brigid

Ohio State University
West Baker Hall
April 20, 1969

I know it's not my turn to write yet, but I just wanted to quickly send my monthly note even though we just saw each other. Between the funeral and Easter and family time, we girls didn't have too much time, but what we did have, I appreciated. The whole two weeks were very strange to me, not at all what I expected. The Easter Resurrection liturgies at Mount Carmel and the display of patriotism at Martin's funeral touched me deeply. Instead of feeling bitter and sad like I thought I would, for some reason I came away feeling connected to something greater than myself and I felt at peace. No, I am not high. Brigid always talks about faith, family, and friends, and for once, I get it, I really do. The hope at Mass, the faith from Martin's family, and the love from you girls, it all got to me. Martin's death is devastating, but we will see him again, and we are still here. I am more committed now than ever to changing the world. Love you both.

Rosie

University of California at Berkeley
Ida Sproul Hall
April 28, 1969

Friends,

My, my, I had to keep checking the signatures on your letters; it seemed like Rosie wrote Brigid's and vicey versey. Rosie got religious, and Brigid got pissed. Just goes to show how messed up things are.

As for me, my mood is in between both of yours. A part of me is low, low,

low, like Brigid, seeing the dark side of humanity. But the elegance and honor displayed at Martin's funeral did echo within me a call to a cause greater than ourselves. I just keep telling myself that Martin wanted to be where he was; he could have never been happy without serving what he considered his duty. The hole in my heart will never heal, but even now, just two weeks after we buried him, I am already caught in the sway of Berkeley bombast.

There has been a simmering debate over the use of a patch of land in the middle of campus. The administration was supposed to do something with it, I don't even know what, but after they tore down some buildings, they just left it alone and it's been an eyesore for a few months. Apparently, while I was taking those few extra days off for Martin's funeral, students and some store owners decided to develop the land for themselves and build a park and another home for protests and free speech gatherings. Things were going kind of ok and the land was being cleared with dozens of people planting flowers and bushes and other park like accessories. But then the admin said, sorry, we have other plans for the space.

The stage is set for a showdown and I don't think it's going to be an amicable compromise. The campus is crazier than usual, and that, my friends, is very crazy. Maybe I am just using this as a psychological diversion from my sorrow, but man, the vibes of revolution are rattling the earth beneath my feet. National Guard guys are everywhere, students, yippies, hippies, and flippies (that's what Chris and I call freaks who are flipped out on drugs), are all just waiting for something to pop. Stay tuned to the news. If Governor Reagan takes a hard line, well, I don't know what will happen.

I hope you don't take offense to my attitude. Trying not to dwell on Martin, and thought you might be interested in the west coast corner of the world that is so far from the corner of our midwestern world. You two wrote your feelings as soon as you got back to school. I've had a chance to settle in and be engulfed in life, moving farther from the gulf of death.

You are right Rosie, Martin is with us. And you are right also Brigid, the beast eats our soul; I am trying not to feed it too much.

Babs

*

The school year ended in May with the three young women advancing to sophomore status. Rosie's and Brigid's final month was uneventful, but Berkeley erupted into violence and chaos. The community efforts to build a People's Park were foiled by the university and the "low tolerance for protest" policy of Governor Reagan. When bulldozers rolled over the park preparations and a fence went up to prevent further community involvement, hundreds of protesters marched and rallied to knock down the wall and seize control of the land. Police officers, county sheriffs, and the National Guard had orders to prevent the seizure. Shots were fired, people were beaten, and the hell that had been simmering for several years boiled over into mayhem and indiscriminate bedlam.

Innocent people were hurt, and Babs, who participated in what she thought would be a peaceful declaration of support for the park, ended up sitting in a paddy wagon next to bloodied radicals and confused bystanders. She unwittingly involved herself in the pandemonium which Berkeley history would record as "Bloody Thursday."

The incident at Berkeley coincided with the culmination of Richard's Apollo 10 project, the first complete spacecraft lunar orbital mission with a crew of three astronauts. He was totally absorbed in this critical endeavor, and Barbara chose to keep Babs's arrest a secret. She used her NASA influence to erase any record of her daughter's arrest. She then wired plane tickets, arranged for a moving company to pack and send belongings from Berkeley to Florida, and have Babs arrive at Cape Kennedy in time for the May 18 launch which would be the finest achievement of Richard's career. Such is the role of a wife and mother. Such is the reason Barbara's nights were drenched in Dewar's Scotch.

The hellish emotional toll of Martin's death, and the Berkeley riots, collided with the heavenly emotional elation of the Apollo launch and the family spotlight. Babs's psyche could endure no more.

While Apollo 10 splashed down into the Pacific Ocean on May 26, Babs collapsed down onto the Atlantic Ocean seashore: physically, emotionally, and psychologically exhausted.

*

Babs spent the rest of May and most of June in a Florida hospital, in the psychiatric ward, recovering from "acute depression with bouts of severe anxiety."

Barbara and Richard strained to cope with the conflicting realities of professional success and what they perceived as parental failure. They were laid waste with guilt for not recognizing the stress that their daughter was enduring.

"We are sick with blame," Barbara cried to Dar when she called to tell of Babs's condition. "How could we miss the strain on her mind that the Berkeley culture bombarded her with? How could we let her go 3,000 miles away on her own, after burying the love of her life? How could we let our professional ambition blind us to the needs of our child? Oh my God, when I look at the fog in her eyes and the bones of her wrists barely covered by skin, I can't bear it."

"We all think of our oldest daughters as mature and tough," Dar consoled. "We never stopped to think of what this mess of a world has done to these girls. They've all been so strong and seemingly adjusted, but they are confused and hurting by the madness that surrounds them. My God, everything they have ever believed in is being questioned or destroyed. Don't be so hard on yourself. I admire you for getting Babs help. She is in the right place, and the love and support that you and Richard give her will get her through this."

Both mothers were holding back heaves of weary tears. When the conversation ended, they vowed to make sure the friends would have time together for talk and support.

June 1,1969 was the first birthday since the girls met that they were not together. Babs was in Florida, Brigid was still in Milwaukee, and

Rosie was already working at the Cleveland Zoo for a summer internship. Rosie and Brigid had a short telephone conversation which dwelled mostly on Babs's breakdown. Babs could not receive phone calls.

Despite Dar's promise to look after Brigid's well-being, she had to stretch her love and time to the younger siblings. When she and Miklos went to pick up Brigid from Marquette for summer break, the drive home from Milwaukee was filled with talk of Michele's baby, which was due in July. Dar told Brigid that she would be needed to help with the baby. Miklos tried to ease the conversation with comments about how proud he was of Brigid's grades and advancement, but it was clear that Brigid was not the main concern or focus of their plans.

When Brigid finally celebrated her birthday with Rosie at the end of June, it was at Barron's Cafe on Pearl Road, where they feasted on nickel beer and steak burgers.

Brigid asked Rosie, "So are you still in religious and tradition mode, or are you back to your screw everyone attitude?"

"Man, that didn't last long. My last month at school was one crazy thing after another. I don't think we are groovin' as much as Berkeley, but there were rallies and marches and protests going on every day. That stuff is where it's at. I love it. One minute we're throwin' rocks at the National Guard and a few hours later we're partying with them and doing all sorts of stuff. So, no, my holiness left the room as soon as I lit my first joint back on the Oval."

"I'm trying to just enjoy my freedom and have fun," Brigid said. "Marquette is nowhere near as active as OSU and Berkeley. It's perfect for me. A calm dissent. Coming back home is hard. I just don't feel that this is my world anymore. I'm already looking forward to going back."

"Yep, I know what you mean," Rosie agreed. "My mom yelled at me yesterday for giving a little kiss on Amir's cheek when I was saying goodbye to him outside our house. 'You look like a little whore out there,' she said. Holy shit, if she knew what we did on the lawn outside the dorm, she would kill me. Our parents have no idea."

"My mother told me how disappointed she was that I had library books that were overdue," Brigid added. "Disappointed in overdue library books. God help me if she finds my contraceptives."

The birthday girls clanked their beer glasses and toasted their mothers.

*

Brigid became part of an older generation on July 2, when Michele gave birth to John Michael Corrigan, the first male child in the bloodline of the union between Dar and Miklos Nagy. Although they never hinted that the gender of the child mattered to them, the arrival of a baby boy was akin to the birth of royalty. Brigid sarcastically joked that she expected the magi to show up with gifts. Michele was a radiant mother, and her husband doted on her and the baby. The shame of the premarital conception ended, and all was forgiven. The king was born--or if not the king, at least a future Browns quarterback, or Indians ace pitcher.

The baby's christening took place at St. Charles, as did the other Nagy baptisms, and the Hungarians and Irish gathered at the Nagy household to celebrate. Memories of Martin constantly stung Brigid's heart, but celebrating a life trumped the funerals that had dominated the clans' gatherings for the past few years. Though feeling alienated from the family, she did enjoy the gaiety and familial bonding of sisters, aunts, uncles, great-aunts, great-uncles, and cousins. It was a refreshing diversion from the world of war and strife that consumed the globe. Falling into the pits of cerebral anarchy, Brigid struggled deeply with her faith, questioning everything. The perpetuating stability of family life provided her with a sane foundation, even if she thought they were all crazy.

She also found relief in romance. Brigid had started dating Bill Jones, a friend of Ellen Bodnar's brother. Bill was carefree, and honest about not wanting a serious relationship. A summer romance with no strings attached provided a perfect vehicle through which Brigid could have a steady date and still maintain her freedom. It was also the reason she started taking birth control pills. Brigid was nineteen, buxom, and beautiful. Spirituality and faith were not the only things she yearned to explore.

*

Rosie was engaging in a different type of exploration, sinking deeper into drug use.

"Woohoo!" Rosie shouted to Amir as he climbed onto a boat where she was partying with some "friends" that he had never met. Her bra-less breasts bounced freely and uncovered beneath her sheerly fringed orange and green vest. Her tattered shorts were accented by the chunk of fleshy buttocks that hung below the length of the cut. The peace sign on her beaded headband covered more of her body than her entire outfit.

Amir had never participated in this part of Rosie's life. They had smoked weed together, but Rosie had indulged and experimented with other things, and he only now saw the depths of her behavior. He had been willing to accept their differences; freedom was a critical component of their successful relationship. But witnessing the scene firsthand was too much for him.

"Jesus, Rosie, let's get out of here," he begged.

"Well just wait a minute," Rosie screeched. "I got some stuff I gotta do first."

Amir watched as Rosie slithered past a few stoned bodies sitting wild-eyed and oblivious on the floor of the boat. She sat beside a dirty, barefoot young man with matted hair, thick eyebrows, and pupils dilated almost to cover the entire iris. Before Amir could grasp what was happening, the man had laid out four strips of white powder on a table. Rosie picked up a small tubed object, sniffed up the powder, one strip at a time, pausing only for a slight cough in between. She shook her head, caught her breath and ran over to Amir.

"Yeah baby, I feel good. I feel really good. Let's go have some fun."

Bewildered and astounded, Amir grabbed Rosie's arm and led her off the boat. Rosie missed the step between the dock and the boat, lodging her right leg in between. Amir hung on to her as he tried to pull her free. Rosie was laughing uncontrollably, mucous streaming from her nose. When her leg was finally twisted free, it was bleeding and scratched. She continued to laugh, gleefully shouting at Amir.

"It doesn't even hurt hahahahaha, it doesn't even hurt."

Amir pushed her into the car, buckled her seat belt, as she protested the constraint. They went back to Amir's apartment where Rosie eventually slept. When she awoke, her leg was swollen and painful. Amir was drinking coffee in the kitchen, waiting for Rosie. She moved slowly from the bed and buried her head in her hands as she set across from Amir.

"Damn, I feel awful. When I take that stuff, it sends me to a place so high I never think I am gonna come down. But when I do come down all I wanna do is get back up to that high. Man, what happened to my leg?"

Amir gazed at her in fear and anger for a few minutes, then finally spoke.

"Rosie, I had no idea you were doing so many drugs. Last night was the scariest thing I have ever seen. You were lost to me. And then when I got you to bed, I looked through your purse, and found these."

He placed a pile of pills of many colors on the table.

"Rosie, you are in trouble, and I don't know how to handle it. I cannot watch you do this to yourself. I ...."

"Oh Christ, shut the hell up." Rosie yelled. "Everyone is doing this shit. I only do it on weekends and once in a while at parties."

Amir stood up, grabbed her shoulders, gazed into her eyes, and said softly, "You are free to do as you choose, but I can have no part in this lifestyle. There are temptations everywhere and you know damn well the consequences of giving in. I will not sacrifice my education or my body for you; I cannot. I will take you home now. When you are ready to walk away from this path, I will be there for you, but for now, no."

Rosie stared at him with a twisted smile, half smirk and half hurt. "You take the world too seriously, Amir. I have always walked between the wild and the wise. I am certainly not going to change that now. I'm nineteen and freer than I have ever been. I will not sacrifice that freedom for you or anyone or anything. Take me home."

Rosie popped a green pill and they rode to Detroit Avenue in silence.

*

Babs sat with her mother and David behind the VIP fence at Cape Kennedy on July 16, and watched Apollo 11 rise into the skies in a streak of billowing smoke and beautiful orange and yellow flames. Roars of appreciation could be heard throughout the Cape as the spacecraft slowly diminished from sight into the heavens. Richard was in the Command Center, watching with apprehension and awe at the sight of a successful launch that carried three astronauts on their way to a lunar landing.

Babs looked at her mother, who was enjoying the moment, allowing herself a relief from the stress that had sapped the energy from her mind and spirit. When the roar of the engines and the crowd dissipated, Babs spoke to her mother.

"I'm okay, Mom. I will be okay. I am so proud of you and Papa for what you have contributed to this historical moment. I am so happy to be here to share it with you. I belong in this world, this world of space and intelligence and wonder. Thank you for what you have given me. I am okay."

"Thank you, thank you, thank you," Barbara said as she embraced Babs.

Even little David felt the magnitude of the emotion, and joined in the hug.

Babs had recovered in mind and body, and now she must rest both. She and her mother and David would spend the rest of July at Cape Cod. As a belated birthday present, Richard had arranged for Rosie and Brigid to visit Cape Cod for a few days from July 18-July 22, so the friends could watch the moon landing together. He was confident in Babs's recovery, and noticed the pinkish hue that had returned to Barbara's face. He also observed a lighter spunk in David's demeanor. His family was sound, and his career was on the verge of an epic accomplishment.

They had conquered the beasts of war and lawlessness, at least for now.

*

Rosie and Brigid jumped and hugged with glee when they spotted Babs running toward them from the Cape Cod oceanfront villa, the Turyevs' summer home. Wading in the warmth of rekindled friendship, and a bright, sunlit afternoon, they all spoke at once, but not missing a word the other said.

"Oh my God, you look like shit," laughed Rosie as she cupped Babs's smiling face in her hands.

"You look like a raccoon--don't you get any sleep?" Babs jokingly scowled back.

"Looks like I'm the only one around here who escaped unscathed from the ravages of freshman year," mocked Brigid as she squeezed Babs to her chest and rocked back and forth, not wanting to let go.

The soon-to-be college sophomores spent the next few days walking along the beach, eating and drinking and talking, each appreciating the others' stories of the past few months, sometimes expressing concern, sometimes dismay, but always love and understanding. Barbara insisted the girls attend Mass, and they laughed at the power a mother still held over them.

When they gathered around the television set on the evening of July

20, they were silent. They watched in an amazed and awesome hush as the spacecraft edged closer and closer to the moon's surface. Babs grabbed her mother's hand, both of them knowing the science and frantic preparations that lay beneath the calm that they were watching.

Neil Armstrong, with suppressed emotion, soon proclaimed the message, "Houston, Tranquility Base here; the Eagle has landed." A few hours later he would descend from the craft onto the moon, and proclaim the majesty of the event with the statement, "That's one small step for a man, one giant leap for mankind."

People in every corner of the world gasped in astonished unity at the sight of man on the moon. The wars, the strife, the hate, the inequalities, the disasters, and the evils, dwarfed by this moment, when all humanity held its breath and realized for an infinite second, the capabilities of the human race, when minds were in tune with bodies and souls.

On the shores of Cape Cod, three young women, living the plots of their own Bildungsromans, escaped the madness of the last few months, and dwelled in a thoughtful oasis of present peace and future fulfillment.

For Babs, the moon landing was a triumphant affirmation of her family's contribution to history and a personal reminder of what she desired for herself as a mathematician and a woman. It did not go unnoticed by Babs that the key players in this marvelous drama were all men. She was not angry at this. She did not begrudge those brilliant, hard-working risk-takers their success. Their accomplishments were mankind's accomplishments. Their achievements served all peoples. She admired them with an immeasurable esteem. She wanted the opportunity to soar as they did--not in imitation, not in competition, but equal with…perhaps even leading them.

For Brigid, the journey to the moon was a culmination of the human endeavor to expand consciousness, the culmination of gazing at the stars and following the desire to explore the space in which the stars reside, a culmination of embracing an unknown reality and examining the very fabric of that reality. It was a quest not only to achieve, but to express. It was art; it was poetry. All things connect. This was why she wanted to teach--to help her students see the connection of all things, and to facilitate their understanding of these connections. The steps of Neil Armstrong on the moon that night were symbols of the steps of all art: inspiration, creation, expression. The world may be in confusion now, but she will help make it better. She will teach her students to make it better. She will guide them to the Sea of Tranquility, and now more than ever, she believed at the center of that sea, was God.

For Rosie, the momentous evening was yet another reason to get high. She enjoyed the company of her friends and she was touched by the magnificence of a man on the moon. She had not dropped any acid nor snorted any cocaine for the past two days. She had affirmed in her own mind that she had no addictions; she simply liked the euphoria that drugs gave her. So as the others slept, she reclined on the beach looking up at the moon, and matched the natural high of the day's excitement with the manufactured high of a joint.

*

Babs remained at Cape Cod for the rest of the summer and fully recuperated from her collapse. Although her parents had strong reservations about her returning to Berkeley, she convinced them that therapy had guided her through the feelings of angst and despair that she felt from the anarchy of Berkeley and the grief of Martin's death. Her time with her family and their NASA colleagues reignited her commitments to academic and social goals. She sympathized with feminist, anti-war, and civil rights causes, but she would work for change from inside the system.

In Cleveland, Rosie and Brigid continued to spend their time working and dating. With Amir out of Rosie's life, her social life expanded to a more diverse group of friends and dating pool. Her love of animals continued, and she rededicated herself to studying and advocating for their well-being. Mama Rose and MV were grateful to have Rosie around to help with children and the store. They worried about Rosie's mood swings, but attributed them to nineteen-year-old restlessness.

Brigid remained steady with Bill Jones, knowing there was no commitment when she left for school. She enjoyed her job at Higbees, and frequently babysat for Michele's infant. The shakiness of her Catholic faith had solidified, and she again found peace in the ancient traditions expressed in the liturgy of the Mass, even though she disagreed with most of the ideas spewed in the sermons. Her time with her family was still stressful as she felt like a stranger--her sisters and parents seemingly oblivious to a world outside of Parma.

When summer faded into late August heat, the girls were more than ready to return to college life. Before they had left the Cape, although Rosie and Babs had protested, Brigid convinced them to continue their letter-writing.

"It was kinda a pain in the ass," Rosie lamented. "I'd rather just call you once a month. Writing on carbon paper is really queer."

"Do you know how much two long-distance calls a month would cost?" Brigid responded. "Besides, this way, we are all seeing the same messages. It keeps us in touch and literally on the same page."

Babs sighed. "I'll do it. It did help me last year to see those letters in my mailbox every month. I like getting the communications, but I can't say I enjoyed writing them."

But write the letters they did.

*

Marquette University
Cobeen Hall
September 5,1969

Dear Rosie and Babs,

Back in Milwaukee, which is starting to feel more like home than home. I love my classes and, I am still shocked at this new Theology class that has already basically denied the physical resurrection of Christ. My parents would just love to know that they are supporting a Catholic college where Catholic teachings are being thrown out the window. But it is interesting to study this other perspective of our faith. I say "our" because we all do have the same background. Remember your miracle legs, Babs?

You'll notice my address as Cobeen Hall. My new dorm is a former hotel. I am on the 5th floor and Ellen and I are very happy with the accommodations. Most of our friends from O'Donnell are on this floor too.

Speaking of Ellen, she has been telling me all about the Woodstock concert she went to in New York this summer. As a matter of fact, many kids are talking about it. The love-in of all love-ins. Janis Joplin, Jimi Hendrix, Creedence, Buffy Sainte-Marie, The Who .... How in the hell did we not go to this? Ellen said it was the most unbelievable experience of her life. Muddy, dirty, almost everyone stoned (almost, she stressed, not all), thousands of kids, no fights, no toilets, and through it all, she said, 'Music mellowed the whole scene.' I talked to two other kids that were there and they both said the same thing, a surreal festival of music and freedom. One kid focused on the sex and drugs. I'm just in awe that I had no idea this was going on.

I started back to work at Gimbels, I really enjoy being in the city. Things on campus seem pretty calm. One big change is with the black students. It's like they all decided to be African over the summer. And there are quite a few more. They sit together as a group in the Union, except for the ROTC guy who still sits with the Pershing Rifle group. Anyhow, that one black girl who was in a few of my classes last year totally changed her looks. Her hair went from a white girl's flip to a wild African Afro. Still gorgeous, but not so approachable. I'm looking forward to getting to know them better to see what's going on. I mean, we totally missed the hippie Woodstock happening, who knows what else was going on while we slept in Cleveland?

Babs--what's up with that hippie girl from Berkeley who was a member of those crazy Manson murders? Makes me shudder.

I hope all is well with you two,
xoxoxo Brigid

Ohio State University
West Baker Hall
Sept. 15, 1969

Woodstock! Oh man, how I would have loved to be there. So many OSU kids went or tried to go. A lot of them got stuck on the roads. One of my friends who made it said she didn't wear any clothes the whole while she was there and dropped acid for three days. Everyone was trippin. But it was cool, she said it was just so cool. Nobody judged anyone and the music rocked or floated or colored their world and she said the whole scene just let her go inside herself. She was surrounded by heads and someone said there was bad acid goin around but it wasn't really bad it was just strong so she tried to get some. I love hearing her stories.

I know you girls aren't into the trips but damn they keep me goin. Ya know, Amir got pissed becuz I did some cocaine, but I don't do that anymore, and some kids are shootin up, but I stay away from junk. So anyhow, yeah Woodstock was where it was at and we missed it.

I've only been to a couple classes, started an animal behavior class which is going to be the best. Things are shaking all over campus. We have a supply of gas masks in the lobby just in case we want to get crazy. The war has to stop man, we're gonna make it stop.

Brigid, yeah the Negroes are different here too. Oops, we are not allowed to call them Negroes anymore. They are black. Stokely said Negroes is the white man's word. Black is black. Black power. Black is where it's at. Once you go black you never go back. Woowooo black. I have a couple Negro friends from last year and they don't even talk to me now. Some even changed their names. We get together for rallies, but they are more about their own thing than the war. Hell, I'm on their side. We have to end all this shit.

It's going to be a crazy year. I love being here. Your turn Babs, can't wait to hear about Berkeley.

Later,
Rosie

University of California at Berkeley
Stern Hall
September 25, 1969

Dear friends,

Back at Berkeley. Berkeley is still the same, but I am different. My summer meltdown, and the psych therapy that followed, really helped me get my head straight. My parents were very leery about letting me come back here, but I was steadfast in my insistence on returning. This is where I belong. The folks call me every week now, which is fine, it feels good to be connected, and my roommate Chris and I have settled nicely in Stern Hall.

The other day, while trying to cross Telegraph Ave., I zigzagged between protesters who were carrying Ho Chi Minh signs. Ho Chi Minh? Really? I hate the war and I want it to end, but I will never show support for the leader of the army that is killing our guys (love you Martin). Christ, Ho Chi Minh.

Of course, then there's Ronald Reagan, who pretty much thinks everyone on campus is a degenerate anti-American communist (well, maybe he's right about the Ho Chi Minh supporters...), but his attitude is as harmful as the rioters. Rosie, you once said that you were stuck in the middle between the beasts and the angels. I think right now, there are no angels, only beasts. Far right, far left, "and never the twain shall meet." My papa says we are in the middle of an epic battle for the soul of mankind. The moon landing represents our ascent to heaven; the sex and drugs and war represent our descent to hell. Which side are we going to end up on girls?

This summer, after you girls left the Cape, I became friends with some guy from Princeton who was staying at Cape Cod for the summer, and we ended up going see a few movies together. True Grit, Midnight Cowboy, Easy Rider, and The Love Bug. Talk about a schizophrenic society. Traditional heroes and pot smoking heroes, country cowboys and New York cowboys and a thinking Volkswagen. Such is the way of our world; no wonder I got screwed up.

I love hearing your Woodstock stories. I have talked to one girl who was there, but many here are poo pooing the event, saying that the Monterey Festival started it all and the performances there were better. West Coast trumps East Coast every time, so they say. One West Coast trend I have embraced is the no bra fashion. Well, I guess it's a political statement, but I have burned my bra because I hate wearing it. Out here, I don't even get a second look. Some girls wear no bra and no shirts!

My focus here is going to be academic, going to take a spectator view of the protests and social activism, (even though just being on campus places me smack in the middle of history). My father pulled some strings and got me a job in the Physics Dept. Christ, I am breathing the same air as some of the greatest minds in the world. The other day I went to a lecture by Louis Alvarez, who just happened to win the Nobel Prize in Physics last year. He spoke of a variety of topics ranging from radiation and particles in the formation of the universe, to hidden chambers in King Tut's tomb. Kinda makes the rest of the world look small.

By the way, Brigid, the lunar astronauts are going to be at Marquette in November, receiving some University award. Do you want tickets? Let me know. I still can't believe Neil Armstrong had dinner at my house when I was a little girl.

Also Brigid, you mentioned our faith and my "miracle legs." I still do have a deep faith in God and I do believe the healing of my legs was from a spiritual source morphing into physical energy. I am just not too keen on Catholicism. Anyhow, I have started running again. Chris and I run on the beach every morning and it is wonderful. For the record, I do wear a bra when I run.

Rosie, there are gas masks and acid aplenty out here. But be careful, I have seen people lose themselves in both the masks and the pills.

Well, thank you dear friends for keeping up this letter writing. It is good therapy and I treasure your words.

Babs

Marquette University
Cobeen Hall
October 5,1969

Dear Rosie and Babs,

Babs, of course I would love to have tickets to meet the astronauts! Thank you so much. They will be here in early November to receive the Père Marquette Award. A bunch of friends and I are going to Chicago for a wedding that weekend, but I will come back early to see them. There's such a struggle going on between the new wave of thought that pretty much condemns everything America does and the 'my country right or wrong' group who think it's treasonous to say anything bad about our country. And here I am in the middle.

We had a 'guest' in our Theology class last week, one of the Milwaukee 14, a group who broke into a federal draft office and set fire to thousands of draft cards. Our Theology teacher treated this guy like he was a saint; I thought he was going to bow down in front of him. But the man himself, I must say, was pretty cool. Very low key and humble. There's a group of protesters that do this type of thing; break into draft board offices and burn as many cards as they can. They don't run away, they hang around the fire and sing and wait to be arrested. Very Thoreauesque. He said their goal is to cause enough disarray to prevent at least some guys from being drafted. Of all the radicals I have come across, I like this guy the best. Interestingly, our professor told us that most of the people involved in this activity are Catholic. Then he went off on Jesus being a revolutionary and we all should be burning things. Anyhow, it was an interesting perspective.

A couple nights ago a large group of kids and some faculty members marched around the ROTC building (the old gym), and the admin building, first chanting something about not teaching war tactics on campus, then they switched to 'student power' and ended with 'fire Raynor' (the president of MU). Such is our campus's weak contribution to the revolution. Some of my friends joined in just to be a part of it all. Personally, I went and got a meatball sub at Antonio's Pizza with a cute guy from my French class. We ended up at the Ardmore bar, and had a nice romantic evening and watched the evening news report about the unrest on Marquette's campus. They interviewed two SDS kids, neither of whom attend Marquette.

Sometime this month though, there is going to be a peace march, just a way to express a desire for a moratorium on war, all war. I shall participate in that one, in honor of Martin.

My English class is British Literature, oh sweet mother I love this stuff. Started with Anglo-Saxon poetry, then Beowulf, and now Canterbury Tales. Such is the stuff man is made of. Desiring immortality, bemoaning transience, satirizing the wrongs of our faith and government -- hundreds of years and nothing has changed. We all connect.

My Philosophy class, on the other hand, which is supposed to be teaching me logic, is blowing my mind. Some of it connects to Aristotle's rhetorical concepts, but the statements versus propositions, deductive versus inductive, form versus content, good Lord, I may go mad.

Will see you next month at Thanksgiving I hope. Keep running, Babs -- and stop tripping, Rosie.

xoxoxo Brigid

Ohio State University
West Baker Hall
Oct. 15, 1969

It's 2:00 a.m. Just got home from a day of yelling and throwing things. But all in all it was pretty mild. I got in a fight with some girl in the dorm who said people like me were giving OSU a bad name that everyone here isn't a protesting anti american commie. She is a straight bookworm who loves Shakespeare, wears miniskirts and thinks she's cool cuz she drinks beer and oh wait, I just described Brigid! hahahahahhaah Anyhow, some ROTC kid punched one of the guys who was burning the flag and the ROTC kid saved the flag. Big hero on campus now with the country right or wrong group.

I think I'm failing in my classes. Missed a lot. Some days my friends and me just play some music and trip. The other day it took me a very long time to come down and I felt the worse I have ever felt. Took some speed the next day to get my energy up and ran around like a train. My roommate kicked me out because I wouldn't shut up. Hahahahah Did you know alot of the big time movie stars tripped. It was legal. So cool.

Heading home for the weekend, hope to intercept the first quarter grades that they send to my parents. Amir still refuses to answer my calls. Boohoo.

Babs glad you are running again, you should pop a bennie and see how fast you can really go.

Later,

Rosie

University of California at Berkeley
Stern Hall
October 25, 1969

Dear friends,

My, you girls have interesting lives. Marquette sounds like the sanest campus around, so happy for you Brigid that you are intellectually and socially stimulated. You are going to be fine girl.

Rosie Rosie Rosie, I would never put that poison into my body. I did marijuana a couple times but I'm done with it. Seriously I'm easy, I can get high just listening to the Beatles' albums. Maybe because they were high when they made the albums haha. Brigid and I have said it before Rosie, you're going to fry your brains with that stuff; you need to take it easy. How is your Animal Behavior class coming along?

It's funny about the girl with the mini skirt; Reagan was right about one thing, the protesters certainly don't represent everyone on campus. There's a lot of nappy blue jeans and long hair, but also a lot of natty slacks and bouffant hair dos.

Our October 15 Peace Moratorium was pretty much washed out by a heavy rain all day, although the campus did manage to periodically attract hundreds of peaceniks.

But really, my life is now being consumed by Science and Astronomy and Physics. My parents' connections have literally opened a cosmos of physical and astrophysical doors for me. The Berkeley Science labs are on the cutting edge of space exploration, search for extraterrestrial life and intelligence. They have been very involved in designing and constructing radiometers and probes that were used to measure energy emitted from Mars, among other things. And here's me, sitting in lectures with these people, and once in a while even working out an equation. When I talk to my mom, we no longer discuss my breakdown, but rather the thermophysical properties of Martian terrain. Next semester, I will be permitted to observe and perhaps have an internship with researchers who are studying the evolution of molecular clouds and star formation. I can't decide which area of study I want to dive into. The choices are truly infinite. I'll see where my Math brain leads me. It does seem inevitable that NASA is in my future.

So you see, things like the war and the protests, and the human folly that surround me, matter less and less. The universe doesn't disappoint. And as much as I miss Martin, I am beginning to feel that destinies of the mind can diminish the desires of the body.

I am going out for a run. Not sure what we are doing for Thanksgiving yet, but hope to see you both next month.

Babs

Marquette University
Cobeen Hall
November 5,1969

Rosie and Babs,

Babs, your last letter reminded me of a favorite scene from Hamlet when he speaks to his friends: "What a piece of work is a man! How noble in reason, how infinite in faculty! In form and moving how express and admirable! In action how like an Angel! in apprehension how like a god!

The beauty of the world! The paragon of animals! And yet to me, what is this quintessence of dust? Man delights not me ..."

You seek the wonders of the human mind but man himself does not interest you. It is so fascinating to hear what does interest you. But I fear Martin's death still wounds your spirit more than you admit. I am all about the spirit these days. And it appears that Rosie is all about the body haha. Mind, body, and spirit -- together we are indeed the paragon of animals. That is if one believes the whole man is an animal philosophy.

I did participate in the October peace march; it was an unorganized jaunt down Wisconsin Avenue to the war memorial and back. We followed like sheep and sang 'Give Peace a Chance' at least a million times. My psychology professor called us 'pseudo activists.' Of course he also said that people who read while on the toilet are selfish, because psychologically they won't give anything out if they are not taking anything in. Seriously, he said that, I am not joking. And he's a world renowned psychologist. So, according to his logic, I am a selfish, pseudo activist. I can live with that for now, not going to argue psychology with that guy; I need the A.

My roommate, our fearless President of Student Council '68, Ellen, went to Madison with some friends for the peace march. She came back a different person, saying that thousands and thousands of people marched, and that Madison is filled with socialists and communists and anarchists. She actually loved it, but was glad to leave. Ironically, she said that the peace protesters were so violent it scared her. I am going to have to check it out -- can't be that close to such an amazing atmosphere and not experience it.

On a more traditional note, the astronauts were unbelievably cool. The dichotomy of our age was evident. One week kids are protesting the government; the next week kids are welcoming government heroes. Long haired, spacey radicals and short haired, space travelers; what a world we live in. Anyway, Babs, please thank your father for the VIP tickets. I got to be in the reception line and shake their hands! When I told Mr. Armstrong that I was Mr. Turyev's daughter's friend, he almost shook my arm off. 'Wonderful man, brilliant man' he repeated twice. I felt very lucky to know you and your family.

I spoke with my mom this week. It was all about King John, Michele's precious baby. It was actually nice to hear about family life. Easy to forget that people are leading normal lives. Student life is a different reality. I think I could be a student forever.

Although English is by far my most enjoyable class, this modern theological approach to the study of the bible messes with my brain the most. The professor has finally gotten off the civil disobedience kick and we are now reading Schillebeeckx (yeah and we have to know how to spell it). Amazing interpretations of Jesus and the Resurrection and of the various ways the gospel writers viewed Jesus. Makes me question everything...again. But I guess it doesn't make me question my faith, it makes me question what we've been taught.

What I hate is the smugness of the prof. He scoffs at the students who question the interpretations. Liberal scholars are allowed to question traditional thinking; traditional thinkers are not allowed to question the liberal scholars. I find myself on the same theological and intellectual plane of the liberal thinkers, but not on their plane of elitist condescension. God, will I ever be released from this middle quagmire of existence?

Ha, laughing at myself. I never express these opinions in class, I don't feel smart enough. I love writing these letters, very cathartic. And I know of course that you two loveys will never make fun of me. Right Rosie?

I hope we get to see each other back in Cleveland over Thanksgiving break. Rosie, I'm dying to know if you escaped Mama Rose's wrath about your midterm grades.

xoxoxo Brigid

Ohio State University
West Baker Hall
Nov.15, 1969

Yeah, I am screwed. I got home last month, just as my mother was opening the mail. First quarter grades, all Fs and a C in Animal Behavior. I came in and she was sitting at the kitchen table. She studied the paper *and then looked up and studied my face. I expected a blow out, but it was worse, she cried. She stared at me and cried. I stared back, just wishing I was high. "I can explain, ma" I said. She lifted her arm and shook her hand, silently telling me to shut up, she didn't want to hear anything I had to say. The report also showed attendance. I only went to class ten times in two months. I found out later that's what threw her over the edge. No way I could blame the classes for being too hard or the teachers for being unfair. I thought I could lie and tell her I was sick, becuz I did in fact lose a lot of weight. But then I was afraid I would have to go to the doctors and maybe they would take blood and all the drugs and shit would show up. I thought maybe I could tell her I've been depressed about Martin and Amir and just couldn't bring myself to go to class. But I know my mother. I know her face. No excuse would work. I hugged her and told her I promised to shape up and by the end of the semester, I would be passing. I only stayed home for a night, had a family dinner, stayed clean, and we both pretended everything was normal. She didn't tell my father or anyone else. When I left, she drove me to the bus station. She said, "I don't know what the hell is going on with you but you are old enough to fix it yourself. If your attendance and grades don't get better by January, your ass will be working at the store, and if you want a college education you will pay for it yourself." She slipped $100.00 in my palm and told me to buy the damn books for the classes. I kissed her cheek, said good-bye and went back.*

The first thing I did back at campus was use the money to buy some speed. If I am going to be studying, I need to be on high alert. On Monday I went to see all of my teachers and their Teacher Assistants, ya know, the TAs. Not sure how it's all going to work out, but my English TA is a grad student and I heard he was really cool. When I asked him what I need to do to pass the class, he told me to start by unbuttoning my blouse.

I will pass English.

Before I go home next week, I am going to ask all the TAs to sign an attendance sheet for me. They laughed when I asked and made me feel like a junior high shmuck, but at least I can show my mother I am trying. The fact is though that I realized I still don't like being in a classroom. Not sure where I am headed. Hope to see you guys over Thanksgiving.

Later,

Rosie

University of California at Berkeley
Stern Hall
November 20, 1969

Dear friends,

I will be in Florida for Thanksgiving. So sorry that I won't see you two, but we will be in Shaker for Christmas, so Rosie, get your act together so Mama Rose will be in a good mood at the annual bash at your house.

Just so you know Rosie, plenty of kids go through what you are going through. I am begging you not to let yourself burn out. You're at a junction and you have to choose to go the right way. Think of how many animals you can save and how many more doors will be open to you if you have a college degree from Ohio State.

Brigid, use some of your magic religious spiel to talk some sense to Rosie. And don't forget to give her a hug.

I'll be thinking of you two gals while I'm watching the Macy's Day Parade on TV. Happy Thanksgiving.

Babs

Marquette University
Cobeen Hall
December 5,1969

Dear Rosie and Babs,

Such an interesting Thanksgiving break. Rosie, I'm glad we got to spend at least a few hours together. It was great seeing your family, your mom and dad always make me feel good. So sorry about your Buckeyes.

What a loss. I'm thinking no one will be taking vacations to Michigan any time soon.

It was also sweet to be at home with my sisters and mom and dad -- even though I am glad to be back here. I didn't tell my parents much about my classes or college life in general. They are satisfied with my As and "normal" appearance.

Well, here's the big news -- actually life changing for me. Ellen Bodnar got engaged. She had been telling me about this guy she met last summer and she has decided that she wants to get married and finish school in her spare time. I met the guy, really cute and they are a cute couple. But jeeez, cute doesn't make a marriage, does it?

So Ellen told me about the engagement and then she arranged for a bunch of our old classmates to go to dinner on Saturday. She still has that old President of Student Council persona -- big organizer. It was really fun seeing everyone. Jeannette Ward is married and pregnant; Paula married Larry Vargo, her high school boyfriend; Sue and Barb are at Ursuline College; and get this -- Carol is on her way to Hollywood to be a Golddigger on the Dean Martin Show! Looks like her dream of making it in the entertainment business is on its way to being real. Barb and Jane work at the phone company and Mac and Betsy are at Bowling Green, Chris is at Kent. That was the group. I was the only one there who went to an out of state school -- but everyone seemed to be following their hearts and brains. It was nice. We didn't talk too much about college or classes. Mostly it was girl talk about gossip, guys, music, and stuff that we used to chat about at the lunch table. The St. Charles girls talked a lot about Martin-- re inflaming the pain. They all said to say hi to you Babs. Rosie can tell her version of the gathering in her letter. It was fun.

Back to Ellen--she is leaving Marquette at semester. That leaves me without a roommate and without a friend here who shares my roots. Not sure what's going to happen with that.

For the next couple weeks, I am working on three major papers as well as studying for finals. For theology, the topic is, Exegetical Eschatology -- yeah, I just said that to compete with your molecular cloud evolution Babs hahaha. My other paper is for English. It's research on the relationship between Ezra Pound and William Butler Yeats. This will be a joy. Yes, I am in full egghead mode. The final paper is actually a speech for my Communications class. I have to take a stand on whether or not desegregation of schools by bussing kids from one neighborhood to another is a good idea. I have become good friends with a couple kids from Boston, and I am thinking these bussing plans are not going to go well.

Things on campus are relatively quiet. Basketball season has started, snow is falling, and end of semester studying have taken center stage. I am going to the High Ball winter semi-formal with my French class cutie.

See you two in a couple weeks!

xoxoxo Brigid

*

By December 20, the three girls were home from school, and on December 22, the Vanettis hosted the annual Christmas party for the three families. Moon landings, hippies, grandchildren, and the Browns dominated the conversations. There was the annual mini-pilgrimage to Ricky's statue, as well as a special salute to Martin. Father Templeton, the priest who baptized Babs and aided the Turyevs through Babs's illness and healing, also passed away that year. A bit of somber reminiscing entailed, but was quickly replaced by the living voices of the present. Richard's firsthand experience with the NASA accomplishments fascinated the group. This was the first gathering that the men and women and oldest daughters remained in the same room together. What had been fragmented conversations in previous years, now merged into trans gender, trans generational discussions. Miklos led the discussion of what was going on at college campuses, parroting fire house gossip about "long-haired freaks," and "unruly Negroes." Her father's derogatory Negro comments always surprised Brigid. MV steered clear of the college campus talk, but did defend the protest tactics of the Negroes. "I do not encourage violence, but I understand that when voices have been ignored for so long, people feel that just talking is no longer an option."

The discussion was lively and respectful, and culminated in a hopeful, boisterous rant regarding the expectation that the Browns would win the NFL championship. (Two weeks later, the Browns lost.)

Marquette University
Cobeen Hall
January 6,1970

Dear Babs and Rosie,

Wow, it's weird to type 1970 as today's date. 1970, the year we turn 20, yikes, when did this happen?

Rosie, we all really appreciate your folks hosting us every Christmas. It's such a nice holiday tradition and it's fun to see our parents sharing and enjoying each other's company. In psychology class, we learned how important it is to kindle friendships as we grow older. The professor stressed male bonding, of course, but when I see our moms together, I realize how deeply women need to be there for each other and give an ear and a heart. Amazing to me how little attention females receive in the medical studies.

I'm sorry we didn't get to spend New Year's together. Ellen and her guy, and Bill and I, enjoyed a nice dinner at the Brown Derby and then celebrated at Public Square, but I did miss you two that night. It was also very strange and sad saying goodbye to Ellen and even stranger coming back to the dorm and having all of her stuff out of the room. Marquette hasn't assigned me another roommate yet. Everything just feels different.

Well, one thing that isn't different, is that this is a basketball campus! The Warriors are 8 and 1 and looking great. I love going to the games -- such a nice escape from the rest of the world. Ring out ahoya! (That's part of our pep song, but no one I can find, actually knows what ahoya is.)

So, classes are starting for second semester of our sophomore year. My second semester classes are continuances of first semester, except for psych which will now have a bigger focus on educational psychology. Philosophy will be much better as we study human nature and man's search for meaning.

That, plus my liberal theology class, should lead to some serious head games. At least it keeps me on the ascension from the middle state. Of course the class I am salivating with is Shakespeare. Assignment #1 is the role of the supernatural in Julius Caesar and Hamlet. I am in heaven.

I have completed my Math requirements (sorry Babs but I am so happy to be done with it), and rounding out my schedule with French III, and Speech.

I had a date the other night and went to see Love Story. Kinda sappy, but everyone else seemed to really like it. I also saw M.A.S.H. with some friends -- much more of a bite, but I'm uncomfortable with all the sex in movies these days. It's just such a private thing -- seeing it on a big screen seems to degrade the act. Oh Lord, I can see Rosie rolling her eyes as she reads this.

Gotta go. xoxoxo Brigid

Ohio State University
West Baker Hall
January 15, 1970

Yeah, 1970 totally freaks me out. It just seems like being in school is such a wasteful way to spend our time. I managed to pass English, Animal Behavior, and Speech the first two quarters, but I flunked Math, History, and Spanish. I am able to move on in the ones I passed but am retaking the other three. Planning on going to summer school so I can return as a junior, but right now not sure what to do. I love being on campus, but I hate school. Just don't know what to do. And yeah, I am still getting high and yeah I am doing other things that would make you cringe, but I am feeling so free. But I must admit, feeling aimless at the same time. Free and aimless, is that a good combination?

I like our Christmas tradition too. Warm and fuzzy. I followed it with a trip to New York with some of my Buckeye friends. We drove to Times Square New Year's Eve. One of my friends has a pad in Brooklyn and we crashed there and took a subway to the craziness. Not warm, and a different kind of fuzzy. So much fun, from what I remember hahaha.

The football fanatics are still in shock about our loss to Michigan in November. Damn they take it seriously.

The protests here are growing stronger. Governor Rhodes announced a kind of a get tough policy, so even the peaceful rallies are being monitored and controlled by police and National Guard. And I think Nixon is the most hated man in the world. Now, what would I rather be doing, throwing bricks at the Admin. building or learning about Darius and the Persian Empire?

The black kids are more pissed than the anti war kids. They're saying that there are less than 1,000 Negroes enrolled at OSU and the total number of students is like 37,000. Something isn't right. And there are some restaurants that still don't serve Negroes, I'm not kidding. Last week, someone painted KKK on one of the black student's dorm door. No wonder they're mad. Their group is about to pop any minute, and as far as I have heard, the admin isn't doing much to help the situation. Babs, the SDS guys talk about Berkeley all the time but say OSU is also a hotbed for social revolution. Yay for us. Sorry, Brigid, no one talks about Marquette, so you just keep your sexual hang ups and theology classes in Milwaukee haha. Off to class, really.

Later,

Rosie

University of California at Berkeley
Stern Hall
January 20, 1970

Dear friends,

Yes, it was odd typing 1970 as the year. Hadn't thought too much about it until I wrote it. Just think, we've been friends for almost six years. Pretty cool.

Sounds like you gals had a fun new year's celebration. I wanted to call you before I came back, but I was completely buried in family. It was nice to be back in Shaker. Something about sleeping in my old room and my old bed that was very comforting. I spent some time with my old friend Karen Grovac. She is transferring to Kent State this semester.

My New Year's Eve consisted of hanging around with my family. We had dinner with some of my father's old NASA friends from the Cleveland facility, and then came back to our house and watched the ball drop. David and I caught up a little bit. He is so smart. He is eight years old, and discussing jet propulsion. My mother has kept him very Catholic and he is very devoted to the faith. They still go to confession every week. I didn't go to confession, but I have to say, even though I am not nearly as religious as I used to be, Midnight Mass on Christmas Eve still moves my soul, and the Eucharist still gives me a temporary connection of spiritual empowerment.

My father told me that he is retiring this year. He will be seventy in April, and he does look tired. Apparently we are rich, so no one is worried about money. He wants to take the family to Germany next summer; I am looking forward to that. My mom said she is going to continue her research project regarding the Martian atmosphere, and they both agreed that they will be leaving Florida and moving back to Shaker permanently. It's hard on David moving around, but he seems adjusted. We will keep the Cape Cod property and hopefully you two can visit again next year.

So that was my very unexciting but restful Christmas break. The folks seem satisfied that I am no longer on the edge of the abyss. As for me, I am rather astonished that I was content to remain at home and just relax. Didn't even have a date.

But here I am back at Berkeley where things continue to simmer. Rosie, you mentioned the black protests and yes, they are ever present here and in California as a whole. UCLA fired Angela Davis, a black power activist and communist. That is not setting well with the free speech and black movements. Reagan and Nixon continue to antagonize just about everyone on campus, and in general there are protests, arrests, and mini riots on campus every week. You just can't be around this stuff and not feel the vibes that things are changing, and that we are part of an historical evolution in our culture. It's not even specific causes that I get caught up in, it's the tide of human aspirations that carries me away and I just have to once in a while sit and join in on a chorus of "We Shall Overcome."

Classes have begun for second semester and I am continuing my work in the Physics Department. One of our Physics Professors received a Guggenheim Fellowship for his work in 'concepts of pulsed coherent quantum phenomena' (there you go Brigid), and I have the supreme luck of having the opportunity to be a lab assistant. A very lowly lab assistant, but still there. I cannot even begin to explain or even fully comprehend this professor's theories and findings, but I have looked at some of the mathematics and am astounded at the implications this research can yield for the study of quantum physics and in particular, medicine technology. In addition to my emotional "We Shall Overcome" moments, the startling leaps in knowledge going on in science leave me teetering on the edge of the intellectual cosmos. I think Berkeley is truly an epicenter of an intellectual and emotional universe.

I'm continuing my classes in Stellar Atmospheres, Quantum Physics, Mathematics, Astronomy, Latin, and Linguistics. Completed my History requirements. Rosie, think really hard before you give up on school. Read through the course description book at OSU. Do you really want to give all that up? So many opportunities. Lay off the pills and come back to us girl.

Brigid, you will love that tonight my roommate is dragging me to a lecture, as described in the course description book, 'The interrelationship of language, thought, and civilization.' So, if I sit through this, you have to go to a Math lecture!

We won't be seeing each other for a few months; keep the letters coming. Hang in there.

Babs

Marquette University
Cobeen Hall
February 6,1970

Dear Rosie and Babs,

Your dad is retiring Babs? I forget he is a lot older than my folks. He certainly deserves a break. Going to Germany sounds fabulous, can't wait to hear more about it.

I have started playing my saxophone again. Why, you ask? Because my

Shakespeare class has reawakened in me the connection between my love of music and my love of literature. First of all, this professor is amazing. He allows the students to choose the part of Shakespeare's genius that interests them the most. Somewhere in my memory box I have a list of things that make a good teacher -- I have to add this one for sure -- in classical literature, let the students choose what touches them. Well, anyhow, the prof casually mentioned that Duke Ellington wrote a suite pertaining to themes and characters in several of Shakespeare's plays. No, I said. I would have surely known about this. But I didn't know, and he surely did compose it. And so I found a recording of Ellington's work. It's called 'Such Sweet Thunder,' and it relates to twelve of Shakespeare's plays. And I know Rosie is dying to know more information, but all I will tell you is that it made me miss my music, so I have begun playing the sax again and have found a couple people who might be interested in forming a group. I am so excited. This is what a liberal arts education should do, make a connection among the disciplines and encourage students to explore those connections in a way that enriches and expands their knowledge of themselves and their worlds and other worlds. Don't need a pill for this high. This is what I want to do as a teacher.

Sorry to bore you with all this, but it's so cool for me to write these letters and be able to express myself, because even if you're bored, you will love me anyhow. Everything else here is going great. Lots of parties and fun stuff as well as intense studying and work. Here we go again -- the lowly functions of the animal -- eat, sleep, and drink -- versus the lofty aspirations of the divine -- love, learn, and create.

Basketball team is 12 and 2 and we are ranked in the top 10. Now that's what college is all about haha.

xoxoxo Brigid

Ohio State University
West Baker Hall
February 15, 1970

Happy Valentines Day. None of us have a Valentine, do we? Boohoo poor us. But I do have a valentine but it's not red. Sometimes it's a purple haze and sometimes it's mellow yellow hahahahaha.

Brigid I do want to know more about your jazz and Shakespeare shit. I really do. You guys should know that I always admired your school successes. I was always jealous a little but I always like hearing about your damn corny study topics. Here's the thing man, I am not like youz I never have been. I do not like school I have to come to grips with that and mama has to come to grips with that and that's that hahaha. I am trying really really hard to pass my classes but even if I do, I don't think I can come back. Don't get me wrong, the gas masks and the marching and the screaming against the pigs and the war and the racist admins is totally cool. I am all about it. And it's so easy to score I'm like in heaven. I think of my baby brother Ricky and Martin all the time. You know about Ricky he slipped from my arms and died. Dead. Smashed. And Martin slipped from my life. Dead. Smashed.

I cannot drag my ass to class. Ass to class ass to class ass to class hahahahaha. Yep. Bah, i mean bye.

Rosie

University of California at Berkeley
Stern Hall
February 20, 1970

Dear friends,

I am buried in studies. My new schedule is grueling and rather mind blowing. In between dodging rocks from protesters and tear gas from the National Guard, I am entombed in Mathematics. My work in the Physics lab is proving to be rather humbling. The physics component of coherent quantum phenomena is way over my head and I have never felt like that before. But the Math department is bursting with enrollment. Berkeley Physics and Math are gaining national recognition, despite Reagan's confrontational approach to anything we do, and I must say it's damn cool to be a part of it all. I have to make a final decision at the end of this semester as to what my specific major is going to be. Math is my love but theoretical physics is so damn interesting. Sometimes I love being an egghead. I've found a guy here who digs my eggheadedness (good word, yes Brigid?). He's kind of like Martin; I can talk about anything and he listens and seems to value my opinion. Not many guys around who value a girl's opinion. Anyhow, the other night, the northern lights were slightly visible and we drove up to Grizzly Peak. Instead of wanting to neck, he wanted to talk about what we are learning about the sun and how it interacts with our earthly magnetic field. NASA is going to be sending up some kind of space lab in the next few years to study these things up close. In the mountains or looking through the telescope, you can't help feeling the magnificence of creation and realizing how damn stupid the war and the prejudices of humanity are. We are part of something so wondrous and yet we insist on dwelling in hatred. So anyhow, we gazed at the lights and the stars and became one with the universe ... and then we necked.

Rosie Rosie Rosie. You don't sound good at all. There's plenty of kids here who sound just like you. OSU isn't all that different from Berkeley, except that California is just way ahead of Ohio on the cool meter haha. You need to get a grip and I don't mean by swallowing a pill. I've seen kids here overdose on everything from dex to heroin. At best they drop a lot of acid and end up dropping out of school. I'm not going to mother you, I'm just warning you to be careful with what you're putting in your system. It will catch up with you sooner or later. As far as school goes, I guess you have to follow your heart when your brain isn't happy. Does that make sense? Ha maybe I do need a pill (just joking). Anyway, try to get through this year without hurting yourself, physically or intellectually. Think of the animals.

Speaking of animals, I have managed to have fun with the guys in Bowles Dorm. Stern and Bowles do a lot of social and community things together and it's a fun, nice break from the rest of the world.

Brigid, how cool that you are playing your sax again. Some of my egghead friends argue about jazz, how rock n roll has destroyed it. I have no idea what they are talking about because we never learned one thing about jazz in our grand liberal arts education so far have we? Brigid, you need to take Duke's and Shakespeare's 'Sweet Thunder' and run with it. Till then, I'm going to listen to some Creedence Clearwater Revival and Jackson 5.

I still run on the shore. Study, sky watch, dodge rocks and tear gas, listen to music, and occasionally neck, then study some more ... yep, I'm feelin it. Take care.

Babs

Marquette University
Cobeen Hall
March 6,1970

Dear Rosie and Babs,

So we are on the eve of destruction, but here at Marquette it is all about basketball !!!!! Our fearless leader, Coach McGuire, pretty much told the NCAA to go screw itself. He didn't like the Warrior placement (or whatever) in the NCAA tournament, so he said screw it we're taking the team to the NIT. Gotta love this guy. There's a theater here on campus and they are showing the movie 'A Man For All Seasons.' Our English Prof. assigned us to see it and write a comparative essay between Sir Thomas More and Al McGuire. What a great assignment. A modern day man of integrity and a fifteenth-century man of integrity, both obeying their own conscience. Very cool. They are both Catholic too haha.

There's still a smattering of protests on campus, but nothing disruptive. When I go to work downtown, I see more of it, especially the black rallies, but most people just see it all as a nuisance. I did finally get to talk with a girl in my English class who is black and we are becoming friends. Her name is Cheryl. I asked her what it's all about. She said, "I feel like I am waking up from a long sleep. As a people we are finally talking about our history. Our history in America and the history that was stolen from us when the slave trade took us from Africa. We're finally talking about it and it's pissing us off.'

You mentioned jazz Babs. Cheryl was sharing with me some of the history of Congo Square in New Orleans where slaves used to gather on Sundays to socialize, sing, dance, play music and basically hold on to their culture. This is the kind of thing the black students want included in school curriculum. I promised Cheryl that my students would learn it. I am starting to get it now. I still don't like ignorant, violent protests from any one, but Cheryl knows what's up and I am looking forward to hearing more.

The dorm still hasn't assigned me a new roommate, I miss Ellen. I have to start thinking about next year's arrangements. All of my friends are getting houses or apartments. I'm not sure what I want to do yet.

There's a coffee shop on Wells Street where I jam with my little music group. Soothes my soul. Thanks for your support Babs.

Rosie, it was great to talk to you. I just had to call you after your last letter. Hearing your voice put my mind at ease (even though it cost me five bucks!) I can't wait to see you over Easter break.

Lots to do. See you soon.

xoxoxo Brigid

Ohio State University
West Baker Hall
March 15, 1970

Things are poppin here and I don't mean pills. Everybody who is pissed at something is on the Oval everyday. The war, women's rights (I still have to get permission from my parents to be out after 10:30) The black kids are more pissed than anyone. They had a march at the admin building the other day and a couple were arrested. This did not sit well with the brothers. The whole place is tense. Easter break can't come soon enough for the administration.

Nice talking to you too Brigid, great.

I am in charge of gas masks. Not much time to write. Hope to see you in a few weeks.

Rosie

University of California at Berkeley
Stern Hall
March 25, 1970

Dear friends,

I am sending this to your home addresses because I assume you are there for Easter break. Happy Easter! May the peace of the Risen Lord be with you. Good God, remember when we used to say that everyday in religion class?

Sorry I am not joining you in Cleveland this year. As you already know, my parents and David came out here to spend the break with me and although I miss seeing you two ne'er do wells, I have to say it's great to have my family out here on the beautiful west coast. We rented a beach house about six hours from campus in a place called Seal Beach. It's just us and the land, air, and sea and it feels wonderful. Next week we are heading back to Berkeley where the NASA people are having a retirement dinner for my father and my mom is giving a lecture on the Martian atmosphere.

NASA is sending up another moon mission next month, and from here, dad is going to Mission control in Houston and my mom and David are heading back to Shaker. This will be my father's last mission. He looks old. Seventy is old. I am enjoying my time with him. He is still my life's beacon to a higher calling. He and my mother are still very naive when it comes to what is going on at campus. Ivory towers built on moon rocks have provided them with a life of celestial wonders and domestic stability. They accept the earth shattering changes in science, but have no idea as to the significant cultural changes that are being planted right on the doorsteps of their ivory towers. Their presence gives me peace; I don't think many kids my age can say that these days. Ha! I say kids. We are going to be twenty years old in a couple months. Holy hell.

I am hoping to be in Shaker for most of the summer; I may be taking a Math class at Case Western, we'll have to see.

Word on the street is that all hell is going to break loose on campus in

April. I may just camp out in the Math building or the observatory. Happy Easter girls, see you soon.
Babs

Marquette University
Cobeen Hall
April 10,1970

Dear Rosie and Babs,

Easter break was very interesting. Rosie and I went to dinner on Wednesday with some Lourdes classmates -- kinda interesting to see how the outside world hasn't crept into their lives too much. Not much talk of the war or protests. I guess if things don't affect you personally, you just ignore them. Ellen Bodnar is getting married in August. She has gone from a feminist leader to a can't wait to learn how to cook fiancée. She said the feminists are diminishing the role of housewife and she is looking forward to finding fulfillment as a wife and mother. Couldn't stop talking about it actually. I think a true feminist makes room for all choices -- mothers, spouses, careers -- the key is to choose with love. Anyhow, she seems genuinely happy. What a difference a year makes. My sister Michele is also happy. Her baby has given her meaning and self respect and her husband seems to be respectful and hardworking and faithful. She earned her high school diploma at night school. They are so young.

It's so nice that you are enjoying your parents Babs. I am having a bit of a problem with mine. It seems like they are stuck in the 1950s. My mom actually told me that she expects me to come home after graduation, live at home, and help with the bills and the kids. There's no recognition of how I am doing at school or what my personal goals are. I feel like a stranger. We went to Mass as a family, which was nice -- but the priest's sermon was about supporting Nixon - my country right or wrong -- blah blah. I love my country and I hate the crazy protests that get more violent by the moment -- but Nixon? Uh uh.

A young man whom I have known since childhood stopped by to see the family. He has just returned from a Peace Corps assignment in India. The stories of poverty and strife were overwhelming to me. But what I loved was his idealism -- even after being exposed to a part of the world so different than ours. He has me reconsidering my post graduation plans.

Things are quiet here on campus. Small groups are trying to inspire, instigate, whatever you want to call it, but the Marquette Warriors are rather complacent protesters. In Ohio, the kids pretty much despise Governor Rhodes, but Senator Gaylord Nelson here in Wisconsin opposes the war and has at least listened to some of the causes that are being espoused on campuses. He is spearheading an Earth Day later this month to bring awareness to pollution and other things that are damaging our planet. I think it's going to be cool.

Starting to study for finals. And I have made what I know you both will consider to be an egghead decision. I've decided to live in this dorm again next year, in a single room. I may be the only upperclassman in the whole building haha, but I really don't think I'd like living in the same house with a bunch of girls (had enough of that at home), and I dread the thought of shopping for food and cooking and all that. They are eliminating curfews next year so I will be able to come and go as I please, and I feel safe here. So that's that -- go ahead and make fun of me.

Babs, I will be watching that moon launch and be thinking of you. Rosie -- great to see you and hoping you come down before our next visit.

xoxoxo Brigid

Ohio State University
West Baker Hall
April 21, 1970

Whoa whoa and whoa. shit going down here. Brigid, I know you don't like violent confrontation, but guess what man, it's a rev o lu tion. We asked the admin for Black studies and women's studies classes and we asked for the military to get the hell off campus, we got nothin. When talking doesn't work, we have to turn to something else. Bricks, molotovs, whatever gets their attention. A lot of kids walked out of their classes yesterday and I think there will be more of that. We have thousands marching now, it's us agains the pigs. National Guard, tear gas, I think even some bullets, man it's like a war zone. Full scale riot. The large majority of the students don't get involved, but those that do are rowdy and determined. One of my friends just put lawn chairs on the flat roof of her apartment building and had a ring side seat to all of the action. Others just avoided the melee and managed to get to classes. Crazy.

When I was home over break, Mama Rose said she would come and get me if I ever did anything disrespectful to a police officer or a soldier. Oops sorry mama.

There are a lot of plans for the rest of the month. It's very exciting and I am either tripping or floating through the whole show. Not sure how classes are going to fit into all this.

Easter break was fun, we missed you Babs. The ol Lourdes girls are looking good. Miss Hollywood Golddigger getting ready to go to Viet Nam with Bob Hope to entertain the troops. Hooray for Hollywood.

Staying in the dorm when you are twenty. Damn Brigid, that bums me out just thinking about it.

Just a few more weeks of school and throwing bricks. See you two back home next month.

Rosie

University of California at Berkeley
Stern Hall
April 30, 1970

Dear friends,

By now I am sure that your moms have told you that my father had a heart attack. He was in Houston when the Apollo 13 mission went haywire, and the stress took its toll. He had something called bypass surgery where they took a vein from his leg and put it in his heart. I flew to Houston for the surgery. They say he is going to be fine.

Campus and the town here have been taken over by the radical protesters, with thousands of kids just hanging around and watching. Some classes are cancelled and I expect the whole place will shut down soon. National Guard is everywhere, kids throwing rocks and shouting obscenities. I don't know how the Guard guys are restraining themselves. Rosie, I don't feel the excitement that you do at this stuff. I totally support the idea that things have to change, but Christ, how are we different from the people we are revolting against if we behave just as badly as they do? The violence just sickens me and I refuse to call policemen pigs.

Tonight Nixon announced he has been bombing Cambodia. Jesus, these kids are going to go nuts. And in the meantime, we continue to soar upwards with accomplishments in physics and medicine. We are indeed 'The glory, jest, and riddle of the world.'

I have spoken with all of my professors and am exempted from final exams. My grades and my dad's influence have secured permission to get me the hell out of here for the final month. I am going to Houston for the month of May to be with my family. Hopefully I can spend our birthday in Cleveland with you two.

Babs

*

May - September 1970

It was not in the distant, lush swamplands of the Mekong Delta, but on the grassy hills of an Ohio campus, where the Viet Nam War claimed four lives of young Americans. On May 4, 1970, responding to protests and campus fires, members of the Ohio National Guard shot thirteen students at Kent State. Four of those students died. Conflicting stories of the event droned through news accounts and anecdotal broadcasts.

Violent protests on several major college campuses across the United States caused many colleges and universities to cancel classes, some temporarily and some for the remainder of the term. The administration at Marquette University cancelled classes for the term, sending students home. Although the campus had no measure of violent responses, it was feared that the turmoil at nearby University of Wisconsin at Madison would permeate through a volatile environment in Milwaukee. Students ultimately received the grades they had established at midterms. Brigid still maintained a 4.00, A average.

Ohio State closed for two weeks and then finals resumed before summer vacation. Rosie passed English and Animal Behavior, and failed her other classes. Berkeley shut down, not affecting Babs since she had already been excused with a perfect grade point average.

The friends met on June 1, their twentieth birthday. They chose to meet in downtown Cleveland to have dinner at the Pewter Mug. The dinner and conversation shared by the three young women sparkled and simmered with good food and heated discussion. When an appetizer, shrimp cocktail, was served, Rosie pushed the serving away from her and started the chat.

"These shrimp are a food source for other creatures in the sea, you know. We are destroying the oceans with over fishing and dumping, and other atrocities to all life on earth."

"Jeeeeeez," Brigid sputtered, shrimp tail hanging from her lips, "Are we going to start our birthday celebration with anti-establishment garble? Genesis says God gave humans dominion over the creatures of the earth. And this shrimp is delicious."

Rosie was not deterred. "Ever since Martin was blown up, I have really taken a look at this mess of a world. We're killing our air. We're killing our water. We're killing our land. We're killing each other. Our generation has a responsibility to change the way we do things."

"Pass the sauce, please," Brigid groaned.

Babs responded to Rosie. "Does changing the way we do things include burning buildings, hurling rocks at cops, shouting vile obscenities, and disrespecting every establishment that gave us the comfortable lives we have today? What I see this so- called revolution doing is replacing one form of violence with another."

"When words and committees and peaceful protests are ignored, yeah, I agree with the action--burn baby burn. And guess what? Our protests are going to end this damn war sooner than later and maybe one burned building and one rock hurled at a pig will save a life. A life like Martin's."

Brigid's cheeks began to redden. "We all loved Martin, Rosie. You seem a bit self-righteous to assume that your radicalism is the only path to honor him. He chose to fight in Nam. Perhaps you should use another martyr to justify your cause."

"Fine," Rosie retorted. "I'll shout for the thousands of guys who didn't choose to be there."

The argument was interrupted by the waitress taking orders for the main entree. Rosie ordered a salad, Babs a filet of sole, and Brigid a prime rib, medium rare. Brigid glared at Rosie, silently daring her to comment, but Rosie started a new and more daunting topic.

"So now that I have your attention, I will tell you that I am leaving Ohio State. Mama and Dad gave me an ultimatum that I just couldn't live up to. I've never been a great student, and the temptations at OSU are way too strong for me to resist. I learned a lot more out of class than in class, but my parents aren't keen on paying for that kind of out of class education." Rosie laughed. "We had a screaming match and I kept screaming, even though I knew they were right."

"Revolution for the sake of revolution," Babs interjected wryly.

"Yeah, well, anyhow, I will be going to Cuyahoga Community College for at least a year and I'll have more time to fight the fight, pop the pills, and save the seas. After I catch up with school, I will probably go to Cleveland State."

The food was served, and as Brigid cut into her bloodied beef, she took her turn in the circle of revelations.

"OK, so I have some news too. I've made a firm decision to join the Peace Corps after graduation. I just feel I need to give back, and to see more of the world, and to see if I can help make it a better place. Losing Martin thousands of miles away struck my heart in so many ways, and one of those ways was the realization that the United States makes up only a small portion of the globe. Many Americans are impoverished, but I don't think anything compares to poor countries in Africa or cities in India. One of the theological emphases in our Gospel classes is to feed the hungry and clothe the poor. I want to help. One of our highest callings is to simply help others."

"Very cool," said Rosie.

"I can see you making a difference, Brigid," Babs added.

"Thank you so much. Now, on a rather humorous note, I have to tell you what my mother said the other day."

Brigid took a bite of her dinner and continued to talk in between chews.

"We were commenting on how well Michele was doing with her husband and baby. I have to admit she does seem happy. Anyway, when I told my mom I wanted to join the Peace Corps, she was stunned. 'But Brigid,' she said, 'You will be twenty-four by the time you leave the Peace Corps. Your time with the treasured egg will be ticking away.'"

Rosie choked on her salad and Babs dropped her fork in disbelief.

"She did not really say that," Babs said incredulously. "Is she talking about having kids? Seriously, the treasured egg? Well, I hope you can find a treasured sperm!"

"Or more important, a treasured penis!" Rosie gagged with laughter.

The friends giggled like naughty schoolgirls, drawing the attention of the more mature patrons of the restaurant. It took a few moments to regain their composure and when they finally stopped laughing, the waitress brought over a bottle of wine.

"Compliments of the mayor," she explained, as she nodded toward a table across the room, where Carl Stokes was dining with a group of businessmen. "He said that he is happy to see young women enjoying the city. And Rosie, he said to give his regards to your father."

The fact that none of the girls were of legal age to order wine did not matter. If asked, they all had identification cards to indicate otherwise.

"A bottle of wine from the mayor? Pretty damn cool," Babs said.

But Rosie felt uncomfortable and whined over her wine. "It stinks not being able to go anywhere in this city without being recognized as MV's daughter."

"Well, here's to fathers," Babs said as she lifted her glass.

"And Cleveland," added Brigid.

"And fake IDs," Rosie concluded.

The friends finished their meals while chatting and gossiping about classmates, many of whom had already married and started families. Ellen Bodnar was getting married in August. Her fiancé had picked an inconclusive number in the draft lottery which left him in limbo, so he decided to join the National Guard. He would be starting basic training soon, and Ellen wanted to marry before he left. She hadn't yet let any man near the treasured egg.

When the plates were clean and the wine almost gone, it was Babs's turn to share where her life was headed. They all ordered the Pewter Mug's dark chocolate ice cream for dessert, and began to dip into the scoops.

"Well, here's my scoop," Babs began. "First of all, my father is recovering nicely and is under the care of the Cleveland Clinic; doesn't get any better than that. My mother really appreciates the flowers and food that your moms sent. Nothing better than good friends in time of need. It's interesting, though, my dad seems like a very different person. Easily agitated, always trying to prove that he is strong as ever, doesn't want to stick to his diet. It's like his brilliant, logical mind is under attack by the unwillingness of his body to accept reality. A pure fight between the flesh and the spirit in a whole different light."

"Hmmm. I usually vote for the flesh," Rosie said, "but this time I hope his mind wins out. He needs to take care of himself."

"We'll see," continued Babs. "In the meantime, my mom is under so much stress. Moving back from Florida, traveling to Houston, resettling in Shaker. All the while trying to make life easier for David and my dad. And to make things worse, Grandma and Grandpa Schneider have both been ill, so she is trying to take care of them too. She is staying up till all hours doing research for a NASA Mars project. I am really worried about her."

"So sorry, Babs. How does all of this affect you and your plans?" Brigid asked.

"Well, I am not going to take a job this summer. I am going to help mom with David and my grandparents, and maybe take a night Astronomy class at Case, just to keep my mind working. My parents have done so much for me--I have to help them any way I can. And besides, Berkeley wore me out, and although it's been a year and a nervous breakdown ago, Martin's memory clings to my heart like a millstone. It's going to be a summer of family and friends."

"And faith," Brigid whispered.

"Whatever," Rosie snapped.

"Will you be going back to Berkeley in September?" Brigid asked.

"Oh yes, we all agree that I am committed to finish my last two years there. I have decided on declaring my major as theoretical physics and am excited where that may take me. Berkeley's Math and Physics Departments are the best in the world. Not sure how welcoming they are to women, but certainly the tide of history is in my favor." Babs smiled and took another spoonful of chocolate.

"Chalk one up for the revolution," Rosie said with a grin.

"To women," said Brigid, and they clinked their glasses with defiance and determination.

When the young women left the restaurant, they headed toward the Agora club on East 24th Street. The mayor's comment about being happy to see young people enjoying themselves in Cleveland was more than a casual, friendly remark. Cleveland was coasting on an economic and psychological downslide, with a mass exodus of population into the suburbs. Racial tensions, increasing crime, declining steel production, and Interstate 71, had combined with the pervasive funk of the country to incline people to seek solace outside of the big cities. But the music scene in Cleveland was still rocking, and Brigid, Babs, and Rosie were enjoying every beat. The friends used downtown as their meeting place once a week throughout the summer, dancing, drinking, and listening to bands at various clubs and pubs throughout the city.

Cleveland withered around them, but the music bloomed eternal.

August quickly simmered into late summer, and soon it was time for Babs and Brigid to return to campus. All three of the girls had reconnected with their families, growing in the self-awareness that although their worlds and values were taking a different path than their parents may have wanted, the roots of family bonds were firmly and unshakably planted.

Mrs. Turyev regained strength through her daughter's presence. Menopause, her husband's heart attack, her parents' failing health, and her daughter's breakdown all battered her body and mind to the brink of insanity. Barbara told Babs that Babs's decision to devote her summer to family care saved her life. It afforded Barbara the luxury of naps, and professional escapes where she could detach herself from being a caregiver. Her research and contributions to NASA's Mars projects allowed her an avenue of intellectual stimulation that kept her balanced.

It also afforded her quality time with David. Now eight years old, David had already seen, firsthand, historical events, nervous breakdowns, heart attacks, and tragedies. He also felt the stability of loving parents, generous grandparents, and an environment that inspired thought and creativity. His persona emerged as a quiet child, introverted and shy, but his inner self burst with a wild artistry and vision. Unlike others in the family, he chose to draw stars and planets rather than calculate the distance between them. He escaped into his art, and delighted in the time he spent with Babs.

It was the relationship with her father, however, that most significantly influenced Babs. She enjoyed walking with her father through the landscape of the Shaker Lakes, listening and learning about the physical and metaphysical connections between the physics of Newton and the relativity of Einstein. Numbers and equations connected her with a higher level of consciousness that she relished, but anecdotes and tales of old fascinated her. That the story of the apple landing on Newton's head would someday lead to the reality of man landing on the moon was a satisfying notion. Her father would instruct her on the mathematics and the physics, and she would internalize the knowledge and make the transcendent connections. The father-daughter bond was intellectual, but permeated into the spirit.

There was little emotion, but the connection was complete--complete enough for Babs to realize that the vitality of her father's mind was battling to overcome the dying of her father's body.

*

Rosie and her family shared a summer of revelations. Living at home demanded the adherence to home rule, so Rosie attended Mass every Sunday, first rebelliously, then begrudgingly, then, finally, resignedly.

Mama Rose and MV had discussed Rosie's withdrawal from Catholicism and her general malaise. While Rosie was away at school, they could hopefully imagine she was doing fine, but now, daily observation had revealed they were losing Rosie to the lures and lusts of the times. They resolved to use lures of their own to assure that their oldest daughter stayed on the right path, or what they thought was the right path.

They told Rosie that Rebecca, Renaldo, and Robert worshipped her, and asked that Rosie make sure she presented herself as a good role model. Rosie knew the plan was to have her spend more time at home and absorb the old family values of church and community. It worked, a little. She attended church with her brothers and sisters and warned them about the temptations of the world that contradicted what was holy and right. The hold that tradition had on her was a confusing revelation--but the hold that the lures and lusts of the times had on her was also a revelation. She began to realize she was hooked on the latter.

When she was not at church or working at the zoo, she was popping pills and smoking dope. She sped and crashed, sped and crashed, on the Beatles' "The Long and Winding Road," always with Three Dog Night echoing in her conscience, "Momma Told Me Not to Come."

*

Brigid collided continuously with her parents. The loving, liberal façade of the Nagy household began to crumble. Brigid now solidly embraced the concept of Jesus as a revolutionary, and held fast to the idealistic notion that Christ called his followers to break down the barriers of race, gender, and dogma, which organized religion had helped to construct. Dar and Miklos agreed that Negroes should be treated with respect, but live next door? No, that goes against God's order of things. Women should be able to learn and expand their knowledge, but become a professional in the workplace instead of being a mother? No, that goes against God's order of things. (Lest one forgets the treasured egg.) Jesus did preach peace, not war, and love, not hate, but join the Peace Corps and serve in a foreign land? No, that goes against God's order of things.

The disagreements grew more disagreeable, and the tension grew more tense. By the time the last days in August approached, both the parents and the daughter were ready for a separation.

Brigid had, however, grown closer to her sisters, particularly Sally and Suzy. Sally was now twelve and Suzy was eight. Both admired their big college sister who dared to question the order of the household. Michele, though only seventeen, was seemingly happy in her basement apartment, loving and caring for her child and being loved and cared for by her husband. Cindy was the quiet twin, and passively obeyed and marched to the beat of whichever drum was drumming.

Brigid dated frequently, still most frequently with Bill Jones. They were partners in Ellen Bodnar's wedding, but they shared the unpopular notion that marriage was not their path to happiness.

The night before Brigid left back to campus, the Nagy family had a jam session with Dar on the piano, Brigid on the sax, Sally on the flute, and Miklos, Cindy, Joan, and Suzy swinging on the front porch, dancing in the moonlight. It was a perfect ending to an imperfect summer, but it provided a temporary sense of order that Dar craved and Brigid had been fighting to reject.

Music was the catalyst for unity between the upper, middle, and lower states of being ... and the heavenly spheres continued to be in harmony, at least for now.

*

September 1970 - June 1971

Babs and Rosie had decided that the monthly letter-writing was growing tedious and time-consuming, so, under the protests of Brigid, they agreed that they would take turns writing. Brigid assigned Rosie to September, Babs to October, herself to November, and so on. Babs and Rosie greeted the "assignment" with scorn, as they jokingly told Brigid that she was already becoming the type of teacher they did not like. Brigid scoffed at the criticism and warned them not to miss their deadlines. And so began the third year of college correspondence.

*

Hermann Ave.
Cleveland, Ohio
September 10,1970

So, Miss Nagy, here is my first assignment. Letter number one.

Who the hell lives on Hermann Ave.? Well, I do. It was just too hard being under the same roof as Mama Rose and MV and the kids, so I moved in with cousin Beth, just a few blocks away from "home." Beth's only conditions were no drugs in the house, help with cleaning, do my own laundry, and wear clothes outside of my bedroom. Piece of cake.

I didn't fight or have a blowout with my folks and I still see them and have dinner with the family a few nights a week. I am working at the zoo, and taking four classes at Cuyahoga Community College, which basically amount to make-up classes for what I flunked at Ohio State. In January, I will be caught up with Junior status and be able to transfer to Cleveland State, still hoping to major in some sort of animal advocacy program. And, on that subject, I have some really cool news.

You probably are not aware, but our beloved government is planning on doing nuclear testing in Alaska. These tests will present tremendous danger to the animal life in that area not to mention the environment. I went down to OSU last week to see some friends and a bunch of kids are flying out to Vancouver Canada next month for a concert to support a group that is going to get a boat and go protest the nuclear testing. The group is called Don't Make Waves, or Green Peace or something, I don't remember, but I am actually going to the concert. One of my friends couldn't go and already paid for her airline ticket, so woohoo I'm going to the concert! My mom and dad are supporting my going, they think it's safer than the anti-war shit on campus. I think that's pretty funny. Anyhow, I'll tell you all about the trip and the concert over Thanksgiving.

It's weird being back in Cleveland. I ran into Ellen Bodnar the other day. Christ, she's pregnant already. But she looked great and she is happy. I'm definitely not ready to settle down with a guy for the rest of my life.

Hell, I'm not ready to settle down with anything. Haha I am determined to get my damn degree though.

Nothing radical going on around here, but there are some marches and sit ins, especially about Nixon's Cambodia bombings. Just the name Nixon brings out a protest.

Beth hates the war but refuses to badmouth it because we have cousins over in Nam and she says we disrespect them if we disrespect the policies. Hell, one of the main reasons I am doing some of this protest stuff is because of Martin, finest soldier of all. Well, I miss you girls, but am managing to have fun and live life anyhow. The race wars are beginning to have their effects on the music here. Smiling Dog on West 25th is becoming the only place for good jazz, kinda unbelievable to have the west side jammin while the east side Negroes are getting locked out of their own music. The more we change, the more things stay the same.

Gotta study, then party. Wish me luck in my Vancouver trip

Rosie

University of California at Berkeley
Le Conte Apartments
October 10, 1970

Dear friends,

Here's my contribution to Miss Nagy's letter writing assignment.

It feels great to be back in California. Though I absolutely loved relaxing and helping out with my family, nothing can replace the intellectual, rebellious, decadent insanity of Berkeley and the beautiful mountains, beaches, and sunshine of the west coast. Chris and I have a great apartment a few blocks away from my classes. Last year, I am told that several of the professors used a couple of these student apartments for classes, when main campus was disrupted.

And here we go again folks, news from my quest for the perfect academia path. Since I have already tested out of numerous higher level Math courses, my schedule opened up several opportunities to explore other avenues of scholarly endeavors. I have decided on a new and exciting venture. My majors are now Metallurgy and Mechanical Engineering. Can you belch that one out, Rosie? The truth is, while spending so much time in the invigorating shadows of my parents this summer, I felt a strong inclination to swerve off their highways and onto my own side roads. Physics, aeronautics, space exploration--while these nurture my soul, I wanted to create my own niche. I met a guy here who studies nuclear physics and he began a discussion of nuclear reactors, and the applications of nuclear energy on everything from space to treating cancer. Berkeley has a particle accelerator and although I know formulae and equations and abstract theoretical approaches to problem solving, these things open new insights for me into the subatomic world, and will take me places my parents haven't entered.

Metallurgy and Mechanical Engineering will provide a thought process through which I can learn about radiation's effects on minerals and other elements with a possibility that I may be able to participate in some altruistic efforts for the environment and/or humanity. It may also lead to some research that complements my mother's research on organisms on Mars. Rosie, I may be instrumental in addressing some of the concerns of that group you are traveling out west to support.

So, here I am, new major, new world, and maybe a new guy in my life. And get this, his name is Adam. Ironic on so many levels. And, he is cute as all get out. And he runs. And his IQ ranks with mine. I'm feelin it.

By the way, as far as I know, I am the only female Metallurgy and Mechanical Engineering major. We'll see how that goes. My adviser told me that women are simply not expected to succeed in these areas. Remember that Brigid, when you are teaching-- never ever lower expectations for women in any fields of study. We can aspire to the divine just as readily as men.

Rosie, be careful in Vancouver--and Brigid, I look forward to your letter. Don't look now girls, but I think we are growing up.

Babs

Marquette University
Cobeen Hall
November 10,1970

Babs and Rosie,

So nice to hear from you two. Babs, your "new" majors sound so fascinating -- and so out of my realm of understanding. We joke around so much, I tend to forget how mind blowingly brilliant you are. And yet, you make room for Adam ... love it. You never talk about your relationships with guys. Have you let anyone near your treasured egg yet ? haahahahahaha

Rosie, I have heard of that concert, and of that group of activists. They call themselves Greenpeace. I am looking forward to hearing all about your trip (the physical trip to Vancouver, not the acid induced trip to another dimension ...).

As you can see by my address, I have moved back into the dorm. There are a few other upperclassmen here and we are all assigned to the same wing at the end of the hallway. God help me for being such an egghead, but I really like it. A private room, prepared meals, security, and freedom to come and go as I please. Feels fine to me. No guys allowed on the floor, but that's okay with me. I keep my dalliances very private.

I have visited my friends in their houses and they too, seem very happy. Guys are around all the time, dirty dishes in the sink, cats underfoot. As a friend of mine from California once said, "It's whatever you like."

My classes are fantastic. Finished with Math and French and concentrating on my English major and History minor, as well as education classes. I am writing a curriculum plan that integrates history, English, and music. Here's the introduction to the lesson plans:

"Duke Ellington's Deep South Suite expresses universal experiences and emotions, using the tools, methods, and spirits, of the art of music. Similar tools, methods, and spirits, express these same universal experiences and emotions in the art of literature.

"The link between the words of language and the sounds of music is a

valuable tool for teachers to consider as they choose content for their course. Music that is rich in tradition and human experience more readily connects with the other arts than music that superficially reflects the id of human appetites. The music of Duke Ellington epitomizes the link between language and music, and the essence of art itself."

You like? One of the marvelous outcomes of all of these protests is that they have forced administration to look at some very important things that are missing in our pedagogy. The Education department at Marquette is just now branching away from the college of Liberal Arts, and professors are formulating new classes and incorporating more cultural curriculum. They have been very open to my ideas of integrating music, English, and history. I am receiving an independent study credit for my curriculum, and next year I will be able to implement it when I student teach.

Theology is also still dominating my class time. Even though I finished the basic requirement for graduation, I am currently taking a course that studies the role of women in the church and in Catholic history (another result of student protests). It's kind of distressing; the Church has really tainted the pure message of Christ--and yet, I am still faithful to its core message of truth. Still stuck in the middle of my struggle with faith.

I am looking forward to seeing you over Thanksgiving break. These three months have flown.

You're right about growing up, Babs. I think being able to really study what we are passionate about unlocks a sense of maturity in our thought processes. The time feels right to let go of adolescent hangups and behaviors. We'll talk more about that later. I'm off to go have a beer.

xoxoxoxo Brigid

November 25 - December 31, 1970

When the friends gathered for Thanksgiving break in late November, the winds of change that had been howling around the perimeters of their lives finally penetrated into the core of their everyday existence. The day after the holiday, the young women braved the icy Cleveland streets, and trudged through the heavy snowflakes that pounded the cracked concrete of Euclid Avenue. They met at their favorite downtown restaurant, the Pewter Mug, but unlike the warm and congenial conversations of years past, the discussion was edged with a brittle resentment and uncertain aura of fear and anxiety. Babs's grandmother had died on November 11, losing a battle against pneumonia, and a week later, her grandfather died in his sleep of a massive stroke. Both had been ill for the past year, fighting one infection and ailment after another. But the loss of both so close together created a void that removed all the joy from the Turyev household.

The young women quickly placed their orders of salads and wine. Though doubt and sadness pervaded the mood, the dominant emotion became shock, as Rosie defiantly began the conversation.

"This weather is awful. My life is awful. I am going away. The concert in Vancouver took me to another world. A world where people care about the earth, and the animals. A world where institutions don't tell you how to think or act or dress or be. A world where family traditions don't rule your self. We talk about revolution but thousands of people are living it. I want to be a part of it. I want to live it. I am going to join a commune. I will ...."

Before Rosie could finish her monologue, Brigid barged in. "You mean a world where you have no responsibility. A world where you turn your back on people who have provided for you and nurtured you since the day you were born. A world where you lie back and do drugs and do anyone you happen to desire for the moment. A world where children sup from any mother's breast and have no idea who fathered them. You're talking about those hippie communes where people live like animals with no concern for the rest of humanity as long as their base needs are being fulfilled."

"A world," Rosie replied, edging closer to Brigid's face, "where friends don't judge and criticize the beliefs of other friends."

A moment of thick silence followed, then Babs raised her head and with glistening eyes, sighed to her friends. "Well, thank you both for your support. Your sympathy for my grief is simply underwhelming."

Rosie and Brigid looked at each other, and with shame in their hearts hugged Babs until the three friends, with tear-streaked cheeks, broke away from the embrace. They sat quietly and awkwardly, waiting for the other to speak. Rosie broke the silence.

"Screw us, Babs. Your loss should have been the first concern. We loved your grandma and grandpa and we know how much they meant to you and your family. I can't imagine the holidays without them."

"I'm so sorry, Babs," interjected Brigid. "You know we are here for you."

"Of course I know that. Thanks. I was just surprised how our conversation started out. But anyhow, my grandparents were ready to die. They had unwavering faith in God till the end. But you both know, the goodness of God is sometimes very hard to understand. That's why we have friends."

Rosie turned to Brigid. "I need your friendship. It looks like I am deserting everything, but I just need to try something else. Please don't judge me."

Brigid remained pensive while Babs responded. "Rosie, we are more worried about your drug use than anything else. Being on the West Coast, I know of many hippie communes that have sprung up. Some of them exist on beautiful, idealistic notions of community and the common good. Others are drug-infested, orgiastic excuses for running from responsibility. Where will you be?"

Rosie ignored the question. When the salads arrived, the conversation switched to men and music.

"Well," said Brigid, "my main squeeze, as they say, is getting married to someone else. Bill Jones has decided that marriage is for him after all. And so it goes ...."

Rosie commiserated. "Losing your hometown honey is a tough

one. I still miss Amir. But no doubt Marquette is loaded with possibilities. As is Berkeley. How about Adam, Babs? Do tell."

"Yes, do tell," Brigid echoed.

Babs became visibly nervous, with a quiver in her smile, a twinkle in her eyes, and a blush on her cheeks. "I love him."

In an instant, the engineer, the teacher, and the hippie, morphed into squealing schoolgirls.

"Oh my God, are you going to live with him?"

"No."

"Is he Catholic?"

"No."

"Have you told him?"

"No."

"Have you done it?"

"Oh my God, NO. Good Lord, so much for being grown-ups. But the fact is, I do love him. He is a smart, kind, man, and he makes me feel good on all levels of my existence. And, no we have not 'done it,' and yes, I am a virgin."

"Whoa!" said Rosie.

"I wish I was," said Brigid.

"After Martin was killed, I reaffirmed that I only wanted to share that important, intense moment with someone I could trust with my heart and soul, as well as my body. Yes, in this day and age, that sounds incredibly corny, and in Berkeley, the word virgin is not even in many people's vocabulary. But it is how I feel. And Adam respects that feeling. Although, I must say, it's getting harder and harder."

"Well, if it's getting harder and harder ..." Rosie quipped.

Rosie's comment ended, as many of their discussions about men ended, with raucous laughter and the snorting out of whatever liquid they were attempting to drink at the time.

Before they left the restaurant, Babs informed the girls that she was not coming home for Christmas. Her parents were spending December in California, visiting friends, and sharing the holidays with Babs in Berkeley. They were anxious to shed the aura of illness and death that had lingered over the Shaker house since the death of Barbara's parents. The early Cleveland winter had been dank and dreary, leaving Richard with a yearning for sunshine and warmth.

*

Richard and Barbara, Miklos and Dar, and Rose and Massimo, dined before the Turyevs left for California, feasting on Hungarian cuisine in a little restaurant on Buckeye Road in Cleveland's east side. The Hungarian newspaper, the *Szabadság,* endorsed MV as a political candidate for County Commissioner, so the Vanettis liked to patronize the Hungarian bakeries and restaurants. Miklos was happy to oblige, and the Turyevs appreciated the proximity to their home in Shaker.

These families had laughed and cried together for seven years. This holiday season was the first without a member of any of their parents' generation present.

Dar spoke softly as she reflected. "It's so sad to think that their wonderful generation is slipping away from us. They have given us so much in the way of love and life's lessons. What rich gifts of culture and wisdom and courage they blessed us with."

"Our generation is next to go," lamented Richard in a voice tinged with thoughtful wistfulness.

Silence prevailed until Rose cracked, "We're not going anywhere until we figure out what to do with that oldest kid of mine!"

Worried chuckles spread around the table.

"What are you going to do, Rose?" asked Barbara. "Babs said Rosie is leaving next month, for God knows where."

Rose gulped down a heavy sigh and MV replied to Barbara's comment.

"We cannot stop her from going, but we are certainly not giving her our blessing or our money. We told her in no uncertain terms that it is unacceptable to us that she is selfishly withdrawing from responsibility. She has always been taught to help others, and improve herself. A hippie commune does neither of those."

He tried to continue, but it was obvious that tears and emotions would soon escape from his heart into his words. He lifted his hands in a gesture that communicated he could say no more.

The conversation shifted to the annual discussions of the Browns, the war, and the other children, particularly the Nagys' grandchild. Miklos and Dar proudly shared photographs and anecdotes about baby John. When the couples said goodnight, they departed, feeling a satisfaction that sharing burdens with friends often bestows. Throughout the years, these parents had nurtured an understanding and camaraderie that did not allow judgment or scorn. They lived the tenets of their faith that beckoned them to love unconditionally and support wholeheartedly. Together, they grieved for Barbara's parents, worried for the Vanetti's oldest child, and blessed the Nagy's grandchild. They were secure in their faith for the souls of the Schneiders, but concerned for the soul of Rosie.

*

The Turyevs flew to California shortly after Thanksgiving; Babs back to Berkeley, and Barbara, Richard, and David to Los Angeles to visit friends, where they stayed until meeting Babs and Adam for Christmas and New Year's at Seal Beach. Barbara perceived an intense goodness in Adam that soothed her anxiety about Berkeley disorder.

Brigid went back to Milwaukee, depressed at Rosie's choices and the thought of spending the holidays without Babs or Bill. She delved into her studies, preparing for her final exams and her curriculum planning. Gimbel's gave her extra hours, and the Warriors burned up the basketball court. Protests occasionally sputtered, but the dominant mood was stable, and when she returned home for Christmas, she settled into an uneasy peace of relaxation and feigned interest in family affairs. For reasons she could not explain, she still cried profusely at the singing of "Silent Night," at midnight Mass on Christmas Eve. And for reasons she could not explain, she could sense that her mother took solace in her tears.

The Hong Kong influenza epidemic crept through the Vanetti household, canceling the annual Christmas get-together and crippling the holiday celebrations. Each child and adult was stricken; when one recuperated, another fell with the illness. As the house sweltered in fever and malady, Mama Rose observed Rosie's behavior. Rosie caressed, cleaned, comforted, and consoled the children and her parents, as each struggled through the burning bodies and soaking sweats. Mama allowed herself to sink into the delirium of the flu, rejoicing in the faith that Rosie may stray for a while, but her core would bring her home.

On New Year's Day, Beth drove Rosie to the Greyhound Bus Station where Rosie boarded a bus that would take her 3,000 miles to California. None of the Vanettis were there to say goodbye. Mama Vanetti and MV hugged their daughter before she left home, and the other children quietly said farewell, sensing a sadness, but not understanding the scope of the departure.

Beth slapped a gentle pat on Rosie's shoulder.

"I think you're a jackass for doing this. Good luck, and come home soon. Oh, and bring me some good weed."

*

Marquette University
Cobeen Hall
January 10,1971

Dear Babs,

It kind of hurts not to include Rosie in the letter's greeting. She called me yesterday, collect of course, to let me know that she made it to California. Apparently she picked up some "friends" in Nevada, and they are planning on "touring" the west coast from Big Sur to Spokane. I had no idea what she was saying. I have heard her talk when she was high before, but this conversation was just too far out for me. She said she was "just gonna breathe the air, feel the wind, and touch the heavens." Christ Babs, when did we lose her?

Well, back to the real world. My New Year's Eve was just awful, thank you very much. It's the first time in years that I haven't had a date, so I took my sisters downtown to Public Square and rang in the new year with them. Darn depressing for me, but they loved it and my mom was happy to have me do family things.

I guess I don't fit into this new feminist mold that tells us we don't need men. This course I am taking has really opened my eyes about how the voices of women writers have been silenced, and how females have actually been defined by males. All of the paradigms we use, including language, have been shaped by men. It is exciting to explore a feminine consciousness, at least in literature. But, getting back to my point, I still like to date haha. My parents have raised me to be a strong woman--I would never let a man dictate to me who I should be, but goodness, we all need a kiss once in awhile. Yes? No? It has nothing to do with man versus woman. I think it just boils down to hormones and genuine human companionship.

My friend, Cheryl, the black girl I have told you about before, is struggling with kind of the same thing. The more she learns about her history, the angrier she becomes. But she said she now has slowly realized that she can't hold on to the anger from the past, without endangering the hope for the future. It's a hard bridge to cross, we have to see the good in people as well as the bad. We have some great discussions about it. Between my English, Philosophy, and Theology courses, hopefully I'll be able to figure things out before I graduate. Or I can just solve the problems of the world over a couple bottles of Pabst Blue Ribbon and a blast of the blues on my sax.

It is hard for me to believe I am scheduling my classes for Senior year! I've been accepted into the (new) Department of Education, and it looks like I will be doing my student teaching in a public school next year. That should be interesting, having been in the Catholic education system for fifteen years. This semester I am observing in a Milwaukee public high school so I can get a feel for the school environment.

So, how is the beginning of this new year for you? Did your parents like Adam? Did Adam like your parents? Looking forward to hearing from you.

xoxoxo Brigid

University of California at Berkeley
Le Conte Apartments
February 10, 1971

Brigid,

Yes, it is sad not to be including Rosie on these letters. I have not heard from her. I suppose she didn't want to call with my parents around. Interesting that she started her journey at Big Sur. There used to be big commune there, but people tell me it closed. I wish I knew exactly where Rosie was going to be, I would make it a point to see her. There are many settlements on the coast that range from orgy loving druggy hangouts, to self sustaining farms and peaceful living. I am hoping her Greenpeace ties will keep her grounded in an altruistic environment, but I can't say I am optimistic. We're all exploring our inner selves and questioning our intellectual and spiritual roots. She's just taking a different path. Hopefully, she will emerge whole, and the path will lead her back to faith, family, and friends.

I loved your insights into male-female relationships. How's this for a profound statement: We can't live with them and we can't live without them.

I've always found that cosmology, math, and science satisfied me, but Adam has helped me balance the flesh and the spirit. Soul mates do exist, and I am convinced he is mine. My parents loved him. My mom said she felt he enhanced the best in me, and my dad was overjoyed I was with a man with whom he could converse on the highest intellectual level. We brought in the new year discussing Differential Equations; Topology; Numerical Analysis; and Abstract Algebra. So romantic.

Adam has been accepted to the Master's program at Purdue University in Indiana. I am already missing him, as I think of spending my Senior Year at Berkeley without him here.

My number one focus is still my double major and astronomical observations. This course on the history of metallurgy is a wonderful reprieve from cold formulae. It's a study of how mankind's scientific and mechanical approach to determine the composition and uses of metals affected and continue to affect the culture of humanity. Add that to my mechanical engineering courses and I am a happy camper. An interesting topic of severe plastic deformation and nuclear reactors now has my attention. There's such an infinite amount of discoveries, I do find it difficult to concentrate on one discipline.

A long time ago, you mentioned something about a Quixotic quest. I think that sums up all of our evolutionary progress; constantly moving toward something that may or may not be real, something that is just beyond our reach, something that is both noble and absurd, something that is science, art, and spiritual. Man, and we think Rosie is off the deep end. Hahaha

The campus is still seething with protest, ideology, and art. The protests and ideologies are predictable and I am hearing that Spring is going to erupt in massive marches. I mention art because Adam and I went to the new art museum to see its premier film offering of Akira Kurosawa's Dodeskaden. Amazing cinema.

The campus is worlds away from Euclid Ave. I do love it. Even when I don't shake with its tremors, I groove with its vibes.

Well, this has certainly been a hodge podge of thoughts hasn't it? Stay well Brigid.

Babs

Marquette University
Cobeen Hall
March 10,1971

Dear Babs,

Loved your last letter, and am so happy for you and Adam. It will be tough having him in Indiana though. I guess you'll see what you two are made of with a couple thousand miles in between. It's great that your parents like him too.

I have nothing serious going on romantically. I do date a lot and am totally enjoying school, parties, dates, the whole scene. Marquette has been perfect for me; sometimes I feel guilty because there is so much strife in other people's lives and in the world. Some people would call it being blessed, but I never thought that was a fair statement. Does that mean God likes me better than others who aren't "blessed"? I think I'm just darn lucky. Or they say God never gives us anything we can't handle. Well, maybe God knows I am a weenie and I can't handle much. Whatever--I am enjoying life.

This semester I began my school observations. There is so much that my wonderful life has shielded me from. It is, of course, a known fact that neighborhoods are segregated. In Cleveland, East is black, West is white. And now I see in Milwaukee, North is black and South is white, with both a physical and metaphorical bridge separating the two. But it is not the racial reality that startles me; it is the economic reality. My God, the black neighborhoods, well at least the school I am at, are poverty stricken. We've seen those words, but now I see the faces, and what I see most deeply is a sense of hopelessness. I spoke with one boy, sixteen, who flat out told me he didn't think he would ever get out of the ghetto, because the white man wants to keep him there. He said his mother "worked her ass off" to save enough money to buy a house across the bridge, but real estate people kept showing her houses outside the white neighborhoods. They have been burglarized three times this year. He said he only comes to school to eat.

So, we have Americans who are trying to improve themselves, but live in a culture with rampant crime, committed by people in their own community. And there's the teacher, trying to connect them to Shakespeare. It's all so much more than teaching. But I think it can be done. I want to try. I want to tell the classroom teacher that perhaps she should be more understanding of the outside of the classroom needs.

My education instructor told me not to offer any suggestions. "Don't ever dare to presume to tell a veteran teacher what to do," he said. "The biggest mistake you can make as a new teacher is to think you know more than the teacher who has been in the classroom for ten years or more. You don't. You have no idea. So, observe what works and what doesn't. You are there to observe and learn, not judge. And when you get a job, keep your mouth shut at staff meetings. No one wants to hear from a twenty-two year old, fresh out of college, inexperienced, brainiac. Work hard and succeed, live in the real world for awhile. Then you will have earned the right to offer suggestions to others."

Well, okay then. Yes sir!

So that's what I've been doing in my education observations. My literature classes are bits of paradise. I have reread The Invisible Man, Bury My Heart at Wounded Knee, and Jane Eyre. Each one takes me deeper into the world in which I breathe, but not the world in which I've lived. My parents sometimes have said that reading is an escape from the real world, but it isn't. It so isn't. Literature places us squarely in the real worlds of emotions and ideologies and good and evil. When I teach, I hope I can help students connect all of these worlds and help them articulate how they fit into these worlds and how they can make it better, and themselves better. But first, of course, I have to figure it all out myself. Which, let me tell you, my theology classes are not helping me with.

Do you want to mess with your mind and reexamine everything you ever thought or learned? Read The Genealogy of Morals by Nietzsche. I'm getting an A in the course, not because I understand the content, but because I am honest with the professor about how Nietzsche's philosophies and ideas fascinate me and scare me at the same time. One of his ideas suggests that our memories as human beings evolved from pain, and that in fact, our consciences evolved from pain and punishment. When you study this, and relate it to Catholicism, it gets to be really messy, seemingly true. If he's right, our religion is just a secular evolutionary result of trying to survive as humans; nothing to do with an all good Creator. If civilization ever gets to the point where every behavior is tolerated or acceptable with no painful consequences, there will be no moral code, and really, no more "us." As much as I want to side with this intellectual, logical argument, somewhere in my spirit I "know" that there is a God; there is an ultimate truth and a supernatural goodness. But damn, these atheists sure make a case for themselves.

Warriors are 24-0. Ohio State is next!

No word from Rosie--my mom says Mama Rose hasn't heard from her in over a month....

See you in April.

xoxoxo Brigid

University of California at Berkeley
Le Conte Apartments
March 20, 1971

Brigid,

Just a quick note to let you know I will be spending Spring Break in Indiana with Adam's family. My parents aren't too happy about it, but I am looking forward to meeting them and also seeing the Purdue campus where Adam will be living next year.

So many kids go to the beaches for Spring Break. It's sort of funny that we would never even think of doing that. Parental control cuts deep with us.

Still nothing from Rosie.

I will give you a call over Easter. Even though we don't see each other, we can chat. I won't mention the Warriors' loss to the Buckeyes ...

Babs

University of California at Berkeley
Le Conte Apartments
April 27, 1971

Brigid,

Sorry I didn't get a chance to call. April has flown by. I hope you had a good Easter break. I haven't heard from Rosie or any word from home, have you?

Lots to talk about. First of all, I loved Purdue, and I loved Adam's family. I will tell you more about that when I see you, hopefully in June. I will be coming to Shaker and staying there until July 5, when I will return to Berkeley for summer sessions. I am hoping to graduate early, in December, and then head to Purdue to pursue further studies. But before we discuss the future, let me tell you about other happenings this month.

Adam and Chris and I went to San Francisco last week and joined the giant anti-war march. It was unbelievable Brigid. I am guessing there were over a couple hundred thousand people--and not just hippie type activists, but mothers, and Viet Nam Vets, and people from all types of backgrounds. There were some radicals who were mean spirited, but mostly people who just wanted the killing to stop and to bring our boys home. It felt good. We hugged soldiers, we hugged everybody--I know, not my usual style, but the Mai Lai massacre, the Laos bombings, the Kovic testimony, Jesus. I think Martin would have been right there with me if he was still around.

So, anyhow, my April was filled with decisions and revelations. I am looking forward to next month when I will be concentrating on math, chemistry, and metallurgy and the effects of hydrogen on metals and hydrogen explosions in nuclear reactors.

Let's plan on a birthday celebration June 1 at the Mug. Hopefully, we will hear from Rosie before then.

Babs

*

May - September 1971

The shrill ring of the telephone pierced the midnight silence of the Vanetti household on May 13. Massimo warily picked up the receiver, with Rose already leaning over his shoulder to hear the conversation.

"Collect call from Simi Valley California to anyone. Will you accept the charges?"

Head clouded with slumber, MV sleepily replied yes, and turned to Rose. "Collect call from California."

"Oh my God, it's Rosie."

The caller spoke. "This is Dr. Schultz from the Simi Valley Free Clinic. To whom am I speaking please?"

"This is Massimo Vanetti."

"Are you the father of Rosie Vanetti, twenty years of age from Cleveland, Ohio?"

Massimo's skin lost all color and mouth lost all fluid. Rose clutched his shoulder, sensing his fear.

"Yes, I am."

"Mr. Vanetti, your daughter arrived at our clinic with an acute case of Hepatitis A. She is suffering from liver failure and severe dehydration. We have transferred her by ambulance to Simi Valley Hospital. She was barely alert, but asked us to notify you."

Massimo swallowed dry air, and attempted to ask more questions, but the reply was swift and to the point. "We are not authorized to provide any more information over the phone. You may call or go to Simi Valley Valley Hospital for more information."

Massimo hung up the phone, relayed the information, verbatim, to Rose. Within an hour, suitcases were packed, Aunt Kookie was at the house to babysit, and a red-eye flight was booked to California. Massimo talked to admissions at the hospital who confirmed Rosie was on her way, but no other information was available. Massimo identified himself, provided insurance information, and told them that any or all expenses would be covered, not to skimp on any services, tests, or care.

Massimo and Mama Rose walked into Rosie's hospital room at 7:00 a.m. Pacific Time. The sight of Rosie's sallow body and intravenous tubes weakened Mama Rose's strength to the brink of fainting. She grasped the chair by the side of the bed, sat down, and reached for Rosie's hand. Massimo walked to the other side of the bed, put his hand on Rosie's forehead, and silently prayed.

Rosie opened her yellowed eyes, which immediately filled with tears as she spoke.

"Mama, Dad, I am so sorry. I am so happy to see you."

The tears slipped out the corners of her eyes as she looked from her mother to her father.

Mama Rose hushed her and said. "Nothing else matters but your getting better. Nothing else matters."

MV calmly spoke. "We are here now. You will be fine. Then we will talk about life, liberty, and the pursuit of happiness."

With closed eyes, Rosie smiled, and whispered, "That's my dad, always the statesman."

When Massimo was certain Rosie was sleeping soundly, he went looking for a doctor. Mama Rose did not leave her daughter's bedside.

Fortunately, Rosie's resident was still making his rounds and met MV in a conference room.

The doctor spoke quickly and matter-of-factly. "Your daughter has contracted the Hepatitis A virus. We have traced the origin to contaminated water that she drank at a, umm, a so-called hippie fest, which occurred in Ballarat, California a few weeks ago. Other cases have been reported from that event. Now, normally, this virus runs its course and there is only a slight chance of complications. But your daughter's case is compounded by previous drug use and dehydration, which have weakened both her immune system and her liver. These things will impede her recovery."

MV managed to interrupt with a question. "When you say drug use, do you mean heroin? I have read that ...."

"No," the doctor replied. Although heroin is often associated with hepatitis, it is not the A virus. Your daughter had no traces of heroin, nor external evidence that she has ever used heroin. However, she has admitted to frequent use of LSD, marijuana, and other drugs. Add indiscriminate sexual activity and venereal disease to that mix, and she is a very sick young lady."

MV shakily replied, "It will not be necessary to share all of this with Rosie's mother."

The doctor nodded, then continued."She is receiving antibiotics for gonorrhea and a saline solution for the dehydration. Rest and a nutritious diet will speed up the healing of the hepatitis. Apparently your insurance will cover a hospital stay of three days; I recommend she remains here for that duration."

The professional detachment of the doctor's manner contrasted with the emotional implosion occurring in MV's brain. His oldest daughter--gonorrhea, hepatitis, LSD. He could barely breathe. He thanked the doctor and left the room. Instead of returning to Rosie and Rose, he attempted to walk away the heaviness that was sinking his heart.

His thoughts churned in his soul. *When did this happen? How did this happen? Where do we go from here?*

The answers awaited in Rosie's room. He hesitantly walked through the door. Rose seemed to have aged ten years in the last ten minutes. Red-eyed, weary, wary, she turned to MV and said, "She has told me everything that she has done in the past four months. Now, she is sleeping ... but I may never sleep again."

The parents, who had given their children everything they thought was needed in life, sat holding hands, wondering how they ended up in this hospital room with a drugged-out, promiscuous, sick daughter.

Finally, MV spoke. "This isn't about us. This is about Rosie. She needs to decide her path. We will be there for her today and every day, regardless of the choices she makes."

For once, Mama did not comment.

*

Babs and Brigid arrived at Rosie's home on June 1 at 2:00 p.m. They had decided to celebrate their twenty-first birthday with a lunch of Big Boys, fries, and cole slaw, which they picked up from Manners Restaurant on their way to the house. Barbara and Dar had shared information of Rosie's health with their daughters, but did not offer specifics. The girls only knew that Rosie had contracted hepatitis from contaminated drinking water and that she had been very ill. They assumed the details of the unspoken remainder of the story.

Mama Rose greeted them with a hearty hello and a "Oh my God, look at my big girls--so beautiful and grown-up."

Although Rosie was recuperating and gaining strength, Babs and Brigid cringed inwardly when they saw her. Rosie was as thin as they had ever seen her, and the dark circles under her eyes betrayed the shadows of despair that she had lived through.

Brigid nervously laughed. "Well, don't you look tip-top!"

Rosie raised her middle finger while simultaneously wrapping her arms around Brigid in a crushing hug.

"I've been sick," she said. "What's your excuse?"

Babs joined the exchange with a faux cheery, sardonic inquiry. "So ... what's new, Rosie?"

And so began the conversation among the young women, on their twenty-first birthday, their seventh-year celebration of friendship.

Rosie provided all the sordid details of what she referred to as "life on the road." The friends listened quietly--Brigid aghast with dropped jaw and incredulous gasps, Babs with controlled grimaces and downcast eyes. Rosie concluded by saying not all of the communes were drug-infested and she had met many wonderful, "earth-conscious" folks.

"The drugs did me in physically and mentally," she said. "And the sex made me feel worthless. But even after all this, I'm not sure, even now, if I can resist the temptations." She started to cry.

"You can," Babs assured her and held her shoulder.

"You will," Brigid said defiantly.

Rosie's full recovery started with a bite from Big Boy, and a buoy from big girls.

*

Babs and Brigid celebrated their birthdays all month long, often at jazz clubs, where Brigid and her saxophone swung in all-night jam sessions. Before Babs returned to California, they visited Rosie one more time to offer encouragement and support. They laughed that the right to vote had finally been granted to eighteen-year-olds...now that they were twenty-one. Rosie took pride in any civil rights strides, feeling she had contributed to the cause. She planned to keep in touch and stay informed on campus protests.

Babs commented that letter-writing might be too time-consuming since her academic schedule loomed ominously with chemistry, engineering, and metallurgy classes consuming her life. Not to mention Adam. She promised to call and keep in touch. Rosie and Brigid said goodbye to Babs, excited that the next time they saw her, she would be a college graduate.

Brigid accepted a job as an English tutor and teacher's aide for summer classes at St. Ignatius High School, a prestigious all-male school not far from Lourdes Academy and across the street from her Grandma Nagy's old house on Carroll Avenue, near the West Side Market. The wages for tutoring were one dollar per hour, sixty cents less than she was making at Higbees, but she relished the chance to work with English curriculum. The fact that the classroom teacher was a young, tall, dark, and handsome Greek god, more than made up for the decrease in pay. His name was Paul. He was working on his Master's thesis, which focused on the universality of Joseph Campbell hero's journey in literature. This study of monomyth had always interested Brigid and she took pleasure in sharing knowledge on the topic.

Brigid and Paul formed an intellectual bond, and although Brigid would not have objected to a bit of flirtation, Paul never seemed quite interested in moving the relationship in a romantic direction. He never talked about his personal life but since he did not wear a ring, Brigid assumed he was unmarried. One day, he asked Brigid if she could remain after class and work in his office to help with some research.

"I know this isn't in your job description, but I could really use an extra insight into some of these feminist interpretations of Campbell's work. And, I hope you don't mind, my little girl will also be with us."

The casual tone indicated that he assumed Brigid knew he had a child.

Brigid, trying desperately not to vomit her lunch, nonchalantly responded, "Glad to help, and of course, no problem that your little girl is there too."

"Good," Paul said. "I have to pick her up from her grandmother's house. I will meet you in my office in half an hour. Perhaps you would join us for dinner when we are done working?"

Damn it, he's a cheater, Brigid thought. "Will your wife be joining us?" she asked, with an edge that did little to mask her dismay.

Paul's face reddened. "Brigid. I am so sorry. I thought you knew. Please sit down."

Brigid sunk into a desk and Paul continued. "I was married for two years, when my wife passed away from breast cancer. She was only eighteen when we were married, and only twenty when she died. We have a little girl, Tamara, who is my reason for living. We live with my mother, and I plan on moving out when Tammy starts kindergarten.

I really figured you knew. Everyone talks around here about everyone else."

Brigid reached for Paul's hand. "I had no idea, and I am so very sorry for bringing it up. I will meet you in your office. I look forward to meeting your precious daughter."

Paul kissed her hand gently and left.

Brigid's mind was already in turmoil when the contents of Paul's office plunged her into a surreal state. She had never been to his office; they had always worked in the classroom. The first item she saw was a double picture frame on his desk. She stared and shook. Looking back at her, was a photo of a beautiful, dark-haired little girl, with a Buster Brown page boy haircut, and bottomless brown eyes. Next to that photo, was obviously the mother, a beautiful, dark-haired young woman, with a Buster Brown page boy haircut, and bottomless brown eyes. Brigid recognized the face immediately: it was her childhood friend, her blood sister, Patti DeSantis.

She would succumb to the irony later, but now, sadness overwhelmed her. Patti was dead. Brigid had always hoped that they would reconnect one day, and again share the soulful friendship that dissolved too soon. Brigid had thought of Patti during every major event in her life. And now, not Patti, but Patti's husband and child crossed her path.

Despite the sadness, Brigid's mind turned to selfish thoughts as she realized she could never again be attracted to Paul. He was Patti's husband. He was raising Patti's child. They would be friends, maybe even close friends, but she could never allow the romantic sparks to catch fire.

When Paul returned, Brigid told him of her shared past with Patti. He was touched when he heard the stories of their childhood. Patti had told him the blood sister tale, and he was deeply appreciative to have another bit of Patti in his life. Brigid and Tammy warmed to each other quickly. Paul and Brigid became friends and taught, researched, and laughed together throughout the summer. When they parted in late August, it was unclear if their relationship would continue, but they were both satisfied with a sense of closure, not with each other, but with Patti.

*

Two days before Brigid jetted back to Milwaukee, she and Rosie met for breakfast at the Egg Palace on Detroit Avenue, not far from Rosie's house. Rosie eagerly shared her summer thoughts with her friend.

"Lots to tell you," Rosie began. "My parents have been paying for me to go to a shrink for the past six weeks. At first I hated it, of course. The guy seemed like a real dweeb. But Brigid, honest to God, it's been great. He listened while I talked, and after a few weeks, we hit the jackpot."

Rosie paused and Brigid could see a fresh pain emerging from Rosie's eyes.

"Rosie, it's okay if you don't want to tell me," she said. "You don't need to bring up the pain. I'm just happy to know you're getting better."

"No, no. I want to tell you," Rosie continued. "A lot of—well, most of--my destructive behavior was a result of the guilt I was carrying."

Again, Rosie paused, and Brigid reached for her hand.

"I always blamed myself for Ricky's death," Rosie continued. "I pushed it deep down, but it lingered in my mind and in my soul. Add that guilt to the guilt of my miscarriage and my lack of self-esteem, and put me smack in the middle of drugs and radicals, and bam; I lost myself. And then there's the fuckin' war, and Martin, and it all just weakened me almost to the point of oblivion."

The heaviness of the moment sunk into silence.

"Well, I don't want to seem judgmental," said Brigid.

Rosie stiffened, and Brigid continued.

"But when, pray tell, did you start using the F word?"

The friends looked at each other, each understanding the pain and love of the other. A tearful laugh and gentle holding of hands ensued. Brigid sensed that Rosie had at last risen from the kingdom of the beast.

*

Marquette University
Wells Street
October 20, 1971

Dear Babs and Rosie,

Thank you both so much for the phone calls last month. I loved hearing from you. Babs, you are on the way to being a famous scientist and engineer--your studies sound absolutely fascinating--and to think in a few months you will be a Berkeley graduate and a candidate for a Master's Degree at Purdue. And maybe a bride?

And Rosie, Lord, you never cease to make me smile. Working in your parents' store but still managing to protest the war and advocate for your animal friends. Excellent.

As I told you, I am living in a house with three other Seniors, and I can't say I am loving it, but we are all very busy and seldom home at the same time, so it's working out. We do get along.

I began my student teaching, and well, I already have had my ego slashed to bits. (Thought you might like that Rosie!) My school is an all female Catholic school in a rather affluent section of Milwaukee. (My Marquette advisor didn't think I was ready for inner city engagement.)The curriculum is outstanding, and the girls are very well behaved in the classroom.

So ... I gave my first lecture. It was on Aristotle's ideas of tragedy, the tragic hero, fatal flaw ... you know, the stuff that all high school students live for. I filled the blackboard with outlined notes of profound significance, and dazzled my Marquette professor (who was there to evaluate my competence) with my knowledge of classical literature and its link to modern, thematic trends.

One of the areas of evaluation is student response, so after talking nonstop for forty minutes, I was excited to see a young woman raise her hand to engage in what I was certain was a relative insight or question that aroused her interest in my intriguing lesson. The rest of the class was silent, most likely, I thought, because they were absorbing the essence of the knowledge they obtained.

"Miss Nagy," the girl began in an enthusiastic, querulous tone. "Are you worried about all the chalk that you got on your new black suit?"

Yep, that was the student feedback that I received on my first ever lecture designed to stimulate intellectual conversation in my students. Nothing about Aristotle or noble thought or unity of time--the students wondered about the damn chalk on my damn suit.

But oh, wait friends, it gets better. The next day, on my own, with no classroom teacher or observers present, determined to make the she-devils accountable for their time in my classroom, I gave a pop quiz on the lecture. It was fair, but difficult-- designed to determine if they paid any attention.

After I collected the quizzes, as they silently read their in-class assignments, I graded the papers, and to my surprise, each and every student received an A. Well, I guessed I was better than little Miss chalk on my suit gave me credit for. When class dismissed, as I straightened the desks, I happened to look at the blackboard (to which I had my back turned during the entire class). The board had never been erased. My entire lecture screamed like a giant cheat sheet off the chalked slate.

And that, is how the Summa Cum Laude, National Merit Scholar, la de da fashion guru, begins her illustrious teaching career.

As Rosie would say, screw me.

xoxoxo Brigid

University of California at Berkeley
Le Conte Apartments
November 1, 1971

Friends,

I am writing because I couldn't bear to talk about this. It's not as bad as all that, but still disappointing. Apparently there has been gross miscommunication between me and the admin office. They will not award my degree until May, 1972. I won't bother you with the details of the mess, but needless to say, I am in disarray, not to mention Adam's distress. So, instead of celebrating my graduation this Christmas, I guess we'll just stick to celebrating Christ's birth.

There is somewhat of a silver lining though. Protests and discontent have solidly branched off from the anti-war campaign and become more effectively focused on other issues. I have been asked to serve on a committee to investigate and improve female participation and enrollment in male dominated areas of study. Also, next semester, I will be involved in an independent study of structural alloys and nuclear reactors. I will also still have access to the telescope. I am hoping these activities will keep me busy and the next six months will speed by as I make my way to Indiana.

Brigid, your student teacher exploits made me laugh out loud, even as I wallowed in my own self-pity. I know that you will be an outstanding teacher someday and these initial lessons will serve to strengthen your ability to empathize with those not as gifted as you.

Rosie, you probably know that your mother has graciously invited Adam to our annual Christmas party at your house. He and my parents are coming out here for Thanksgiving, so I won't see you until December.

Till then, my friends.

Babs

November 24 - December 31, 1971

Brigid flew in to Cleveland on the day before Thanksgiving, and flew back to Milwaukee on Thanksgiving night. Swamped with education classwork and student- teaching obligations, she could barely concentrate on anything else. She did have time to observe the swiftness of her sisters' growth and maturity, and the rapid development of her nephew.

Ellen Bodnar (now Ellen Epstein) drove Brigid to the airport, and Brigid was struck by the beauty of Ellen's baby girl, Darlene, and the contentment that glowed from Ellen's smile. The reality of the passage of time stunned Brigid's psyche, and a feeling of melancholy shadowed her mood. By the time she finished her final exams, she was ready to return home and pass some of that precious time with the people who shared her genes.

Babs, too, enjoyed her family in a different manner than usual. Her aging father, her maturing brother, and her withdrawn mother awakened in her a sense of inevitable change. Perhaps the realization of the upcoming rearranging of their lives had begun to settle in her mind, and she wanted to hold on to the present moments that would soon flicker into the past.

Contrary to her friends, Rosie always lived in the present. These moments to her were like any other moments and as always, she seized them. Whether playing Monopoly with her brothers and sisters, or gossiping with cousin Beth, Rosie enjoyed life. Babs and Brigid sensed that a happy, fulfilling part of their lives was ending; Rosie sensed only beginnings. All of the girls anticipated a joyous gathering at the annual Vanetti Christmas bash. They were not disappointed.

The presence of Adam generated fresh conversations of love and fidelity. The embarrassment these conversations burdened him with was of no matter to the parents.

Mama Rose started with: "We always wondered what type of men our daughters would bring home. So far you seem to be the only keeper."

Dar patted his shoulder, continuing the barrage. "You are well built for such an intelligent young man. Brain and brawn. This is good."

Miklos threw an apple from the fruit bowl and Adam caught it. "Good hands," he said. "The Browns could use a guy like you."

Then Adam plummeted into no-man's land.

"I'm a Steelers fan," he said.

Not a creature was stirring.

"Did I mention Adam is studying nuclear physics at Purdue and has been awarded a twenty-thousand-dollar fellowship when he completes his studies? And that he volunteers at an orphanage on Sundays, and that he is converting to Catholicism?" Babs babbled.

"That isn't the only conversion we will be expecting," Richard retorted.

The hush gave way to the antics of baby John who trotted his two-year-old cuteness into the conversation by reaching for Adam to hold him. The toddler was wearing a Browns jersey, and laughter and gaiety returned. Adam knew that the family was only joking about their football animosity ... but Michele's husband warned him that they were only half joking.

The joys and traditions of Christmas pervaded the evening, culminating in the backyard scene by the Italian statue where homage and remembrances were shared in memory of Ricky and other deceased family members, and Martin.

Rosie said a special prayer, thanking the spirits of Ricky and her grandma for sending her forgiveness and relief. Mama Rose, MV, and Rosie walked hand in hand back to the feast that awaited them. They could not know that this would be the last time the families would all be together at Christmastime.

Babs travelled to Indiana to celebrate New Year's Eve with Adam before returning to Berkeley. Brigid and Rosie spent the evening babysitting for baby John, providing a much-needed break for Michele and her husband.

"Who would have guessed we would be spending our twenty-first New Year's Eve babysitting?" laughed Brigid.

"Last year at this time, I was spiraling toward hell," said Rosie. "I'll take this baby over the baby I was doing then."

"Out with old, in with new," they said in unison as they welcomed 1972 with the clank of champagne glasses, and a sing-along with the tune playing on the radio, "I've Got a Brand-New Pair of Roller Skates."

Hermann Ave.
Cleveland, Ohio
January 21,1972

Hey girls - - hmm I guess we're women now.

Hey women!

Well, you may have noticed I am back on Hermann, living with Beth. Don't worry, I am still on a straight and narrow path. My parents have been unbelievably wonderful to me. But I just can't take the rules of the house. Here was the clincher. Last week, I went to midnight Mass at the cathedral. Yes, Mass. I actually left a club early to go to Mass. It felt good. But that's not the point. So I go to Mass with a guy I met at the club, and I get home about 1:15 (a.m.). I walk in, liquor on my breath, strange man in the car outside, and my mother is sitting at the table with a glass of wine. I say hi and tell her I just went to the cathedral for Mass, thinking to myself, "Yay this will make her happy." But noooooooooo.

She looks me up and down and says, "My God, I cannot believe you wore slacks to church."

Yeah, that's what I am dealing with. I love her. I appreciate her. In many ways, I wish I could be like her. But seriously, I cannot live with her. So Beth took me in. I am still going to the shrink and working at the store, and I hooked up with a group of other dropouts from OSU, and we're doing some volunteer work for the George McGovern campaign. He is probably going to enter the Ohio primary. I really love him and I love working on a campaign again. It's been good for my parents and me too. They don't like his stance on marijuana (I love it), but they like him so it's a safe topic.

Just wanted to fill you in a little bit. I know you're both worried about me, but I'm taking care of myself, bathing, running around with decent people, and not popping any pills. The shrink is helping me sort things out. It's all good.

Rosie

Come Home America !

Marquette University
Wells Street
February 20,1972

Babs and Rosie,

February, 1972. Lord, it seems unreal. I remember reading in my First Communion book in 1957, the Table of Movable Catholic Feasts went up to the year 1970. I couldn't imagine that day ever coming. And here it is,1972.

And here I am. My semester ended splendidly. I learned so much. The teacher from the school where I student taught gave me so many good tips and lessons. She said I was one of the smartest student teachers she ever had--offered me a job as soon as I graduate. But she also gave me plenty of advice on where I need to improve my teaching skills. Apparently I appear to be a tad "aloof," and I have to relate to the students more, not by lowering my standards, but just simple things like walking around the room, greeting students when they enter the classroom, saying goodbye when they leave, being aware of what they do outside of the classroom, etc. By the end of the quarter my relationship with the girls was great and it was a wonderful feeling. I am still planning on joining the Peace Corps, but no doubts, the classroom is where I will end up.

Now that student teaching is done, I can enjoy my classes. I am enrolled in two Education courses and two English courses, and am also doing an independent study, polishing up my Ellington curriculum. I finally gave up on Theology. Thank you Jesuits, for compelling me to question every physical and metaphysical fabric of my mind, body, and soul.

After all of the protests and demands for change, I am seeing some results in the inclusion of multi cultural classes and women's studies. There is a solid philosophy here of respect for excellence, no matter where or who it comes from. I like that and I shall teach by that philosophy. One doesn't have to tear someone down to build someone up.

I had a bit of an awakening though last week. I happened to be on a date in a lovely secluded, romantic restaurant about twenty minutes south of town. There, snuggling in a candle lit corner and gazing into each other's eyes, pawing at each other's necks, were the President of the School Board, a Barbie doll caricature with an IQ to match, and the Assistant Superintendent of Schools, a hoary headed jock caricature with the morals of an alley cat, from the suburb where I did my student teaching. They are married--but not to each other. It shook me a bit to see such brazen immorality from two educational leaders of children.

The uneasiness morphed into physical nausea when the next night I attended the school board meeting, and listened as the President unblinkingly announced to the audience: "The value of the month is Fidelity."

Seriously. I talked about it to my Professor, but he said to just let it go. Chances are, people are just looking the other way and it wouldn't be worth it to stick my neck out. Whew, this is the world. Even with all of the liberal theology I've studied, I still think the Ten Commandments are the best foundation for a successful society. "Thou shalt not commit adultery" is a biggie, no? I despise cheaters.

Rosie! So happy to see you are doing well. Wisconsin is going crazy for McGovern. "Come Home America" indeed! It's wonderful that our first vote can be cast for a dove. Very exciting. Glad to hear that you appreciate your parents, even though you can't live with them. Sounds like you have struck a healthy balance.

Well, Babs, just a couple months left of undergrad. What a ride. I love Marquette, (Warriors are 21-0) and I know you've loved Berkeley. Soon you will be with Adam, and I will be with ... who knows where the Peace Corps will send me.

Oh well, off to play my sex. Oh my God, I mean sax!!!

Hahahahahahahahah

Love you both! xoxo Brigid

University of California at Berkeley
Le Conte Apartments
March 20, 1972

Friends,

I was going to give you both a call, but then I realized this will probably be my last conversation from Berkeley, so I figured I would end like I began; with a letter. Thank you again, Brigid, for nagging us to write. It has been cathartic, and even now, I can't help smiling when I see letters in my mailbox from you two.

Campus has been relatively quiet, though I'm sure Nixon will think of something to anger the rebels. I have continued to escape into my studies. I have more free time now that Adam isn't around, but I do long to be with him. Plenty here to keep me occupied though. You are correct Brigid, I have loved Berkeley. Even though I never really embraced the culture of the protests and riots (most of the time even thinking they were a nuisance), I am grateful I was a witness to it all. And, I will have an arrest story to tell my grandkids.

The biggest blessing has been the academics and exposure to the geniuses in Physics and Engineering, and Science that walk this campus. Truly they have taken me to a higher cerebral plane then I ever imagined. You may not know that Einstein believed "the separation between past, present, and future is only an illusion." The physics and math behind that conclusion is daunting, but thinking over my life, I understand the reality of it, because everything seems as one. The "now" is also the past and future. We travel through space in certain directions, but really there is no time. Yeah, I need a break from school.

You said you were shocked at the immorality of your education officials Brigid. My God, the immorality goes deeper than we can imagine. Deeper than interpersonal relationships. During these past few weeks of my final courses here, I have served on a committee that is, in essence, investigating gender inequality in education. The initial data was staggering to me. Fewer employment opportunities, fewer promotions within employment, fewer acceptances to graduate studies. In the areas of Science and Math it's the worst. The size of the disparity is such, that the causes cannot be considered random or chance. There is a systemic discrimination against women, and I think it begins long before girls apply to college. This will be a fascinating avenue of research. Hopefully by the time our daughters (if we ever have any) arrive, we will have equalized the playing field.

However ... Brigid, you said it nicely when you said we can't build something up by tearing something down. We are so lucky to have mothers who have put their children before all else. They chose to forego careers and be housewives and full time moms. As a result there is ... us. What a paradox. Hopefully, we can create a world where women can have the opportunity to choose fairly what is best for them. What a great time to be alive, and make a difference.

Adam and my parents are returning here for Spring Break, so the next time I see you will be for our birthday celebration in June, at which time I shall hold a Bachelor of Science Degree from the University of California at Berkeley, and be an official graduate student at Purdue University.

Rosie, I see that Greenpeace is organizing a sailing protest against the nuclear testing. I look forward to your thoughts on this.

Till June,

Babs

P.S. And yes, "Come Home America!"

Marquette University
Wells Street
April 20, 1972

Dear Babs and Rosie,

Our last letters ... sounds like Einstein got the whole time thing right Babs. It does seem like just one moment from birth to where we are now. As Shakespeare said, "And so our virtues lie in the interpretation of time."

Although graduation is dominating my thoughts and activities, I do have to comment that Spring Break was dreadful. A group of us had decided to stay in Wisconsin and just party for our last hurrah, but my mom made such a fuss about my not coming home, and I, the twenty-two-year-old, summa cum laude, about to leave the country graduate, capitulated to mommy's whims, and spent Easter at home, with my sisters and parents. This time there were no comforting nostalgic moments. It was, for the most part, hell. My parents said if McGovern gets the nomination, they are voting for Nixon. Why? Because McGovern "favors hippies and pot smokers." They are turning their backs on everything I thought they held dear. Unions, workers, peace. Good Lord, I just can't believe they would vote for a Republican. I guess I have been away too long. Anyhow, you can guess how those conversations progressed.

It was nice however, to see my Cleveland pals. Ellen Bodnar Epstein is a happy homemaker, and little Darlene is adorable. Anyone else who didn't go to college seems to be working at the telephone company. An eclectic group, we young women.

Rosie, you looked fabulous. So nice to see you happy and healthy.

Babs, I absolutely love that you are on that committee investigating discrimination against women. Going to Lourdes protected us from the ugliness of gender bias; the faculty and our folks did such a great job of keeping high expectations and eliminating obstacles. I have learned a great deal about women writers and the struggles they have had throughout the ages. Women have been defined in literature written by men. Here's a little tidbit from Virginia Woolf in her novel, A Room of One's Own: "If woman had no existence save in the fiction written by men, one would imagine her a person of the utmost importance (...); as great as a man, some think even greater. But this is woman in fiction. In fact, as Professor Trevelyan points out [in his History of England], she was locked up, beaten and flung about the room."

Yeah, and now I have to get ready for a date! Hahahahaha I am dying in dichotomies.

xoxoxo Brigid

*

Chapter 7

May 1972-September 1972

Rose Margaret Vanetti (Rosie) became a convention delegate for presidential candidate George McGovern on May 2, 1972. McGovern received almost forty percent of the democratic vote in the Ohio primary election, earning sixty-five delegates. Rosie was one of them.

Massimo, Mama Rose, Rosie, Rebecca, Renaldo, and Robert celebrated the election by attending Mass the following Sunday, and then a feast of Italian proportions at Bucci's Restaurant.

The events of the past year of Rosie's life remained unmentioned, but hung like gossamers over the banquet. It was Rosie who broke through the webs, as she raised her glass of Merlot and proposed a toast.

"A year ago, I was a sick animal, lost, afraid, and dying. I drink to my family, who have saved me from the beast and nourished my body and soul. And I drink to George McGovern who hopefully will do the same for America."

Massimo and Mama Rose were the first to shout, "Hear, hear!"

*

Brigid Delia Nagy graduated from Marquette University, Summa Cum Laude, with Honors in English, Education, and History, on Sunday, May 22,1972. Miklos, Dar, Joan, Michele, Suzy, Sally, and Cindy attended the ceremony.

The commencement concluded with an anti-climactic speech by

the chairman of the board of General Motors Corp. Brigid thought the choice of speaker was odd, considering the deep-seated mistrust of institutions and big business that Marquette had planted in her consciousness. However, the pomp and circumstance enthralled the Nagys, and when the family convened at the front doors of the Pabst Theater after the ceremony, Brigid could sense the pride emanating from her parents' tears and smiles. Miklos spoke softly with controlled emotion.

"I am so darned proud of you," were the only words he could eke out.

Dar spoke more poignantly. "Brigid, you must have known that I was hesitant about your going away to college. Your brains and success at school have always made me feel distant from you. I could just never relate to that part of who you are, mostly because it is something I could never be. Oh, I don't know if I am making sense. I just want you to know that I am sorry if I ever discouraged you from following your dreams. I want you to know that I have never felt closer to you than right now. My oldest daughter, my college graduate, my young, successful woman. I can imagine all Brigids in heaven right now applauding and whooping up a giant Irish hoorah."

One can accomplish the highest and most notable achievements the world has to offer, but nothing can touch a girl's heart like the full approval of her mother. Brigid breathed in the hot, hop-soaked Milwaukee air, and for the first time, ever, allowed herself to be truly proud.

*

Barbara Ann Turyev (Babs) graduated from University of California, Berkeley Campus, Summa Cum Laude, with Honors in Physics, Mathematics, and Engineering, on Sunday, May 22,1972. Richard, Barbara, and David Turyev attended the ceremony, as did Adam Schwartz. The Departments at Berkeley provided individual ceremonies with prominent guest speakers such as Chief Justice Earl

Warren in the History Department, Nobel Laureate Professor Emilio Segrè in the Physics Department, and California Assemblyman Willie Brown in the Education Department. Babs received her diploma from the College of Materials Science and Engineering; she was the only female in the program.

The speaker, Dr. Donald H. McLaughlin, impressed her, not so much for his science and engineering expertise, but for his approach to the changing social world. McLaughlin had been one of the Berkeley faculty who refused to sign the loyalty oath when the Free Speech Movement was sweeping the campus, citing the insult to integrity he felt it implied. Yet, although embracing the students' perspective on free speech, he deplored the ignorance that emerged from youth who ignored and disrespected the accomplishments and mastery of the past. Freedom of speech, he had said, should allow complete expression, but should not espouse ignorance. His insights into the past, present, and future provided a balanced approach for Babs to consider as she moved forward in her studies and her role in society.

The family celebrated with a formal dinner, hosted by a NASA scientist, who also served as an adjunct professor at the university. Though Babs's academic ventures now focused on nuclear energy, and Barbara's research contributed to the Mariner spacecraft currently orbiting Mars, the conversation steered toward lunar exploration, and the December Apollo mission.

Barbara spoke with Babs afterwards. "We didn't talk too much about your achievements, Babs, but you know how proud we are of you. It's just that when men and women get together, the men deem their topics more important."

Babs shrugged. "Why do you let that happen?"

"Because I don't really care. As long as their egos don't interfere with who I am, I just let them talk. They do not define who I am," Barbara replied.

"Don't they?" Babs asked rhetorically.

She said goodnight and then went for a moonlight run along the shore with Adam. The conversation focused on Adam's graduate research.

*

Babs, Rosie, and Brigid celebrated their twenty-second birthday at Stouffer's Restaurant on Public Square in Cleveland. A brisk wind blew in from the Lake Erie waves, as the late, chilly spring hung to the smoggy air. Warmth and clarity overcame the gloom, as Rosie began the event with jubilant congratulations to the college graduates.

"Twenty-two years ago, our moms pushed out three babies destined to become friends. Here we are, celebrating eight years of triumph and tragedy. I drink to you, my friends, and want to tell you how much I appreciate those eight years and how proud I am to call you my friends and how proud I am of your college degrees. We never manage to get cheesy, but damn, I gotta say it; I love you and I just know you are both going to accomplish big things. Screw Notre Dame, screw Harvard, screw Yale, and screw all of those schools whose doors were closed to girls. We don't need them! Cheers to you!"

"And to you, Rosie!" Babs and Brigid shouted.

A clank and a chug, and the evening began. The girls were eager to share the latest news of their lives. Rosie, as usual, started the conversation.

"Brigid, holy shit, my parents got a call from the FBI checking you out because of your Peace Corps application."

"I heard they were calling people," said Brigid. "Ellen got a call too. I hope it wasn't too inconvenient."

"Scared the hell out of my father," Rosie laughed. "After what I put them through, any call from law enforcement makes them nervous. But it wasn't inconvenient. They thought it was cool."

"Well, I am training this summer in the slums of Brooklyn and Harlem. It looks like in a few months I will be headed to India to work in a very poor area. It's all a bit scary to me, and my parents are not happy. But I asked to work with people in poverty. I want to do something helpful and worthwhile. I want to serve." Brigid spoke with a wistful nervousness in her voice, but no trace of regret.

"Still, Saint Brigid," Babs said kindly, not mockingly. "I hope the training prepares you for the culture shock you will experience in India. If you believe the missionary pamphlets, the squalor is beyond our imagination."

"Yes, I am aware. Don't laugh, but I do believe my faith will sustain me," she replied.

"Want me to sneak some weed in your suitcase just in case your faith isn't enough?" Rosie joked.

"Good Lord, some things never do change," Brigid said, rolling her eyes, trying to stifle a laugh.

Rosie became serious. "You noticed, I hope, that I toasted with Coca-Cola. I haven't had much to drink for a year, and although I do occasionally take a hit of pot, it's not often and it's not much. My liver is still recovering and I am taking care not to have a flare-up. So, when I say things like that about weed, I am totally joking. Well, mostly joking."

Babs looked at Rosie and said, "I admire you, Rosie. It's tough to give up that stuff. Good for you."

"Couldn't have done it without you two," Rosie whispered, on the verge of a crying jag.

"Well," said Brigid. "So I will be in slums and ghettos. Where will you be this summer Babs?"

"Ahhhh…drum roll, please. I have secured an internship with the Delco Remy in Anderson, Indiana where I will be involved in research to improve metallic compounds for various uses. It's a whole new world of science for me, not at all what I planned for, but I am really excited to be doing something different. It's a little over an hour from Purdue and I will be living in an apartment half way between the two places.

Adam will stay in West Lafayette near campus. Mom was hoping I would come back to Ohio, but I convinced her that the four-hour drive from Cleveland to Indiana is still much closer than the four-hour plane ride to Berkeley. What I didn't tell her is that the guys at U.S. Steel in Cleveland told me that they had no place for female engineers, and then they offered me a clerical job. I showed them my academic record and research work, and they just smiled and sent me on my way. Yeah, we've got a long way to go, ladies. I am anxious to take the first steps."

"Screw U.S. Steel," Rosie barked. "Babs, I cannot wait to see the things you will do. Congratulations on your internship. What is your Master's focus going to be at Purdue?"

"Thermonuclear engineering," Babs replied.

"Of course," said Brigid. "What else would a woman who conquered the Math, Physics, Astronomy, Metallurgy, and Engineering curricula at Berkeley focus on?"

Laughing, Babs turned to Brigid, and said, "And where else would a saxophone- playing Shakespeare lover go but to the slums of India?"

Rosie concluded the talk of future plans by adding, "And where else would a recovering druggie, dropout dreamer go but to the Democratic convention?"

Laughter ensued, glasses clanked, and dinner was served. When the chat geared toward men, as it always did, Rosie asked Babs, "So, about you and Adam. Are you going to live together at Purdue?"

"No. And in answer to your next question, no."

"Damn," Rosie said.

"Why? Or, I should say--why not?" Brigid asked.

"Ugh," moaned Babs. "I have explained to you before. First of all, living together is out of the question. I have seen other girls move in and out of apartments and living conditions with their boyfriends. It's like pretending to be married without any security or commitment. The girls usually get the raw end of the deal. Frankly, the pain that it would inflict on my parents would not be worth any convenience or pleasure I would get from it. As far as sex goes, I have simply made up my mind that there will only be one man that I shall be intimate with, and that man will be my husband. Adam knows this and so far, he is willing to wait. Such is our love. And such is my privacy. It's funny to think that eight years ago we would not be having this conversation. Just think how things have changed."

"Well, good for you, Babs. You and Adam are lucky to have found each other." Brigid ended the conversation, knowing Babs did not want to discuss the topic any further.

By the time dessert arrived, a pall of silence hovered over the group. The unspoken reality began to take shape. No one knew when they would meet again. They were all silently attempting to think of some grand or hilarious way to end the evening, but they were trapped in reveries of things past and things to come.

Then, the waiter politely lit Rosie's cigarette, then dropped the lit match on the table napkin, which shot up in flames, which made the girls scream, which caused the waiter to throw a pitcher of water over the table, which doused the flames, which caused all of the patrons to stare at them, which caused the ultimate, most satisfying, gut- wrenching, pants-pissing fit of laughter that they had ever experienced.

The manager sent a bottle of complimentary champagne, along with a paid in full check. They lifted their glasses and through tears of laughter and anticipation, said in unison, "To us."

*

Babs settled in Indiana a week later, saying goodbyes to her parents and David, all of whom were supportive and a bit sad. They had helped her into her new apartment, and expressed satisfaction that the drive proved to be quicker than they had thought it would be.

David especially seemed grateful, whispering in Babs's ear as they hugged, "I'm so glad you will be closer to us. I miss you. Please come home often."

Her little brother, now almost ten, was maturing into a different sort of child than Babs. He was reserved, cautious, and poignantly artistic. His drawings of the solar system earned numerous awards from the Cleveland diocesan art contests for their accuracy and detailed features. Whenever he drew people, however, a distinctive pattern of outsiders emerged. He drew groups of sports teams, Boy Scouts, altar boys, and other bands of brothers, but there was always a boy outside the circle engaged in another activity--painting, playing an instrument, or reading. David never spoke about his drawings; he was quiet and unassuming. Babs looked forward to seeing him more, and getting to know him better.

Adam also said goodbye, having obligations at Purdue. They shared a warm embrace, holding on a little longer than usual. "We'll be fine," he said, as he kissed Babs's forehead and turned away.

The last person to say good-bye was Karen Grovac, Bab's first friend from Shaker. Karen recently graduated from Kent State with a nursing degree. Charity Hospital in Cleveland hired her, and before she started working full time, she wanted to share a few moments with her old friend, so she helped in the move. Still puffing on Taryton cigarettes, Karen reminisced about the days at Our Lady of Peace.

"Remember when you punched that rotten kid in the nose on the playground? I think that's my best memory from grade school," Karen said.

"You taught me everything I know," Babs replied while giving Karen a pat on the back. "We've come a long way from that school yard, and have thrown a few more punches along the way."

"Yeah, and we've taken some punches too, haven't we?" Karen sighed. She was on campus when the Kent students were killed in May,1970. "Good luck, Babs. I'm glad you're in driving distance now; I hope we get to see each other more often."

"Good luck to you too, Florence Nightingale." With a hug and kiss on the cheek, Babs said goodbye to her dear friend.

*

Babs started her work the following Monday and immediately realized she was not in Berkeley anymore. The Midwest had not caught the liberation spirit.

Babs expected some flirtations, as a woman working in a traditional man's arena, but she was shocked at the cat calls and incessant sexist comments that spewed her way as she walked the factory floor of the plant. Though unsettling, the atmosphere did not deter her from providing and obtaining valuable research which added to her arsenal of knowledge and skills. Despite some gender disparagement, the internship proved invaluable in both professional and personal experience.

In the evening, she jogged around the park near her apartment, and at night, she found contentment where she always had, in the night sky. She started going to Mass on Sundays, more for the social connections, but also with a hope that her waning spirituality would be rekindled.

Her family visited frequently, and on occasion, her father would visit the plant. His reputation was well known, and the respect shown to Babs when she walked with him through the factory was palpable. Although she was proud of her father, Babs found the double standard deplorable.

Her oasis in this desert of testosterone appeared on the Purdue campus where she spent her weekends with Adam. He barely sympathized with her plight against the male behavior, advising that it should serve as a warning to what she might expect in her field. Babs did not view his attitude as patronizing; rather, she saw it as honest and helpful. Adam and she grew as equals in mind and spirit, and both were content.

She never made the trip home to Cleveland. Between the job, the romance, and the family stopovers, time passed quickly, and in August she moved into her apartment near Purdue. The only communication from Rosie or Brigid came through her mother who stayed in touch with Mama Rose and Dar.

*

Brigid's last efforts in Parma before she entered Peace Corps training resulted in a stronger bond with her sisters and her family. Determined to fill in the gaps of her collegiate absence, she talked, walked, shopped and doo-wopped with each of her sisters.

Michele seemed to exhibit the most self-assured identity: a wife and mother who settled into the role of loving homemaker for the nuclear family she created. Michele also became the daughter on whom Dar depended--a role which Brigid knew had been expected of herself. Michele confessed that their mother often bemoaned that Brigid had consistently chosen to engage in activities away from the family. Brigid made sure that Michele knew how much she appreciated her and how proud she was that Michele had overcome the difficult beginnings she faced. As far as her choices, she had no regrets.

Sally had grown into a strikingly beautiful young woman. Now fifteen, she was a cheerleader for Valley Forge High School, and a Candy Stripe Volunteer at Parma Community Hospital. She confided to Brigid that she was Brigid's biggest fan, and recited to Brigid every crush, every date, every accomplishment, every heartbreak, and every music concert Brigid ever performed. Pangs of guilt stabbed Brigid's conscience. She realized how little attention she had given to this growing adolescent, this sister. She vowed that she would always be aware of Sally's journey to fulfillment and she would always share and encourage her on the way to that fulfillment.

Joan, an 8th-grader suffering through the blemished awkwardness of being thirteen years old, had hidden herself in music. She was an accomplished flutist, earning the coveted first chair in band, as well as selection in the All State of Ohio Youth orchestra. Social norms dictated that she was not "pretty," but Brigid assured her that inner beauty emerged with every word she spoke and every note she played. Joan's self-esteem solidified in the few days she spent with her oldest sister.

Brigid described the twins, Cindy and Suzy, as "rascals," while noticing that the ten-year-olds were the darlings of her parents, and everyone else in the family. They were the athletes, the mischief-makers, and the proverbial babies of the family who received whatever they wanted, whenever they wanted it. Time spent with them consisted of playing Wiffle ball, swimming, Barbie dolls, and front room dancing to the very unNagy-like music of Peter Frampton, Slade, and Alice Cooper.

Finally, Brigid spent almost every evening with Dar and Miklos, trying to make them understand why she was leaving for the Peace Corps.

"Why?" asked Dar. "I just want to know why you have to go so far? There are poor people here. There are people who need help here. We've invested so much in your education and your upbringing. Why can't you stay here and share it?"

Miklos, too, was confused. "We just always thought you would come back and be part of the family. It seems like college has changed you so much. Now, to go to such a dangerous part of New York, of all places. Then India. My God, I just don't understand."

Brigid understood the confusion. Her parents had seldom ventured away from Ohio and what her dad had seen in the war convinced him that foreign countries should never be a preferred destination. She tried to help them see her point of view.

"I appreciate everything you've done for me. So much," she began. "But always, always I have felt the need to help people in a special way, in a global way. I just feel that my faith, and my education, and my brains can help relieve the world of some of its sadness. Martin sacrificed his life for his country. I feel like I have to serve my country in a special way, and the Peace Corps is it. I will be back, Mom and Dad, and no matter how far I go, I will always be a part of this family."

These weeks and conversations provided closure as she ventured toward a new destination in her life--a destination that she would later refer to as her "descent to purgatory."

The descent began in New York City where the Peace Corps sent her for training to become acquainted with a "slum-like" environment similar to where she would be assigned in Bombay. The training started pleasantly with classes at Columbia University, where she studied community development and the cultural and linguistic history of Hinduism. The International House where she stayed offered comfortable accommodations, but the field experiences in the South Bronx and Harlem carried Brigid to a world far away from the academic haven of the university.

Two muggings in Central Park stripped her of some of the courage she had depended upon to survive in New York. During her first week in New York, mugging number one, a frightening intimidation by two teenagers taunting racial slurs and sandwiching her between their muscular bodies, resulted in the loss of a few dollars and her identification card. This occurred at 11:00 a.m. The second mugging, at 11:00 p.m. involving a gun pointed at her head held by a Spanish-mumbling, scarf-headed, middle- aged man, resulted in the loss of jewelry, a credit card, her social security card, and twenty-five dollars. It also resulted in the loss of her willingness to ever again walk through Central Park alone.

Incidents in the park were the prelude to what she encountered in the field. The field experiences opened her eyes to existences that she had heard spoken of, but never imagined or believed existed. Brigid often worked in New York churches where drug addicts and recovering drug addicts frequented, not to pray or be counseled, but to vomit, urine, scream, and writhe.

She also brought food to tenements and was greeted, or rather groaned at, by children caked in dirt—filthy, ragged young girls, holding filthy, miasmal-smelling babies. Water was often not available, air conditioning was unheard-of, and people simply breathed--nothing more, nothing less. While in Harlem, she walked daily (and quickly) past a Black Panther headquarters where scowling, angry men stood guard. She never looked them in the eye. In the South Bronx she sat in and observed meetings between white gang members, church leaders, and government mediators, all with what she thought was the shockingly shared goal of eliminating the drug dealers from neighborhoods. As she walked down the stairs after the meetings, she would overhear the gang members planning to "gank" the first "civilian" they saw on the street. One minute talking crime prevention; the next minute talking crime planning.

For several weeks, Brigid had struggled to convince herself that she could, indeed, complete her task--that she could face the depravities of poverty and crime and contradictory human behavior, and come away from it all with her idealism intact. She was losing the struggle. The realities of evil forced themselves into the depths of her psyche. She could not force herself to enjoy the other reality of New York. A reality of art and music and dance--the reality that existed side by side with the horrors. Realities separated by just a few blocks.

One night, she remained in her room as the members of her training group escaped to a concert. Brigid crashed to her knees, and screamed silently in her mind to God.

"Where are you? Where are you?"

No answer.

The next day, her roommate, Marcie, a seemingly hardened veteran from the rough streets of Los Angeles, informed her that she had decided to leave the program.

"I have thought and thought and reflected and argued and drank myself silly and I have come to the conclusion that I do not have to go to Bombay to help people. I am going back to L.A. where there's plenty of this shit I can help with. The time here has convinced me that my own people need me. You have been a peach, Brigid. I am proud to know you and I know you will be a great help wherever you end up."

Brigid could not find words to express the sadness and hopelessness she felt. Marcie had frequently offered her strength and consolation. It seemed impossible to imagine continuing without her. She finally said, "When in doubt, hug," and offered a warm and lasting embrace.

Marcie prepared for a quick departure, and Brigid's day was the worst day of her training. One of the families she was helping with food and hygiene had a one-year-old baby living in the apartment. Brigid often fed and bathed the little girl, whose name was Maria. Maria and her mother shared a bed in the crowded apartment. During the night, the mother had rolled over and unknowingly smothered the little girl, killing her.

When Brigid arrived, she sensed the unusual quiet that pervaded the customary cacophony of tenement malaise. Climbing the stairs, she found the baby's-three-year old sister sitting on the stoop, rocking back and forth.

"El bebé está muerto, el bebé está muerto," the little girl kept repeating.

Brigid hugged the dazed child, then ran to Maria's apartment where she found the mother and other five siblings sitting silently on the floors and worn couch. The mother, still in a dazed shock, explained what had happened. Brigid prepared the milk and oatmeal she had brought with her, and stayed with the family, consoling, cleaning, and discussing arrangements with the neighborhood pastor, passing time until a social worker brought in dinner six hours later.

The chief Peace Corps trainer was waiting for her outside the tenement. Brigid broke down in his arms.

They walked back to the International House with minimal conversation. Before he left her at her room, he said, "We are going to dinner tonight, the whole group. We will dine at a nice restaurant and then go to the Vanguard and soothe our souls with gin and jazz. Be in the lobby at 7:00 p.m."

Physically and emotionally exhausted, Brigid collapsed on her bed, and as she did, a crudely made wooden picture frame with beautiful calligraphy within its glass fell to the floor. She picked it up and read the card that was taped to the back.

"Didn't have time to buy a nice gift, but I thought that you might appreciate this. My mother gave it to me many years ago. I want you to have it. Remember me. Remember why we were here. Love, Marcie."

Brigid read the framed writing:

Flower in the crannied wall,
I pluck you out of the crannies,
I hold you here, root and all, in my hand,
Little flower—but if I could understand
What you are, root and all, and all in all,
I should know what God and man is.
by: Alfred, Lord Tennyson.

A purgatorial epiphany seized Brigid's soul. For an infinitesimal moment, Yang conquered Yin; Michael the Archangel conquered Lucifer the Archangel; Humanity conquered Beast. Faith conquered Doubt.

She was ready to serve ... after the gin and jazz.

*

Rosie simmered through another Cleveland summer without her closest friends. This time, however, her self-confidence and self-esteem had finally developed to a point where she was strong enough to resist the lures of acid trips and promiscuous dalliances. The McGovern political machine hired her as an area campaign director in Cuyahoga

County, and Rosie relished the responsibility. She developed a circle of friends who steered her away from anarchist revolution, toward systemic revolution. McGovern's calm and intelligent approach to conflict inspired Rosie to seek solutions within the structures of government and not within the subcultures of communes.

The Democratic Convention in July startled Rosie with its diversity and conflict. Miami, Florida, the location of the convention, buzzed and bubbled with parties, arguments, and wheeling and dealing. She hobnobbed with Hollywood stars and famous activists during the day, and danced and walked the beach with her friends during the night. The formulation of the Democratic Platform as well as the feminists' quarrels regarding support for black candidate Shirley Chisholm, allowed Rosie to witness momentous changes in American politics. The efforts of established politicians, black and white, to reduce Chisholm's delegate count shocked Rosie, but her main focus was, as always, to end the war. George McGovern was her candidate, and her hope. Though Rosie identified with the plight of women, and supported the black people's fight for equality, she did not want to divert her attention from the main reason she supported McGovern's candidacy. As she observed the behind the scenes deal making, one aspect of American elections was clear: men ruled the roost.

The topic of abortion loomed in every discussion in the women's caucus. Rosie struggled with the issue, respecting women's rights, but deploring the willful destruction of human life. She was relieved, when, under McGovern's directions, his people blocked a pro-abortion clause from the platform. When it became obvious that McGovern would not support it as a Democratic premise, her opinion tentatively swayed to the anti- abortion side. She felt a twinge in her stomach, somehow suspecting that Brigid was sending cosmic applause.

Each evening offered new insights into the political world. One of these insights came in a metaphorical bag of what became known as "Nixon's dirty tricks."

Many of the delegates stayed in a hotel in Key West, and would be bussed to the convention in Miami. On one such bus ride, the driver pulled over to the side of the road, and exited the bus. Another car picked him up. This left the bus and the delegates stranded. Stunned, the group chose two delegates to walk the few miles to a gas station to call Democratic headquarters for help. When they finally arrived at the convention, crucial votes in the rules and regulation committees had already taken place. They learned, much later, that the bus drivers had been paid off by the Nixon committee. Rosie learned that this was one of many manipulative shenanigans perpetrated by that group.

Senator McGovern's acceptance speech made these shenanigans of little importance to Rosie. When he spoke the words, "And then let us resolve that never again will we send the precious young blood of this country to die trying to prop up a corrupt military dictatorship abroad," Rosie stood on the convention floor, surrounded by screaming, cheering delegates, and cried. It was a cathartic cry that soothed her with a knowledge that she was helping her country, serving in the opposite way that Martin served it, serving in a way that would bring all of the Martins home. For, even if McGovern was not elected president, his voice would be heard, his message would be absorbed, and the war would end sooner than later. These were her thoughts and hopes.

On the flight home, Rosie read the newspaper accounts of the convention. Most were critical of the infighting, the mishandling of choices for vice-president, and the mismanaged convention that took the acceptance speech out of prime time television and into the middle of the night. She wished that everyone could see past those logistic errors, and understand the essence of McGovern's message--an essence of peace, hope, and equality. The convention served as a moment where the realism of politics connected with the idealism of possibility. That moment sustained Rosie through the grueling task of campaigning.

Rosie spent the remainder of the summer and autumn in an endless movement of knocking on doors, stuffing envelopes, and calling registered Democrats to go to the polls in November to vote for George McGovern. It was already obvious, from her contact with the voters, that he was not going to win. Longtime, traditional, steadfast democrats did not like the new era of America that McGovern was promoting.

"Christ, Nixon was right about the silent majority," Rosie moaned to a campaign volunteer. "People are turning away from the party. They see George as a super liberal, anti-white, anti-America hippy. Damn, he's as straight as you can get. I just don't understand."

The campaign worker just shrugged. He was there to meet girls.

*

Though the outlook was grim for a McGovern presidency, Rosie managed to make contacts with interesting and devoted people, including some who were active in crafting the Animal Welfare Act of 1966. She looked forward to developing those contacts after the election.

Much to Mama Rose's and MV's delight, Rosie's favorite contacts this summer resided on 61st and Detroit, in her childhood home. All of the Vanettis actively participated in the campaign, and Rosie enjoyed being part of the family unit again. She still lived with Beth, but many hours of her days and nights were shared with Rebecca, now eighteen, and Renaldo, fourteen, who helped with stuffing, mailing, and canvassing. Lost in her own world for the past two years, Rosie did not share with Rebecca many of her adolescent experiences.

"Damn, Becky. I can't believe how mature and grown-up you are," Rosie said one day as they stacked McGovern pamphlets in piles on the campaign office floor.

"Yeah, and I smoke and drink too!" Rebecca laughed.

"Well, not too much, I hope," Rosie responded, not laughing. She hesitated a bit to give advice on drugs and alcohol.

"Jeez, Rosie. Don't worry, we all learned a lesson from you. Even though they tried to hide it from us." Rebecca laughed. "I am going to stay at my operator's job at Ohio Bell for two years, save some money, and then marry some cute little Italian boy and live happily ever after."

Suddenly, Rosie felt old. Twenty-two years old, listening to her little sister talking about work and marriage seemed like a dream. Taking a look over at Renaldo, who at fourteen was already a football hero at St. Edward's High School where he was a freshman, she recalled the carefree years at Lourdes Academy and mused about how things had changed. She remembered the day little Robert came home from the hospital, bringing the joy of life into a household grieving for a fallen president.

The family bonded closely that summer of the campaign, and the love of faith and family again brought Rosie peace and stability. Yet, somewhere in the stirring of her soul, she knew it would not last.

*

Chapter 8

September - December 1972
Babs and Rosie

Purdue University boasted a record breaking year in 1972, when for the first time in its history, women filled over one-third of the enrollment. The Thermonuclear Engineering graduate studies had one female student, Barbara Ann Turyev.

Professors respected Babs's academic and intellectual prowess and held for her the same classroom expectations as her peers. There were some exceptions to the treatment, however. Since there were no female predecessors, there were no female restroom facilities in the main building. Babs had to leave the building to relieve her bowels and bladder. Her mentor, the only female engineering faculty member, also shared this inconvenience. When these two women petitioned to have a restroom in the building set aside for females, a unanimous vote from professors and student committee members said, "Nay."

After her summer internship experience, Babs knew that women were not considered to be viable candidates for advancement in the field, but she nevertheless continued to be astounded at the degree of discrimination.

The female professor warned Babs not to expect career advancement in thermonuclear studies.

"I've published twice as much as some of the male faculty, and yet I have been skipped over time and time again. I have been told I will never achieve the status of full professor."

"Why do you stay?" she asked.

The mentor replied, "I am not here to make a feminist statement. I am a scientist and an engineer, and this is an excellent place to explore the knowledge and wonders of those disciplines. Purdue has not opened all doors, but they have opened enough to satisfy my most serious goals of intellectual curiosity and practical application of science and mathematics. I have no complaints against the treatment I have received from my colleagues when it comes to personal and academic respect. Professionally, they are victims of their times. You and I, and women like us, shall end those times, not by burning bras or buildings, but by successfully solving equations and finding solutions."

"I never considered men as victims," Babs said, skeptically.

"Every institution man has built in the Western world has been based on some untruths. People who have believed those untruths are victims of it. However, there are also truths embedded in the foundations, and they will survive. We are witnessing the crumbling of the lies. When truth prevails, it will reveal all victims."

Babs appreciated the essence of these insights, though unsure of the specific applications. She held those thoughts as she progressed in her field of study, achieving high marks, particularly in problem-solving. Her experiments and research of flow blockages in fast-breeder reactors would eventually rocket her to a highly acclaimed leader in that field of expertise.

Babs remained in Indiana for Thanksgiving, celebrating with Adam's family. She and Adam had decided to share the holidays--Thanksgiving Day with Adam's relatives, Christmas Day with Babs's. Two weeks after Thanksgiving, Babs's mother came to visit. She was alone, without her usual traveling companions, Richard and David. Barbara slowly walked up the sidewalk as Babs watched from her apartment window. Babs had not seen her mother in almost two months, and was alarmed to see how frail and thin she had become in that short of time.

Barbara had celebrated her fiftieth birthday in autumn, but with her wrinkle-free face and toned body, she was often mistaken to be in her forties. Now, Babs thought, her mother appeared much older.

Babs welcomed her with a hug, and a bottle of Coca-Cola, and the mother and daughter, scientist and engineer, sat on the only two chairs in the small kitchen. Babs immediately expressed her concern.

"Mom, you look so tired. Is everything okay?"

Barbara answered, as always, directly and to the point. "I am fine dear, but yes, tired. Your father's heart is failing. He is not well. Although he makes great effort to be strong, each day he sinks weaker and weaker into an existence of sitting on the davenport, reading or napping. He doesn't enjoy visitors anymore because he doesn't want anyone to see him looking so feeble."

"Well, this happened rather quickly. He seemed fine when I saw him last. Well, what can the doctors do? What's the prognosis? I have read that they are working miracles with heart health and drugs and surgeries, and ...." Babs didn't take a breath as she spoke. She didn't want to be interrupted, because she feared what the interruption would reveal.

Barbara spoke softly. "He is seventy-two years old, not a good candidate for any of the miracles you speak of. He is dying, Babs. He may have a year at most."

She paused and reached for her daughter's hand. "I was wondering if you could spend your entire Christmas break with us, at home, in Shaker, as a family. Adam is more than welcome to join us."

Babs rested her other hand on top of Barbara's. "Of course, Mother, of course," she sobbed.

Not wanting to dwell on the sad news, Barbara quickly turned the conversation to Babs's studies. The mother's demeanor changed significantly when discussing her daughter's work and research. In perfect reciprocity, the daughter gave the mother life. They exchanged ideas and thoughts on topics ranging from Martian atmosphere to the metallurgy of nuclear fuels. Babs wanted to discuss her relationship with

Adam, but just as she began, the door buzzer sounded. It was Adam. She had forgotten that she invited him over to share the afternoon with her and her mother.

The afternoon passed pleasantly and quickly. December darkness had already stolen the light from the short winter's day when Barbara said goodbye. She walked a bit more briskly and her smile grinned a bit less wanly after an afternoon with her daughter.

Adam stayed behind. He, too, had something to discuss with Babs.

"I'm so very sorry about your dad's poor health," he began. "It kind of relates to what I want to talk to you about."

Babs had sensed something in Adam's attitude lately that she could not quite articulate. Something was on his mind. She guessed now is when she would find out what it was.

"Go on," she said.

Adam cleared his throat and beckoned Babs to sit next to him on the couch. His long legs and longer torso did not fit comfortably on the small kitchen chairs.

"Babs, you know, someday, I am going to ask you to marry me," he said, with a nervous, crackling dryness in his throat.

God, it's the marriage talk, Babs thought.

"I know we agreed to wait until we both have our Master's degrees, but this semester is tough, leaving here late at night, or your leaving my place late at night, and some days not being able to see each other at all. And the abstinence is getting unbearable. It just doesn't make sense to me. I love you, Babs. I'm ready for the commitment of marriage." He spoke with a finality that Babs found annoying.

"I don't know how many times I have to say it." Babs garnered up her own tone of finality. "I don't want to get married yet."

Adam looked disappointed but not dejected. "You have never really said why. Do you think you can't remain faithful? Am I lacking in something you need? What? Why?"

"Adam, when I want to stay in the library till four in the morning,

I can. I can because I am free to do so. There is no one waiting for me to come home. When I do come home, let's say, after a tedious day of classes, I don't have to cook. I pour a bowl of Frosted Flakes and some milk, and I am happy. No cooking, no mess, no stress of what to make for dinner. I hate to cook; I hate to clean; I hate to iron ... shall I continue? I am not wife material. You would never be happy with me. It has nothing to do with love. I adore you. I know I shall never meet anyone who makes me as happy as you do. But you will become a husband, I will become a wife, and those labels entail automatic expectations."

"So, you think I want to marry you so I can have a maid and a cook?" Adam was incredulous.

"I don't think that's why you want to marry me, but I do think that's what you will expect. All of my friends who have married, all of them, have fallen into that pattern. It's the order of things. I don't think it's bad. I just don't think I can do it." Babs sounded cold and distant.

"Well, first of all, your study in physics and observations of life should tell you that the order of things is changing," Adam responded. "And second of all, I have no doubt that we can create a mutually satisfying order. And third of all ...." He hesitated. "I have tasted your roast chicken, and I am not very eager to trust my appetite to your cooking ability."

At this, Adam grinned, and pulled Babs toward him, embracing her firmly, and kissing her gently. Her first urge was to break away, but the kiss was so genuine and loving that it reminded her of every reason why she should marry him. The cooking remark deserved a kick in the pants, but sometimes, she thought, truth, even condescending truth, is funny. So after the kiss and embrace, she murmured, "I'll think about it."

Later, before Adam left, it was Babs who brought up the subject again.

"So, what if you ask me again, and I say no?" she asked him, while holding onto his waist preparing for the goodnight kiss.

Adam did not hesitate. "I will keep asking until you say yes."
They kissed goodnight, and he went back to his apartment.

*

Rosie languished on the Democratic Party campaign trail throughout September and October. In November, she joined other staff members in South Dakota to support each other through the pending slaughter, and to be near Senator McGovern, whose unwavering integrity somehow made the defeat more traumatic. Nixon's crushing defeat of their candidate demoralized the Democratic Party, especially the young, idealistic campaign workers, who never fully comprehended the cavernous divisions that alienated the young from the old, the rich from the poor, the dove from the hawk, and the white from the black.

Since the convention in July, Rosie had become more disdainful of politics and more skeptical of the institutional foundations upon which government teetered. A burglary by Nixon's campaign staff at the Watergate complex in Washington DC, as well as the dirty tricks she experienced firsthand, cemented her personal assessment that politics was no longer an honorable endeavor. The inclusion of minority delegates, insisted on by McGovern, exposed chasms of racism and sexism that prevented the unified solidarity needed to win the election. One of Rosie's coworkers, a 65-year-old woman whose grandson was killed in the war, observed to Rosie, "A broken party can never mend a broken country."

"This is true," said Rosie. "But a president who breaks the law also cannot fix a broken country."

The woman responded, "Don't give up on the system, young lady. Nixon will get what's coming to him. Mark my words."

*

After the election, Rosie returned to Cleveland. McGovern's campaign continued to keep her on the payroll until the end of November as she completed paperwork and follow-up phone calls at the Cuyahoga

County headquarters. Shredding documents and correspondence provided her with closure. This was the end of her political involvement in national politics. George McGovern, to Rosie, represented everything that was right about America. His decisive defeat, she thought, was a signal that Americans had grown weak in discernment, and the effect would be debilitating to the core foundation of American values.

Rosie spent the first two weeks of December sending out resumes to various organizations that focused on animal protection. Campaign activities had introduced her to several people who worked in the business of animal advocacy, and she had secured a dozen references and recommendations. Her plan was to gain employment outside of Ohio. The restless hankering to be on the move conquered her nostalgic hankering to remain in Cleveland. Cousin Beth's declaration that she would be getting married in a year solidified Rosie's plans to venture into new territories. It would be rude, Rosie knew, to live in a house with newlyweds.

*

The Vanettis hosted the annual Christmas party on December 18,1972, and the households of Turyev and Nagy again joined with their Italian friends for an evening of celebration. Dar and Miklos barely hid the sadness they carried for the absence of Brigid, eight thousand miles away. Barbara and Richard masked Richard's health problems with talk of space flights and Mars explorations. The Vanettis did not mention their unnerving at the November election. Everyone had agreed that they would focus on the blessings in their lives, not the troubles.

Babs and Rosie barely found time for a moment of sharing, each staying close to their parents, and each missing the presence of Brigid. Babs also missed Adam, who would not arrive in town until Christmas Day.

The evening ended early with hugs and holiday wishes bestowed upon all. Babs noticed that the hugs for Richard hung with more emotion and love than in years past.

*

The Turyev family exchanged gifts early Christmas morning. In a scene filled with tears and the most tender of affections, David presented his father with a painting he had made. His eyes fluttering, his hands quivering, he handed the painting to his father.

"I found a picture in the library, of a lithograph printed in 1900. It shows the December sky. It was Germany, Christmastime, and the year of your birth. I couldn't believe it. Father, it took me three months to paint this. Each detail of each star reminded me of how lucky I am that you are my father. I am proud of being a German; I am proud of my Jewish blood, and most of all, I am proud to be the son of a star gazer. I was so happy to paint what the sky looked like on your first Christmas. Merry Christmas, Father."

Babs and Barbara sat motionless, stunned at the passion David expressed, and moved by the depth of meaning that the gift itself expressed. One never knows what children absorb from their environment. It was obvious that David absorbed the greatness of his father's accomplishments, and the inevitability of his father's mortality.

Richard, for whom every moment now carried a significant value, stared at the painting for several minutes. He thought of missed opportunities to show appreciation to his son, who was so different from the rest of the family. His son, not the scientist of the physical components of the stars, but the painter of their beauty.

Finally, allowing his tears to fall, he grasped his son's hand, moved it in a strong, firm, handshake, gazed in David's eyes and said, "You are a fine young man, a fine son."

Richard then forced the strength to carry the painting across the room and place it on the mantel.

*

Adam arrived shortly after. The Turyevs greeted him with a smorgasbord breakfast feast of Belgian waffles, liverwurst, Eggs Benedict, bagels, homemade jam, bacon, ham, fresh strawberries, melons, dates, and syrups. Barbara and Babs prepared the feast at the request of Richard, whose appetite was waning, but who still desired a special Christmas treat for his family. This was their gift to him.

Food, gifts, and familial bonding continued throughout the day. Adam and Richard withdrew to the study, where Richard clandestinely enjoyed a few puffs from a cigar that he had hidden in his desk drawer. The doctors had forbidden him to smoke, but Richard knew a cigar now and then would have no influence on the length of his days, so he frequently escaped to the study to have a drag.

"He thinks I don't know," Barbara grimaced. "I play his game. He deserves any enjoyment he can steal."

Babs smiled, but changed the subject. "Mother, I think Adam is going to ask me to marry him, sometime soon."

Barbara, obviously pleased, expressed her excitement. "Oh, Babs! He is a wonderful man. Does he make you happy? Are you confident in his love?"

Babs answered somewhat hesitantly. "Yes, and yes. It is not Adam's love or fidelity that worries me. It is marriage itself that worries me."

Reaching for her coffee, Barbara sipped, and then slowly and thoughtfully sighed aloud. "Marriage can devour you, but you and your husband must make sure that doesn't happen. I will tell you right now that you must never change who you are. But I will also tell you that marriage will change who you become."

"I'm not sure I understand," Babs replied.

"Well, look at me. I love my work, my research. I love the knowledge we can glean from the heavens. That is a big part of the essence of my soul. Our marriage strengthened that and nurtured it. Yet, my priority was and is and always will be the happiness of my children and my husband. As a result, I could not 'become' a famous scientist. What is important has remained; what could have been is gone. This is not bad, not good; it just is. It goes for men and women."

"And yet Father got to keep who he is and what he wanted to become," said Babs.

"I could have chosen to pursue my career more exclusively. It was my choice not to. Maybe someday the choice won't be so difficult, but now it is. So, make sure you and Adam agree on priorities beforehand. Your love will then see you through it."

"I can't cook and I hate to clean, and I hate having to be accountable to someone," Babs lamented.

Barbara laughed. "You'll get over it. And I hasten to add, Babs, a strong faith is a critical component. For all my love of the natural world, my faith in something supernatural is what sustained me. At the core of your marriage should stand the Lord."

Yikes, Babs thought. "Ooooookay. Thanks. I am going over to say Merry Christmas to Karen. I'll be back soon. Love you, Mom."

*

The day after Christmas, the mailman delivered a letter from the American Humane Association in Washington DC to the Vanetti house, informing Rosie that the organization wished to hire her as a communications assistant in their home office. Rosie waited until after Christmas to share the news with her parents. She simply handed the letter to Mama Rose at the dinner table.

"Massimo," Mama Rose said after she read the letter. "Our Rosie is going to Washington DC. She is following the dream she has had since she was a little girl. She is going to help save animals from abuse and abandonment."

MV looked at Rosie. "That is wonderful, Rosie! We are so proud of you! Jobs in DC are hard to come by. You must have made quite an impression on those people. Well done."

"Can I come to visit you?" asked Rebecca.

"Will you be working with elephants?" Robert said innocently.

"You're going to miss my football games," Renaldo mumbled.

Rosie soaked up the attention, realizing that family mealtime was what she would miss the most. She answered all questions, relieved that the conversation exalted the situation, rather than criticizing it.

*

Chapter 9

January - June 1973
Babs and Rosie

Within a few weeks, the Vanetti family packed up a few pieces of furniture and all of Rosie's clothing, and drove to Washington DC. Rosie had arranged to share an apartment with a Senatorial intern for George McGovern whom she had met during the campaign. After unloading and unpacking, the family toured the city together. At each landmark and each building, the excitement and pride bubbled over into animated discussions of American history and government service.

Rosie, who had vowed to remove herself from a political environment, found herself in the hub of a political mecca.

*

Work at The Humane Association inflamed Rosie's passion for caring for and saving animals. For the first few months, her job consisted of answering phone calls and redirecting the constituents to departments that could help them. As the number of calls increased, Rosie assumed more personal responsibility for solving or investigating situations of animal neglect. Cockfighting, abandonment, starvation, natural disaster rescues; these were a few of the conditions Rosie attempted to improve. The reports and complaints concerned the treatment of house pets, to animals in film, from cities and farms to the mountains and the oceans. She arrived early, and stayed late, overwhelmed by the atrocities that people perpetrated on animals. She again wondered who were really the beasts--the humans or the animals.

The plight of animals garnered little concern outside the walls of the Association. Too many other global issues dominated attention. President Nixon had agreed to a cease-fire in Viet Nam and ended the war at the tables of the Paris Peace Accords. The pangs of Martin's death ached in Rosie's heart. Memories of the past five years flooded her soul. She relished the news of peace, but could not escape the hurts of war. The lack of trust in the peace agreement hovered over every word the president muttered. While speaking to her mother in a late-night phone conversation, Rosie aired her opinion.

"Our Secretary of State, Henry Kissinger, was bombing the hell out of Viet Nam all the while he was sitting at the peace table. Really? I can't stand any of them. There is no peace, and there is no honor. I just can't stand any of them."

"So happy to hear that my sweet child is still true to her kind and gentle ways," Mama Rose said.

*

During many evenings, Rosie and her roommate, Jacqueline Espy, unwound at the plethora of bars and pubs in the DC area. Their favorite was Cellar Door, a music bar where, on any given night, they could hear rock and roll, rhythm and blues, or jazz, performed by some of the best musicians in the country. Cellar Door was a short taxi ride from their apartment in Georgetown, and provided a setting that soothed the sickening stories that Rosie suffered through all day at work.

Jacqueline and Rosie enjoyed each other's company, and nurtured a growing friendship of trust and camaraderie. Rosie would share stories from her job and Jacqueline would take those stories back to the Senate offices where legislation for the treatment of animals was being proposed and discussed. In turn, Jacqueline would tell Rosie anecdotes about McGovern, and Washington political intrigue. The buzz about Watergate grew deafening.

One evening in February, after gulping down three whiskey sours, Jacqueline gossiped to Rosie.

"Rumors are rampant around the Senate that those burglars who were convicted in the Watergate break-in had links to higher-ups."

"Higher-ups? How high?" Rosie answered. The only political talk she enjoyed more than McGovern's accomplishments was political talk about Nixon's troubles.

Jacqueline took another sip of her fourth drink, and paused. She was a South Carolina native, speaking in a slow southern drawl, and moving even slower. Her demeanor presented a stark contrast to the fast-talking, fast-moving Cleveland girl who performed every task and every conversation speedily and breathlessly.

"How high up?" Rosie repeated, in a slightly higher pitch.

"You northern gals are always in such a hurry," Jacqueline teased.

Rosie growled.

"Well, the rumors are that there are lists and phone records that provide evidence that some of the president's own men were involved in some illegal activities."

"Damn!" said Rosie. "Do they think the president is involved?"

"No one is saying that out loud, but all signs point to the Oval Office."

Before the conversation continued, two young men sat down with the girls. Jacqueline shushed her scuttlebutt. They finished their evening with their own style of rocking and rolling.

*

Watergate talk dominated the Washington conversation in every corner of the city. Rosie listened, but kept her focus on the tormenting scenarios that crossed her desk every day. The Humane Association relentlessly approached the task of safeguarding animals, but Rosie already grew weary of desk and paper work. Despite the pride in the numerous successes, she longed for more active engagement with the issue. A phone call in late March diverted her attention from her work and play.

"Rosie—hi, this is Babs," chimed the familiar voice.

"Hi, Babs! Oh my God, I've been thinking about you, girl. How the hell are you?" Rosie bellowed excitedly. They had exchanged a brief letter, but no phone conversations in the past few months.

"I am fine, Rosie, and I hope you are the same. I am calling you with some news, and a favor."

A guffaw sputtered from Rosie's mouth. "Uh-oh, you're not pregnant, are you? Oh wait, I forgot who I was talking to."

Babs breathed a lighthearted sigh. "We really should talk more often. You're always so ... so unkindly amusing. The reason I am calling you is to tell you that I am getting married and I would like you to be my maid of honor."

A long pause ensued.

"Rosie? Are you there?" Babs asked.

Finally, Rosie responded. "Ho-ly shit. Congratulations, Babs, and oh my God, thank you. Just tell me when and where, and I am there. Oh, umm--who are you marrying?" Rosie grinned so widely that Babs could almost hear it.

"So amusing," said Babs, with a grin as wide as Rosie's. "The wedding is April 28 in Shaker. There will be Mass and then a dinner. I'm sorry, lovey, but you'll have to wear an ugly bridesmaid's dress."

"I love ugly dresses; I wear them every day to work." Rosie laughed. "But I gotta ask, Babs, why so soon? I didn't pick up on any wedding plans when we saw each other at Christmas. What's the rush? And pleeeeeeease don't tell me it's a consummation thing."

Babs laughed again, but then changed to serious mode. "Well, the main reason is that I am out of excuses not to get married. Even more compelling, my dad is growing sicker by the day, and I'm afraid he won't be around much longer. He is thrilled with my choice, and I just want to make sure he is able to attend the wedding."

Another long pause was finally broken by Rosie.

"You're a good daughter, Babs. And a good friend."

"Let's hope I'm a good wife," Babs added.

"Eh, screw that. You'll just get on-the-job training. Adam loves you, that is obvious. Things will be fine. Hey--on another topic, have you heard from St. Brigid? My mom talked to Mrs. Nagy and she said Brig hardly writes."

"No, I haven't heard anything, but really it's only been a few months. I sent her a letter today, telling her about the wedding. I sure wish she could be here."

"I'm sure she will wish that too," said Rosie.

"Alrighty, on that note, we shall bid adieu. See you in April, Rosie. I'll get the dress and other info to you as soon as I can."

"Thanks, Babs. This call meant a lot to me. Say hi to dear ol' dad for me."

*

Cherry blossoms bloomed in full splendor in the springtime of 1973, and Rosie breezed through Washington DC with a feeling of freedom and contentment that she had never before experienced. The chimes and churning of the city easily compensated for the lack of excitement in her daily routine of the drudgery of reports, research, and rumors.

When MV came to the city for a political business trip, he doted on Rosie, treating her and Jacqueline to fine restaurants, and inner-circle conferences. Legislators, senators, lobbyists, international ambassadors--Rosie met them all with grace and respect. The pageantry and pomp that accompanied the dinners and gatherings impressed Rosie, not because of the glamour, but because of the rot she knew slithered beneath the façade. Nevertheless, she enjoyed the attention from her father, and beamed at the consideration these men gave his ideas. She thought of Babs's situation and the looming passing of Richard, and she made sure to express her love and admiration to her father.

"Dad, I know I have put you through a lot. Please know how much I love you. How proud I am. And how much I appreciate you. You never gave up on me. You're the only politician in the world who still keeps it an honorable profession. I'm so glad you're here."

She stuttered with affection. MV heard and treasured every word. Their time together culminated at Mass in the National Shrine of the Immaculate Conception where their Catholic faith manifested their spiritual bond.

During his visit, MV was afforded a driver to transport him around the city. His name was Samuel Scarponi, whose family had migrated from Italy two generations ago. When he left MV at the airport, Samuel drove Rosie to her apartment. On the way, he asked if she would like to dine with him that evening. She accepted, and so began a courtship that never ended.

Rosie and Sammy, as she called him, meshed immediately. His driving job provided a steady income while he completed his graduate studies in Journalism at Georgetown University. They discussed politics and the press; protesting and proselytizing; philosophy and philanthropy. He enthralled her with information he gleaned while interning at The *Washington Post* and told her without a doubt, Nixon would be indicted for his role in the Watergate scandal. The fact that he said this with glee thumped Rosie's heart. Sammy, too, was enthralled, listening intently as Rosie shared her daily litany of animal cruelty. They magnetized each other, attracting on all levels of physical and emotional energies.

This is it, thought Sammy.

Whoa, thought Rosie.

*

Wedding bells clanged as Barbara Ann (Babs) Turyev married Adam William Schwartz on Saturday, April 28,1973 at Our Lady of Peace Catholic Church in Shaker Heights, Ohio. Fifty guests attended the ceremony, including the families of the bride and groom, and the Vanetti, Nagy, Pentello, Grovac, and Armstrong families.

Richard held his daughter's hand as his wife guided him in his wheelchair down the aisle to give the bride away. Rosie Vanetti served as maid of honor; Karen Grovac and Christine Gallik served as bridesmaids. David Turyev served as best man. Ray Magaldi and Anthony Toth, Adam's friends from Indiana, served as groomsmen.

Babs garbed herself in a tea-length white gown with a beaded bodice, and a chai necklace. A white lace mantilla covered her head and flowed down her temple to her shoulders. She carried three white roses, one to honor each of her grandmothers, and her mother.

The bridesmaids wore lilac-colored dresses above the knee, and each carried a bouquet of lilacs with a spray of baby's breath. Karen and Rosie restrained their giggles when Babs solemnly walked to the statue of Mary to proclaim her purity and dedication. Rosie, unsmilingly masking her sarcasm, whispered to Karen, "Last of the 22-year-old virgins."

Babs and Adam then recited traditional vows.

Leaving the church, the family and friends dined and partied at the Top of the Town restaurant in downtown Cleveland. After tearful farewells, Babs and Adam flew to Silver City, New Mexico, where they honeymooned, and spent their nights gazing at the dark night sky, joined by amateur astronomers whose feet remained on the soil, but imaginations rose to the stars.

Their nights were filled with other wonders. Babs sent postcards to Rosie in Cleveland, and Brigid in Bombay. The picture on the postcard depicted a rocket soaring through a dark tunnel of the Milky Way vortex.

On the back, Babs wrote simply, "I'm glad I waited."

*

Sammy and Rosie grew closer every day. When Sammy spent time with the family at Babs's wedding, the Vanettis accepted him immediately as one of their own.

Sammy went back to DC immediately after the wedding. Rosie remained in Cleveland for a few days, and asked Mama Rose if she would be her guest for lunch at Higbee's downtown in the Crystal Room restaurant, a favorite dining place for both of them.

Aware that her daughter had never offered to pay for a meal in her life, Mama looked at Rosie and asked, "Are you pregnant?"

"No, Mama, for heaven's sakes, can't a girl take her mother out to lunch with no strings attached?" Rosie whimpered.

Mama thought, *No,* but smiled and said, "Sure. I have errands to do first, so I will meet you there at noon."

The next day, during a meal of chicken salad on a flaky crêpe with a side of frosted melons, Rosie pulled out the attached strings.

"So, Mama. You have seen that Sammy and I love each other very much. We are sure that we were meant to be with each other forever. And so, to save money and get to know each other better we are going to share an apartment, probably sometime in October. I know that you have old-fashioned ideas about this, but I am almost twenty-three and on my own now and this is what I would like to do, and I trust him, and we will probably get married next year anyhow when he is done with grad school and has a job, and I just wanted you to know."

Mama Rose bit into her frosted melon, then sipped some lemonade, and responded.

"Yes, you are almost twenty-three, and you are on your own. And if old-fashioned means that one must make a commitment before God and witnesses to sanctify the union and love of a man and a woman, then yes, I am old-fashioned. You can do what you feel is right."

She took another bite of a melon, another sip of lemonade, then completed her reply.

"Sharing an apartment means shacking up, fornicating with no responsibility, pretending you are married. I will simply introduce you to people as my oldest daughter, the concubine."

*

Sammy, having received a similar, perhaps less blunt, reaction from his parents about living with Rosie, suggested that they "play their parents' game" and stay in their separate apartments. As it turned out, his course work exhausted him, and he was content to live alone with his chaotic schedule. When an internal power struggle waged within the Association, Rosie's workload also intensified. She enjoyed the freedom that came with having a place away from her boyfriend and a roommate to discuss girl talk; she found herself begrudgingly appreciating Mama Rose's insights.

*

Adam received his Master's Degree in Nuclear Physics from Purdue University in May. He had opted out of attending the ceremony, because Babs's father suffered another heart attack, one that he would not survive.

Richard Turyev died in his sleep on May 24, 1973. The foggy aftermath of funeral preparations, services, and burials swirled by, as Barbara, Babs, and David motioned their way through the mandatory activities. Babs wrote and presented the eulogy, ending with the most profound and rewarding insight her father had upheld throughout his life.

She spoke with a strong, steady voice, that camouflaged her weak, aching heart.

"As I look out over this congregation, I see men who have travelled to the moon-- men and women whose work and vision have made it possible for satellites and ships to travel the stars. My father viewed mankind as travelers through both the corporeal world, and the spiritual world. He continually reminded his children that from an evolutionary perspective, we began as animals. But we are animals who have the ability to choose. We can either wriggle and wallow with the wild beasts, or we can aspire and ascend with the angels. Whether it be science, or music, or the arts, or love, we must always, in every situation, choose to be a beast no more."

*

Chapter 10

June - December 1973
Babs and Rosie

Babs and Rosie postponed their birthday celebration until two weeks after the funeral. They went to Cleveland Municipal Stadium on June 6 to watch the Minnesota Twins defeat the Cleveland Indians. The long game gave the young women time to talk. Babs shared two communications she had received from Brigid. Both were in the forms of simple gifts: a hand-woven basket as a wedding gift, and a mala, Hindu prayer beads, as a token of sympathy when Richard died. A short note was attached to each gift, expressing love and sorrow and a sense of longing.

For the wedding: "I am overjoyed at your finding a soulmate with whom to spend your life. My heart yearns for your friendship. xoxox Brigid"

For the funeral: "My heart breaks. For your family and our world. Will see you in a year's time. xoxox Brigid"

*

Westinghouse Division of Nuclear Energy hired Adam as a chief nuclear physicist researcher and Babs as a summer intern in the Metallurgy Lab. The presence of Adam eased the sexist, snide, and frequent vulgar remarks that haunted her last year, but did not completely eradicate them. The workplace did not offer a welcoming environment for a female genius. Nevertheless, Babs not only prevailed, but succeeded in offering insight and problem solving in the study of flow blockage effects on coolant pressure and temperature in nuclear reactors.

Babs welcomed the return to class in September. Barbara and David came to Indiana for Thanksgiving and Christmas, escaping the memories and constant specter of Richard's legacy in Shaker Heights. Barbara accepted a full professorship at Case Western Reserve University, to begin in January. David withdrew further into his art, opening up only to Babs about his sense of loss without his father in his life.

*

The Vanettis did not host the annual multifamily Christmas celebration. The Turyevs would not be present and Brigid would also be absent again. Rosie and Sammy had garnered enough independent determination to spend the 1973 holidays of Thanksgiving and Christmas together in San Francisco. Sammy received a grant to investigate the ivory trade, which posed a significant threat to elephant populations around the world. Rosie had presented a proposal to the Association asking for funds, which would allow her to research the scope of the trade and theorize the direct effects on the elephant populations. The Association refused, so Rosie went to the newly formed Humane Society, which had recently split from the Association. They accepted Rosie's proposal, and offered her a job. She had a month to research, and then report to her new position as Wildlife Abuse Researcher and Field Supervisor.

Sammy's grant and Rosie's new job provided a solid foundation for a fulfilling and successful endeavor on the shores of the Pacific Ocean. Most of their time was spent in Chinatown, where the ivory trade emerged as one of the leading areas of imports, second only to New York. The vast quantity of ivory and the stories of slaughtered elephants sickened the pair, and they returned to DC with a firm commitment to pursue protection for the magnificent beasts. They also deepened their commitment to each other.

*

Chapter 11

January - June 1974
Babs and Rosie

The harsh winter soon thawed into a soft spring. Rosie's new employment mushroomed with possibilities for her to explore. The Convention on International Trade in Endangered Species of Wild Fauna and Flora (CITES) and the recently passed Endangered Species Act opened opportunities for possible world travel. Those opportunities also arose for Sammy, and the two plotted and planned hopes for their future. No wedding plans would be announced yet; Beth planned a July wedding, and Rosie would do nothing to upstage that.

Jacqueline constantly fed Rosie with political scoops, and it seemed certain that with the revelation of Nixon's knowledge of White House involvement in the Watergate scandal, he would be impeached or forced to resign.

"Seriously," Rosie told Jacqueline, "can my life get any sweeter?"

Jacqueline laughed. "Now, now, let's not relish another's downfall. Senator McGovern is being very gracious. So far his only comments have been questioning why it took so long for the investigation on Watergate to catch hold of public attention. He is also generally bewildered by the motive for the break-in."

"Whatever. Bye-bye Tricky Dicky," glowed Rosie.

Political and spring storms thundered through April and May. Georgetown University awarded Samuel Scarponi a Master's Degree in Journalism, and Rosie applied for a field assignment in Kenya, Africa, the purpose of which was to establish programs that would aid and advise native Kenyans on the importance of elephant preservation. Samuel received offers as a freelance writer that ranged from salacious politics to species protection. He knew exactly which one he would choose.

Samuel and Rosie would spend June 1974 engaging in independent research for their upcoming projects. He rented a room in Lakewood, in a boarding house on the shores of Lake Erie. She stayed at home with her family.

Rosie had not directly heard anything from Brigid since Brigid left for India, although there were "hellos" given through Dar. Brigid would be home soon, and both Rosie and Babs would be there to greet her.

*

Babs completed her Master's studies at the top of her class. Having no interest in accolades or ceremony, she skipped the May commencement activities. Westinghouse offered her a lucrative position for the summer, starting in July, and Purdue granted full tuition paid as a Doctoral candidate in Thermophysics for the 1974-75 school year. She and Adam, who had accumulated four weeks' vacation time, decided to spend June in a rented house overlooking Horseshoe Lake in Shaker Heights, less than one mile from her childhood home where Barbara and David still lived. Barbara still had not cleared out Richard's things, and Babs wanted to help her mother sort through her father's belongings. She also felt a need to share some time with David.

Adam stayed true to his commitment of minimal expectations.

He had not yet spoken the words, "What's for dinner?"

*

Chapter 12

September 1972 - June 1974
Brigid

One can read about, and listen to stories about, and see pictures about, people living in poverty. But until one looks directly into the eyes of human suffering, the scope of pain and desperation that impoverishment hosts can never be understood.

Brigid arrived in Bombay, India on September 25, 1972. The bus ride from the airport to downtown introduced a view of humanity that Brigid had never imagined. The training in New York did not prepare her for the sea of people and animals that crowded the roads and the fields. No taxi driver in a Manhattan traffic jam weaved and dodged in between cars like this bus driver who weaved and dodged in between children and oxen and cattle. The bus carried fifty Peace Corps volunteers. Some, like Brigid, were fighting nausea and fatigue, as the odor of human and animal excrement oozed through the open windows.

To add to the physical discomfort, Brigid's emotions teetered on tears. While departing the plane, she had learned that her saxophone had been "lost" in transport. Her Peace Corps supervisor later told her that "lost" was the common euphemism for stolen. As the bus twisted and turned through the trail of travelers, Brigid convinced herself that tears of self-pity had no place in her new life. She closed her eyes, breathed deeply, and prepared herself to bring what she naively called the hope of human triumph to the hopelessness of beastly defeat.

Downtown Bombay overflowed with people. As Brigid and another volunteer explored the streets, the warnings issued during training took human form. Beggars on every corner, many of them missing limbs or maimed in some other grotesque fashion, all pleading for money. The mutilations resulted from a variety of sources. Sometimes gangs collected money from the beggars and would chop off limbs if a quota was not met. Sometimes parents maimed children because there was more sympathy, and thus more money, for disfigured beggars. Seeing the reality of the plight of the poor children of Bombay overwhelmed the idealism of the middle-class girl from Parma. Brigid went back to the hotel and collapsed on the bed, and wept until the anchors of sleep tugged on her drooping eyelids, sinking her into a restless slumber. When she awoke, she felt tired, but determined.

"I am here to help. And I will do that in any way I can," she said aloud, to no one.

After three days of orientation and attempting to grow accustomed to this new world, Brigid and her colleagues moved into their tenement, a few miles from downtown, in the belly of the slums. Worli Chawls, the assigned living quarters, housed other Peace Corps volunteers, including two young men who chose to serve their country in India rather than Viet Nam.Thousands of Indian families crammed into tiny rooms at night, and trudged through rat-infested garbage dumps during the day to escape the squalor from within. The "tenants" that dominated Brigid's thoughts, however, were the hundreds of cockroaches that accompanied her daily activities.

Organized opportunities that she had hoped for did not readily become available. Direction from the Peace Corps came in the form of a supervisor who advised Brigid to "find something useful to do." She finally settled on an assignment that consisted of helping local women sell their homemade crafts and jewelry at a tourist center near a cruise ship dock.

Extreme dysentery attacked her digestive system, and head lice ate at her hair and scalp. Her only solace came in the company of her roommate, Elizabeth, who shared equally in the agony, but possessed a tougher survivalist instinct. When a rat wiggled across Elizabeth's bed one night, Brigid stayed awake all night shaking in fear and disgust, while Elizabeth quickly fell back to sleep. The next day, Elizabeth returned with a pet mongoose, and comforted Brigid with the promise that the store owner assured her this was the "best rat-eating creature in the world."

Brigid said a prayer that the store owner was correct, and secretly wished she had never left Parma.

Time, however, flowed as quickly in Bombay as it did in Ohio. Soon, it was Christmas time, and the Peace Corps changed the women's work assignments and living quarters. The Chawls had become a hotbed of racial and economic revolution, led by the Dalit Panthers, a radical group of revolutionaries from the "untouchables," a group considered too low in stature to be in the caste system. Modeled after the Black Panthers in the United States, the Dalits rebelled against the system that offered them nothing but a life of desolate deprivation. The rebellion made the Chawls a danger zone for the young women. Elizabeth and Brigid moved away--Elizabeth into a neighborhood house hosted by an Indian family, and Brigid into a private apartment. The women remained in close contact, Elizabeth serving as a community assistant, and Brigid serving in an orphanage.

Brigid had only written to her family once since arriving in India. That note was brief, informing them that she had arrived safely. By December, she had decided she owed them further details.

December 5,1972

Dear mom and dad and sisters,

I am sorry I have not written more often. It has been a rather overwhelming adjustment and I am just now feeling comfortable enough to share some thoughts with you. I miss you all very much, and I also miss toilets and water that does not need boiling. But I do not spend my days "missing." I spend most of my time absorbing this fascinating land of cultural madness. I say madness because it does seem crazy here, but crazy in the sense that it is so different from America. Oh mom, the poverty here is ever present. I am currently living in what back home we would call the slums. You cannot imagine the unsanitary conditions and hunger, and general shabbiness of these people's lives. But not to worry. I am safe, and the people are so very kind.

My roommate is an earthy, stouthearted type of gal. She keeps my spirits up and is helping me become more street smart. For instance, there are beggars on every corner here. She figured out that we should choose one to contribute to and then the others will leave us alone. She is smart that way, reminds me of Rosie. Her name is Elizabeth.

Next week we are moving from the slums. I will be in a tiny apartment, but it will have a toilet, not just a hole, and I will have rattan furniture, and a desk. I will also be sharing a cook and a house cleaner with a couple of other volunteers.

For these past two months, I have been selling jewelry made by some Indian women. It has not been a very rewarding task, and certainly not what I was trained to do. My satisfaction has come from getting to know the culture and the people, by independently riding the busses and trains around the city. The trains are gender segregated, that is, men in one, women in the other, it is not a mandatory segregation, so I do still ride with the men sometimes. Anyhow, I get to come and go as I please, and I do savor that freedom. American women get away with a lot more than Indian women. A couple of the other female Peace Corps girls have already taken to wearing saris, but I find them too hot and cumbersome.

I received two of your letters and I appreciate the candy, although some of the items you mentioned in your letters must have been "lost." I love the photos of Joan, Sally, Suzy, and Cindy and especially of Michele and little Johnny. I've only been gone a few months and already it seems like they have grown so much.

It was very sad to hear how ill Mr. Turyev has become. Of course, as

Christmas draws closer, I am thinking about the wonderful holidays we have shared. Please tell the Turyevs and Vanettis that I think of them often.

You asked about church. I must confess that I have only been to Mass once--in the downtown cathedral. It's funny, but I feel closer to Jesus when I walk among the beggars and lepers on the streets than I do in the golden glow of the man made structures. I am the only Catholic in the Peace Corps group. I will probably attend Mass when I am more comfortable traveling alone.

I will write again soon. I am looking forward to my new assignment and living arrangements. I love you all very much and more and more I appreciate everything you have given me and what God has blessed me with.

I hear the sound of much needed rain falling, time to go.

With all of my love, Brigid xoxoxox

The sound of "rain" that Brigid referred to was, in reality, the plop plop of roaches falling off the walls. There was a standard joke relating to the contents of information that went back to families. It was called "the things we don't tell Mom."

Other things Brigid "didn't tell Mom" included the feverish virus that heated her body to 103 degrees and forced her to spend two weeks in November sweating on a bed in a doctor's house. The Peace Corps provided two doctors for all the volunteers in India. Brigid was fortunate that one of them was stationed in Bombay. When she stumbled to the doctor's house to get help, he placed her in his own bed where he and his wife monitored and cared for her until the fever subsided. An old high-fidelity record player softly echoed sounds of a Doris Day Christmas album while Brigid slipped in and out of delirium. When the fever finally broke, she thanked the doctor for his kindness and walked shakily back to her new apartment, alone and weak with weariness and angst. This nadir of her Peace Corps journey passed quickly, and day by, month by month, Brigid grew in love and appreciation of the country and of her colleagues.

Once she realized the irrelevance of her Peace Corps training and the shattering of her idealistic expectations, Brigid opened her mind and heart to her surroundings. The children at the orphanage eagerly soaked in her affection and storytelling, and her jaunts to the city offered new experiences of fun and enrichment. She explained some of these in her next letter to her family in March.

March 3, 1973

Dear mom and dad and sisters,

Happy New Year--albeit a couple months late! I missed all of you over the holidays. I did receive your letters and treats. Thank you so much. Much has happened since my last letter. Hard to believe I have been here for six months already. My new living arrangements are much cleaner, and more conducive to rest. My apartment is sparse, but I have learned to live with only the barest of necessities. I am often reminded of what I now consider the excesses of American life. I think of wedding showers I attended back home, where pots and pans and dishes and towels are so abundantly present. Here, the women use the same pot to cook, scrub floors, and bathe the baby. Please don't think I'm being judgmental of my American friends. We all simply respond to our environment.

The environment here presents an interesting array of daily surprises. Yesterday at the train station, I bought a Coca Cola from a machine. When I placed the money in the slot, a thin, brown hand emerged from the dispenser and handed me my bottle of Coke. Apparently, the machine was broken and it is cheaper to hire someone to dispense the purchase, than to pay the cost of machine repair. These are the kind of delightful twists that make me love these people. And, oh dear, there are so many, many, people.

I am still not accustomed to the caste system here. The cook will not sweep; the sweeper will not wash the sink; the mattress fluffer will not make the bed ... it is truly amazing.

The children in the orphanage are a blessing to me, as I hope I am to them. There are only two workers for dozens of children, so anything I do is appreciated. There is a Catholic missionary across the street staffed by a dozen nuns. Those children are much better cared for, and it is sad to see how sometimes our children look forlornly over there. One thing that has remained constant in my psyche, is the ubiquitous presence of life's dichotomy. One side of the street hope, the other side, despair. I do miss my saxophone dearly. Every corner of this place screams the blues.

My Peace Corps friends and I have grown very close. They are a fun loving, kind bunch of people. I have also dated a few Indian men and manage to watch some of our American guys play basketball at a court near my apartment. All in all, not a bad gig, although it is difficult to constantly see the poverty and massive abuse of lower caste women.

It does seem like I have plenty of "down" time when I am not actively engaged in Peace Corps work, but I still haven't found time to write to Rosie and Babs. I cried when I read about Babs's engagement. I am so happy for her and truly wish I could be there for her. Please tell them I think of them often and look forward to being with them again. I do plan on sending Babs a gift.

I love hearing about the family. Please keep writing. It's funny- family and church played such a big role in my life and now I am so distant from both of those influences. I don't know how I will emerge from all of this. Surprisingly, my closest Peace Corps friends are atheists. Flat out non believers. I don't think I ever had a serious discussion with an atheist before I came here. We have had some great conversations.

Time again to go.
I love and miss you.
Brigid xoxoxo

The things Brigid "didn't tell Mom":

In the train station, on the far edge of the platform, a little beggar girl relieved herself, and then ate her excrement. Such was the level of poverty, hunger, and neglect of the untouchables.

When walking amongst the population of masses that filled the streets, buses, and trains, women were continuously groped, pressed against, squeezed, and fingered through their clothing. This was commonplace. Neither women nor the government defended against it.

The lightest-skinned American women were prized possessions of the Indian men, who showered them with gifts and travel "opportunities."

*

News of Babs's wedding and Mr. Turyev's death reached Brigid in mid-August. These blasts of news from home yanked her back to a different reality, hitting her with the reminder that her life in India was only temporary. The death of Mr. Turyev cast a depressing gloom in her spirit. Missing the major life events of her friends and family imparted the only regrets she harbored regarding her decision to join the Peace Corps. However, India succeeded in sucking away the depression, and Brigid soon shed the gloom to focus on her orphans and other adventures.

The Peace Corps offered forty-five days of vacation time to the volunteers. Brigid and her colleagues took full advantage of the offer, and used the time to travel. After an October training session in Kashmir, they decided to rent a houseboat and remain there for two weeks. Surrounded by the splendor of the Himalayan Mountains, and the beauty of Dal Lake, Kashmir awarded them a respite from the overpopulated quagmires of city life. The government issued warnings regarding the skirmishes on the Pakistani-Indian border, but these travelers did not encounter any troubles or mishaps. A cheery mood transcended the sight-seeing and conversations of the group, sometimes interrupted by the sounds of distant gunfire. The starry evenings often led to philosophical and spiritual musings.

Elizabeth, always prodding Brigid about her faith, gazed at the stars and said, "The universe is full of wonders, Brig, I'll give you that. But how can you possibly believe in a loving God after seeing the crud and suffering that is everywhere?"

"Whew," sighed Brigid. "I'm glad you didn't ask me about the infallibility of the Pope!"

"Hell, I won't even start on Catholicism," laughed Elizabeth. "No, I mean in general. Science is growing closer and closer to explaining the universe as well as human behavior. It seems to me that the people who say man created God, not the other way around, have it right."

"Science changes its theories every hundred years or so," Brigid answered. "I've had this discussion many times. I don't argue, because I can't win. It's a matter of faith. We either live in a universe created by an all-knowing, benevolent being, or all of these wonders we experience are the product of randomness and chance. There's deep theories in between, particularly in this part of the world, but that's the gist of it. Purpose, or randomness. One is just as logical or illogical as the other. Amongst the crud and suffering are hope and love. I think the crud and suffering are the results of man's choices. We have it in our power to live in mindful paradise, but we continue to choose a fleshy hell."

Brigid's thoughts leapt to Mr. Turyev with whom she had had this same discussion.

The other colleagues spouted their opinions, and as from the beginning of history, the answer to the query of God remained nebulous. Brigid enjoyed these conversations because they forced her to consider and articulate her faith. Here, in the distant grandeur of the Himalayas, she and her friends spoke the name of Jesus. Though Brigid considered some of the talk blasphemous, she still found the conversations comforting. She also found it comforting that she could love and respect atheists. Sounds of the groaning of nuns rumbled through her soul.

When they returned from Kashmir, the Peace Corps supervisor informed them that they would be the last volunteers to serve in India. Apparently the political tension resulting from India's policy toward Pakistan did not coincide with the desired policy of the United States, so ties were being loosened, and eventually would be cut.

"Kinda cool that we will be the last," Elizabeth said as she and

Brigid weaved their bicycles through the human traffic on their way to meet two of their Indian male friends for lunch.

"I'm not sure how much good we actually did here. Certainly not at all what I expected." Brigid puffed as they pedaled up a hill.

They stopped at a café where their friends were waiting. The men were members of the Parsi community who long ago fled to India to avoid brutal persecution by Muslims who invaded their homeland of Iran. Brigid told them of the Peace Corps decision, and expressed her doubts about her contributions to the people of Bombay. Abadi, who had been Brigid's companion for several months, addressed her concerns.

"Brigeed, you have brought many smiles to the faces of the young and old. Bringing just one smile would have made your time here worthwhile. Do not belittle the much joy you have bestowed."

Elizabeth added, "And hey, I wrote newsletters informing women how to kill rats and roaches, not to mention a few other tricks."

"A successful mission to be sure," said Rahim, the other man at the table.

*

The winter months afforded more travel time. Brigid crossed the country to the exotic mysteries of Nepal and back to the crowded beaches of Marine Drive and Juhu. She shared some of her sights with her family.

January 21, 1974

Dear mom and dad and sisters,

Hello! I hope you received my postcards showing some of the marvelous places I have seen. I received your "care packages" and appreciate them very much. The photographs of the family are still amazing to me. Sixteen months and the kids have changed so much.

I hope you had a Merry Christmas. I celebrated Christmas in Goa where I attended Mass at the Basilica of Bom Jesus. Saint Francis Xavier's relics are buried there and the community celebrates his sainthood every December. The festivities reminded me of a grand version of the carnivals at St. Charles.

Goa possesses many beautiful churches; it was a pleasure to feel the beauty and ancient history of the church that each one presented. It seems like forever since the spirit of Catholicism ignited my soul. The majesty of the ceremonies and the sacredness of the traditions reawakened a much needed sense of the supernatural.

But truly, the astronomical observatory in the city of Jaipur, Rajasthan, transported me to the heavens. My God, Babs would love that place. An ancient masterpiece symbol of man's connection to the stars. Everywhere I look in this world I see what man can be as opposed to what man has chosen to be.

I also visited Kerala in southern India. Much different from Bombay in that the people were quite literate and educated--but still tainted by the scars of poverty.

My last few months here will have a bit more traveling, but my friends and I will put most of our efforts into finishing up projects and helping people in any way we can. We will be the last Peace Corps volunteers in India, and I want us to be remembered as people who made a difference, and as Americans who cared. I'm the sappy one of the bunch they tell me.

This time will pass quickly and I will see you in June. Love to all of you.

Brigid xoxox

June 1974, Brigid would be returning home after twenty-one months in India. Dar and Miklos were planning a welcome home party. Babs and Rosie would be there.

Chapter 13

Egg Palace
Detroit Avenue Cleveland, Ohio
June 1, 1974

On June 1, 1974, Brigid Delia Nagy, mother of Brigid Delia Nagy; Rose Margaret Vanetti, mother of Rose Margaret Vanetti; and Barbara Ann Turyev, mother of Barbara Ann Turyev Schwartz, met for lunch at Egg Palace restaurant, a few blocks from St. John's hospital, where twenty-four years ago they had given birth to their firstborn children.

Since their daughters could not be present to celebrate their birthdays, the mothers decided to do it for them. They had not been together since Richard's death, and they welcomed the opportunity to catch up on each other's joys and sorrows.

"How are you coping?" asked Dar of Barbara, laying a hand on Barbara's shoulder.

"I am amazed at the gaping hole in my life that his absence creates. My work has offered a refreshing diversion, as has David, and the outpouring of love and invitations to dinners and memorials from friends and colleagues have filled my days and evenings. But at night, when I lean over to his side of the bed, I feel like I am falling into a cavern of aloneness from which I shall never escape."

The three women fell silent for a moment, empathizing with their friend.

Mama Rose changed the mood. "He was here long enough to see

his children on the right path to happiness and to accomplish things that history will remember him for. Let's hold on to that."

Dar added, "And today we are here to remember that day, twenty-four years ago, when our lives crossed paths and our oldest daughters entered the world."

"And God knows we haven't been the same since," smiled Mama Rose.

"True, that," smiled Barbara.

The glasses clanked, the women drank.

They began to prepare for the coming-home party.

Acknowledgments

The following people provided personal support or information, assuring the completion and authenticity of the story.

Ray, Phyllis, Jacqueline, Darlene, and Melanie: Support extraordinaire.

Phyllis and Nick Toth I; Mary and Mike Zone: Models for the loving marriages of characters Dar and Miklos, Mama Rose and Massimo Vanetti. May they rest in peace.

Kate Alexander, Marcia Kramer, Bessie Tyrrell, Anne Williams: Pioneer Peace Corps pioneers whose insights and tales of their time in India informed and inspired.

Christine Bernhard: Registered nurse and dear friend who informed on medical jargon, and offered undying support.

Peggy Zone-Fisher: CEO of the Diversity Center of Northeast Ohio. Treasured best friend who provided lore and details about life in Cleveland's west side, Ohio State's 1960s campus life, and the McGovern campaign.

Dwayne Hunn: Executive Director of the People's Lobby. Friend of the Toth family since the 1950s, and Peace Corps pioneer who provided the stories for "The things we don't tell mom." Author, *Every Town Needs a Castle.*

Gail Kline: NASA scientist at the Jet Propulsion Laboratory who helped pave the way for female scientists and engineers at Purdue University and NASA. Her history and professional expertise were critical in shaping the professional character of Babs.

Dean Smith: Researcher at The Bancroft Library, UC Berkeley, Berkeley, CA.Researcher who provided details, facts, and tidbits which enhanced the narrative of the drama unfolding on the Berkeley campus in the 1960s.

Susan B. Stawicki-Vrobel: Archival Technical Assistant, Department of Special Collections and University Archives, John P. Raynor, S.J. Memorial Library Marquette University. Took the time to scour the records, providing curriculum and academic historical information about Marquette University.

Todd Stoll: Vice President of Education at Jazz at Lincoln Center. Educator espousing the beauty and power of jazz. His influence is seen in the character of Brigid.

Nick, Mike, Sally, John, and Suzy Toth: Always there when needed most.

Women of Lourdes Academy Class of 1968, who continue to amaze and inspire.